ENGAGING
THE ENEMY

REESE RYAN

VENGEFUL
VOWS

YVONNE LINDSAY

MILLS & BOON

First Published in Great Britain 2019
by Mills & Boon, an imprint of HarperCollinsPublishers,
1 London Bridge Street, London, SE1 9GF

Engaging the Enemy © 2019 Roxanne Ravenel
Vengeful Vows © 2019 Dolce Vita Trust

ISBN: 978-0-263-27178-2

0419

MIX
Paper from
responsible sources
FSC™ C007454

This book is produced from independently certified FSC™ paper to ensure responsible forest management.

For more information visit: www.harpercollins.co.uk/green

Printed and bound in Spain
by CPI, Barcelona

ENGAGING
THE ENEMY

REESE RYAN

To all of the fantastic, supportive readers in my
Reese Ryan VIP Readers Lounge on Facebook.
You've made this journey truly remarkable. As long
as you keep reading my stories, I'll keep writing them.

To Johnathan Royal and Stephanie Perkins,
thank you for being not only loyal readers,
but such vocal advocates. You enthusiastically
champion my work and introduce new readers to it.
I am tremendously grateful to both of you!

To Charles Griemsman, you're a patient,
insightful editor. You challenge me in ways
that deepen my characters, strengthen my
story and make me a better storyteller.
I'm glad we're a team.

One

Parker Abbott pulled into the parking lot of the two-story building that had definitely seen better days.

Better decades even.

He parked, turned off the engine and groaned.

Kayleigh.

His high school nemesis and the one person in town who was most likely to head up the Parker Abbott *not-a-fan* club.

Usually he enjoyed negotiating deals for their family-owned distillery. But the thought of negotiating anything with Kayleigh made a knot form in his gut.

Perhaps because, deep down, he still saw her as the girl with curly pigtails and thick glasses who had once been his closest friend. Until a falling-out had made them bitter adversaries.

Parker heaved a sigh, pushed open the car door and climbed to his feet.

Waiting five more minutes, or even five more days, wouldn't make the task ahead any easier.

Parker straightened his tie and grabbed his attaché from the back seat of the car. He wasn't that preteen boy with a killer crush on Kayleigh Jemison anymore. He was a god-damned professional, and he was going to act like it, even if it killed him.

As Parker approached the shop, he caught sight of Kayleigh's shock of coppery-red curls through the window. She was gorgeous, as always, with her honey-brown skin and expressive coffee-brown eyes.

Kayleigh was laughing with a customer, but as she waved goodbye to the woman, she caught a glimpse of him standing outside, gawking at her.

Her deep scowl and hard stare confirmed exactly what he'd expected. Kayleigh Jemison was going to give him hell.

He reached into his pocket, flipped the top on a tube of antacids and popped two into his mouth.

Kayleigh Jemison folded her arms as she stared through the window of her small handmade-jewelry-and-consignment shop.

What the hell was he doing there? It wasn't Christmas and his mother's and sister's birthdays weren't imminent. And the uptight, Wall-Street-wannabe certainly wasn't the kind of man who'd wear her hand-tooled jewelry. So why was he here? And why on earth was he staring at her like she was a museum exhibit?

Kayleigh involuntarily dragged her fingers through her wild red curls, trying to create some semblance of order.

It was a slow weekday, so she'd been in the back, stamping and hammering metal pieces to be shipped to customers across the country. She wore a faded old T-shirt and a tattered pair of jeans stained with leather dye. A black bandanna pulled her hair back.

In short, she looked a hot damn mess.

Of all the days for him to show up at her shop... Kayleigh sighed, giving up any hope of redeeming her look.

What did it matter anyway?

As far as Parker was concerned, she was beneath the mighty Abbotts. They were the family with the keys to the kingdom in their growing small town of Magnolia Lake, Tennessee, a gem situated in the foothills of the picturesque Smoky Mountains.

The Abbotts, owners of King's Finest Distillery, the largest local employer, were well-known and beloved by everyone in town.

Except her.

The little bell over the entrance tinkled when Parker yanked open the door, holding it for the customer who was leaving. The woman was juggling her purse, her bags and an unruly toddler.

So he does have manners. He just uses them selectively.

"Parker Abbott, what brings you into my shop today?" Kayleigh stood straight as a rod and tried to relax her involuntary scowl.

She'd returned to Magnolia Lake to start a business after going to college in Nashville and then living in Atlanta. Waging an outright war with the Abbotts would be detrimental to her interests. Besides, despite her disdain for Parker and his father, his mother and sister were nice enough. They'd been longtime customers and had referred lots of other clients. They'd even invited her to sell a few of her higher-end pieces on consignment at the distillery gift shop.

It was a lucrative partnership. So despite her utter disdain for the man who'd once been her closest friend, but betrayed her without the slightest hint of an apology, she would play nice.

For now.

"I wondered if you planned on coming in or if you were auditioning to be a living statue."

Okay, maybe not exactly nice, but close enough.

He glared at her with his typical Parker Abbott glare, but then he did something beyond strange.

He actually *smiled*.

Or at least he was attempting to smile. He looked like Jack Nicholson as the Joker.

She kept that observation to herself, but she couldn't help the smirk that spread across her face.

"Good afternoon, Kayleigh," Parker said in a tone that was unnaturally cheerful for him. "I was hoping I could have a few minutes of your time, if you're not too busy."

Kayleigh scanned the empty store, but bit back a flippant response. "Sure. What can I do for you, Abbott?"

Parker relaxed and his smile looked a little more natural. "Actually, I'd like to do something for you."

"Is that right?" Kayleigh folded her arms, one eyebrow raised. "Now, what would that be?"

Parker indicated the two chaises placed back-to-back in the center of the store. "Would it be all right if we sat?"

Kayleigh shrugged. "Sure."

After Parker took a seat on one of the chaises, she sat at the opposite end and turned toward him, glancing at the leather cuff timepiece on her wrist. "You were saying?"

Parker was one of the most impatient men she knew. Why, for God's sake, wasn't he getting to the point? She had orders to complete and ship.

"I'd like to buy your store."

"What?"

Surely she'd misheard him. Why on earth would Parker want to do that? The man had no use for her jewelry; he only wore a watch. In fact he collected high-end timepieces purchased at seizure auctions and estate sales. But that was the extent of his jewelry collection, as far as she could tell.

Kayleigh schooled her features, determined not to show her surprise. "I'm sorry, did you say you want to purchase my store?"

Parker straightened his tie and made another attempt at a smile. This one was better. "Not the store, per se. What we're after is the building. You'd be free to reestablish the store wherever you'd like."

Kayleigh almost laughed. She pointed to the worn floorboards beneath her. "You want *this* building?"

She loved this place, but the old girl was falling apart at the seams. She'd bought it five years ago, expecting it to be a long-term fixer-upper. But the building had required expensive repairs to the foundation, new plumbing and electrical rewiring. All of which had cost a bundle but had done little to improve the aesthetics.

The ancient roof had been patched more times than she cared to admit, and the HVAC system for the store was just about on its last legs. The nicest part of the building was the apartment she rented out upstairs. Her apartment, also upstairs, had plenty of shabby but very little chic.

"Why would you want to buy my building? The distillery is ten miles from here. And if you want a building in town, why not one built in that new multipurpose shopping center your brother is building up the road?"

There was a tick in Parker's jaw and his mask slipped. He seemed to be making a real effort to hide his annoyance, but it flickered in his dark eyes.

"We have plans for it."

It was evident that Parker didn't want to share those plans. At least not with her.

"Thank you for the offer, but my building isn't for sale," Kayleigh said politely, rising to her feet.

"You haven't even heard my offer." Parker stood, too.

"It doesn't matter what you're offering because the building isn't for sale." She folded her arms again.

"Despite its current condition, I'll give you the tax-assessed value of the building."

Though she knew the information was public, it made

her skin crawl to think that Parker had gone through her records. She scowled. "Thanks, but no thanks."

She walked behind the counter, hoping he'd get the hint.

"Kayleigh, you're being unreasonable. I'm making you a generous offer." When she didn't reply, he waved his large hand around the room. "My God, look at this place. No one in their right mind is going to give you full value for this building in the condition it's in now."

"I plan to fix the place up. Flip it, eventually."

"We both know that's not something you can afford. If you could, you surely would've replaced that old, leaky roof by now."

Kayleigh's face stung. It was one thing for her to disparage her old, run-down building; it was another thing altogether for the high-and-mighty Lord Parker Abbott to do it.

"You don't know anything about me or what I can afford," she seethed, her pulse racing.

"Then why haven't you—"

"I'll replace the damn roof when I'm good and ready."

Parker sighed, clearly exasperated that she hadn't fallen to her knees and kissed his expensive Italian loafers, thanking him for his "generous" offer.

"It's your first property and it's where you started your business. You're sentimental about the place. I get it. I'll offer you five percent above tax value."

"No." Kayleigh peered at him.

"Ten percent above."

"No." Her heart jackhammered in her chest. Partly because she was indignant that Parker Abbott thought he could just walk in off the street and steal her building right from under her. As if she was an inconsequential bug he could squash under his heel and then keep it moving. Partly because she realized she was acting contrary to her own best interest.

Parker was right. No one else would want this building

in its current condition, and they certainly wouldn't give her the tax-assessed value for it.

"Dammit, Kayleigh, we're being more than generous here. You're just being obstinate for the sake of it. Forget for a moment that it's me making the offer and just think about it. You can move to that new shopping center that's going to get all that tourist traffic. It's a win-win for both of us."

"Is there a better way for me to say this? Hmm... Let me see... Hell to the no, Parker. My building isn't for sale."

Parker sighed heavily, as if the words he was conjuring were causing him physical pain. "All right, Kayleigh. What if we pay fifty percent more than the assessed value?"

Kayleigh's ears perked up. If cheap-ass Parker Abbott was offering to overpay for her building, he wanted the place desperately. Which meant she was the one with the leverage. This was the opportunity she'd been waiting for. A chance to reclaim some of what Duke Abbott had stolen from her family.

While she and her older sister, Evelisse, were away at college and her father was deathly ill, Duke had paid her mother a mere pittance for the land she'd inherited from Kayleigh's maternal grandfather. He'd taken advantage of her mother at her lowest point and robbed them of land that had been handed down in their family for generations.

Kayleigh stood taller, her chin tipped up as she met his intense gaze. "It would be nice to move my shop to the new mixed-use center, but as I'm sure you already know, leasing space there won't be cheap. And there's something else you haven't considered..."

"And what might that be?" Parker, the unofficial president of the Hard-core Perfectionists' Club, looked indignant at her insinuation that he'd overlooked something.

"This building doesn't just house my business. It's also my home. Then there's the rental income from the other apartment. While your offer seems generous on the surface…all things considered…it's a hard pass."

"That's why I'm offering you way more than this… *place*…is worth."

"But not enough if you expect me to move my shop, studio and apartment while also recouping lost rental income."

"No one's lived there since Savannah moved out three years ago," Parker said, referring to his sister-in-law and Kayleigh's closest friend.

"I make even more off it as an Airbnb," she said casually.

"Okay, fine. What figure would you consider adequate compensation?" Parker shoved his hands in his pockets and widened his stance.

Kayleigh's gaze was automatically drawn to the panel over his zipper and the outline of his…

Nope. Uh-uh. Hell no.

"Give me twice the tax-assessed value and I'll gladly hand the building over to you today. Lock, stock and barrel."

Parker looked like a volcano about to erupt. "Are you insane? Seriously, Kayleigh, you should be paying me to take this friggin' money pit off your hands. Like, right now, before the whole damn building falls down around us." He gestured wildly.

Before she could tell him exactly where he could shove his last offer, her phone rang. She blew out a hard breath and whipped her phone out of her pocket.

Kira Brennan.

Kayleigh hadn't seen or heard that name in more than seven years. She hadn't expected to ever again. So why was Kira Brennan calling her now?

Two

Kayleigh's back stiffened and her heart beat in double time as she stared at the number on her phone.

Kira was her ex-boyfriend's younger sister. And during the three years she'd dated Aidan Brennan, she'd been closer to Kira than she was to her own sister. But they hadn't spoken in years. What could she possibly want?

Kayleigh considered not answering the phone. Maybe it was best if she just let it go to voice mail. Then she could listen to the message and answer later, preferably by text.

The last time they'd spoken, Kira had been bitter and resentful. Kayleigh and Aidan had been together three years, and he'd started to hint at the possibility of marriage. But Kayleigh couldn't imagine herself as a member of the Brennan family.

Neither could their matriarch, Colleen Brennan.

Aidan's mother had told her, in no uncertain terms, that she'd merely tolerated their relationship as a phase Aidan needed to get out of his system. But she would never welcome Kayleigh into the Brennan family.

Mrs. Brennan had told Kayleigh that if she really loved

Aidan, she'd do what was best for everyone and end the relationship, before things got any more serious between them.

Kayleigh had walked away. Not because his mother had asked her to, but because everything the woman said was true.

Except for Kira and Aidan, who both loved her, everyone else in the Brennan clan had seemed irritated and uptight every time she had shown up at another of their family functions. More important, as much as she'd loved Aidan, she just hadn't fit into his world.

She hadn't turned down his offer because she was intimidated by his mother; she'd done it because she'd genuinely believed it was in both their best interests.

She'd explained her position to Aidan, but chosen not to disclose her talk with his mother. He'd been crushed by her decision to walk away, and so had his sister.

So why was Kira calling her now?

"Kayleigh? Is everything all right?" Parker's voice was laced with what almost sounded like genuine concern.

"Absolutely." The last thing she wanted to do was reveal a chink in her armor to a shark like Parker Abbott. "And if you're not willing to meet my number, the answer is still no."

"But, Kayleigh—"

Her phone rang again. *Kira.*

Panic gripped her chest. If Kira was so determined to reach her after all this time, there had to be a reason. Her brother had moved on. He'd found someone else. Someone more to Mrs. Brennan's liking. They'd gotten married and had their first child all in the space of one year.

But maybe Kira was calling because something had happened to her brother.

"I need to take this call." Kayleigh held up a finger. She turned her back to Parker and walked a few paces away.

"Hello?"

"Kayleigh! Thank God you answered! I hate leaving voice mails. I never know what to say, especially on an occasion like this."

Kira was still an energetic chatterbox. And even after all this time, she knew she didn't need to identify herself. That Kayleigh would just know who she was.

"It's good to hear from you, Kira." Kayleigh smiled. "Especially after the way we left things—"

"I know... I was a stupid kid. I didn't mean any of those awful things I said, but I was so hurt and angry. I know that's no excuse, but—"

"It's okay, Kira. I realize how hard it must've been for you to understand why I did what I did."

"I do understand. Mother told me about the conversation she had with you after Aidan asked her for our grandmother's wedding ring. I only wish you'd told us instead of just walking away."

"Does he know?" Kayleigh cast a glance over her shoulder at Parker, who was pacing the floor.

He tapped on the face of his black Hermès watch with a double leather strap.

Kayleigh considered holding up a different finger, but held up her index finger instead and dipped behind the curtain to her studio space in the back.

"No. She wouldn't have told me, but I figured it out from something she said when she was a little...shall we say tipsy? The next morning she begged me not to tell Aidan, and I caved. Mostly because I know how much it would hurt him. And about Aidan—"

"I don't want to talk about Aidan." Kayleigh ran her fingers through her hair, probably making it look like even more of a crow's nest than it already did. "What's past is past."

"No problem. That isn't why I called anyway."

"So why did you call? Not that I'm not glad to hear from you."

"First I want to apologize for my behavior and for what my mother did."

"Apology accepted." Even if Kira was no longer in her life, it felt better knowing that the air between them had been cleared. "And what's the other reason?"

"To tell you that… I'm getting married!" Kira finished her sentence with a squeal. "Can you believe it?"

"Oh honey, that's wonderful news. I'm so happy for you."

"That's not even the best part…" Kira took a dramatic pause. "I want you to be in my wedding!"

"Me? Why?"

"Because my fiancé has a ton of brothers, and I want my bridesmaids to be people who have been truly important in my life. Not just some random, distant cousin filling up a spot. Our relationship meant so much to me. I want you to be there to share my day."

Kayleigh hesitated for a moment. "Are you sure this isn't just about pissing your mother off?"

"Well, there's that, too." Kira laughed. "But seriously, you mean a lot to me, Kayleigh."

"And Aidan and his wife won't be upset?"

"I guarantee you that Aidan's wife won't raise any objections." The humor was gone from her voice. "And neither will my brother. In fact I'm sure he'll be glad to see you again."

"I don't know, Kira. When's the wedding?"

"In two and a half months. And get this…my fiancé's family owns a private island in the Caribbean. That's where we're getting married. And we're flying everyone out for the entire week, all-expenses paid."

An all-expenses-paid vacation on an island in the Caribbean for an entire week? That was something to consider.

"Kira, I'm honored that you'd ask me to be part of your wedding—"

"Then you'll do it? Awesome! Just text me the name of your plus-one and all the information my wedding co-ordinator will need to book your flights. You're the best, Kayleigh. Bye!"

Kira had ended the call before Kayleigh could tell her she'd *think* about it and that she most certainly didn't have a plus-one.

She scrubbed a hand across her forehead and sighed. The truth was that, as reluctant as she was to do this, she'd always had a soft spot for Kira. So they both knew she'd eventually cave.

Besides, maybe by the time the wedding rolled around, she would actually have a plus-one prospect.

She shoved her phone into her back pocket and returned to the front of the store, where Parker looked fit to be tied.

Parker stared at Kayleigh. He'd bet she took that call in the middle of their negotiations just to tick him off.

If that was her aim, she'd succeeded.

He was a busy man. He'd scheduled exactly thirty-five minutes for this meeting. It was already going on forty-five minutes and they hadn't agreed on anything.

Kayleigh was being stubborn. No, downright ornery. Was she really going to allow her disdain for him to prevent her from accepting his exceedingly generous offer?

"So, where were we?" Kayleigh seemed distracted and her hair looked even wilder than it had when she'd disappeared behind the curtain. As if she'd just tumbled out of bed and she hadn't been alone.

He swallowed hard, fighting off the image of Kayleigh in bed that immediately filled his brain.

Focus, Parker. Focus.

"I'd offered you fifty percent more than the assessed value."

She froze for a moment, cocking her head before a smirk curled one corner of her mouth. "I remember now. You asked what figure would make me happy, and I said—"

"I know what you said, Kayleigh, and it's unacceptable."

"Then buy someone else's building instead." She stared at him defiantly.

The number-one rule of negotiating was be prepared to walk away. Every salesperson understood that. But his family hadn't given him that option. This building had once belonged to his mother's family. They'd run a tiny café here, and now his father wanted to help his mother reclaim a portion of her family's history by creating a flagship restaurant here, branded with the King's Finest name.

It was going to be a surprise. His mother didn't know, but his father had already purchased the two other buildings on the block and made the sellers sign confidentiality agreements. But without Kayleigh's building—the cornerstone of the entire project—it simply wouldn't work.

Closing this deal was the leverage he needed to make his father realize that naming his older brother, Blake, as his successor at King's Finest, simply because he'd had the good fortune to be born first, would be a grave mistake.

Blake was a good person, a great brother and an excellent operations manager. But neither Blake nor their brother Max possessed the killer instinct the CEO position called for. His sister, Zora, did have that killer instinct. More so than he, perhaps. But what she lacked was the ability to control her emotions. With Zora, everything was personal. She was much like Kayleigh in that way.

He had to have this building, but Kayleigh didn't know that. So maybe if he showed her that he was willing to walk away, she'd come to her senses.

Parker stooped to pick up his attaché. "Sorry we couldn't

come to an agreement. Maybe it would be better if we went with new construction in that shopping center. I'm sure my brother will give us a good deal."

Parker crossed the room under Kayleigh's cold stare, waiting for her to stop him.

She didn't.

He turned the doorknob and stepped one foot onto the sidewalk, the bell jingling above him.

Still nothing.

"You really don't have anything else to say?" Parker turned back to her.

"Don't let the doorknob hit you where the good Lord split you." She grinned, her eyes shimmering with amusement.

Parker blew out an exasperated breath and stepped back inside. "Look, there has to be *something* we can do to sweeten the deal for you. I can do the one-point-five and throw in renovation of your new space so that it meets your specific needs. Or maybe an all-expenses paid vacation."

"What did you say?" She narrowed her gaze at him.

He now had Kayleigh's rapt attention.

"I said we can renovate your space so it fits your needs."

"Or…"

"Or throw in an all-expenses paid vacation." Something in Kayleigh's expression unnerved him. The wheels were definitely turning in her head.

"That." She shook a finger in his direction, her gaze not meeting his, as if she was still working everything out. "I want the all-expenses paid vacation, but you won't have to pay for it."

Parker scratched the back of his neck. Kayleigh Jemison had confounded him for years. He didn't think it was possible, but today she was more confusing than usual. "That doesn't make any sense. The whole point of the offer is to—"

"I know how negotiations work, Abbott," she said dismissively. "Just listen and don't panic while I tell you the rest."

Now Parker was really alarmed. He set his attaché on the floor again and shoved his hands in his pockets. "I'm listening."

"You pay me twice the property's assessed value. That will allow me to lease a new shop and buy a nice condo in the same complex."

Parker had no desire to overpay for Kayleigh's crumbling building, but his father had insisted that he do whatever it took to acquire the property. It was to be his anniversary gift to Parker's mother, and a sound investment for their business.

"I'll consider it," he said gruffly.

"But there's one more thing I need."

"In addition to us overpaying for the property?"

She didn't acknowledge the comment. "As a condition of our deal, you'll need to accompany me on a one-week, all-expenses paid trip to the Caribbean."

He stared at her for a moment, waiting for the punch line.

"But you despise me." When she didn't disagree, Parker leaned against a display case, his arms folded across his chest as he studied her. "Why would you want me, of all people, to accompany you?"

He wasn't always the best at reading people, but there was definitely something that Kayleigh was having a hard time getting out.

"You have to pretend to be my fiancé." She cringed as she said the words.

"What?" Parker pressed a hand to his forehead, stunned by her request. "You're not serious."

"You need this building for whatever your next big venture is, and I need a fake fiancé for a week. It's not as if I'm asking you to trade murders, Abbott. This isn't *Strangers on a Train*. Do you want this building or not?"

"There are escorts for this sort of thing, or have you not seen *The Wedding Date*?" he retorted. She wasn't the only one who could throw around a film reference to make a point.

"You're no Dermot Mulroney," she mumbled under her breath. "This isn't some romantic fantasy, and I have zero interest in sleeping with you. So if that's what's worrying you, let me put your mind at ease."

Kayleigh Jemison evidently had no compunction about taking a Louisville Slugger to his ego.

"We'll pay double, without the pretend fiancé thing. Final offer."

"Then no deal." She folded her arms. She'd gone from sheepish to defiant again. "The fiancé thing is nonnegotiable."

He'd thought she'd thrown that in as a bargaining chip just to get him to agree to double his original offer, but she was serious.

Dead serious.

"Then we'll pay one and a half times the assessed value and I'm sure one of my brothers would be happy enough to get a free vacation and play your fake fiancé for a week."

"Twice the value and *you* play fake fiancé for a week. Am I not being clear about this? Because I really feel like I am." She smirked, a hint of victory in her voice.

Parker ran a hand over his head and groaned.

"You're dreaming if you think I could even begin to pull this off. You know I was a terrible liar when we were kids. That hasn't changed."

"Then you'd better learn, Abbott."

"Why can't you take Max or Cole? Either of them would be thrilled to go on an all-expenses paid island vacation. I'm sure Cole would be more than happy to share a bed with you." His brother Cole, the one sibling who didn't help manage the distillery, seemed determined to sleep his way through half the town.

"No one said anything about sharing a bed. That's what makes you a pretend fiancé, *genius*." Kayleigh clenched her fists, her chest puffing out.

"You expect me to fake intimacy? We were friends once, but we hardly know each other now. And you think I'll be able to pretend well enough to fool someone who was your close friend? You're being completely unreasonable here." Parker took a cloth from his pocket and cleaned his glasses. "Even for you, and that's saying a lot."

She sneered at him, then sighed. "You're right. We'd never fool Kira with this." She gestured between them. "She'd sense that we're virtual strangers."

Parker breathed a sigh of relief, returned his glasses to the bridge of his nose and picked up his pen again. "So in lieu of the whole pretend fiancé thing…"

"No in lieu of." Kayleigh shook her head vigorously and a few of her bouncy red curls spilled from the bandanna. "I didn't say we weren't doing it—I just said it wouldn't work the way things stand between us now. That means we need to put some effort into it. We have ten weeks to get to know each other."

"Kayleigh, how do you expect—"

"That's the deal, Abbott. Take it or leave it." Even the insidious grin slowly spreading across her face couldn't dim her beauty. If anything, the sly smile highlighted her perfect cheekbones.

Acquire this building, no matter what it takes.

He could hear his father's words in his head. When his siblings on the King's Finest board had laughed, insisting he wouldn't be able to cut a deal with Kayleigh Jemison, he'd taken it as a personal challenge.

Parker loved his mother and knew how much owning

this piece of her family's history would mean to her. Still, it was a lot to ask.

His teeth clenched and one fist balled at his side. "I'll have the contract and confidentiality agreements drawn up and let you know when they're ready to be signed. For now, though, this deal stays between us."

Kayleigh could barely contain a grin as she gave him a two-finger salute. "Pleasure doin' business with you, Abbott."

Parker grunted in response as he headed to his car.

Now he was saddled with a broken-down building and a fake fiancée who hated his guts.

His siblings were going to get a kick out of this.

Three

"Are you all done?" Parker sat at one end of the conference-room table, fuming as his father, brothers Blake and Max, and sister, Zora, laughed so hard that tears came to their eyes. "If so, I'd like to get back to the business at hand."

"That Kayleigh is a shrewd businesswoman." His father dabbed his eyes with a hankie, then stuffed it into his pocket. "You have to give her that."

He could think of things he'd like to give Kayleigh Jemison. A compliment wasn't one of them.

She'd turned him into the family punch line and seemed determined to make the next few months of his life a nightmare. They still had to iron out the details, but he'd have to spend the next few months getting to know her. It'd be like two betta fish being placed in a single bowl.

"C'mon, Parker, don't try to act like you're not secretly looking forward to a little alone time with Kayleigh." Zora wiped away tears with her knuckle. "It's no secret you have a little—"

"I'm not and I don't." He addressed his sister—the baby

of the family—pointedly. "Now, if we could get back to the details of the contract."

"Savannah won't believe it when I tell her this." Blake chuckled.

"Neither will Mom," Max added, shaking his head. "Once we finally tell her. But I'm sure the prospect of marrying off another one of her kids will thrill her to death."

"No one is getting married." Parker's voice came out shriller than he'd intended. He straightened his tie and released a slow breath. "I'm glad I could provide you all with a bit of amusement today, but we can finish this around the dinner table on Sunday." He tapped his Bvlgari Roma Finissimo watch. "Right now we're on the clock and I need to get the team's agreement on the details of this contract so I can get it revised and signed before Kayleigh changes her mind."

"Parker's right," his father said, with one final chuckle. "Time is of the essence. I think I speak for all of us when I say, we gladly accept Miss Jemison's terms."

Of course they did.

They weren't the ones sentenced to spend the next three months in hell.

"So, when were you going to tell me you proposed to Parker?" Savannah Abbott asked as Kayleigh slid into her seat in their favorite booth at the Magnolia Lake Bakery.

"First, I did *not* propose to Parker. Second, he said I wasn't permitted to talk to anyone about the deal, so I couldn't tell you."

"I had to hear it from Blake." Savannah's hazel eyes danced. "I thought it was an April Fools' joke."

Savannah was Parker Abbott's sister-in-law. When she'd come to town three years ago, she'd loathed the Abbotts as much as Kayleigh did. But while carrying out her plan to prove that half of the King's Finest Distillery rightfully belonged to her grandfather, Martin McDowell, Savannah had fallen for Blake Abbott. In the end it turned out that neither of their grandfathers had been completely honest about what had happened to their partnership all those years ago.

They'd both fessed up and Joseph Abbott had felt guilty enough to give McDowell and his two granddaughters—Savannah and her younger sister, Delaney—a share of the business. He'd also written Martin a seven-figure check.

"Honestly, I was kind of relieved that I couldn't tell you about my deal with Parker. It's embarrassing to admit that I needed to barter for a date to my friend's wedding."

"Why did you feel you needed to?" Savannah employed the same patient, soothing tone she used when trying to reason with her nearly two-year-old son, Davis.

"This isn't just any friend's wedding. She's my ex's younger sister."

"The guy you moved to Atlanta with after college?" Savannah looked up from sipping her coffee.

"Aidan." Kayleigh confirmed with a nod. "He's married now. To a gorgeous woman from the right family. Last I heard, they had a couple of kids together." Kayleigh gripped her mug tighter in response to the tightness in her chest.

"I'm starting to get the picture." Savannah squeezed her friend's hand. "But, sweetie, you were the one who walked away. You have nothing to prove to him or anyone else."

"I know, but the thought of being the only one there alone while everyone else on the island is boo'd up…" Kayleigh heaved a sigh and raked her fingers through her curls. "I couldn't bear for Aidan to look at me and feel like he dodged a bullet by not marrying me. Or worse, that he'd pity me."

"If he thinks that, he's a fool." Savannah gave her hand one last squeeze before picking up her mug and taking a sip of her vanilla decaf latte. "So I understand why you felt compelled to take someone as your date, but why Parker? I thought you couldn't stand him."

"I can't." Kayleigh's eyes met her friend's. She blew out a long breath. "But this was going to be awkward, no matter who I brought along. I figured that at least with Parker, I know exactly who I'm dealing with, so there won't be any misunderstandings. This is a business deal, not a hookup."

The corner of Savannah's mouth lifted in a smirk. She brought the mug to her lips and mumbled under her breath, "If you say so."

"You don't actually think I *want* to spend an entire week sharing a room with Parker Abbott."

Savannah shrugged as she sipped her latte. "You two do have pretty passionate feelings for one another."

"It's pure, unadulterated loathing. Nothing more. Now can we change the subject?"

"After you answer a few more questions." Savannah set her cup down and leaned forward, folding her arms on the table. "Since you went for broke and declared that you were bringing your fiancé, won't it become painfully obvious that you two dislike each other?"

"Like I said, I may not have been thinking clearly." She shrugged. "I figured I'd put together a backstory of how we met. And we can fill out a couple of those questionnaires to get to know each other. You know the kind that ask about your favorite color and your ideal date?"

Savannah practically snorted. "*That's* your game plan?"

"Pretty much." Kayleigh's cheeks heated beneath her friend's stare. "I mean, we do have two and a half months to memorize this stuff."

"Kayleigh, sweetie…" Savannah took a deep breath as she returned her mug to the table. "Parker is supposed to be your fiancé, which means you two should look like you're head over heels in love. No basic questionnaire is going to get you two to that point. Not in a way that will convince anyone who spends more than three seconds with the two of you." Savannah sighed, but her hazel eyes were filled with warmth. "Are you sure that you should bring Parker on the trip? Can't you just say that your fiancé couldn't make it because of a business obligation?"

"It'll look like I made the whole thing up."

"Which you did."

"Sometimes a girl has to do what a girl has to do. You, of all people, should understand that." Kayleigh took a sip of her coffee.

Savannah's eyes widened and she lowered her gaze to her cup.

Kayleigh's cheeks stung and her gut twisted in a knot. "I'm sorry. I shouldn't have said that."

Savannah gave her a small nod, her eyes not meeting Kayleigh's.

Savannah and Blake had fallen in love and had managed to work things out, despite their rocky start. Still, Kayleigh knew her friend harbored guilt over the way she'd deceived Blake and his family in the beginning.

Kayleigh squeezed her friend's hand. "I didn't mean to sound bitchy and judgmental. I just thought that you'd understand that sometimes the ends justify the means. Your grandfather would never have gotten what was rightfully owed to him if it hadn't been for you. And he might never have rectified things with his old friend or gotten to see his great-grandson before he passed."

"I was trying to restore my grandfather's legacy and dig our family out of debt," Savannah said sharply. "I didn't do what I did just to make my ex jealous."

"Now who's being bitchy and judgmental?" Kayleigh raised a brow and drank the last of her coffee.

Savannah sighed. "This is important to you. I get it. But it still goes back to what I said before. You won't fool your ex or his sister with your sad little 'I love red and he loves green' routine."

"Then help me. Please." She flashed her best sad, puppy-dog eyes at her friend.

"Fine, but only if you'll do *exactly* what I say. I won't invest my time in this little scheme of yours if you're planning to half-ass it."

"Thank you, thank you, thank you!" Kayleigh bounced in her seat. "I'll do whatever you say. I promise. Parker on the other hand—"

"Don't worry about Parker." Savannah waved a hand dismissively. "Leave him to us." She pulled out her phone and opened her text app. "I'll enlist Blake and Benji to make sure Parker understands exactly what's at stake."

If Parker Abbott cared about her feelings, they'd still be friends.

Kayleigh's face burned and tears stung her eyes as she remembered the day in sixth grade when their friendship had ended. She'd caught Parker repeating things she'd confided in him about her father—the town drunk—to a chorus of laughter from the popular kids with whom he'd chosen to ingratiate himself.

"When do we start?"

"Right now." Savannah shoved a monogrammed pen and pad across the table. "Make a list of everything you like about Parker."

Kayleigh frowned. "Can't we start with something easier? Like a list of reasons he's incredibly irritating?"

"Do you want my help or not, Ms. Thing?"

Kayleigh pouted. "This is harder than I thought."

"You're not trying. Parker may be annoying, but he's brilliant. And he's determined when he believes he's right."

"Which is always," Kayleigh muttered. She jotted down *smart* and *determined*.

"You know, you and Parker have a lot in common."

"That's a low blow." Kayleigh dropped the pen. "Name one way I'm like Parker."

"You're both stubborn smart-asses who can be exasperating. You're both extremely good at what you do, and you're both carrying king-size chips on your shoulders."

"I said *one* thing." Kayleigh held up a finger. "The rest was completely unnecessary."

Savannah grinned. "Just keep working on that list. I'm going to grab something to eat. Want anything?"

Kayleigh shook her head as she studied the list.

She closed her eyes and pictured Parker's face. Beneath that constant scowl was a strong jaw, dark, piercing eyes and sensual lips framed by a neat, full goatee. Kayleigh's eyes opened suddenly as her cheeks flushed with heat.

Some women might find Parker hot—with or without his glasses.

She scribbled *fairly attractive*, *gainfully employed*, *wealthy* and *family-oriented*.

"You're making progress." Savannah set down a warm sticky bun and slid into her seat.

"Speaking of progress…doesn't that defeat the purpose of yoga this morning?"

"I'm allowed a few extra calories." Savannah broke into a slow grin and pressed a hand to her belly. "I'm pregnant."

"Savannah, that's wonderful!" Kayleigh hugged her friend.

She was thrilled for Savannah. She had the dream husband, a career she loved, an adorable little boy and another little one on the way. And she'd never have to worry about money again.

Still, Kayleigh envied her friend's happiness. Wanted a piece of it for herself.

"Thanks, but please don't tell anyone," Savannah said as they returned to their seats. "Blake and I will share the news with his family at dinner on Sunday. Then I'll call my sister."

"I won't say a word." Kayleigh forced a smile. "When is the baby due?"

"November." Savannah reviewed Kayleigh's list as she nibbled on the sticky bun. "This is a good start, but it's just the basics. And right now they're empty words. If you have any hope of pulling this off, you and Parker have to spend time getting to know each other."

The knot in Kayleigh's stomach tightened. "Are we talking about a couple of get-to-know-you sessions?"

"Sorry, babe." Savannah pushed her plate aside. Her grin indicated she wasn't sorry at all. "I'm talking full-on dating…on steroids."

"What's Option Two?" Kayleigh slumped in her seat. Her mouth went dry and her palms felt clammy.

"Tell your friend the truth. There is no fiancé and there never was one."

"Fine." Kayleigh dragged a hand across her forehead. "If you can convince Parker to do this, I'm in, too."

"Perfect." Savannah's Cheshire Cat grin faded. She placed a hand to her mouth. "I'm going to be sick."

Me, too. Kayleigh buried her forehead in her hand as her best friend made a beeline to the restroom.

Her saving grace was knowing Parker would never go for it.

Four

"Now you expect me to date Kayleigh Jemison, too? Have you all lost your freaking minds?" Parker paced the floor in the conference room. "It's bad enough I have to spend a week pretending to be her fiancé."

"You know this plan will never work the way things stand between you and Kayleigh now," Savannah said calmly. "Besides, it'll give you two a chance to finally hash things out."

"Your sister-in-law is right, son," Duke piped up. "This feud between you two has gone on for too long."

"It isn't a feud," Parker clarified. "She hates my guts. End of story."

"You hurt her, Parker, and you never even apologized," his sister pointed out. "What do you expect?"

"For the hundredth time… I didn't say anything she hadn't said herself."

"I love you, Park," his sister said. "But you can be an asshole sometimes. You're so determined to prove yourself right that you're not giving the slightest consideration to Kayleigh's feelings."

"Let's not stoop to name-calling, baby girl," their father said sternly, glancing around the room at all of them.

He came to stand beside Parker in front of the conference room windows and placed a hand on his shoulder.

"Son, I realize that I'm asking a lot of you, but this is important to me because it's important to your mother. She's put her heart and soul into supporting my father's dream and into raising this family. This is our chance to help her revive her father's legacy. It's something she's dreamed about for years, and now we finally have the opportunity to make it happen. I'm sorry that the bulk of the load will fall to you. But this is important, Parker. Not just for your mother, but for King's Finest, too."

Parker groaned as he stared out the window. They had no idea what they were asking of him.

Kayleigh Jemison loathed him, but despite what his family believed, he didn't despise her. He was angry with Kayleigh. Maybe even hurt by her unrelenting disdain. But spending time with her at Blake and Savannah's wedding had made it clear that he was still very fond of her.

Being forced to spend a week with Kayleigh would test his will in more ways than they knew.

"I'll do it for Mom." Parker nodded. "And for the sake of this deal."

His father clapped a hand on his back and smiled. "Thank you, son. This means a lot to all of us."

His father was counting on him. Hell, his entire family was counting on him to make this deal happen. He'd been given a gift. He wanted to prove that when it was time to name a successor to the King's Finest throne, he was the obvious choice. What better way to show his fitness for the role of CEO than by proving that he'd go beyond the call of duty to ensure the company's success?

Their receptionist, Lianna, called the conference room

to announce the arrivals of Kayleigh and their attorney, Lane Dennings.

"Speak now or forever hold your peace." Max could barely contain his grin as Blake and Zora dissolved into laughter in response to his marriage pun.

Parker wouldn't give his siblings the satisfaction of reacting. He simply ignored them.

"Ready, son?" His father held back a smile.

Parker nodded and sat at the table.

"I'll clear the room. Go ahead and send them up, Lianna," his father said. "I'll meet them at the elevator."

"You're putting us out?" Zora groused.

"We don't want to intimidate her. Parker, Lane and I have to be here, and Kayleigh requested that Savannah stay."

"Well, I'm going down to the day care to spend some time with Davis before I go back to work." Blake looked especially happy. He leaned down and gave his wife a quick kiss before exiting on the heels of Max, Zora and their father.

"Right this way, ladies," his father was saying.

Parker's eyes met Kayleigh's as she entered the room. His pulse quickened and his mouth went dry.

He'd expected her to show up in tattered jeans and a T-shirt, with her hair a mess. But she hadn't.

Kayleigh was stunning in a simple white blouse and a plain black skirt with a hemline that hovered just above her knees. Her hair fell below her shoulders in bouncy curls that swayed with every movement.

He'd barely managed spending a single day with her when he'd been charged with escorting her down the aisle at Blake and Savannah's wedding.

Ten weeks and ten dates?

He was an absolute goner.

* * *

Kayleigh Jemison was not easily intimidated. But there was something unnerving about Parker Abbott's appraisal as she entered the conference room.

His eyes widened with surprise as his gaze met hers and then slowly trailed down the length of her body.

Savannah had been right. Dressing the part was a good choice. It'd thrown Parker for a loop.

What she hadn't expected was that she'd find his reaction unsettling. Her cheeks felt warm and there was a fluttering low in her belly.

Parker scrambled to his feet and buttoned the heather-gray suit jacket that fit him so well. He offered a stern nod.

Kayleigh returned the gesture before turning her attention to Duke Abbott, who stood beside his son.

"Ladies, please have a seat." Duke gestured toward the chair beside Savannah. "Kayleigh, thank you for agreeing to meet us here."

She smoothed down the black A-line skirt that skimmed her thighs before taking her seat next to her friend, who squeezed her arm reassuringly. "Thank you for agreeing to my price and terms."

Kayleigh insisted that the purchase agreement for her building clearly spell out that the deal was contingent on Parker fulfilling his end of the bargain. Duke agreed readily, assuring her that he was a man of his word, as was Parker.

In her experience, neither Duke nor his son were trustworthy. But she needed both of them for now, so she'd play nice.

"I appreciate your willingness to accommodate my unusual request." Kayleigh tucked her hair behind her ears to keep it from falling forward.

Parker cleared his throat. "Ready to sign the contract?"

"My attorney went over the agreement thoroughly, but I'd prefer to schedule the ten agreed-upon dates *prior* to signing the agreement."

A deep frown creased Parker's forehead. He opened his leather-bound planner. "For the sake of simplicity, why don't we make it the same day and time each week?"

"What if we already have an event planned that day?"

Parker shrugged. "Then we make that our 'date.'" He used air quotes.

Kayleigh wasn't looking forward to combing through her calendar to schedule ten dates with Parker Abbott any more than he seemed to be.

"That's a reasonable way to settle this, but I think we should allow for flexibility on the time of the 'date.'" She used air quotes, too.

Parker grunted his agreement without looking up.

"How about Sunday afternoons?" she offered.

"We have our family dinner on Sundays." Parker frowned. "How about Wednesday evenings?"

"In the middle of the week?" Now it was Kayleigh's turn to frown. "That's when I do most of my metalwork, and I'm in the studio pretty late, so that won't work for me."

Parker stared up from his datebook. "Saturday afternoons?"

"I can make Saturday work." Kayleigh opened the calendar app on her phone. She'd gotten some part-time help on the weekends; otherwise she would've had to work on Saturday afternoons.

Parker stroked his goatee as he contemplated the calendar. Kayleigh couldn't help studying his handsome features. Neat, thick brows framed his pensive, dark eyes. Full, kissable lips tugged down in an ever-present frown. His slim-cut gray suit accentuated his long, lean frame.

Okay, so she could definitely see why some women might consider Parker Abbott's handsome-geek-chic look hot.

"How long will these dates be?" Parker skipped the air quotes this time, but his tone indicated that they were implied.

"We should allow for flexibility, but two to three hours on average should give us time to rehearse our story and get to know each other."

"Agreed." Parker made careful notes in his datebook. "How do we decide what we'll do on each date?"

"We'll take turns choosing." Kayleigh shrugged.

"Seems fair." Parker nodded. "Why don't you choose first?"

"Actually, I have a suggestion for your first date," Savannah interjected.

They both turned toward her.

"Blake and I want you to come to our house. Nothing fancy, just homemade pizza and a friendly board game or two, after we iron out your story."

"Story?" The lines in Parker's forehead deepened.

"How you two met, why you fell in love with her, your plans for the wedding. The kinds of questions that Kayleigh's friend and her—" Savannah paused when Kayleigh frowned and subtly shook her head "—family are sure to ask."

"I have an excellent memory." Parker tapped his temple.

"It's not about repeating data verbatim, Parker." Savannah was remarkably patient with him. Perhaps because she was the only person in the room accustomed to managing the whims of a toddler. "You must be convincing when you say it."

Parker didn't acknowledge Savannah's statement, but he didn't object either. In Kayleigh's book, that was progress.

"Besides, it's a low-stress way for you two to ease into this arrangement," Savannah added.

"Sounds reasonable." Parker jotted the appointment down in his book. "What time should we be there?"

After the time was set, Duke stepped in to move the process along. He reiterated that the confidentiality agreement prevented her from discussing the deal with anyone other than Savannah or the six members of the King's Finest executive board: Duke, Blake, Parker, Max, Zora and founder Joseph Abbott. She wasn't even permitted to discuss the arrangement with his wife, Iris. Though they wouldn't share the details of the project, it was to be a surprise for her.

"Won't she wonder why Parker and I are suddenly spending so much time together?" Kayleigh frowned.

"She's always hoped that you two would try and repair your friendship." Savannah smiled warmly. "So, as far as Iris is concerned, this is Project Friendship."

Kayleigh had zero interest in trying to resurrect a friendship that had been in tatters for far longer than it had existed. But if that would make Iris feel better, fine.

Once the paperwork was signed, Kayleigh shook Duke's hand, then Parker's.

There was something in his firm handshake and piercing gaze that sent a shiver down her spine. She hugged Savannah and quickly excused herself, eager to make her way back to her Jeep. When she did, she sank into the driver's seat and leaned against the headrest.

Had she really been ogling Parker Abbott? And had he been doing the same?

No, of course not. She despised Parker and he obviously felt the same way about her. It wasn't attraction; it was nerves, plain and simple. She'd insisted on Parker being the one to escort her to Kira's wedding because with him there would be no blurring of the lines. She could count on Parker to keep their dealings strictly business. And she needed to do the same.

Ten dates, then one week together on the island. Afterward they'd both walk away with exactly what they wanted.

Negotiating the deal had been the easy part. Getting to know each other well enough to make Kira and her family believe they were a couple in love and engaged to be married…that was the hard part.

But she'd do it, no matter what. Because the looks of pity she'd garner from her ex and his family if she arrived alone were something she simply couldn't endure.

Five

Kayleigh pulled into Blake and Savannah's driveway and parked her mud-spattered Jeep beside Parker's pristine blue BMW. She wasn't sure how he managed it, but the rims always gleamed and the car always looked like it had just rolled out of the car wash.

Kayleigh studied the gorgeous, timber-frame home situated on a lake.

Parker was right; the Abbotts were on an entirely different spectrum than she was. She had a little shop, one part-time employee and a vehicle that was well over ten years old.

As she stepped out of the Jeep, her legs felt unsteady.

She hated to admit it, even to herself, but she was genuinely nervous about this first date with Parker. It was less of a date and more of a strategic-planning session. But that didn't stop the fluttery feeling in her stomach or the zing of electricity that trailed down her spine when she remembered how their palms had touched when he'd shaken her hand. Or the heat in his dark eyes as he'd surveyed her in her little black skirt.

It was Parker Abbott, for God's sake. The man she'd spent most of her life despising. She needed to get a grip.

"Kayleigh." Savannah stood in the doorway on their large front porch, with Davis on her hip. Her smile was broad and welcoming.

A little of the tension in Kayleigh's shoulders eased as she allowed her friend to give her a hug.

Davis giggled in response to Kayleigh's customary greeting of tickling his belly.

Savannah put the toddler down and instructed him to go to his father, who was in the great room with his Uncle Parker.

Kayleigh's spine stiffened at the mention of Parker's name, but she forced a smile as she faced her friend.

Savannah practically glowed. Her bouncy curls were shiny and radiant. Her hazel eyes seemed to be lit from within.

"One more day before your secret's out," Kayleigh whispered conspiratorially as she glanced down at her friend's belly.

Savannah's hand went there instinctively. "I know. It's been killing us to keep the news to ourselves."

"What news?" Parker appeared suddenly in the kitchen.

"What can I get you, Parker?" Savannah's tone made it clear that she wouldn't be answering his question.

He shook his glass, filled with ice. "Came to get water, but I've got it. Thanks." He nodded toward her. "Hello, Kayleigh."

"Parker." She nodded back.

There was an uncomfortable pause.

"And this is why we need to practice." Savannah glanced from Kayleigh to Parker and back. "Are you sure we shouldn't try for two dates per week, or maybe three?"

"No!" They both said, simultaneously.

"We're both very busy, so it'd be difficult to find the time." Parker looked the tiniest bit apologetic.

"Absolutely," Kayleigh agreed. "We'll make the time we've already allotted work. Besides, with your help, we'll do fine."

The slightest smile curved one edge of Parker's mouth.

Kayleigh followed her friend to the great room, satisfied with having been the reason for a genuine Parker Abbott smile.

Dinner was remarkable. They fell into an easy, comfortable rhythm. Blake and Savannah went out of their way to keep the conversation flowing, expertly drawing them in and looking for ways to get them talking to each other.

"All right," Savannah said, when Blake took Davis upstairs to give him a bath before bed. "Take out your lists."

Parker opened his datebook while Kayleigh pulled the wrinkled, coffee-stained sheet of paper from her pocket.

"Read them to each other." Savannah beamed.

Kayleigh clutched the wrinkled sheet of paper. "You want me to read it to him? Out loud?"

"Yes," Savannah said resolutely. "Remember, this is a list of all the reasons you truly admire each other. We'll use them to craft the story of how you two fell in love."

"I'll go first." There was a beat of silence as Parker pushed his glasses up the bridge of his nose. He turned his body toward hers, but his gaze didn't leave the page. "I admire Kayleigh's sense of compassion, her determination, her courage and her creativity." He glanced up at her finally. "I also appreciate her unique beauty."

Arms folded, Kayleigh bristled at the term *unique beauty*. Was that his way of saying she had a face that only a mother could love? More important, even if it was Parker's attempt at a backhanded compliment, why should she care what Parker thought of her?

Probably for the same reason she cared about what the Brennans thought of her. She'd spent so much of her life unable to control the narrative about herself and her family. Had been called "poor little thing" either directly or by adults whispering in grocery aisles who didn't think she'd heard them. So now she managed as much of other people's perception about her as she could and convinced herself she didn't care in the instances when she couldn't.

"That's a great list, Parker." Savannah seemed to sense her uneasiness. "But let's get more specific about why you admire those qualities in Kayleigh."

Her face felt hot and her eyes widened as she met Parker's gaze. His cheeks and forehead flushed; he looked as panicked by the prospect as she felt.

This could go sideways fast.

Parker was sure his heart was attempting to beat its way out of his chest as his eyes met Kayleigh's. She'd narrowed her gaze and folded her arms when he'd described her beauty as *unique*. So though he'd meant it as a compliment, she obviously hadn't taken it that way.

Strike one.

He opened his mouth to launch into an explanation of how she'd misunderstood him again, but Benji's advice to him over drinks with the guys the night before echoed in his head.

Don't be a jackass.

Max had suggested that he make it his motto and tattoo it on the inside of his wrist, if need be.

Parker swallowed hard and held Kayleigh's gaze. "I like that she demonstrates compassion through volunteering and activism. I admire the courage it must've taken to start her own business and keep it going."

Kayleigh's arms relaxed and her gaze softened. She

seemed stunned that he could string together a complete sentence that didn't inadvertently insult her.

"Her creativity is evident in the jewelry pieces she designs, and her unique style sets her apart from anyone else I've ever known." He dropped his gaze from hers for a moment. "And she's gorgeous. But in a way that makes her stand out as different. Which I appreciate."

When Parker was done, neither Savannah nor Kayleigh spoke. They exchanged looks and then stared at him again.

Had he screwed up again?

"Was that bad?" he asked his sister-in-law.

"No, Parker. It wasn't. It was beautiful." She beamed at him with an expression similar to the one she employed whenever his young nephew acquired some new skill.

"Kayleigh, how about you? What do you admire about Parker?"

Kayleigh silently consulted her wrinkled, stained sheet of paper again before raising her eyes to meet his. She adjusted in her chair, sitting taller.

"Parker is brilliant. He excels in math, science, business and just about anything he puts his mind to. I admire his focused determination and his commitment to his family and their business." Kayleigh ran her fingers through the long, curly ponytail hanging over one shoulder. "He's tall, but not too tall. And handsome, despite always scowling. Oh, and I like the goatee. It suits him."

Savannah looked up from the notes she was scribbling. "I'm gonna check on the boys and let Benny and Sam out. Why don't you two go over your lists again, but this time I want you to speak directly to each other. Be back in a sec."

Parker frowned. Maybe this was Savannah's way of getting a little payback from the time he'd been hell-bent on having her tossed in jail because he thought she was stealing from the King's Finest archives.

"I'll go first again," he said, finally.

"One more thing," Savannah called from above as she leaned over the railing. "Hold hands this time."

"What?" Kayleigh looked up at her friend.

"Why?" Parker asked simultaneously.

"You don't expect to spend an entire week pretending to be engaged without a little hand-holding or an affectionate kiss or two, do you? Hate to break it to you, puddin', but that's part of the sell. So…" She clapped. "Again. Holding hands. Like you mean it. Let's go!"

And that was why Savannah was such a good fit for their family and business. She'd never been intimidated by what people perceived as his perpetual grouchiness. And she'd never been afraid to challenge him or anyone else in their family, including his father and grandfather.

"I hadn't thought of that," Kayleigh muttered, more to herself than him. "With this emotional distance between us…there's no point in even doing this."

Was she calling the whole thing off? Because that was an idea he could get behind, even if it meant paying a little more for her building. "So does that mean—"

"No, you're not off the hook, Abbott." She sighed, then rose to her feet and faced him, her hand extended.

Parker wiped his palms on his pants legs and stood, too. He placed his much larger hand in her outstretched one.

Her skin was soft and warm and he inhaled her subtle vanilla scent that reminded him of buttercream frosting.

Kayleigh met his gaze. "Parker, I admire your intelligence, your focused determination and ability to see the endgame when everyone else is just getting suited up. I love how close you are to your family. You obviously love them. And…" She sighed softly. "You're very handsome—with or without your glasses."

"Thanks, Kayleigh." He tightened his grip on her hand. "I admire your strength and tenacity. When you have a goal in mind, you don't let anything stop you, not even your own fears. I admire the creativity required to take what's essentially scrap metal and a few rocks and turn it into something…magnificent. And I love that you have your own sense of style. You own your unique beauty instead of buying into someone else's."

Kayleigh stared at him with surprise and then thanked him.

"Not bad, you two." Blake carried Davis downstairs in his cartoon-character pajamas, with Savannah on his heels.

"Thanks," Kayleigh muttered, yanking her hand from Parker's and stepping away. As if they'd been caught making out.

He shoved his hands in his pockets, his cheeks warm.

"Little Man wanted to say good-night to Uncle Parker and Aunt Kayleigh." Blake looked at his son proudly.

"Good night, Davis." Kayleigh tickled the boy's belly and kissed his cheek. For a moment Parker was envious of little Davis as he squirmed and giggled in response.

"Good night, Little Man." Parker mussed the boy's soft curls. "See you tomorrow at Grammie and Grandpa's house."

Davis called good-night to them repeatedly as his father carried him up to bed.

"That wasn't too hard, now was it?" Savannah grinned. "No one died, and the earth is still spinning on its axis."

"You didn't say you'd be listening." Kayleigh jabbed the air with an accusatory finger.

"Didn't say I wouldn't, either." Savannah shrugged. "I just thought you'd both feel less self-conscious without observers."

"Though clearly we had an audience." Parker pushed his glasses up the bridge of his nose.

"As you will at the wedding," she reminded them. "So you need to be able to say it like you mean it, whether it's in front of two people or two hundred."

Parker was a straightforward kind of guy who said what he meant, even if people sometimes misconstrued his words. Putting on a show for Kayleigh's old friend didn't sit well with him.

If they were *really* friends, she should be able to tell the woman the truth without judgment. But then he certainly hadn't been a shining example of how a good friend behaved, had he?

"I doubt we'll need to pull this shtick in front of many people. No one but Kira and her immediate family will care."

"Still, it's better to be prepared." Savannah nodded toward him. "Since Parker looks a little green, I'd suggest you try again until you can both recite the words comfortably. When you're done, there'll be cake." She winked.

Parker turned toward Kayleigh and extended his hand. "We'd better try a few more times before the overlord comes back."

"I heard that!" Savannah called.

"We wanted you to!" Kayleigh responded.

Parker couldn't help smiling as Kayleigh put her hand in his.

Six

Kayleigh pulled her flame-red Jeep, with the hardtop removed, into Parker's driveway. He glanced down at the fancy sports watch on his wrist and frowned as he rolled his mountain bike out of the garage. He was wearing a black long-sleeve sports shirt that revealed a more impressive chest and biceps than she'd have expected of the pencil pusher. His black mountain-biking pants had a loose fit but highlighted his strong legs and surprisingly impressive hindquarters.

Not that she cared.

"You're late," Parker groused, as if she wasn't already aware.

She bit back her smart-ass comeback as she hopped out of the truck and met him at the back, where her bicycle was strapped onto the bike rack. "Danette needed help locating one of the orders that had to be shipped out today."

"Don't you have some sort of organizing system to keep from losing orders?" Parker lifted his bicycle and strapped it onto the rack and she secured it.

She nodded toward his garage—organized with high-end cabinetry on one wall and a paneled system of shelves, hooks and baskets on the opposite and back walls. "I'm clearly not as organized as you are."

"Organization is the key to efficiency." Parker opened the passenger door and nearly jumped out of his skin when her three-year-old golden retriever, Cricket, barked from her perch in the front seat of the truck.

"Are you afraid of dogs?" Kayleigh strapped on her seat belt. "Is that why Blake and Savannah kept poor Benny and Sam in the den while we were there last week?"

"I'm not afraid of Benny and Sam." He seemed insulted by the question. "I'm just not a big fan of keeping pets indoors."

Parker folded his arms and stared at Cricket, who growled at him disapprovingly. "Is he gonna move?"

"*She* called shotgun on the ride over, so that's a no, chief." Kayleigh grinned before breaking into laughter at his look of outrage. "I'm just kidding, Abbott. Geez, relax. You look like you're about to crap a diamond."

Parker's eyes widened, then narrowed as he stared at her.

Kayleigh kissed Cricket's nose and petted her head. "Go to the back seat, girl. It'll be all right. Despite the mean mug, Parker here is relatively harmless."

Cricket climbed onto the back seat begrudgingly and barked again to make sure Parker understood how displeased she was.

He dusted bits of Cricket's hair from the front seat before getting in and using a phone app to close his garage door.

"Thanks for the ride," Parker said after a few minutes on the road together in silence.

"You obviously weren't going to put a bike rack on the back of that shiny Beamer. I didn't have much of an option if I wanted you to come along." She stared ahead at the road. "Nice bike. How often do you ride?"

"My family bought it one year for my birthday." He

shrugged. "Every now and then, one of my brothers decides we all need to go riding. Usually it's Cole."

That explained it. Parker didn't seem like the kind of guy who hit the bike trail regularly, though he certainly looked the part in his expensive gear.

"Honestly, I think the outdoors is overrated. I never fared very well trekking in the woods with my brothers as a kid." He absently grazed the scar she knew he had just above his knee from when he'd tumbled down a hill as a boy. "And then, of course, there's my schedule."

"I hate to break it to you, but camping is on the agenda in a few weeks. I planned the trip months ago, but you said that if we already had something on the books—"

"I know, I know." Parker clearly regretted that decision.

"Do you have a tent and camping gear?"

"Wait…you mean old-school camping? As in sleeping on the ground rather than in a cabin or RV?"

"My dad loved camping, and we always roughed it." Her lips curved in an involuntary smile. Those annual family camping trips were the highlight of her childhood. "Since I've been back home, I kind of keep up the tradition."

"Oh." Parker cleared his throat. "I never got a chance to say how sorry I was about the loss of your dad and then your mom. She was a really sweet lady, and she had an amazing smile. Same as yours."

"Thank you." Kayleigh's chest felt heavy.

"Since it's a family tradition, is Evvy coming, too?"

"No." Kayleigh's back tensed. Her strained relationship with her older sister, Evelisse, was another sensitive topic.

"I haven't seen Evvy since—"

"My mother's funeral," Kayleigh said sharply.

"Where does she live now?"

"She got a job in LA after college. Been there ever since."

"You adored Evvy when we were kids. What changed?"

"I realize you don't always pick up on body language, Parker, so I'll be direct." She managed to keep her voice even, despite her irritation. "I do *not* want to talk about my sister."

"We're supposed to be engaged," he muttered. "Seems like something a fiancé would know."

Now he wants to be helpful.

"Fine." Kayleigh heaved a sigh. "Evvy is desperate to erase our family's past history. She's still embarrassed about our dad. Ashamed of how poor we were growing up. She doesn't want any part of this town or anything that reminds her of the humiliation she endured here."

"Does that include you?"

She gripped the wheel so tightly, her knuckles ached. "It would seem so."

"I'm sorry, Kayleigh." Parker spoke after a long, uncomfortable pause. "I honestly didn't know."

"Well, now you do. So let's not talk about it anymore."

Cricket growled at Parker and then barked twice.

"Seems your dog doesn't want me to talk about it anymore either," Parker muttered.

"Her name is Cricket, and she's an excellent judge of character."

"Meaning?"

"She senses how anxious you are around her, which is why she distrusts you. And she senses how anxious you're making me. As you can see, she doesn't like it."

Parker glanced over his shoulder at Cricket. "Has it been scientifically proven that dogs can sense emotions, or are you basing this on anecdotal evidence?"

"It's a real thing, professor. Google it or something." Kayleigh rolled her eyes and sighed. She just wanted to get through the day without attempting to strangle Parker Abbott. That was looking less likely with each passing minute. "Maybe we should try for some meaningless small talk."

"All right. Maybe you could tell me why we're *really* doing this pretend fiancé thing?"

Parker obviously didn't understand the concept of small talk.

"I don't want to be the only person going solo at a romantic-destination wedding." She kneaded the Parker-induced knot forming in her neck. "I already explained this."

"You *implied* it," he clarified. "But I'm not buying it."

"Why not?" Kayleigh hit a bump in the road intentionally. Parker could use a good jostling.

"You don't usually care what other people think. Especially not enough to go through such an elaborate ruse."

Parker knew her better than she thought.

"And last week, Savannah was about to say something, but you cut her off. You obviously didn't want me to know."

"Then why are you asking about it?"

"I'm being forced to jump through a flaming hoop like a trained poodle. Don't you think I deserve to know whose benefit I'm doing it for?"

Actually, she didn't.

But Parker was as stubborn as she was. He wouldn't let this go, so she might as well level with him.

"The bride-to-be is my ex's younger sister."

"You're doing this for some guy?" He sounded profoundly disappointed in her for being so shallow.

"He's not just any guy. He was going to ask me to marry him."

"He was your *actual* fiancé?" Parker turned his body toward hers.

"I didn't give him a chance to ask," she said tersely.

"Why not?"

"I loved him. Very much. Maybe if the circumstances between us had been different—"

"Different how?"

"The Brennans are a wealthy, old-money Irish family. Part of the Atlanta aristocracy with the storied sugar plantation to prove it." Kayleigh shifted gears as they climbed into steeper terrain.

"And?" Parker seemed genuinely perplexed as to why any of that made a difference.

"His mother wasn't keen on the idea of a brown-skinned girl with no family or fortune to speak of making her way onto the illustrious Brennan family tree."

Parker's hands curled into fists on his lap. "If that's the kind of people they are, you made the right decision not to marry into their family."

"Don't get me wrong, she was never overt about it. And don't get the wrong impression of Kira or Aidan. Neither of them is like that. So much so that I don't think either of them recognized it in their mother."

"Do you regret not marrying Aidan?" Parker asked after a few moments of awkward silence between them.

"It was the right choice for both of us." Kayleigh shrugged, trying to shut out the painful memories of the decision she'd made that day. "He got married a couple years later. Last I heard they were happily married with two kids."

"And you?" His tone was softer.

Kayleigh focused on the road ahead. She couldn't bear to see the same pity in Parker's eyes that she heard in his voice.

"I'm better off without the hassle. Now story time is over. Unless you want to see Cricket do a mean imitation of an attack dog, I suggest we steer the conversation away from all of my failed relationships."

Cricket growled in response, and a smile slowly crept across Kayleigh's face.

Good girl, Cricket. Good girl.

Parker pulled out a cloth and cleaned his glasses without responding. He was reasonably sure Kayleigh was joking, but with her growling dog in the back seat, who obviously wasn't a fan, it seemed better not to test the limits.

Still, he felt a sense of satisfaction at getting Kayleigh to open up to him a little. When they were kids, she'd talked to him about everything, especially her family.

He'd missed those conversations and the easy friendship they'd once shared.

He glanced over at Kayleigh. His eyes were drawn to her strong, toned thighs, visible in her distressed, cut-off denim shorts, which were about an inch and a half too long to be considered Daisy Dukes. Her fitted baseball tee highlighted her ample breasts, and the deep vee offered a peek of her cleavage.

Not that he was looking. He just happened to be a very observant guy who noticed things.

Parker glanced around at the rugged terrain. "We're biking in the mountains?"

"You've got a pricey mountain bike and hard-core biker gear. Don't you want to put it to good use?"

Not particularly.

He ignored her question. "Do you often ride up here?"

"As often as I can. Savannah's ridden up here with me a few times. But it looks like we won't be doing that anytime soon." Kayleigh pulled into a parking lot for the mountain trail. "I hear you're going to be an uncle again."

"Seems that way," he said absently, studying the trail up ahead and calculating whether he'd brought enough water.

"If you're not up to this, we can take the beginner trail," she offered.

He hadn't been sure what possessed his family to purchase the bicycle in the first place. It certainly wasn't his ideal way to spend an afternoon. But he'd accepted the gift gratefully and gone for a ride with them whenever the occasion arose.

As much as he wanted to accept Kayleigh's offer to bike

an easier trail instead, there was no way he'd give her the satisfaction of believing that he was incapable of tackling a trail that she and Savannah managed without difficulty.

"No, this is fine." Parker frowned, stepping out of the truck.

Kayleigh hopped out, opened the back door for Cricket and pulled out a backpack. She put it on as she watched him take his cycle down from the rack.

Kayleigh reached for her bike, but he engaged his kick-stand, then took the bike down for her.

"Thanks." Kayleigh grabbed the handlebar and seat. Her hand accidentally brushed his and she quickly withdrew it, as if her skin had been burned. She glanced up at him momentarily, cheeks flushed.

Parker ignored the zing of electricity he felt when her skin touched his. The same sensation that had crawled up his arm when he'd shaken her hand at the office, the day she'd signed the deal.

"How are you going to manage her while you're rid-ing?" Parker nodded toward Cricket, who gave him her death stare.

Kayleigh indicated the metal bar extending from her seat. An extendable leash was attached to it.

"Clever." He watched as she connected it to Cricket's collar, then patted the dog's side.

Kayleigh strapped on her helmet and mounted the bicy-cle. The position drew his attention to her generous bottom.

Good Georgia peach.

Heat prickled his cheeks, and his face suddenly felt hot, despite the cool, early spring temperature.

"Everything okay?" She stared at him, her eyebrows drawn.

"Yes, of course." He put on his helmet and gloves, then mounted his bicycle, too.

"We'll take the easier of the two mountain trails," Kayleigh called over her shoulder as she rode toward it.

"Not necessary. Whatever you do normally is fine."

"You're sure?" Kayleigh didn't sound convinced.

"Positive."

"All right." She changed direction and headed toward the entrance of the advanced trail.

It was his second big mistake of the day.

"Parker, are you sure you don't want to go back?" Kayleigh stopped her bike and put one foot on the ground after they'd been riding for about forty minutes.

"I'm…good," he coughed, barely able to get the words out. Sweat ran down his face and stung his eyes.

"God, you look like you're about to pass out." Kayleigh put the kickstand down and hopped off her bike, looking alarmed. "Your face is red, you're practically hyperventilating and I'm pretty sure you're melting."

"It's no big deal. I'm fine."

"You are *not* passing out on me." She pointed a finger at him. "I'll leave your ass up here—I swear. You're too damned heavy to carry back down that hill. Get off the bike and sit down for a while." She indicated a wooden picnic table. "You brought water, didn't you?"

He nodded, still trying to catch his breath while Kayleigh wasn't even breathing heavily. Parker collapsed on the bench, took out a bottle of water and downed it.

Kayleigh poured water in her hand for Cricket to drink, then sat next to him on the bench, finishing the bottle off.

"I didn't consider how tough this trail is for someone who isn't very physical. We should've stayed on flat terrain."

"What do you mean someone who isn't physical?" He frowned, opening another bottle of water.

"I mean you spend most of your day at a desk. Physical

labor isn't your thing, and there's nothing wrong with that. We've all got limitations."

"I'm fine." Parker stood quickly, his head spinning a little from the sudden movement. He wavered and she reached out to steady him. She pulled him down on the bench beside her and his thigh grazed hers.

"You are not fine, and I don't want to be the one who has to explain to your parents that you died on the side of this mountain because you didn't want to be shown up by a girl. Seriously, Parker, we're not ten. Get over the chauvinist bullshit."

He was more embarrassed by her accusation than he had been by his inability to keep up with her on the trail.

Don't be a jackass.

Kayleigh was right. He'd gone soft. He spent most of his day sitting behind a desk and it showed.

From the look of her toned body and the endurance she'd shown on the trail despite the steep inclines, Kayleigh Jemison was no stranger to physicality. Parker swallowed hard, heat spreading through his face and chest at the thought.

"You didn't do badly, this being your first time." Kayleigh nudged him with her elbow and smiled.

"Thanks." He drank more water. His breathing finally slowed enough for him to speak normally.

He was melting in the hot sun like the Wicked Witch in *The Wizard of Oz.* Meanwhile Kayleigh glowed, with a light sheen on her forehead and chest, and smelled like sunshine and vanilla.

She reached into her backpack and handed him a protein bar. "It tastes like cardboard coated with peanut butter and chocolate, but it'll give you enough fuel to get back down the trail."

Parker accepted it gratefully, opened the package and took a bite. She'd been generous with her description of the taste. But if it would give him a boost of much-needed energy, he'd eat three of the damn things. "How often do you bike this mountain?"

"Every chance I get. It's a good place to enjoy the peace and quiet and get out of my own head. Forget whatever is bothering me."

"Like?"

"You wouldn't understand." Kayleigh gave Cricket the last of her bottle of water, then tossed all of the empties into a nearby recycling bin.

She put her backpack back on and walked over to her bike.

"Why wouldn't I understand?" He sat on his bike and released the kickstand.

"Because…you're one of the Mighty Abbotts. You guys don't have real-people problems." Her tone was sharp.

"That's not fair, Kayleigh. I've never purported to be better than you or anyone else."

"You don't have to say it. It's evident in how you deal with people. In how your father treated my mother when he lowballed her on that property you all expanded on. Or how you walked into my shop with your nose in the air, like you had a right to my property, whether I wanted to sell it or not."

"My father doesn't lowball people. He pays everyone a fair price. He always has. And we were more than generous with you, despite your unorthodox request. After all I'm here, aren't I?"

There was sadness in her brown eyes. "Then I guess I should be grateful, huh?"

Kayleigh took off down the trail on her bike, without waiting for his response.

Dammit.

Parker groaned as he followed Kayleigh and Cricket back down the hill, hoping she wouldn't decide that leaving him on that mountain to die was a pretty good idea after all.

Seven

Kayleigh parked her truck on the grass, along with the cars of the other friends and family members who'd been invited to Duke and Iris's place for a joint birthday party for Blake and Savannah's son Davis, who'd turned two and Benji and Sloane's twins, Beau and Bailey, who'd turned one.

Every muscle in her body was tense, her heart raced and her stomach was twisted in knots. The last thing she'd wanted to do was step foot in the lair of the devil himself, Duke Abbott. Sitting across from him at a conference table when she'd clearly had the upper hand was one thing. Stepping inside his home and playing nice at a social gathering was something else altogether.

She wanted to start up the Jeep, turn around and leave. Make some excuse as to why she couldn't stay. But this was her and Parker's fifth date. More important, Savannah had enlisted her to do crafts with the children. It was a service she'd intended to add to her business menu, and this was the perfect chance to promote her newest offering.

Kayleigh got out of the truck and hauled her case of art

supplies out of the back seat while also struggling to retrieve all three birthday gifts.

"Can I help you?"

The husky, sensual voice startled her. She quickly stood up straight and turned around.

"Cole Abbott." Kayleigh folded her arms. "You were staring at my ass, weren't you?"

His sensual lips curled in a smirk. "You looked like you were struggling, but if you'd rather carry everything in yourself—"

"No, I could use your help." She chose to ignore his nonanswer; instead she handed him the stack of colorfully wrapped gifts.

She grabbed her purse and the art case, then followed Cole to the front door of the grand home. The exterior was made of gray stacked stone and shakes made of poplar bark. The house overlooked the gorgeous Smoky Mountains.

Cole studied the exterior as if he was critiquing the home his company had built.

Kayleigh scanned the structure. "You do amazing work, Cole. This place is incredible, and the views must be breathtaking."

"You've never been here?" Cole seemed genuinely surprised.

"I've been to the barn on the edge of the property for different events. But no, I've never been to the house proper."

His eyes lit up. "Then you have to let me give you a tour of the place. It's still my favorite house that I've built."

"I'm sure you'd much rather enjoy the party." She followed Cole through the ornamental wood-and-glass front door.

One part of her loathed the idea of oohing and ahhing over Duke Abbott's lavish home. Another part of her was curious to see how the other half lived.

The large entrance hall had gleaming wood floors, high ceilings and large decorative windows that let in lots of light.

He set the gifts on the entrance table and dodged two little girls who giggled as they darted through the space.

"It won't take long." Cole took the art case from her and sat it in the corner of the adjoining dining room. He headed toward the stairs. "Come on, we'll start upstairs."

Kayleigh glanced around, hoping that Parker, Savannah or someone else would appear and need her. Her curiosity had gotten the better of her. She honestly did want to tour the place, but it felt odd to traipse through their private rooms without Iris's permission.

"My parents love showing off the house," Cole assured her, as if he'd read her mind. "They won't mind—I promise."

"All right. Lead the way." Kayleigh followed him up the stairs.

Cole Abbott was the unabashed flirt of the Abbott family and a certified skirt chaser. He seemed to relish the reputation he'd earned. Kayleigh kept enough distance between them to make it clear she had no intention of being among his conquests.

The home had four bedrooms and a lovely bonus space upstairs. As they came back down the stairs, Cole was explaining how the site itself had inspired the design and materials he'd selected for the project.

"Cole. Kayleigh." Parker stood in the entrance hall, his hands balled into fists at his side.

"What's up, Park?" Cole greeted his brother cheerfully. "I was just showing Kayleigh the house. She's never been here. I was just about to show her the downstairs."

Parker's fists unfurled, but he still scowled. "Actually, Savannah sent me to find Kayleigh. We need to set up the art project for the kids," he said gruffly.

"My supplies are in the dining room." Kayleigh pointed.

"I'll grab them," Cole offered.

"No." Parker held up his large hand, palm facing his brother. "I've got it. And I'll show Kayleigh the rest of the house when we're done."

Cole frowned. "Everything okay, Park?"

"Of course." Parker relaxed his scowl and shoved his hands in his pockets.

"Since you have everything under control, I guess I'll see you guys out back." Cole turned and walked away.

"What was that about?" Kayleigh whispered loudly as she followed Parker to the dining room to retrieve her case.

"What are you talking about?" Parker shrugged innocently.

"You know *exactly* what I'm talking about. We're not on the island yet, so you can relax the whole jealous-boyfriend act."

Parker looked at her sharply, then frowned. "You don't know my brother like I do."

"Everyone in this town knows your brother's reputation." Kayleigh walked quickly to keep up with Parker's long strides. "You don't need to protect me from your brother. I've got a hell of a right hook and I can knee someone like nobody's business. Besides, he was just showing me the house."

Parker turned to look at her. He opened his mouth, then snapped it shut, as if there was something he wanted to say but couldn't. He shoved a hand in his pocket. "Sorry. I didn't mean to come off as some macho jerk."

Parker Abbott apologized?

The town should declare it Parker Abbott Apologized Day and make it an annual celebration.

"I appreciate your concern, but honestly I can take care of myself. Been doing it most of my life." She took the case from Parker. "Thank you, anyway."

Parker nodded without comment, led her to where she needed to set up for the kids and then left.

As Parker walked away, she couldn't help wondering what it was he hadn't been able to bring himself to say.

Parker sipped his bourbon-spiked sweet tea as he watched Kayleigh guide the children through a painting project. His cousin Benji's fiancée, Sloane Sutton, helped her twins, the youngest of the children.

Kayleigh was beautiful. It wasn't even summer yet, but her skin had already started to tan. The sunglasses she wore shielded her eyes, forcing him to focus on the sexy little pout of her Cupid's bow mouth. Her strong, toned arms were visible in the tank top she wore, which had an unusual cutout design at the neck and back. Tattered blue jeans offered peeks of her skin through holes at the knees and over her thighs.

Her long red hair had been in loose, shoulder-length curls when she'd arrived, but she'd swept it up in a high ponytail as she worked with the kids.

Kayleigh wiped her face with the back of her wrist, but managed to get blue paint on her face anyway. She was adorable.

This was their fifth of ten dates. Yet, rather than being happy that he was halfway through his contractual obligation, he was disappointed by how quickly their time was flying by. The realization startled him.

He'd begun to anticipate spending Saturday afternoons with Kayleigh Jemison. If he was being honest, the time he spent with Kayleigh was the highlight of his week. But maybe he was giving her too much credit. Perhaps it wasn't so much about Kayleigh as the fact that he'd spent the last weekends doing something other than working or dealing with his family.

Maybe he just needed to get a life.

"Dude. Close your mouth before something flies in it."
Benji sat in the Adirondack chair beside Parker's with a
beverage of his own. "At least *try* to play it cool."

Parker scowled at his cousin. "I'm watching the kids.
That's the point of this party, after all."

"C'mon, Park." Benji chuckled. "You can do better than
that. Or…"

Parker met his cousin's gaze, anticipating what he would
say next. "Or what?"

"Or you can tell Kayleigh how you really feel about her."

Parker turned away from his cousin. He searched for another glimpse of Kayleigh before gazing out at the impressive mountain overlooking his parents' patio.

He tried to ignore his cousin's pointed stare and the feelings that had flared in his chest when he'd seen Kayleigh
coming down the stairs behind Cole earlier.

It was jealousy. Plain and simple. Raw and uninhibited.

He had no claim on Kayleigh's affections or her body.
She could do whatever she wanted with whomever she
wanted. Still, the thought of Cole putting his hands on her
had sent Parker into a brief irrational rage, even if it was
only in his head.

"Ignore me, if you want, but I'm not going away." Benji
poked his arm. "Neither are your feelings for her. Face it,
Park, you've always had a thing for Kayleigh."

Parker narrowed his gaze at his cousin before surveying the scenery again. "You know why I'm doing this. But
I just can't turn it on and off as easily as she can."

"I think you're wrong." Benji nodded toward the table
where Kayleigh and the kids were. "I don't think she can,
either."

When Parker glanced in her direction, his eyes met hers.
She smiled, holding his gaze for a moment before returning her attention to Davis's work of art.

He swallowed hard, his heart thumping in his chest.

"See what I mean?" Benji stood, hovering over him. "Kayleigh is smart, gorgeous, adventurous… She won't stay on the market forever, Park. What happens when someone else comes along and sweeps her off her feet? You'll regret not making peace with her and telling her how you feel."

Benji walked over to the table, kissed Sloane on the cheek and then sat down to help his son Beau.

Parker heaved a sigh and finished his spiked tea. Maybe he did have feelings for Kayleigh. But that didn't mean it was in his best interest, or hers, for him to act on them. They were just too different.

Kayleigh was a free-spirited, wild child who railed against the very tenets that were the foundation of his life and the keys to his success.

They wanted very different things in life. And then there was her animosity toward his father that was bubbling just below the surface. An issue his father was well aware of, but unwilling to address.

He had absolutely no reason to believe that he and Kayleigh would make a good match. That either of them would be willing to bend enough to make a friendship, let alone a relationship, work.

His head was clear on all the reasons he shouldn't want her, and yet…he did, with a growing desperation that made his chest ache just thinking about her, which he did often.

Parker went to the outdoor bar, where Zora had set up as the unofficial bartender.

Zora shuddered. "Looks like you could use a refill, stat."

She took his glass and filled it with sweet tea before topping it off with King's Finest bourbon and stirring. Zora handed the glass back to him.

"Want to tell me what the long face is all about, or are we just going to pretend you're not pining over a pretty little redhead?"

"Don't you start with me, too," Parker grumbled, taking a sip of his tea. "That's really strong, Zora."

"Good. You could use some mellowing out and a dose of courage," she remarked without apology.

"You let me handle my business, and I won't ask how things are between you and Dallas."

Zora's cheeks flushed at his mention of her best friend, Dallas Hamilton. "Dallas and I are just friends. Always have been. Don't try to change the subject. How is the whole dating Kayleigh thing going?"

"Fine. Better than expected, actually," he added under his breath.

Zora's eyes lit up. "Does she feel the same way?"

Parker shrugged. "We've talked about lots of things. How we feel about each other isn't one of them. Which is probably why we've been getting along so well."

"Good. I don't have to remind you how important this deal is to all of us, or how much it's going to mean to Mom when Dad surprises her with it."

"I know what's at stake here." Parker nodded. One more reason he and Kayleigh needed to keep things strictly business between them. He was all for repairing their friendship, but anything more could derail their deal. "I won't do anything to jeopardize it. Which is why it's a bad idea to—"

"Zora, I'd love a bourbon punch, if that's possible." Kayleigh said as she joined them.

Zora glanced at him quickly before turning her attention to Kayleigh and smiling. "Pull up a seat. I just need to grab a few more lemons from inside." Zora looked at her brother pointedly. "I'll be right back."

"That looks good." Kayleigh indicated Parker's drink. "What's that?"

"Sweet tea with about a sidecar worth of bourbon." He chuckled. "Zora was a little heavy-handed for my taste."

"May I?"

He nodded, watching as she avoided his straw and sipped from the glass.

"It's good," she declared. "Strong, but good."

"Then it's yours." He put a square drink napkin in front of her and turned on the stool, his back against the bar. "The kids certainly seem to be having a good time."

"They were so adorable and their pieces all came out well. I'm going to surprise their parents and frame their pictures so they can hang them at home."

Parker couldn't find the slightest appeal in having a piece of art created by a toddler hanging in his home, but their parents undoubtedly didn't share his view.

"I'm sure they'll appreciate it. But when will you have time to do that?"

"After we eat, they're going to put on an outdoor movie for the kids. That should give me time to frame each painting."

"The point of this whole exercise is that we spend time together." Parker straightened his shirt collar. "So I'd be happy to help."

"Thanks, Parker. That'd be great. I'll look for you after dinner." She rose from the stool, lifting her glass. "And thanks for the drink. Tell Zora thanks anyway."

"Kayleigh." He caught her hand in his and it seemed to surprise them both.

"Yes?"

He took a napkin, rubbed it against the condensation on the glass and wiped at the blue paint stain on her cheek. "You've got a little paint here."

Kayleigh thanked him, then headed back to the party, leaving her sweet scent in her wake.

Time slowed as everyone moved around Kayleigh.

Iris and Savannah cut the cake, and Sloane handed pieces out to the children. The men sat around the bar, joking with each other, and the other women sat on the patio, gossiping and catching up on each other's lives.

She'd known the Abbotts her entire life, as just about everyone in town did. But even when she and Parker had been school-age friends, their families didn't move in the same circles. In fact her family was the antithesis of the Abbotts.

They were wealthy, world-famous local royalty and beloved by all. Her family had barely skated along between utility shut-offs and vehicle repossessions. Her father's notoriety had been a perpetual stain on all of them. He'd been the most despised man in town, and everyone regarded her, her mother and her sister with a pity that clawed at her soul and burned her skin.

Leaving town hadn't solved the problem. The damage had been done. It had burrowed its way deep inside her consciousness and infected her psyche. Only once she'd moved back to Magnolia Lake had she been able to work out the demons that had haunted her. Little by little, she'd come to love the town and its people again.

Still, she hadn't extended the need for peaceful resolution to Parker Abbott or his father, Duke. She'd held onto her resentment of them like a warm blanket that warded against the cold winds of doubt that sometimes crept back in. But the past few weeks with Parker had slowly been chipping away at that protective armor.

Her close friendship with Savannah had given her occasion to get to know Blake and Zora. But she'd stayed clear of Parker and politely declined whenever her friend had invited her to functions at Duke and Iris's home.

Seeing all of the Abbotts and their extended family together this way made them seem more human. More real. The love they had for each other was evident, even in the teasing between the siblings. Duke and Iris were doting grandparents who were deeply affectionate toward their children and grandchildren.

There were so many of them. All of the Abbotts were here, including their grandfather Joseph. Sloane, Benji and their twins, along with her mother and grandfather, and his parents, sister and niece. Even Savannah's sister, Delaney, and her young daughter, Harper.

And she had…no one. Maybe she never would.

Tears burned her eyes suddenly. She'd never have her parents again, and even when they'd been in her life, their family was nothing like the Christmas-card-worthy Abbotts.

It was one more thing they had that she never would. Maybe Aidan had been her one chance at having a meaningful relationship and children of her own. Kayleigh's hand drifted to where the tears were spilling down her wet cheek. She furtively glanced around the space, hoping no one had noticed. The only thing worse than being alone in the world was being pitied because of it.

She turned around and collided with a hard body.

"We've gotta stop meeting like this, darlin'." Cole wore a good-natured grin—and his slice of cake, which she'd smashed into his pricey designer shirt.

"Cole, I'm so sorry. I ruined your shirt."

"Not one of my favorites anyway." He shrugged, licking icing from his fingers.

"I should've been paying attention. I'll get something to clean it before the stain sets."

"It's no big deal. I'll throw it in the wash and grab one of Dad's shirts." He swiped the wetness from her cheek. "Seriously, it's nothing to cry over. It's just a shirt."

Her face stung with embarrassment and the sound of her heartbeat filled her ears.

"What did you say to her?" Parker was there suddenly, and now half of the adult eyes at the party were focused on the three of them.

"Nothing. It was an accident—that's all." Cole wiped frosting off his shirt with a napkin.

Parker looked to her as if he needed her confirmation. "I'm sorry, Cole. I'll pay for the shirt. Excuse me."

Kayleigh wished she could disappear, or at the very least go home. But she'd promised to frame the kids' art. So she made her escape to the craft room on the lower level of the spacious home. When Kayleigh closed the door behind her, she couldn't contain the tears.

As shitty as it had been to grow up poor with only a few friends and a father who was the laughingstock of the town, it had made her strong. Impenetrable, even. Losing her father had been painful, but not unexpected, given his lifestyle. But losing her mother…that had broken her.

That had left just her and her sister. But Evvy's way of dealing with the pain was to throw herself into her new life, thousands of miles from this little town. Between school and work and the small acting jobs her sister was able to garner, they'd simply grown apart. But Kayleigh had gotten through it.

She'd met Aidan at a time when she'd felt incredibly alone. He'd been warm and supportive, and Kira had been like a sister to her. But then she'd walked away from the two of them.

The door opened and she expected Savannah, but it was Parker.

"I came bearing cake and libations." He held up a plate in one hand and her bourbon punch in the other. "Pick your poison. Or don't. You can have both."

"Thanks, Parker. Maybe later." Kayleigh swiped away the dampness on her cheeks, not meeting his gaze. "Could you just leave them?"

"Oh, sure." He put both the cake and the drink down on the work surface, away from the kids' art that Blake and Benji had transferred there earlier.

Parker opened the door to leave, but closed it again. He walked over to her. "Are you sure Cole didn't do anything…

inappropriate? I saw him touch your face, and you seemed agitated."

"It wasn't because of anything Cole did. I was already upset and in tears. I was trying to leave before anyone noticed. That's how I ended up running smack-dab into Cole. Which, of course, drew everyone's attention." She sighed. "If anything, he should be angry with me for ruining his expensive shirt."

Parker stepped closer, extending a handful of napkins to her. "Then why the tears?"

She accepted the napkins, decorated with colorful balloons, the words *Happy Birthday* emblazoned on them. She wiped her cheeks, then shoved the crumpled napkins in her pocket. "You wouldn't understand."

Parker stepped closer still, his gaze trained on hers. "How do you know?"

"Because you have all of this." She gestured around them angrily, fresh tears stinging her eyes. She wiped at them, her cheeks heating with embarrassment. "And because you still have your parents, and you're surrounded by your siblings, and that's great. But you have no idea what I'm feeling right now, and I hope you never do."

He stepped closer, his voice low and his expression sincere. "I would never have invited you here if I'd realized how it would impact you."

"It isn't your fault." She sniffled. "And I'm not normally like this. I can't remember the last time I cried about anything. Besides, I'd already promised Savannah that I'd come to the party before they decided to have it here. I couldn't miss Davis's birthday."

Parker's eyes were filled with what seemed like genuine compassion, as awkward silence stretched between them. He stepped close enough that his enticing scent tickled her nostrils and his heat enveloped her. His dark eyes locked with hers as he took another step forward.

He slowly lifted his hands and cradled her jaw as he lowered his head, closing the space between them.

Kayleigh squeezed her eyes shut, her heart beating faster.

His lips met hers in a kiss that was tender and sweet. Yet her body burned for him as she leaned into his touch, her hands pressed to his firm chest.

She knew that he'd kissed her out of a sense of pity. She didn't want Parker's pity, but she did want this. His firm, sensual lips on hers. His strong hands gently cradling her face. His hard body braced against hers.

He tilted her head back, and she parted her lips in response. A soft murmur rose in her throat when his tongue swept between her lips.

Warmth filled her chest, and her belly fluttered as he deepened their kiss. His mouth tasted rich and sweet. Like bourbon, sweet tea and buttercream frosting.

Parker's hands dropped to her waist and she gasped when he lifted her onto the table, without breaking their kiss.

His hands found her lower back as he pulled her closer to the table's edge. The ridge beneath his zipper pressed against the growing heat between her thighs, making her want things with Parker Abbott that she shouldn't.

Her pulse raced as Parker's large hands slipped beneath her shirt, his fingertips skimming her back.

She wrapped her arms around his neck, pulling him closer, desperate for more of the unexpected connection between them.

The door opened suddenly, startling both of them. They turned toward the sound.

"I'm sorry, I didn't mean to… I just wanted to make sure Kayleigh was all right," Savannah stammered. "I'll just go. Let me know if you need anything."

Her friend was gone before either of them could respond.

Kayleigh's face stung with heat and her heart raced. She

didn't meet Parker's gaze as she slid off the table and out of his reach. She folded her arms over her chest, shielding the evidence of her body's intense reaction to his.

"We should get the framing done." She moved toward the back of the room, where the frames were lined up.

Parker ran a hand over his head and sighed. "I know I shouldn't have done that, but—"

"Let's just consider it practice. You know...in case the situation arises while we're at Kira's wedding." She tested the paint on the children's artwork to see if it was dry without looking up at him.

"I'm sorry about your parents and about you and Evvy." His voice was warm and reassuring. "If there's anything I can do—"

"Thank you, but I'm fine now." She glanced up briefly before returning her attention to the paintings. "Now, if we work together, we can get all of these framed in no time."

"Just tell me what you need."

What she needed was...him. The comfort of his embrace. The warmth of his kiss. To not feel alone.

She asked him to hand her one of the frames instead and tried desperately to convince herself that she didn't want Parker to kiss her again.

Eight

Kayleigh sat across the booth from Savannah at Magnolia Lake Bakery after yoga, sipping her mocha latte.

Savannah still looked stunned, despite the fact that they'd broken down the kiss between her and Parker, as well as everything that had led up to it.

Who could blame her? Kayleigh had had two days to digest and rehash the events and she was still just as surprised.

"Does that mean Project Friendship has now become Project Relationship?" Savannah sipped her peach-mango smoothie.

"As far as I can tell, neither of us is looking for a relationship. I'm not even sure we'll come out of this as friends exactly." Kayleigh shrugged. "But I do know that, for the sake of the deal, we both need to remain focused on our objectives."

Kayleigh sipped her mocha latte and returned the oversize cup to the table. "Getting through Kira's wedding without incident is my only concern, and it should be his, too. The deal hinges upon it. Anything else is an unnecessary complication neither of us can afford."

"Believe me, I understand where you're coming from. This is supposed to be about what your head wants, not your heart." Savannah sighed. "But I also understand how quickly a plan like this can go off the rails when you're battling your emotions and physical attraction. It isn't easy to ignore feelings like that, whether it's love or desire."

"Whoa, no one said anything about the *L* word." Kayleigh held up a hand.

"So maybe love isn't an issue…yet." Savannah looked at her pointedly, one brow raised. "But from what I saw, the other *L* word, *lust*, was definitely in play. Who knows how far you two would've taken things if I hadn't interrupted you."

Kayleigh's cheeks burned, the possibilities flashing in her brain. "Things wouldn't have gone that far. Not there," she added.

"But you and Parker have that camping trip coming up this weekend. He's just spending one night at the site, right?" Savannah pulled off a piece of her warm sticky bun and practically purred when she put it in her mouth.

"Actually, there's been a change of plans and a compromise." Kayleigh had hoped the topic wouldn't come up.

"What kind of change?"

"I've agreed to accompany him to New York for the weekend when he attends one of his industry events in a couple of weeks, so he thought it would only be fair if he stayed the full weekend when we go camping."

"Right. That's the week our whole family will be in the Bahamas." Savannah nodded, then hiked an eyebrow as she leaned back, arms folded. "Wait… Parker *volunteered* to spend an entire weekend at a campground site with public bathrooms and an outdoor shower? That's surprisingly charitable of him. What's the compromise?"

"That we *don't* spend the weekend at a campground site with a public bathroom and an outdoor shower." Kayleigh sipped her latte slowly, allowing the large cup to shield much of her face.

"I thought you were a purist when it comes to camping." Savannah could barely hold back her smirk.

"I am when I'm paying for it," she muttered. "Parker insisted on the upgrade, so he's paying the difference."

"And what about when you two go to New York?"

"Separate rooms, of course." Kayleigh didn't meet her friend's gaze, didn't want to see the questions and implications there. "And King's Finest is paying for my flight and hotel since I'm accompanying him to an industry event."

"Just be honest with yourself and each other about how you feel. I know Parker comes off as this curmudgeonly turtle with a hard shell who only peeks his head and limbs out when it's absolutely necessary, but he's more vulnerable than he believes he is, especially when it comes to you. What happened Saturday proves that he's a lot more into you than either of you might realize."

"I never asked Parker to run interference between me and Cole. Nor did I ask him to kiss me."

"And yet he did." Savannah nibbled another bite of her sticky bun. "He's already in way over his head, but he still thinks he's standing safely on the shore."

"You've got a soft spot for Parker." Kayleigh cut her muffin in half. "Even after he tried to toss you in jail?"

"To be fair, he thought I was a corporate spy trying to steal proprietary information to sell to their competitors," Savannah said, her tone serious. "So I can't much blame him for being angry at the time. Or for his initial objections to his grandfather giving my family what was rightfully owed to us. But that was three years ago. Our relationship has come a long way since then."

"You've been charmed by Oscar the Grouch." Kayleigh teased.

"Well, you kissed him, so I'm pretty sure I'm the one

who's winning." Savannah giggled, drinking the last of her smoothie.

"Good point." Kayleigh laughed. "I'll admit, I'm seeing Parker in a new light the more time we spend together. I'll keep what you've said in mind. I promise."

"That's all I ask." Savannah smiled sadly. "You're both family to me. I don't want to see either of you get hurt."

Kayleigh's heart swelled. Savannah, having lost her parents at a young age in a fire, understood Kayleigh's pain and loss. Perhaps even more deeply. So saying that she considered them to be family... Savannah understood just how much that meant to Kayleigh. That it made her feel a little less alone in the world.

Nine

Kayleigh stood in Parker's driveway with Cricket by her side as he loaded his duffel bags into the back of the Jeep. The golden retriever still wasn't a fan of Parker's, mostly because he usually ignored her, but at least she wasn't growling and baring her teeth at him.

So…progress.

Since they wouldn't be needing the tents, sleeping bags, heater or propane stove, there was plenty of room for his oversize bags.

"You do realize we're only staying for the weekend and formal attire isn't required?" Kayleigh teased as he loaded the last of his things into the back.

"In the event of a zombie apocalypse, I've got you covered," he said, nearly straight-faced.

"Can't argue with that logic." She laughed.

Parker had just referenced her favorite television show and he wasn't taking himself too seriously. Also progress. Maybe their weekend together wouldn't be so bad.

"Hey, Cricket, how are you this morning, girl?" Parker waved at her, smiling.

Cricket turned to Kayleigh, seemingly as surprised by Parker's direct address as she was.

Kayleigh patted the dog's back to ensure her that the zombie apocalypse hadn't arrived and left them with a zombified version of Parker Abbott.

Cricket walked over and sniffed the part of Parker's leg left bare by his navy cargo shorts. When Cricket seemed satisfied, she looked up at Parker.

Kayleigh laughed. "It seems you passed the sniff test. I believe she's waiting for you to pet her."

Parker patted the dog's side twice. "Good girl. Ready for our weekend adventure?"

Cricket barked, then jumped into the back seat when Kayleigh opened the door for her.

"Guess that means she is." Kayleigh closed the door behind her and opened the driver's door. She stared at Parker, who'd already gotten in on the passenger side. "I was up late finishing a few orders before our trip. Interested in driving?"

"You'd trust me to drive the Cricketmobile?" He straightened his glasses.

"We both know that, of the two of us, you're the safer driver." Kayleigh tossed Parker the keys and they traded places. She strapped on her seat belt.

Parker got into the driver's seat. He reviewed the location of the turn signals, windshield wipers and hazard lights. Then he asked about the brakes and inquired about when the oil was last changed. Kayleigh was starting to regret her decision to let Parker drive, but then he finally pulled onto the road.

They'd been driving in silence for a bit when Kayleigh summoned the nerve to broach the topic they were both avoiding.

"So, about that day at your parents' place..." It was a lame but effective opening line. "That was weird, right?"

Parker tightened his grip on the steering wheel and his expression tensed, but he didn't take his eyes off the road.

"It's weird that a guy would want to kiss you?"

"It's weird that *you'd* want to kiss me. It's not like you're my biggest fan." She studied his expression, hating that she could only see half of it.

"I'm not the one who declared war, Kayleigh." There was a sadness in his tone that stabbed at her chest. "But to your point, it wasn't something I set out deliberately to do. It just sort of…happened."

"That's why I thought we should talk about it before we spend the next two weekends together." Kayleigh tried to keep her tone upbeat. "Because I think it's best if we don't have any misunderstandings."

"Like?"

"Like I don't want you to think that this is some convoluted scheme designed to—"

"Get me into bed?" Parker smiled slyly.

"Or into a relationship," she added.

He frowned. "If I offended you, I'm sorry."

"You didn't offend me, Parker." She touched his arm. It seemed to startle him, so she withdrew her hand. "And I obviously reciprocated. I guess what I'm saying is…we shouldn't get caught up in the moment, because this is just a temporary arrangement."

"I agree." Parker nodded. "I'm not a person who acts on emotion, and I didn't intend to kiss you. I just…" He glanced at her quickly before returning his attention to the road. "You were incredibly sad. I just wanted to console you. Honestly, I'm not sure what I was thinking. Guess I wasn't. But I'm glad we can move past it. I know you're going to like this cabin. The view is amazing, and it's quiet and secluded."

Kayleigh was grateful Parker had shifted the conversation back to safe ground and that they'd come to an understanding. Now that they'd gotten that practice kiss out of the way, they just needed to follow the same rules they'd learned in kindergarten: keep your hands and lips to yourselves.

Then everything would be just fine.

Parker readjusted his pillow and checked his watch. It was well after midnight, and though he'd turned in for the night two hours earlier, sleep had yet to find him.

He threw an arm across his face, shielding it from the sliver of moonlight visible through a gap in the curtains.

The logical option was to get up and pull them closed, but his weary, aching muscles refused to comply.

Despite Kayleigh's claims of being tired, she and Cricket possessed a boundless well of energy he simply didn't. For the first full day of their trip, Kayleigh had insisted on hiking the area, taking photographs of foliage, wildlife and the landscape. She collected interesting rocks and pieces of wood for future projects.

She hadn't compelled him to go. In fact she'd suggested the hike might be too much for him. Which, of course, made him more determined to show her that he wasn't the lethargic desk-sitter she imagined him to be.

The only problem with his plan was that he was indeed a lethargic desk-sitter. His work in his home gym had toned and carved his muscles, but his aversion to cardio and sweating revealed itself in their fourth or fifth mile of hiking.

He'd nearly fallen face-first into his plate during their late dinner, excusing himself afterward for a long soak in the tub.

But after a couple of hours of fitful sleep, he was awake again. Visions of Kayleigh danced in his head. He'd spent hours trudging behind her as she hiked in those enticing khaki shorts that accentuated the shapely curve of her perfect bottom. The length of the shorts made her legs appear to go on for miles, despite the muddy, worn hiking boots she wore.

The racerback athletic shirt highlighted the long, lean column of her graceful neck and the muscles of her back. Her curly red hair swung in a ponytail that peeked through the back of the khaki baseball hat pulled down low over her eyes. And her thighs…

Parker sat up abruptly against the headboard. He pressed the heels of his hands to his tired eyes and heaved a sigh.

Kayleigh had been clear that, from her perspective, nothing had changed regarding the temporary nature of their arrangement. This was all simply research for the roles they would play in just a few weeks. Then things would go back to the way they were. Reliving his spectacular view of Kayleigh's curves during their afternoon hike was counterproductive to that objective.

He threw off the sheets, pulled on a T-shirt, and stalked across the hardwood floor and down to the kitchen for a warm glass of milk.

When he entered the kitchen, half of the large deck, visible through the kitchen window overlooking the mountains, was lit. The lights were on in the room that housed the indoor swimming pool.

Parker followed the sound of water splashing.

"Kayleigh?" He stood beside the heated, indoor pool. "I can't believe you're still up. I would've expected you two to crash after the day we had."

"One of us did." She pointed to Cricket, who was lying in the corner, sleeping peacefully. "But I couldn't sleep."

She went back to swimming laps in the pool. Her lean, strong arms effortlessly sliced through the water; she had a beautiful freestyle. When she reached the wall, she went directly into a backstroke.

Parker stood beside the pool, mesmerized. There was

something simply entrancing about the movement of her body whether she was in the water, on foot or on a bicycle.

Kayleigh finished the last of her laps and climbed the stairs out of the pool, giving him a full view of her red halter bikini.

She looked…incredible. Narrow waist, toned abs, strong arms and lean, muscular thighs that he kept envisioning wrapped around his waist.

"Parker." She'd said his name as if she'd called it more than once to get his attention. "Would you hand me a towel, please?"

She removed the band that kept her hair up in a topknot and wrung the excess water from it.

"Thanks." Kayleigh wrapped the towel around her loosely, tucking it beneath her arm to secure it. She put her hair back in a much looser topknot before nodding toward the hot tub in the far corner. "I'm getting into the hot tub. You should join me. I worked you pretty hard today, but you were a trouper."

He swallowed hard. *Mind out of the gutter, Park. Mind out of the gutter.*

"I'm not wearing my trunks, but I'll keep you company."

"I thought you went to bed hours ago. Did I wake you?" She wrapped her damp hair in a second towel.

"Couldn't sleep. I came downstairs for a warm glass of milk."

"I couldn't sleep either." She bit her lower lip and glanced away momentarily. "I think I'm too wound up after today. And this place is amazing. I've never stayed in a cabin this nice. I still can't believe it has an indoor pool, a game room and this amazing view."

Kayleigh stepped closer to the wall of glass windows facing the mountains. She turned to him suddenly. "I've got just the thing to knock you out. I'll be right back."

He should go to bed. Leave her to her hot tub while he

got some sleep and tried not to think of her in that bikini. But he stayed rooted in place, because the truth was that he was eager to spend more time with her. Even if that meant keeping her company while she soaked in the hot tub in the wee hours of the morning.

Kayleigh returned, her flip-flops slapping against the stone floor. She held a jug he recognized as one of the moonshines they'd released to commemorate the King's Finest Jubilee three years earlier.

"You held onto that bottle all this time?" He grabbed two of the stemless silicone wine glasses stored behind the poolside bar.

"Savannah gave it to me one year on my birthday. I'd been saving it for…" Her cheeks suddenly turned pink. "I thought I'd bring it along to thank you for the upgrade. I might have been wrong about this whole glamping thing. Camping in luxury isn't so bad."

She handed him the jug, kicked her flip-flops off and slid into the warm water of the hot tub. Parker opened the bottle, poured a little in each of their glasses and handed her one.

"You know, drinking makes you sleepy, but it doesn't actually help you sleep better. It's been proven to interfere with sleep patterns." He dragged one of the heavy chairs closer to the hot tub and sank onto it.

"Humor me." She sipped her drink. "Mmm… Savannah was right. The peach cobbler is amazing."

"It's my favorite, too." He inhaled the luscious peach aroma before tipping the glass and allowing the slow burn to spread through his body. "But drinking it always makes me feel like a cliché. A rural Southern person camping in the mountains and drinking moonshine. How original."

"Don't be so high-and-mighty, Abbott. Your family wouldn't be sitting on that wad of cash now if it wasn't for the moonshine operation your great-grandfather ran in these very mountains back in the day."

"True." He sipped from his glass. If it weren't for King Abbott's moonshine operation, his grandfather Joseph Abbott would never have started a legitimate distillery. Parker set his glass down on a nearby table. There was something else he'd much rather talk about. "Kayleigh, can I ask you something?"

"You can ask." She set her glass down, too. "But I reserve the right not to answer."

"Fair enough." He scooted toward the edge of the seat. "This Aidan guy and his sister...you said they were important to you."

"They were." She frowned. "We covered this already. Do I need to call Cricket over?"

"Cricket is sleeping," he reminded her.

Kayleigh groaned, taking another sip from her glass. "Okay, so what is it that you so desperately need to know about my relationship with Aidan?"

"If you loved him so much, why didn't you fight for your relationship, or at the very least tell him what his mother did and let him decide?"

She narrowed her gaze and pursed her lips. "It was a no-win proposition. If he chose me, then there would always be tension between his mother and us. If he chose her..." Her words faded and she emptied her glass before returning it to the ledge and sinking deeper into the warm water.

"You were afraid that if you gave him a choice, he wouldn't choose you." Parker spoke softly, saying the words more to himself than to her.

Kayleigh climbed out of the hot tub, slipped on her flip-flops and wrapped the towel around her again. "It's late, and I'm suddenly very tired. I'll see you at breakfast."

"Kayleigh." Parker gripped her hand. "I didn't mean to upset you."

"Then why do you keep asking about my relationship with Aidan when you know I don't want to talk about it?"

"Because I'm trying to understand."

"Trying to understand what?" Her shoulders tensed.

"You're a fighter. You always have been. So I'm just trying to understand why you won't fight to save your relationships with the people you care about."

Kayleigh snatched her hand from his. "A few dates and suddenly you think you've got my entire life figured out? Well, you don't, Abbott. You don't know anything about who I am or what I'm willing to fight for."

"I know you were willing to dig your heels in and fight me and my father—even when it wasn't to your advantage. Yet you weren't willing to fight for your relationship with Aidan, Kira or Evvy…or your friendship with me."

Kayleigh's eyes widened and her brows furrowed. The color seemed to drain from her cheeks. Her chest hitched as she shook her head. "I should never have asked you to do this."

She turned and hurried away from him, her wet flip-flops slapping against the stone.

Parker jumped to his feet to go after her, but Cricket, who was up and on Kayleigh's heels, barked at him, then growled before following her mistress out of the room.

Don't be a jackass, Parker.

He had one rule to follow. Yet he couldn't seem to manage it. Kayleigh didn't want to talk about Aidan or Evvy. She'd been crystal clear about that. But he hadn't been able to help himself. He was compelled to understand her and why she'd written off their friendship without even allowing him to explain.

Parker dropped back onto the chair, wishing he'd stayed in bed and kept his big mouth shut.

Ten

Kayleigh pushed herself, running as fast as she could for the final mile back to the cabin. The cool, brisk early morning breeze was a relief against her heated skin, damp with perspiration.

She'd gotten up before the sun rose and hit the mountain trail as soon as there was enough light, hoping to avoid Parker.

Fucking Parker Abbott.

Once a jerk, always a jerk.

Aside from the still inexplicable kiss, things had been going pretty well between them. They were getting along, even enjoying each other's company. And Cricket was just beginning to come around to Parker. But deep down he was still that persistent little boy who would pick at a sore, pulling off the scab and wrecking the healing process.

She understood why Parker had some curiosity about the Brennans. After all, he was attending Kira's wedding and had been roped into an elaborate scheme for their benefit. So she'd allowed for his first round of questions about her relationship with the family and tolerated the second. But, as always, Parker Abbott just didn't recognize when she was at her limit. And the guy was still terrible at taking a hint. Even when she'd spelled it out for him pretty plainly.

She'd been so angry, she'd wanted to take Cricket and hop into her truck in her wet swimming suit and drive back to Magnolia Lake, leaving Abbott to fend for himself.

Maybe he would've gotten the hint then.

Kayleigh gasped with relief when the cabin finally came into view. Her muscles ached and sweat dripped into her eyes. Her feet hurt and she had calluses. And she was thirsty enough to drink from a trough.

But at least she'd given herself some distance from Parker. Some time to decide what she should do next. She hadn't been perceptive enough to add a Parker's-a-total-jerk clause to the contract.

Would she be able to pull out of the contract, even if Parker hadn't violated it in any way?

Kayleigh collapsed on the front steps of the large porch, her chest heaving as she tried to catch her breath.

Her head was pounding, her body ached, and she and Cricket needed water. But she honestly wasn't sure she could move another muscle.

The front door creaked opened, but she didn't turn around. She hoped Parker would get the hint and go away. When the door clicked shut without a word, she squeezed her eyes closed and released a long breath. Partly in relief, partly in disappointment.

"I know you're thirsty, girl." Kayleigh rubbed Cricket's soft fur, then patted her side as the dog panted. "Give Mama a moment to catch her breath."

A few seconds later, the door creaked open again. This time the sound was followed by Parker's footsteps as he descended the stairs and placed a bowl filled with water on the ground for Cricket. He sat on the step above Kayleigh and extended a cold bottle of water to her without saying a word.

Kayleigh raised her eyes to his and sighed.

She wanted so badly to tell Parker Abbott exactly what he could do with that bottle of water, but she was desperate for hydration.

"Thank you," she muttered, lowering her gaze to the bottle as she accepted it. She unscrewed the cap and drank until the bottle was empty.

Parker took the empty bottle from her hand and screwed the top back on it before leaning back on his elbows. "How far'd you run?"

She checked her fitness watch. "Six and a half miles."

"Without water?" He turned to her and frowned.

"I had water for both of us. I just didn't expect to run so far." She readjusted the baseball cap on her head and wiped the perspiration from her eyes with the back of her wrist.

"You were that angry with me, huh?" He held her gaze.

Kayleigh stood quickly, prepared to make her escape, but her right calf cramped.

She sat back down on the step and rubbed the pained muscle.

"May I?" Parker set the bottle aside and indicated her leg, his large hands hovering just above it.

Kayleigh sighed, nodding. Her cheeks stung with heat. She couldn't even pull off a decent dramatic exit.

Parker turned toward her and gently placed his hands on her leg, extending her calf.

"Pull the toes toward your knee. That'll help relieve the cramp."

Parker supported the weight of her leg as she did the extensions repeatedly.

"That's good. Now just relax your leg." He rested her leg across his own, his strong hands massaging her calf.

His hands moved deftly, alleviating the pain and causing warmth to spread along her skin, culminating in the space between her thighs.

She was suddenly conscious of her hardened nipples, accentuated by the rapid rise and fall of her chest.

"Thank you." She halted his motion and withdrew her leg. She was able to stand easily, but some of the pain lingered.

"It feels much better. I'm going to hop into a nice, hot shower."

"Actually, you should ice it first." Parker said. "When the pain has diminished, then you can take your hot shower."

"Thanks." Kayleigh put weight on her right leg as she climbed the next step, but she winced in pain.

"I've got you." Parker stood, sweeping her up in his arms before she could object.

She gasped in surprise, her hand pressed against his strong chest as he carried her up the remaining stairs and into the cabin.

Kayleigh wanted to insist that he put her down. She was hot, sticky, sweaty and smelled like the great outdoors. Parker was a germophobe. She could only imagine how grossed out he must be. But he didn't flinch or complain as he took her inside, then carried her up to her bedroom on the second floor and set her down on the edge of the large soaking tub.

"Sit tight. I'll get some ice." He returned with a plastic bag full of ice, wrapped it in a towel and handed it to her. "Let me know if you need anything else. I'm going to order us some breakfast. Eggs, waffles, bacon, sausage and orange juice?"

"That'd be great." Kayleigh positioned the ice over her calf. "Thank you, Parker."

He nodded and left the room while Cricket lay down at her feet on the cool terra-cotta bathroom tile.

She didn't understand Parker, and maybe she never would.

One moment he'd accused her of being a coward who was too afraid to fight for the people she loved. The next he was caring for her and Cricket as if he…

No, she would not give him credit for imitating a decent human being. Parker was all about business. His actions were sweet and thoughtful on the surface, and she appreciated what he'd done. But this was all about the deal for Parker. He'd done what he felt he needed to do to ensure that their deal was still on.

Kayleigh set the ice in the sink and turned on the shower, reminding herself to never forget that.

Eleven

Parker carefully unpacked their breakfast and laid it out on the table on the back deck overlooking the mountains and lush green forest. He glanced up as Kayleigh approached.

A short, flared white skirt showed off her strong, feminine legs, while a black off-shoulder blouse accentuated her toned shoulders and graceful neck. Her hair, still wet from the shower, appeared much darker and hung in perfect ringlets.

"This looks and smells amazing." She surveyed the spread and sat in the seat he'd indicated. She waited until they were both settled at the table before she took her first bite and groaned with pleasure.

The sensual sound vibrated through his chest and settled below his belt. He gulped some of the freshly squeezed orange juice.

"So, about last night," Parker said after they'd enjoyed most of their meal in relative silence.

Kayleigh frowned and sipped her juice. "Maybe it's better if we forget about last night."

Parker hesitated for a moment, but then put his fork down and scanned her pained expression.

"I didn't intend to make you angry."

"I believe you, Parker." Kayleigh nibbled on her last piece of bacon. "I guess I got so angry because..." She shrugged. "Maybe there's some truth to what you said."

Kayleigh was conceding to his observation?

He was speechless.

"So this awards event next weekend in New York..." Kayleigh finally said after another stretch of silence. "I assume I should dress up for it."

"If you'd like." He shrugged. "I'm only staying at the gala long enough to collect the award."

"For?"

"Distillery executive of the year." He drank the last of his juice.

"That's quite an honor. You're just going to accept the prize and bounce? Seems rude." Her tone made it sound more like an observation than an accusation. And she was probably right.

"I don't care much for large social events. I spend the entire evening checking my watch and calculating the appropriate time to make my escape." Parker chugged the last of his orange juice.

"What's your biggest fear about attending them?" Kayleigh's dark brown eyes assessed his.

"Other than the fact that I don't enjoy spending my evenings making inconsequential talk with strangers?"

"It's an industry event. You must be acquainted with some of your competitors and vendors."

"I am." He rubbed the back of his neck. "But that usually means enduring long, painful conversations. A vendor once cornered me and showed me photos of all twenty of his grandchildren."

"You're a real charmer, aren't you?" Kayleigh rolled her

eyes and sighed. "It's called building relationships, Abbott. You get to know them. You allow them to get to know you. Then they're more inclined to purchase from your company in the future. It's a little thing we like to call networking, and it's an essential part of every business."

"Fortunately Max, Zora, Blake and my dad excel at it."

"But they won't be there next weekend. You will. Who knows what type of connection you might make, if you're willing to make the effort."

"You sound like Zora." Parker groaned.

"It's no different than what you've been doing with me the past few weeks. Asking questions about my life. At least feigning interest—"

"I *am* genuinely concerned about your life and about what you've been through," he said abruptly. Was he that much of a bastard that even now she still didn't believe he was genuinely interested in her?

"I appreciate the effort," she said. "And I'm sure that the people you'll encounter at the event next week would, too."

"Point taken, but there's one more thing…" Parker frowned, remembering the awkward dance he and Kayleigh had shared at Blake and Savannah's wedding reception. "You already know I'm not much of a dancer. If I hang around too long at these things, someone inevitably asks me to dance. I either hurt their feelings by turning them down or make a fool of myself by attempting to accommodate them. Neither situation is ideal."

"That was a painful experience," Kayleigh groused. She shook her head at the memory. "But you don't need to be Usher or Fred Astaire. A little hip swaying should get you through the night just fine. All you need is a couple of moves and a little bit of swagger."

"I'm pretty sure I don't have either. When it comes to dancing," he clarified.

"You can learn them." Kayleigh stood, gathering their

plates. She paused and glanced over at him. "How long before we need to check out of the cabin?"

"I booked it for tonight, too. Just in case you wanted to stay until later this evening. We could even leave first thing tomorrow morning, if you'd like."

She froze, pinning him with an incredulous stare before returning her attention to gathering the plates. "That was very generous of you, Parker."

He stood and collected the remaining food, then followed her to the kitchen.

"Give me a few minutes to load the dishwasher. Then meet me beside the pool for your dance lesson."

"I appreciate the offer, but I'm sure you'd rather spend your last few hours here relaxing and enjoying the view."

"I'm not going to let you accept that award and dash out next week. And if I'm getting all dressed up, we're staying and dancing," she replied. "So I'm doing this for my own safety."

He'd stepped on her foot inadvertently and they'd nearly stumbled during their last dance together.

"Fair enough. What time would you like to check out?" He asked the question nonchalantly, hoping it wasn't too obvious that he wanted to spend another evening with her. This time he'd keep his observations about Kayleigh's life to himself.

"Why don't we play it by ear?"

Parker's jaw clenched involuntarily. He was practically allergic to spontaneity, a fact Kayleigh was well aware of. She seemed hell-bent on bashing in every single wall of his carefully constructed comfort zone with a steel battering ram. But he would do his best to adapt.

He nodded. "Sure. Why not?"

Kayleigh seemed stunned that he'd agreed so easily. She nabbed one last piece of bacon before he shut the lid on the container. "See you on the dance floor in five."

Twelve

Parker stared at his feet and repeated the line dance steps in his head. Patterns he understood, so he could easily remember what he was *supposed* to be doing. But once he tried to move in sync with the music, everything fell apart.

"It's pointless." He stopped his painfully uncoordinated movements and ran a hand over his head. "Dancing isn't my gift. I've made peace with it."

Kayleigh paused the song on her cell phone. "You know the steps. Just stop thinking so much and connect with the music."

"I'm trying to move with the beat."

"And it looks painful." Her warm tone and sweet smile took the sting out of her words. "So let's try something less structured."

"What do you have in mind?" He was grateful for the reprieve.

"A basic step, touch." She demonstrated the move.

He watched her do it a few times, then moved in sync with her. "This is easy enough. Why didn't we start with this?"

"It's too early to get cocky, Abbott." She stopped dancing and faced him, indicating that he continue as she assessed him. "Soften your knees and take smaller steps. Don't stomp your foot. You're not killing bugs. Just tap your toes lightly. You'll be lighter on your feet and you can easily shift your weight in preparation for the next step."

He felt awkward dancing while Kayleigh critiqued him. But he tried diligently to incorporate each new instruction.

"Much better." She switched to a mellow love ballad. Her brown eyes twinkled and one side of her mouth quirked. "My big toe may never forgive me for this, but why don't we take another stab at dancing together?"

Parker placed one hand near the top of her back and gripped her hand with the other, holding it high. He could still remember his grade school phys ed instructor barking at them to hold the frame.

"We're not doing the waltz, so this position feels too formal. Loosen up a little. Also, I won't bite, so you don't need to leave enough space between us to set up a lemonade stand."

"Loosen the hold and hold the lemonade stand. Got it." He catalogued her instructions in his brain. Parker stepped closer, glided his palm down her back a little and lowered their clasped hands. "Like this?"

"Much better." Kayleigh pressed her hand to his back. "Let's go back into that step, touch move."

They practiced to one song, then another, until he felt more confident.

"Better, but you're still a little stiff. You realize your hips are capable of movement, right?"

"Obviously." He smirked.

"Not *that* kind of hip movement." Kayleigh's cheeks flushed. "Maybe we should practice hip circles."

"That's a definite no for me." He came to a stop and released her. "But if you'd care to practice hip circles, I'm happy to critique you."

"That's a great idea. But don't just assess them— practice them with me." She huffed in response to his adamant refusal. "Okay, you don't have to. Just try to *feel* the music."

"I'll try to do a better job of keeping time with the music. How's that?"

"Close enough." Kayleigh scrolled through her phone. The opening chords of Marvin Gaye's "Got to Give It Up" played and she set it down. "This is perfect. It's up-tempo with a really funky, sexy groove."

Strung together, those words didn't make sense to him. "What exactly am I supposed to be doing?"

"Same as before." She started the step, touch again. "Just remember, you're not a utility pole, so your hips and waist shouldn't be stationary."

Parker followed her lead and tried to be more relaxed, like Kayleigh. Arms raised and hips rocking, she snapped her fingers and sang along. He was mesmerized.

He concentrated on the music and Kayleigh's movements—smooth, hypnotic and sexy as hell. Little by little, each move felt more natural.

"All right now!" Kayleigh grinned, her body swaying. She turned, giving her back to him as she swiveled her hips.

She was close. Close enough for her signature vanilla scent to tickle his nostrils. Close enough for him to feel the heat radiating from her freshly scrubbed skin. But not close enough to touch.

Yet that's exactly what he wanted. To wrap his arms around her waist and haul her body against his as they danced together.

"Awesome job, Parker." She high-fived him when the song ended. "Now we'll do the same thing back in partner position to a slower song."

"Got it." He mentally reviewed everything he'd learned as she selected the next song. Another Marvin Gaye tune: "I Want You."

Apropos choice.

He took her in his arms and they swayed to the song, which she played on repeat.

"You're doing terrific, Parker." The encouragement in her voice warmed his chest and made him want to try harder.

Next she showed him how to use the gentle pressure of both hands to guide her as they made their way across the floor.

"You're actually going to let me lead?" he teased.

"Don't let it go to your head, and don't make us look bad." Her body fit snugly against his as she pressed her cheek to his chest.

It was a welcome sensation.

Parker cradled her soft curves against him and rested his chin against the top of her head, inhaling the sweet scent of her shampoo.

"So, what's the verdict?" he asked. "Am I ready for prime time?"

"Definitely." Kayleigh looked up at him. There was something in her tone and expression he couldn't quite read. She pulled out of his embrace and turned off the music. "That's enough practice. I'll go pack so we can get out of here."

"Kayleigh." Parker caught her hand when she turned to walk away. "Was it something I said?"

"No." She shook her head, not meeting his gaze. "It's nothing like that."

"But it is *something*." Parker stepped closer.

Kayleigh bit her lower lip. Her chest rose and fell quickly, as if she was in distress.

"Talk to me, Kayleigh." He needed to see the depths

of those brown eyes to make sure he hadn't sabotaged the progress they'd made. He gently lifted Kayleigh's chin, and her gaze met his. "Why are you suddenly so agitated?"

"It's nothing. I…" She sighed heavily as she slipped her hand from his. But rather than pulling away, she clutched his shirt with both hands and lifted onto her toes. Her eyes drifted shut as she pressed her lips to his.

Kayleigh Jemison was sure she'd lost her freaking mind. She was kissing Parker Abbott. *Intentionally.*

Parker seemed stunned at first. He'd gone still, allowing her to take control. But then his strong hands drifted to the back of her neck. His thumbs rested against her cheekbones as he kissed her.

The kiss started off tame and sweet as they felt each other out. But their tentativeness slowly gave way to the heat growing between them. He sucked on her lower lip before tilting her head, sliding his warm tongue inside her mouth and gliding it against hers.

She welcomed it with an involuntary sigh.

Parker was an excellent kisser. She could add that to the long list of things about him that surprised her.

He'd been utterly adorable as he'd struggled to learn to dance. But as they danced to a slow song together, in full contact, hips in motion, his lean, fit body pressed to hers, she couldn't help wanting him to kiss her again. Something she'd fantasized about since he'd kissed her at his parents' house.

The memory of that first kiss often flooded her brain, the sensations washing over her with the same intensity they had that day. Each time, she dismissed the prospect of repeating their mistake.

It was a colossally bad idea that would only complicate their arrangement. Yet she couldn't help wanting him.

She wanted to feel his strong hands on her bare skin, and to run her fingertips along his. She wanted to trace the muscles of his calves and biceps, which she'd ogled shamelessly during their hike through the mountains. And she desperately needed to know if his abs and ass were as firm as their perfect outlines, visible through his clothing, led her to believe.

Her pulse raced and her temperature rose in response to his deepening of their kiss. A spark of electricity danced along her spine as he trailed one large hand down her back. Her nipples pebbled as they brushed against his firm chest.

As delicious as his kiss was, it only made her want more than was possible with the two of them still fully dressed. Kayleigh fumbled with the buttons on Parker's shirt. She'd unfastened two when he pulled his mouth from hers suddenly.

He seemed thrown off by her taking control again. He studied her, his chest heaving. But he didn't speak. Nor did he halt her progress as she unbuttoned the remaining buttons.

She slipped the fabric from his shoulders. His hungry gaze locked with hers as he allowed the shirt to fall to the floor.

Kayleigh sank her teeth into her lower lip and sighed softly as she studied his lean, muscular frame.

Parker certainly hadn't earned those pecs and biceps from sitting at his desk all day, crunching numbers.

His hands dropped to her waist, then drifted up her rib cage as he lifted the hem of her blouse and tugged it over her head.

Her chest rose and fell heavily and her belly tightened beneath his gaze as he studied the sheer black bralette that did little to hide how aroused she was by him. Parker glided the backs of his fingers up her stomach, then teased one of the pebbled nubs with his thumb.

He grazed the hardened peak with his teeth through the lacy fabric, then sucked. Her knees went weak and she held on to his shoulders so she wouldn't topple over. Parker wrapped his other arm around her waist, steadying her as he tugged the material aside and tasted her skin. He swirled his tongue around her painfully tight nipple.

"I've imagined this moment so many times," he muttered between licks and sucks that made her increasingly hot for him.

Just when she thought she'd combust, he pulled aside the fabric and released her other breast, lavishing it with the same attention.

Her legs shook and her breath came in quick, shallow pants that made her slightly light-headed. Suddenly he gazed up at her. There was something warm and liquid in his eyes. Like warm maple syrup.

God, the things I could do with a warm bottle of maple syrup right now.

Parker backed her up until her legs bumped the edge of one of the sturdy poolside lounge chairs. He lay her down and pressed his warm mouth to hers. One hand skimmed down her side, then slipped beneath her skirt.

He squeezed her bottom, most of which was exposed by panties that straddled the line between a thong and a brief. Kayleigh drew in a deep breath, breaking their kiss when he palmed the space between her thighs. Parker's gaze met hers, his nostrils flaring.

"Damn," he muttered, evidently pleased by the indisputable evidence of her desire for him.

Any lingering hesitancy between them dissipated.

Parker claimed her mouth in another bruising kiss. A steady pulse built in her core and her breath hitched as he teased the bundle of nerves and the sensitized flesh surrounding it.

"Parker, please. I need you," she whispered, hating the truth of those words as much as she anticipated the fulfillment of them.

He dragged the damp fabric down and off her legs with urgency.

Kayleigh released a soft cry when he plunged his fingers deep inside her and curled them, allowing him to reach the spot where she needed him so desperately.

Her breathy sighs came faster and her head lolled back as the overwhelming sensation built inside her like a storm growing in intensity. When he added the sensation of his thumb gliding across her sensitive nub and slick, swollen folds, her legs trembled from the intense pleasure.

Her stomach clenched and her core convulsed. Kayleigh squeezed her eyes shut as she rode the wave of pleasure that left her quivering and aching for more.

She heaved a sigh, her eyes drifting open.

Parker lay beside her. One edge of his sensuous mouth quirked in a half-smile that sent a prickle of heat to her already aching nipples.

"That was incredible." She sheepishly met his gaze. "But what would be even better is…" Kayleigh loosened his belt buckle. Her pulse pounded in her ears as she inched his zipper down.

Black boxer briefs.

She wouldn't have expected anything else from Parker Abbott. Kayleigh licked her lower lip as she studied the bulge in his shorts from its base to the damp circle over its tip.

Kayleigh swallowed hard, her heart beating wildly as she ran her fingertips along the fabric shielding him. She pressed soft kisses to his chest as she slipped her hand beneath his waistband and wrapped her fingers around his thick shaft.

Parker's eyes drifted shut. A shudder rolled up his spine as Kayleigh's hand glided up and down his length.

He took slow, measured breaths, each descending into a

throaty exhalation. Though he realized it was impossible, it felt as if his heart would pound right out of his chest as she brought him closer to the edge.

It was a hand job, and he wasn't some hormone-filled teenage boy. But Kayleigh Jemison made him crazy with want. Everything about her stoked a fire deep inside him. In her absence, he felt a deep ache in his chest. In her presence, he was overcome by an overwhelming hunger for her. And what she was doing to him at the moment might drive him over the brink.

His urgent need for her was irrational and very much unlike him.

He prided himself on staying cool, being logical and maintaining self-control, even if he couldn't control the circumstances around him. But Kayleigh had a talent for shattering that.

He'd come to the cabin determined to be on his best behavior. To keep their relationship strictly business. His resolve had been hanging on by a worn thread all weekend. When she'd kissed him, every remaining ounce of it had disintegrated.

Parker met Kayleigh's gaze, hazy with lust. Needing another taste of her sweet, warm lips, he kissed her with a desperation that felt foreign, and yet deeply satisfying. He swept his tongue inside her mouth, savoring her kiss. Her hand continued to pump his shaft, the sensation building until he could barely hold on another moment.

Grasping her wrist, Parker stilled Kayleigh's hand. He dragged his mouth from hers, his breathing ragged. It required every ounce of determination he could muster to hold on. That hadn't happened since he'd been a bumbling teenage boy learning to navigate sex and the female body.

"You don't like it?" Kayleigh looked hurt and confused.

An expression he knew well. It had been burned into his brain for the past two decades.

"No, that is definitely not the issue." His cheeks and forehead stung with heat.

"Oh." Her eyes widened with realization.

"I just thought you'd rather…" He indicated the chaise. "You know."

"Have sex?" Kayleigh seemed amused by his avoidance of the word. Her eyes twinkled as she stared at him intensely and smiled. "I would. I assume you have a condom in your wallet."

"Actually, a wallet isn't an ideal place to keep them. It's much safer to store them in—"

"Parker." Kayleigh's tone was sharp. "Do you have one?"

"I do."

"Could you get it? Like now?"

"Of course." He pressed an awkward kiss to her cheek and trotted upstairs to retrieve the strip of condoms from his shaving kit.

Parker caught a glimpse of himself in the mirror. He was shirtless, his cheeks were red and his pants were unfastened.

He enjoyed sex as much as the next guy, but what set him apart from his libido-driven counterparts had always been his ability to exercise logic and good sense.

At the moment, he was employing neither.

Sleeping with Kayleigh was a thrilling prospect. She was sexy and beautiful. Maddening, yet amusing. And he admired the hell out of her for her strength and tenacity. But the deal between Kayleigh and King's Finest was the most important thing in his world. And this could ruin everything.

He'd be taking one hell of a risk. A risk neither of them could afford.

This deal was too important to everyone involved.

Parker gripped the edge of the counter and cursed. *Kayleigh.*

She'd be madder than a wet hen. But it was the right decision. He was sure of it. Hopefully when she calmed down, she'd come to the same conclusion. Maybe she'd even be glad he'd stopped them from taking this any further.

Parker's steps felt leaden as he returned to the spot where Kayleigh waited for him partially undressed. A sight he'd never forget.

Kayleigh studied him as he walked toward her. Her expression went from a soft, hazy lust to one he could read quite easily.

Animosity.

"You've changed your mind, haven't you?"

"Kayleigh, I'm sorry. I just think—"

"Save it, Parker. *Why* doesn't matter." Her cheeks flushed as she scrambled to her feet quickly. She tugged her skirt and bra back into place.

He stooped and retrieved both of their shirts from the stone floor and handed Kayleigh hers.

"God, I'm such an idiot." She swiped the garment from his hand and slipped it over her head. "I can't believe I did this, that I thought you…" She stopped short. Her gaze was filled with resentment.

Kayleigh searched the floor. Presumably in search of the black lace panties he'd stripped her of earlier.

Parker spotted them beneath the chaise. But before he could retrieve them, she'd stormed off toward her room, saying she'd be leaving in an hour, with or without him.

He was surprised she hadn't shoved him into the pool. After stooping to pick up her panties, he shoved them into his pocket and then dropped onto the chaise.

Kayleigh wasn't the idiot. He was.

He wanted to be with her. Desperately. But there was

one thing he wanted more: to be named the next CEO of King's Finest.

Sleeping with Kayleigh Jemison could put his chances of that in serious jeopardy.

They were nearly back to his house and Kayleigh had barely uttered two words, other than "You drive," as she'd chucked the keys at him, narrowly missing his head.

Slumped against her seat, and wearing a faded T-shirt and tattered jeans, she'd spent the entire drive either staring out the window or scrolling through her phone.

"Kayleigh." Parker said her name softly as the car idled at a light. "I'm sorry, but it just wouldn't be prudent for either of us to jeopardize this deal. It has such large implications for both of us. The exposure was just too great."

She snapped her attention in his direction. "Seriously, Parker, are you trying really hard to be a dick, or does it just come naturally to you?"

"I don't under—"

"Of course you don't." She waved her hand dismissively. "Look, forget it. It was third base, not a marriage proposal. So let's pretend it never happened."

"Do people over twenty still say *third base*?" The light changed and he pulled off.

"God, you can be so…infuriating." She clenched her fists as she drew in a deep breath and released it, lowering her voice. "I asked you to drive because I was afraid that if I did, I'd be tempted to pull over and dump your body in a ditch. Now, please, just let it go. You learned how to dance and we're ready for the event next week. That's all that matters."

"So, the deal is still on?"

"It's like you said—it's too important to both of us." Kayleigh tossed her phone on the dashboard. "I didn't appreciate it at the time, but you're right. Sex would only complicate the deal. Neither of us needs that. So we each fulfill our end of the bargain and we walk away. No regrets."

Parker nodded as he turned onto the street that led to his neighborhood. He was glad Kayleigh recognized the logic of his decision. But she was wrong about one thing. Despite knowing all the reasons he shouldn't be with Kayleigh, he deeply regretted not making love to her.

It was a chance he'd never have again.

Thirteen

Kayleigh sifted through spools of jewelry wire stored in her studio supply room. She had another idea for the new line of jewelry she was designing, based on her weekend stay at the cabin with Parker.

The sun had gone down, but her mind still buzzed with ideas. She'd already made a few necklaces with matching bracelets and earrings, but another design was knocking around in her head, if only she could find that damn sheet of pink lace variegated brass leaf. It would create beautiful contrasts on another design that would be ideal for fall.

"Kayleigh."

She dropped the spools of copper and silver wire and nearly toppled the cabinet. Parker was standing in the doorway between the shop and the back room.

"Parker? What the—"

"I didn't mean to scare you." He held his hands up in surrender. "I worked late tonight and decided to grab a bite to eat before the pizza shop closed. I noticed your light was still on in the studio."

Kayleigh retrieved the spool of copper wire from the

floor and Parker held out the roll of silver wire, which had rolled to his feet.

"Thanks." She accepted the spool, then quickly turned and shoved it back into the bin. "Is there something you need?"

"No, I just…well, they were offering a deal on the extra-large pizzas that didn't seem prudent to pass up, but it's more than I can eat alone. I thought maybe…" He shifted his weight from one foot to the other, looking as uncomfortable as she'd felt the night he'd left her half naked on that chaise and suddenly decided he didn't want to sleep with her.

Good.

It didn't begin to make up for the humiliation she'd felt in that moment. She considered herself confident, but a rejection like that could take a hammer to even the most self-assured woman's ego.

"You thought maybe…*what*?" Kayleigh folded her arms, eyeing him impatiently. She was eager to get back to searching for materials for her project.

"I thought maybe you'd like to split it with me." Parker unbuttoned the top button of his crisp white shirt and loosened his navy printed tie before shoving a hand into the pocket of slim, gray pants that seemed tailored to his lean, muscular frame. "Have you eaten dinner yet?"

"No." She'd nibbled on a granola bar she discovered in a drawer five hours earlier. "Pizza would be great. I can grab a plate from upstairs if you want to leave me a couple of slices."

She searched through the cabinet for the metal leaf again.

"I guess I didn't explain myself very well. I thought maybe we could eat *together*." Parker squatted beside Cricket, who'd walked over to greet him. He rubbed her ears and ruffled the fur on either side of her head. Cricket looked uncommonly content.

Traitor.

"I'm working still." Kayleigh gave Cricket a side-eye before rummaging in the cabinet again.

"Then we could have a working dinner. Right here." He gestured toward her work space.

"Look, Parker, if this is a pity thing, it's completely unnecessary." She turned to him, her arms folded. "That thing that didn't happen between us? I've put it out of my mind."

"This isn't a pity thing." Parker's cheeks flushed. "It just didn't make sense to waste half of a perfectly good Hawaiian pizza—"

"You ordered Hawaiian pizza?" She raised a brow. "I thought you said ham and pineapple on a pizza was disgusting."

Parker shrugged. "I tried a slice. Just to prove to myself that it was as awful as I thought."

"And?"

"It was one of the best damn pizzas I've ever eaten," he conceded with a half smile.

"Fine." Kayleigh huffed, sure she'd soon regret her decision. "If you don't mind me working while we eat."

"Of course not. I'll grab the pizza from the car." He opened the door and turned back toward her. "When you're working late like this, you really should lock your door."

"We live in Mayberry," she scoffed. "Nothing remotely interesting ever happens here."

"Even in Mayberry there was crime," he countered.

She folded her arms again, her jaw tight. "If I'd locked the door tonight, I wouldn't be having this conversation about locking the door with you now. So there is that to consider."

He pressed his lips together and his mouth curved in a partial smile. "Don't lock me out, in case you were considering it."

"Of course not." She *totally* was. "How else would I get my Hawaiian pizza?"

* * *

"Maybe I was just incredibly hungry, but Margot's pizza was exceptional tonight," Kayleigh declared after unapologetically polishing off her third slice.

"It's her new chef," he confirmed. "I've noticed subtle improvements in their menu since she hired him."

Awkward silence stretched between them for a few moments. Kayleigh couldn't take it anymore. She stood suddenly and wiped her hands on a napkin.

"Thank you for the pizza, Parker. But I need to get back to work, and I still haven't found that metal leaf. Besides, I'm sure there's something else you'd rather be doing tonight."

Parker didn't acknowledge her polite and apparently too subtle attempt at saying *you don't have to go home, but you've gotta get the hell out of here*. He walked over to the storage cabinet she'd been searching. "How do you ever find anything in here?"

"I generally know where everything is." Maybe she wasn't as organized as him, but she had a system. Sort of.

"What were you looking for?"

Kayleigh described the thin metal sheets she was searching for and Parker helped her go through the shelves, which were overflowing with jewelry-making components.

"Is this it?" Parker held up a shipping envelope from the company that supplied her metal leaf.

"Yes! Thanks. I could kiss you right now." She took the envelope from him excitedly. Then, realizing what she'd said, she added, "Don't flip out—it's just an expression. You're in no danger of me kissing you again. *Believe me*." She muttered the last part under her breath.

"I understand." Parker frowned and shoved his hands back in his pockets.

"Well, thank you for dinner and for helping me find

this." Kayleigh held up the envelope after an uncomfortable lull between them. "I'd better get back to work."

Parker nodded, but didn't move toward the door. "I'd love to see what you're working on."

She furrowed her brow, her head cocked as she studied him for a moment. "Why?"

"I thought I'd get an early start on shopping for my mother's birthday this year. I'd love to get a first look at your newest designs."

Kayleigh seemed to find his response reasonable. She directed him to an arrangement of three necklaces with matching bracelets and earrings.

"These are incredible, Kayleigh." He studied the pieces, one by one. Using gold-and-silver wire, she'd recreated some of the flowers and leaves they'd seen during their hike. Each piece was more stunning than the last. The third set was embellished with precious stones.

"This one is particularly beautiful." He admired the wire-wrapped stones and her intricate work. "I'd never really noticed what exceptional work you do. I'd like to buy this set."

"I'm not quite finished with it, and I'm not sure how much I'll charge for it when I'm done."

"Well, when you decide, I'd like it." He shoved his hands in his pockets.

Kayleigh narrowed her gaze at him and then waved her hand. "Consider it a gift."

She was wearing tattered jeans and an old T-shirt. Her hair was pulled high in a lopsided bun that a light breeze could've blown apart. Yet he could barely take his eyes off her. And he couldn't stop thinking of the taste of her mouth or how it had felt to hold her in his arms.

"No, I couldn't."

"You paid for the upgrade to the cabin and King's Finest

is covering my travel expenses this weekend." She swept aside a few stray curls that had tumbled free of her loose bun. "It's the least I can do."

"You let me know when you decide on a price for that set." He didn't acknowledge her offer again as he turned to leave. "Be sure to lock the door this time." He gave her a faint smile. "Good night, Kayleigh."

She followed him to the door, wished him a good night and locked it behind him.

Parker squeezed his eyes shut against the vision of Kayleigh at the cabin that day, wishing he'd made a different choice.

Fourteen

Kayleigh studied herself in the full-length mirror. Her hotel room was gorgeous, as was the hotel where Parker's national distillery trade organization was holding their conference and gala. He'd arrived earlier in the week, while she'd arrived the previous day.

Parker had planned a day of sightseeing for them, and as much as she hated to admit it, it had been fun. She'd been to New York before, with Aidan, but she hadn't visited any of the touristy sites like the Empire State Building or the Statue of Liberty. Which was something she'd mentioned to Parker when he'd proposed this trip.

He'd arranged for her to visit both, and earlier that day they'd gone on one of those cheesy television-show tours. She'd loved every minute of it. And despite himself, Parker seemed to enjoy it, too. He'd been genuinely disappointed when she had other plans for lunch.

She raked her manicured fingernails through her shiny, silken coppery curls and tugged her hair over one shoulder, hoping he'd be pleased when he discovered how she'd spent the afternoon.

Kayleigh removed her dress from its silk hanger and stepped into the soft, buttery gold satin, sliding it up her body. The floor-length dress had a deep V-neck, a low-cut back, spaghetti straps and a thigh-high slit.

It wasn't something she'd typically wear, but Savannah had gotten teary-eyed when she'd tried the dress on and insisted that this was the one. So Kayleigh had trusted her hormonal friend and ventured outside of her comfort zone.

There was a knock at the door that separated her hotel room from Parker's.

"Perfect timing." She opened the door and turned her back toward him. "Can you get this zipper for me?"

Parker set something down, then zipped up her dress. "Kayleigh, you look…absolutely stunning."

"Thank you." She surveyed his charcoal gray Michael Kors tuxedo and pristine white tuxedo shirt. "You look quite handsome, too. Except…"

She adjusted his black bow tie a smidge. It was the kind of thing that she normally didn't notice, but would drive Parker insane. "Perfect."

"Ready?" He checked his watch. A Bvlgari with a black alligator strap, an eighteen-karat rose-gold bezel and a transparent dial that revealed its black gears. The watch had to be worth more than her truck. Maybe even when it was new.

"Yes." Kayleigh stepped into the gold, peep toe Betsey Johnson stilettos she'd picked out to go with the dress. The four-inch heels were studded with crystals and had an ankle strap. She picked up her cell phone. It was all she planned to carry.

"Before we go…" Parker retrieved the box he'd set down when he'd zipped her dress. It was wrapped in shiny gold paper and had an organza bow. He handed it to her. "This is for you."

"What is it?" Kayleigh studied the beautiful box. It was almost too pretty to open.

He shrugged. "Only one way to find out."

Kayleigh carefully loosened the bow, set the box on the bed and opened it. She gasped. "This is the Alexander McQueen clutch I admired in the shop window yesterday. You went back for it?"

He shrugged, as if buying her a bag that cost more than her mortgage payment was no big deal. "You liked it, and you said you didn't have a handbag for a formal event."

Kayleigh glided her fingers over the crystal-studded black calf leather and the hinged clasp with its signature skull and embellished four-ring knuckle-duster. "Parker, this was incredibly sweet of you, but it's much too expensive a gift. Besides, I thought you didn't like it."

"I didn't at first. But the more I thought about it, the more I understood why you love it. It's edgy, yet beautiful. Classic, yet modern. It suits you, Kayleigh." He lifted the black leather clutch from the box and extended it to her. "So I want you to have it. It's that simple."

Parker Abbott was an enigma she might never understand. He could be infuriating, but he could also be sweet and insightful. "I don't know what to say other than…thank you."

She pressed a quick kiss to his cheek, then wiped off the smudge of lipstick left in its wake.

They made their way down to the beautifully appointed ballroom. Kayleigh tensed the moment they stepped inside. Most of the women were dripping with diamonds and wearing expensive, high-end designer ball gowns. Many were wearing red-bottomed heels.

She'd felt confident and beautiful when she'd stepped on that elevator, but now she felt like she was on the JV team when everyone else here was clearly varsity.

Parker slipped an arm around her waist. "You'll do fine,

and you look amazing." He guided her to their table and pulled out her chair. "Can I get you a drink?"

"A dirty martini, please."

"Coming right up."

Kayleigh watched Parker walk across the room. He looked incredibly handsome in his tuxedo and there was something about the swagger of his walk that…

No. Nope. Stop it.

Kayleigh reminded herself of all the reasons she shouldn't be thinking of Parker Abbott that way.

Parker surveyed the crowded room as he moved toward the bar. He reached inside his tuxedo jacket for his wallet when the bartender requested his order. "A manhattan and a dirty martini, please."

"I hope that dirty martini is for me," a sultry voice whispered in his ear.

"Elena." His spine stiffened as he turned to face her. "How are you?"

"Better now that you're here." Her brown eyes twinkled.

Elena Mixon was the kind of woman who commanded attention anywhere she went. The kind of woman that just about any man would want on his arm. But Elena was no man's arm candy. Nor would she ever consent to being a trophy wife. Much to the chagrin of her parents.

She was as dedicated and driven as any man he'd ever met, and like him, she was determined to prove that she was the one who should be running her family's distillery. An opinion her old-school father, traditional mother and six siblings—five of whom were male—heartily disagreed with.

"And I was afraid it was going to be boring this year." She trailed a finger down his arm, her brown eyes gleaming.

They'd last seen each other at an event two years ago. And they'd seen every inch of each other.

"Actually, I brought a date this year."

She smacked her lips as if it were the most preposterous thing she'd ever heard. "I thought you didn't believe in dating."

"Generally speaking." He shoved one hand in his pocket and leaned against the bar.

"What makes this girl so special?"

"She just...is." Parker glanced in Kayleigh's direction. Their eyes met and she smiled. It warmed something in his chest.

He checked his watch. *What the hell is taking the bartender so long with those drinks?*

"How long have you two been dating?" Elena parked herself on the stool beside him.

Parker groaned quietly. Elena was worse than he was at taking hints. "Not long, but we have history. We were best friends in grade school."

"And what prompted the change in your relationship?"

"Is there a reason you're so interested in my love life?"

"The thing is, I didn't think you had a love life. That's why I didn't press for anything more than industry-event hookups. But when you change the rules of the game, darling, it isn't fair to not inform the other players." Elena crossed her legs and one long, shapely leg peeked through the high slit of her dress.

"We haven't seen each other in two years. You're upset because I'm here with someone else?" He was honestly baffled by Elena's reaction. "Why? Neither of us expressed an interest in a relationship."

Elena sighed. "I understand, but if I'd known there was another option—"

"Another option for what?"

"Don't play coy with me. You know good and well that—"

"Hi, babe. I thought I'd check on our drinks." Kayleigh suddenly appeared beside him, her clutch in hand.

He blinked. Had she just called him *babe*?

"Parker can be so…well, you know… Parker." Kayleigh smiled at Elena. "Hi, I'm Kayleigh Jemison. I'm Parker's—"

"Fiancée." The word escaped his mouth abruptly, taking all three of them by surprise.

"Fiancée?" Elena echoed.

"Yes." Kayleigh stared up at him lovingly, after quickly recovering from her initial shock at his sudden declaration. "I'm his fiancée."

"But no engagement ring?" Elena tapped her long fingernails against the oak bar.

Parker and Kayleigh exchanged glances. It was something they hadn't considered.

"I'm a jewelry designer, so I'm hard to shop for." Kayleigh smiled at Elena sweetly. "But I'm confident we'll find the right ring."

"Yes." Parker wrapped his arm around Kayleigh's waist and pulled her closer. "I know we will, sweetheart."

She wasn't the only one who could throw around terms of endearment.

After an awkward silence between them, Parker spoke. "My apologies, ladies. I should've introduced you from the outset. Kayleigh, this is Elena Mixon. Her family owns Mixon Whiskey. And Elena, you already know that Kayleigh Jemison is—"

"Your fiancée." Elena sounded completely unconvinced.

"It's a pleasure to meet you, Elena." Kayleigh nodded, then turned toward the bartender, who'd finally brought their drinks and apologized for the delay.

"What was that about?" Kayleigh asked once they'd taken their leave and returned to their table. "The look you gave me… I could tell you needed an escape from your friend over there, but I didn't expect you to pull the whole fiancée thing out of the hat."

"Neither did I." Parker gulped his drink. He still wasn't

sure why he'd said it. But if the encounter with Elena was any indication, their fake-fiancée experiment was going to go up in flames before they unmoored the boat from the dock.

"I guess it's only fair." Kayleigh sipped her martini. "You're playing my fake fiancé for a week—the least I can do is play yours for one night." She set her martini down. "It's good this happened. Elena brought up a very good point."

"The ring. I know. I hadn't thought of that either."

"I cannot go there with a fake ring. Aidan's mother and sister would spot it from a mile away. Maybe I can find a really nice ring at a pawn shop here."

"Don't worry about the ring." Parker swigged his manhattan, then set the glass on the table. "I've got that covered. A friend owes me a favor."

"Thank you, Parker."

The relief and gratitude in Kayleigh's eyes made him sit a bit taller. He liked being someone she could count on.

"Parker, it's so good to see you."

He stood as Malcolm and Sarah Mays, the owners of a gin distillery in Washington State, joined them at the table. He accepted a hug from the kindly older woman and then shook her husband's hand.

"And you must be Parker's fiancée." The woman grinned.

Kayleigh nearly choked on her martini. She set her glass down and gave him a panicked look before her smile fell back into place. "Yes, ma'am. It's a pleasure to meet you."

Parker searched the room for Elena. She was talking with a group of industry execs and pointing in their direction.

By the time the night was over, the entire room would know.

Fifteen

"You've been practicing." Kayleigh looked up at Parker as they swayed together on the dance floor. She was surprised at how light and confident his steps were.

"I'll neither confirm nor deny." He chuckled. "Maybe I just had a really good teacher."

"Well, that's for sure." She grinned. There was a beat of silence between them before she blurted out, "I'm sorry this whole fiancé thing got out of control. I should've stayed at our table and let you handle your friend over there."

"It isn't your fault. I'm the one who told her. I just didn't think she'd make it her mission to tell everyone here."

Kayleigh's cheeks heated. They'd been congratulated by countless distillery owners and execs, as well as several of the vendors. And more than once the photographer had asked to take a picture of the award winner and his fiancée. Photos that would hopefully go into a single email or, better yet, be buried on someone's hard drive.

"Congrats again on the award." Kayleigh was anxious to change the subject. "Your acceptance speech was heartfelt and witty. You even made us laugh. I was impressed."

She grinned. "I know your family is enjoying themselves in the Caribbean, but it's too bad they couldn't be here to see you tonight."

"Thankfully I wasn't alone."

There was something so warm and open about his expression. It caught her off guard and made her belly do a little flip. Suddenly she was keenly aware of the placement of his large hand low on her back and how their bodies moved together. It stirred up all of the feelings that had led her to kiss him that day at the cabin. Something she couldn't stop thinking about, no matter how hard she tried.

This is a business arrangement. Real feelings have no place in a fake relationship. Because the only person who would get hurt was her. Again. Parker would go on with his life as if nothing had happened. Experience had taught her that.

"Everything okay?" Parker frowned.

"Yes." She stopped swaying and took a step away from him. "It's been a long day."

"And it's been a long week for me." Parker looked disappointed, though he managed a cursory smile. "We stayed a socially acceptable amount of time, and I danced. Seems like a good time to call it a night."

Kayleigh forced a smile and slipped her arm through his, disappointed that their weekend together was coming to an end.

Kayleigh said good-night to Parker and closed the door behind her. She pressed her back against the cool door and sighed. Just a few more weeks and then they could go back to the way things were. Hopefully she and Parker wouldn't be enemies. But they wouldn't need to spend time together, either.

She tossed her clutch on the bed and kicked off her heels.

Her feet ached, and she remembered exactly why she preferred a broken-in pair of cowboy boots.

A knock at the door between their rooms startled her. She swung the door open.

"Yes?"

Parker didn't speak right away. He just stared at her for a moment. "Need help with that zipper again?"

"Oh, yes. Thanks." Kayleigh tried to tamp down the disappointment in her voice. She turned her back to him and swept her hair over one shoulder.

He stepped forward and slowly unzipped the back of her dress. When he was done, he didn't move and neither did she. Kayleigh stood there, heart racing, the sound of her heartbeat filling her ears.

Parker slipped his arms around her waist and pulled her against him as he leaned down and kissed her neck.

Kayleigh's eyes drifted closed at the delicious sensation of his lips grazing her heated skin. She relaxed against Parker's hard chest and felt his heart thudding against her back.

She allowed her head to fall back, granting him complete access to her neck and bare shoulder. Her entire body shivered as he planted soft kisses along her skin.

A soft murmur escaped her mouth when Parker's hand glided up the front of her body and cupped her breast. She leaned into his touch, wanting more.

He turned her around and captured her mouth in an intense kiss. One hand was pressed to the heated skin of her bare back; the other was wrapped around her waist, pulling their lower bodies closer.

Kayleigh slid her hands beneath his jacket and wrapped her arms around his back, desperate for more contact between them. Parker obliged. His strong hands eased down her body, gripped her bottom and hauled her against him. His growing length was pinned between them.

Kayleigh's eyes opened abruptly at the memory of the humiliation she'd felt when Parker had suddenly changed his mind. She couldn't do that again. And there was no way their business relationship could recover from it a second time.

She did have a modicum of pride.

Kayleigh pulled away and shook her head. "No, Parker. You don't get to do this to me again. You made it clear that it's a bad idea for us to sleep together. Have you changed your mind?"

Parker frowned. "Assessing the situation objectively, I know it's risky."

Kayleigh's cheeks burned. Her fingers drifted to her lips. "Then why'd you—"

"Because I want you, Kayleigh." He planted his hands loosely on her hips, his intense gaze pinning her in place. "I can't stop thinking about you or that night. I can't stop wishing I'd made a different choice. For once in my life, I don't give a damn about doing what's logical. I just know I want this...that I want you."

Kayleigh's hands trembled slightly. She sucked in a deep breath and slipped one strap then the other from her shoulder. The silky material glided onto the floor.

Parker's mouth twisted in a sexy grin when she gripped the lapels of his jacket and pulled him down for another kiss.

The fire grew in his belly and spread through his limbs as Parker kissed Kayleigh, palming her round bottom and hauling her against him. His body was strung tightly with a desperate need for this woman. Thoughts of Kayleigh filled his head constantly now, distracting him from his work during the day and keeping him awake at night.

He kissed her with a hunger that she seemed to feel, too. Until they were both gasping for breath.

Kayleigh pulled away, her chest heaving and her warm brown eyes studying his.

Parker hoped to God that Kayleigh wasn't having a moment of clarity. Because for the first time in a very long time, he didn't care about logic and reason. He simply wanted to give into the sensations that overwhelmed him whenever he was with this woman.

He wanted to feel the heat raging between her luscious thighs as her molten center pressed against him. Her soft breasts, with their pointed peaks, mashing against his hard chest. Her warm hands on his hot skin. Her lips crushed against his. The sense of urgency and the enthralling feeling of spinning out of control.

He was addicted to that feeling and to her. And he didn't want it to stop.

Kayleigh slipped her hand in his and led him to the bed. She helped him out of his tuxedo jacket and dropped it onto the chair before slowly unbuttoning his shirt.

He couldn't take his eyes off her gorgeous face and the deep flush of her cheeks as her fingers nimbly pushed each button through its hole.

As sexy as she was, slowly undressing him, he desperately wanted to kiss her again and glide his hands over her bare skin. And he ached to be buried deep inside her.

Parker stripped off his shirt and pants, hastily retrieving the strip of foil packets he'd shoved into his pocket before he'd knocked on Kayleigh's door. He dropped them onto the bedside table.

"Ambitious." Kayleigh's mouth pulled into a playful grin as she regarded the strip of six condoms.

Parker was neither bashful nor prudish. Yet, somehow, Kayleigh had a gift for making him blush, and she seemed to take great delight in it.

"I wasn't sure that would be enough."

Kayleigh grinned, her eyes twinkling. She sank her teeth

into her luscious lower lip, then lifted onto her toes and pressed a kiss to his eager mouth.

Parker cradled her face as he savored the taste of her sweet lips and the sensation of her tongue gliding against his. He could hold this woman in his arms and kiss her until the sky turned green and the grass turned blue. And still it would never be enough.

He lay her on the bed and hovered over her, his gaze meeting hers. His heart pounded so loudly that the sound seemed to fill the space around him.

Parker wanted to tell Kayleigh everything he'd been thinking these past few weeks. That he cared for her deeply. That he often wished he could go back to that day when they were kids and make a different choice. That he'd do anything to take away the pain she'd suffered during their years apart. But the words lodged in his throat. He stared at her without a word.

Kayleigh traced his cheekbone with her thumb, her eyes drifting closed as she pressed her mouth to his again. He kissed her; this time the kiss was slow and sweet even as heat built between them.

Parker stripped Kayleigh of her pretty black lace strapless bra and matching panties before chucking his boxers, ripping open one of the little foil squares and sheathing himself.

He kissed his way down her chest, flicking her hardened nipple with his tongue. His body tensed in response to her sensual murmur.

There was something so incredibly provocative about Kayleigh. She was sexy, regardless of whether she was wearing a satin gown or tattered jeans and a tee. And she could get a rise out of him like no one else. She'd been the source of joy, anger, frustration and amusement. But lately the feelings Kayleigh engendered in him most were a consuming lust and an affection that grew deeper with every passing day.

This moment was everything he'd dreamed of, and he couldn't wait another minute to be inside her.

Parker guided himself to her entrance, his hips inching forward. Everything about this woman made him feel incredible in a way he hadn't experienced before. His senses were overwhelmed with pleasure intensified by her soft whimpers.

A delicious sensation rolled up his spine as he glided inside her, slowly and deliberately. He was intent on savoring every moment of their connection.

Kayleigh wrapped her arms around him, her freshly manicured nails digging into his back as he circled his hips with focused determination.

He alternated deep and shallow thrusts, allowing her responses to guide him until she tensed, her body trembling as she called his name.

His pulse raced and beads of perspiration trickled down his back as her inner walls contracted around his heated flesh. Parker cursed beneath his breath, his back tensing as he found his release with a few more thrusts.

Parker collapsed on the bed beside her, both of them still breathing heavily. There were so many things he wanted to say to Kayleigh. But instead, he gave her a quick kiss and made his way to the bathroom.

It'd been a long time since he'd been in a relationship. Sex had simply been a biological need. A necessary mutual release. But with Kayleigh, everything felt…different.

He wasn't sure exactly what their sleeping together meant for their relationship. Or what her expectations were. It was something they should have addressed prior to having sex. He'd known that, but it wasn't the head above his shoulders that had won the argument. Which meant they needed to talk about it now.

But when he returned from the bathroom, Kayleigh lay on her side with her back to him. Her rhythmic breathing indicated that she'd fallen asleep.

Parker sighed, relieved they could delay the awkward *what-does-this-mean-for-us* conversation for another day. But it presented another problem. Did he go back to his own room, as he typically would? Or should he crawl into bed beside her?

Neither option seemed quite right.

Parker sat in the chair beside Kayleigh's bed as she slept. He'd checked his email, worked on some spreadsheets and watched a couple of financial news shows. He'd even managed to doze off to sleep.

"Parker?" Kayleigh rolled over, her hand searching the empty spot he'd vacated hours earlier.

"I'm here."

She turned toward him and then sat up in bed. "Did you sleep in that chair all night?"

"I needed to catch up on some work, and I didn't want to wake you."

"Then why didn't you return to your room?" She eyed him suspiciously.

"I thought you'd find it rude if I just left," he admitted. "The chair was a compromise."

A slow smile curled one edge of her mouth, and her eyes twinkled as if she was pleased with his answer. She yawned and ran her hands through her wild red curls. When she spotted the time—barely five o'clock in the morning—she extended a hand to him.

"It's too early to do anything. You're on vacation."

"Actually, it's a business trip."

"Parker." She wiggled her fingers. "Come to bed."

He set his phone on the table and stood, taking a deep

breath before he slid beneath the covers and wrapped an arm around her.

They were both quiet for a moment. Kayleigh raised her head and met his gaze. "Look, I know you're probably freaking out because you think this means we're suddenly... I don't know...a couple or something. It doesn't. We're two sensible adults and this is just...sex. I'm not looking for anything more than this."

"Oh, okay." He wasn't sure whether he should feel relieved or slighted by her declaration.

"But since we've broken that barrier... I'd certainly be open to doing this again. Since you've still got a few left and all." Kayleigh glanced at the foil packets on the nightstand and then grinned. She pressed her open palm to his chest, halting his movement when he reached for them. "After I get a few more hours of sleep and a shower."

"Deal." Parker grinned, lying back down and propping one arm behind his head.

"Parker, can I ask you something?" Kayleigh folded her arms over his chest and propped her chin on her hands. "Are you planning a hostile takeover of King's Finest?"

"What would make you think that?" He frowned.

"I noticed the research you were reviewing when I joined you for breakfast this morning. It was about merit-based family-owned business succession as opposed to succession based on birth order." She tilted her head as she regarded him. "You're trying to leapfrog Blake as the next CEO, aren't you?"

"Yes. Because I think it's in our company's best interest." He stared at the ceiling. "And it wouldn't be a hostile takeover. It would be by consensus. I plan to prove that I'm the best candidate for the position."

"And that's why you were willing to do this. Playing my fake fiancé for the sake of your family's deal...it's a perfect opportunity to prove to your father that you should be the heir apparent." She lay on her back in the crook of his arm.

There was silence between them for a few moments. "You think I'm being unfair to Blake?"

"I think he deserves to know how you feel and so do Max and Zora."

"I plan to tell them, but I wanted to wait until after my parents' big anniversary party."

"In case your brothers and sister don't take the news too well?" Kayleigh laughed. "Because boy would that make the party *awkward*."

"Exactly." He couldn't help chuckling, too.

"Who have you told about this?"

"Just you." There was something oddly comforting about there being a secret that only the two of them shared. "Hey, what do you think about switching to a later flight, if one is available? There's a little gallery in West Chelsea that I'd love to take you to, if we have time."

"I'd like that." Kayleigh pressed her cheek to his chest and settled against him.

Parker pulled up the airline app and switched their tickets. Before he was done, Kayleigh had already fallen back to sleep. Her soft breath skittered across his chest as her limbs tangled with his.

Parker kissed the top of her head and readjusted his pillow as he stared at the ceiling of the hotel room. He wouldn't be leaving anytime soon, so he might as well settle in and enjoy having Kayleigh's warm, lush, naked body pressed to his.

Sixteen

Parker Abbott did something he never, ever did. He called the office, took the day off and slept in.

He and Kayleigh had returned to Magnolia Lake in the wee hours of the morning after taking a later flight back. Besides, between making love to Kayleigh and his insistence on sleeping in that damned chair, he'd gotten very little sleep. He usually subsisted on a few hours. But it needed to be three or four solid hours in a comfortable bed.

He awoke, showered and fixed himself breakfast, with thoughts of his night with Kayleigh still running through his head. Maybe sleeping with her was an ill-advised move, but it was one he couldn't bring himself to regret. In fact his only regret was not taking her to bed that night at the cabin.

Parker had made himself a late breakfast and was loading the dishwasher when his doorbell rang. He peeked through the small windows at the top of the ornate wood door.

"Mom?" Parker swung the door open and she rushed past him, not bothering to give him her traditional hug and kiss. He furrowed his brows and closed the door. "What's wrong? Did something happen at the office?"

"Yes." She looked both angry and teary. "How could you get engaged and announce it to the entire world without telling your own family?"

Shit.

He zeroed in on the sheet of paper she was waving, taking it from her hand. It was the e-newsletter from the trade organization that had put on the event they'd attended over the weekend. The caption under the lead photo proclaimed that the executive of the year was in attendance with his fiancée.

"Mom, I can explain."

Or could he? He couldn't tell his mother about the deal with Kayleigh. It would ruin the surprise his family had worked so hard on.

"I'm listening." Iris Abbott folded her arms and plopped down on the sofa in his great room. "I'd love to hear you explain why you'd tell the entire free world but couldn't be bothered to pick up the phone and share your happy news with your mother."

Parker sank onto the sofa and wrapped an arm around her.

"I told Elena Mixon that Kayleigh was my fiancée to make it clear that there was nothing between us. She made it her business to tell the entire association. Once it spread like wildfire…well… I couldn't very well change my story."

"So you and Kayleigh *aren't* engaged?" His mother seemed disappointed when he confirmed that they weren't. "That's a shame. She's good for you, Parker."

"What makes you say that?" Parker sank against the back of the cushion. "We're like fire and ice. Polar opposites."

He actually wanted to believe that there could be something more to him and Kayleigh. That what they'd shared last night could be the beginning of something bigger instead of the end of their fake-fiancé experiment. But there was too much baggage between them, and they were too different in nature.

Wasn't that a recipe for disaster?

He cared too much for Kayleigh to hurt her any more than he already had.

"I guess you've never heard the old saying that opposites attract." His mother patted his knee.

"I have. It's filed in here—" he tapped his temple "—alongside stories of Sasquatch and alien abductions."

They both laughed when she elbowed him.

"Seriously, Mom, if there's one thing I've learned about relationships from watching you and Dad, it's the importance of a unified purpose. You two have a lot in common. So do Blake and Savannah."

"But we have a lot of differences, too. That's what brings variety and interest to a relationship, sweetheart." Her eyes twinkled. "There's something special between you and Kayleigh. There always has been. It broke my heart when you two parted ways as kids. I've always hoped that one day you two would figure things out and fix your relationship. Good friendships are hard to come by."

Parker nodded. "I know, Mom. These past few weeks with her have been great. In some ways she's still the girl I've always known. In other ways I wonder if I ever really knew her or understood her situation at all."

"Well, whatever it is that you two have… I still see it in her eyes. You care deeply for her, Parker. And despite how hurt and angry she might be over what happened between you two, it appears that she has deep feelings for you, too."

"I don't know. Sometimes I look at her and I think… maybe we could be…something. But other times…" He sighed and ran a hand over his head.

"Life isn't like the data you love so much, honey." His

mother's tone was soothing. "There's no guarantee that two plus two will equal four."

"Precisely. Data is reliable. Two plus two *always* equals four. And if you perform the steps correctly, the data can fairly accurately predict what you should expect. There are variables, but—"

"That's what makes life and love so exciting." She cut off his ramblings, a wide smile spread across her still-beautiful face. "Love is unpredictable. You never know exactly how things will turn out. You have to use your mind, your heart and your instincts to make the right decision when it comes to love."

"Who said anything about love?"

"Romance, relationships, affection. Whatever you want to call it." She waved a hand dismissively.

"The point is that numbers are straightforward. They don't confuse the hell out of you and make you doubt yourself."

His mother placed a gentle hand on his arm. "Maybe she's struggling with her feelings, too."

He hadn't considered that.

Maybe she was grappling with her feelings. Or maybe she'd meant exactly what she'd said. That he shouldn't read anything deeper into their sleeping together, because it was only temporary. Once he'd fulfilled the terms of their contract, they would go their separate ways.

Parker turned to face his mother. "If we were truly compatible, it wouldn't be such a struggle, would it?"

His mother frowned. "Things in life aren't always so straightforward, son. But the effort makes the reward sweeter. So if you truly care for Kayleigh and want a relationship with her—romantic or otherwise—be prepared to roll up your sleeves and work for it."

She didn't wait for his response. His mother kissed his

cheek and walked to the door. "And don't be afraid to tell her how you feel. You might never get the chance to again."

Parker locked the door behind his mother and groaned. He was a man who valued order and control. He liked knowing what came next. More important, he liked being in control of what came next. And of his feelings. But with Kayleigh Jemison, he was never sure what came next or of how she'd make him feel.

A little part of Kayleigh seemed to relish slowly driving him insane and making him want things he shouldn't.

Yet all he could think about was cradling her in his arms and making her his again and again. Shattering her control and allowing her to decimate his.

Parker had monitored his voice mail, email and text messages all week.

No messages from Kayleigh.

It was week ten, their last date before they went away to her friend's destination wedding. It was Kayleigh's turn to choose the place, but she hadn't responded to his text asking where they were going.

Perhaps she'd chosen to skip it.

Regardless of where it began, every date they'd had since New York had ended with the two of them in bed. They'd made love in her hotel room in New York, in her storage room the night he helped her do inventory at her shop, and in his shower and bed after a movie and late-night swim at his place.

Well before that night in New York, he'd begun to anticipate their weekly dates. No matter how hard he tried to focus on work, he couldn't stop thinking of her smile, the sweet sound of her laugh or the way her creamy skin glided against his.

He wanted Kayleigh. Thought of her constantly. Was

driven to distraction by her. But she didn't seem to be as affected by him.

He needed to renew his focus on the priority at hand. Proving to his father, and to his siblings, that he should be the next CEO of King's Finest Distillery. Getting sidetracked by the feelings he'd developed for Kayleigh Jemison was a mistake.

Still, it was Friday evening, and he couldn't help being disappointed that she'd chosen to blow off their final date.

Parker went to the bar overlooking the patio. He'd never be able to look at his pool again without remembering Kayleigh stripping naked, diving into the water and then inviting him to join her.

He dropped brown and white sugar cubes into a rock glass, added both orange and Angostura bitters and a splash of water, and then muddled it. Parker stirred in two ounces of King's Finest bourbon, then two large ice cubes. He finished it off with lemon and orange peel.

The perfect old-fashioned cocktail.

As Parker raised the glass to his mouth, he heard a car door slam. The doorbell rang and he answered it.

"Kayleigh, did I miss your message?"

"May I?" She indicated his glass and he handed the drink to her. Kayleigh took a gulp, her eyes fluttering closed for a moment. She sighed, handing the glass back to him. "I didn't send a text message or an email. I didn't know if I should say what I want to say."

"Come in." He stepped aside and invited her to have a seat on the sofa. Parker handed the glass back to her. "You look like you could use this more than me."

She nodded and took another sip before finally raising her eyes to meet his as he sat on the opposite sofa.

"This is our last date and all week I've tried to think of how I wanted to spend it." She walked over to stand in front of him, setting the glass down on a nearby coaster. "But I only want one thing." She straddled his lap and pressed a palm to his cheek. "I want to spend it making love to you."

Something in his chest fluttered and he felt an overwhelming sense of joy.

"I can't think of a better way to spend it." He cradled her cheek and pressed his lips to hers.

His tongue swept inside the warm cavern of her mouth; she tasted of sugar, citrus and the unique bourbon recipe that had built his family's fortune. He slid his hands up her back to remove her bra, but she wasn't wearing one.

Kayleigh lifted her arms, allowing him to pull the fabric over her head, revealing her firm breasts and hardened brown peaks.

He showered kisses down her neck and shoulder, palming one heavy globe before laving its pebbled tip with his tongue.

Kayleigh pressed her palm to the back of his head and ground her hips against him, causing him to harden painfully.

"You taste even better than I remembered," he whispered against her soft skin between gentle bites and leisurely licks.

"That's just the appetizer. Wait until you get a taste of the main course." Kayleigh gave him a naughty smirk that made his pulse race.

He slid his hands up her outer thigh and beneath her little black skirt.

No panties, either.

She flashed him another mischievous smile and pressed a slow, lingering kiss to his mouth before rising to her feet and walking toward his bedroom.

Parker shed his clothing, sheathed himself and had Kayleigh out of her skirt in the blink of an eye. He wrapped his arms around her waist, pulling their naked bodies together as he claimed her mouth in a greedy, impatient kiss that was fueled by his consuming desire for her.

He wanted her more than he'd ever wanted any woman. And he felt driven to bring her the deepest, most sensual pleasure possible.

Parker settled between her thighs and pressed a gentle kiss to the space between them. She shuddered and dug her heels into the mattress.

He placed another kiss there, relishing her taste: salty with a hint of sweetness. His eyes drifted closed as he parted her with his thumbs and dipped his tongue inside her.

Kayleigh rode his tongue, her soft whimpers escalating until she came completely undone. She shuddered as she called his name in a throaty, raw voice that sent shivers up his spine and made him want to do it all over again.

He made love to her. Tried to get his fill of her, knowing it would be the last time he'd have her in his bed.

Parker was awakened from a deep, satisfying sleep by the jangling of keys. He searched the room in the dark. A figure moved beside the bed.

"Kayleigh?" He sat up and turned on the bedside lamp. "You're leaving?"

"It's late. I should get home."

"Or you could stay."

"We both know you're not comfortable with that. It's fine. Really." Her tone indicated that it wasn't fine at all.

True. Normally he wasn't comfortable with that level of intimacy. But tonight he hungered for it. With her. "I'd really like it if you'd stay tonight…and tomorrow night."

She gave a small nod. "If you really want me to, I'll stay." She rummaged in her purse and then climbed back into bed. "But there's something I need to give you first."

"What's this?"

She shrugged. "Open it."

Parker put on his glasses and opened the box. It was a leather cuff bracelet with a steampunk-inspired skeleton watch with a clear dial that revealed its inner workings.

"Kayleigh, I don't know what to say." Parker traced the distressed brown leather and studied the exquisite workmanship of the piece. "This is—"

"It's not something you'd wear. Ever. I know." She smiled sheepishly. "And I honestly won't be insulted if you never wear it. But you wore that watch with the transparent face in New York, and I noticed that you read steampunk books. Something about that touched me. It reminded me of us as kids dressing up like pirates and space explorers. I wanted to make something for you that felt really personal and captured that little boy who still lives inside you. The boy who was once my best friend." Kayleigh dragged a finger beneath one eye. "Besides, I wanted you to know how much I appreciate everything you've done these past two months, and to leave you with something to remind you of our time together."

"Thank you, sweetheart…" He cradled her cheek and pressed a soft kiss to her lips. "It's extraordinary. I love it.

"That reminds me… I have something for you, too." Parker returned the watch to its box and set it on the bedside table. He got up and rummaged in his sock drawer.

"You've done so much already. I can't accept another gift."

"I think you'll make an exception for this one." Parker retrieved the box and removed the ring, which slipped from his fingers and rolled underneath the bed.

Parker cursed and dropped to his knees to search for it.

"Let me help you." Kayleigh swung her feet onto the floor.

"No, I've got it." Ring in hand, Parker knelt, preparing to stand. When he looked up at her gorgeous face, he was struck by how much he cared for her. How much he wished this was real. "I was going to give this to you right before we left on Monday. But it seems apropos that I give it to you now."

He held up the ring. "My friend came through. He gave me a few options to choose from, but this one just felt like you."

Kayleigh pressed her fingertips to her mouth. "My God, Parker, it's beautiful. I can't believe I get to wear something this gorgeous, even if it's only for a week."

Parker gave her a pained smile and took her hand in his. He slid the intricate, rose-gold ring with a large, round center diamond and several swirled channels of smaller accent diamonds onto her finger.

"Kayleigh Louise Jemison, would you please agree to be my one and only fake fiancée?"

She laughed. "Yes, Parker Stephen Abbott, I promise *not* to marry you, but as your fake fiancée, I will happily wear this lovely ring."

Kayleigh cupped his cheek, leaned down and kissed him.

It was a sweet, tender kiss that reignited the deep passion he felt for her. He lay her back in bed and kissed her, made love to her, held her in his arms until she'd drifted off to sleep again.

But he lay awake for another hour, trying to hush the little voice deep inside his chest that kept growing louder. The one that kept telling him that what he felt for Kayleigh was real.

Seventeen

Kayleigh breathed in the salty air drifting off the Caribbean Sea as she exited the helicopter on the beautiful private island owned by the family of Kira Brennan's husband-to-be, Theodore Patrakis.

Parker offered her his hand as she stepped down. He looked concerned. "Having second thoughts about this?"

She was.

But after all the time and effort they'd put into preparing for it, there was no turning back now.

Kayleigh didn't answer his question. "Thank you." She tucked the clutch he'd given her in New York beneath her arm. "You're going to love Kira. She's the sweetest."

"She means a lot to you." Parker extended his elbow and she slipped her arm through his. "So I look forward to meeting her."

His response left her speechless, as had many of the other sweet and thoughtful things he'd said or done in the past weeks.

They were escorted to a limousine shuttle that took them

and a few other passengers to where they'd be staying. Within ten minutes, they had arrived in paradise.

"This place is amazing." Kayleigh kicked off her sandals and walked through their luxury seaside villa with folding glass doors, a hot tub, plunge pool and a deck overlooking the sea.

"It is," Parker agreed. "Looks like you're the one doing me a favor." He pulled Kayleigh into his arms and kissed her.

"Let me guess…you know just how to thank me." She couldn't help giggling when he nibbled on her ear.

"Nothing as trite as that." He kissed her neck. "Honestly, this is all I've been thinking about from the moment I saw you in that sundress this morning. I sat there on the plane, trying to work out the space and mechanics of joining the mile-high club."

"Parker Abbott, what has gotten into you?"

He cradled her face, his dark eyes staring intently at hers as he leaned in for another kiss. "You. And I'd like to return the favor."

Parker swept her up in his arms and carried her to the bedroom. He made love to her in the well-appointed luxury master suite with a wall of windows overlooking the sea and a small deck with seating.

Kayleigh would've been content spending the entire week lying right there in Parker's arms. But they had to shower and change to make it to the welcome dinner later that night.

"Kayleigh! It's so good to see you!" Kira Brennan's baby blue eyes lit up. Her tousled blond beach waves dusted the fair, freckled skin of her shoulders.

"My God, Kira, look at you. You're gorgeous. You're going to make a beautiful bride." Eyes damp with tears, Kayleigh hugged her friend. Kira had grown into such a beautiful young woman. "Thank you so much for inviting us to be part of your wedding. The island is simply incredible."

Kira grinned up at the tall, handsome, dark-haired, olive-skinned man beside her. "This is my soon-to-be husband, Theodore Patrakis. Theo, this is Kayleigh and her fiancé. Parker Abbott, right?"

"Yes." Kayleigh's cheeks warmed as she glanced up at Parker. Her plan had seemed like a good one until she had to stand in front of Kira and tell her a lie, right to her face. Her hand trembled.

Parker slipped an arm around her waist and pulled her closer, a silent reminder that he was there for her. The tension in her shoulders eased instantly.

"Pleasure to meet you, Theo." Parker shook the man's hand. Then he shook Kira's. "I've heard so much about you from Kayleigh. It's a pleasure to finally meet you and an honor to be part of your wedding celebration."

Kira's eyes lit up and her smile was a silent *I like this guy*.

Kayleigh breathed a sigh of relief…until Kira asked her next question.

"So, I want to know everything. How did you two meet? What made you decide to get married? I want to hear it all." Kira squeezed Kayleigh's hand.

Kayleigh turned to glance at Parker, but he was focused on Kira.

"I've known Kayleigh since we were kids. I didn't know it then, but I fell in love with her when I was maybe nine years old. She was beautiful and fierce and uniquely her own person. Confident in her own skin, regardless of what anyone else said or did. I admired those qualities even then." Parker turned to her. His deep, genuine smile and the dreamy look in his dark eyes made her heart flutter.

"Parker was brilliant, even when we were kids. Maybe too much for his own good." Kayleigh shifted her gaze back to Kira. "We both made some mistakes and our friendship ended badly. But in recent months, we decided to renew our friendship. Things just progressed from there."

"And let me see the ring." Kira held Kayleigh's hand and admired the unique ring that Parker had given her just a few days earlier. "Kayleigh, it's beautiful. And it's perfect for you. Did you pick it out yourself?"

"No." Kayleigh smiled at Parker. "Parker did that on his own. He knows me even better than I thought."

"My God, you're both just so cute and so in love. I'm thrilled for you, Kayleigh. I really am. You deserve to be happy." Kira leaned in and kissed her cheek. "Theo and I need to make the rounds, but we'll catch up more later."

Kira slipped her hand in Theo's as they went over to greet the other guests.

"Relax. You did just fine." Parker's soothing deep voice and warm breath on Kayleigh's ear calmed her.

She released a heavy sigh and nodded, glancing up at him. "Thank you for being here, Parker. I honestly don't think I could've done this with anyone else."

Parker's cheeks flushed. He leaned in and gave her a quick kiss on the lips. "I'm glad I'm here, too."

"Kayleigh, so glad you could make it." Colleen Brennan approached with a flute of champagne in her hand. Her dark hair was a perfect contrast to the icy blue eyes that suited her so well. At nearly sixty she was still stunningly beautiful, and the crisp white linen dress she wore complemented her figure. "And this handsome gentleman must be your fiancé, Parker Abbott. Looks like you found your perfect match."

Parker's back tensed beneath Kayleigh's arm and his expression hardened. She tightened her grip around his waist, a silent plea for him not to make a scene with the bride's mother.

"I have," Kayleigh said simply. "And I couldn't be happier."

* * *

They'd stayed out late and drunk far too much. Parker slept in the next morning, but Kayleigh needed to burn off some of the nervous energy that left her lying awake most of the night while Parker slept soundly.

She'd met the entire wedding party and encountered many of Aidan and Kira's aunts, uncles and cousins again at last night's dinner. The one person she hadn't seen was Aidan. She wouldn't allow herself to ask about him, but she'd found herself glancing around the room and expecting every new person who walked through the door to be him.

"Aidan won't arrive until tomorrow," Kira had whispered in her ear when she joined Kayleigh at the dessert buffet.

"I wasn't looking for Aidan," she'd said quickly as she debated over the tiramisu and crème brûlée.

"It's okay, Kayleigh. It's understandable that you'd both be nervous about seeing each other again after all this time. But there's something I should confess. I invited you to be in my wedding for all of the reasons I told you before. But I had another reason for inviting you. I—"

"What looks good for dessert, ladies?" Parker had appeared beside them suddenly.

"Everything. I've tried them all." Kira had flashed her broad smile and then excused herself to join Theo and his family.

There hadn't been another opportunity to speak to Kira alone, and all night Kayleigh couldn't help wondering what other motive Kira had for making her a part of her wedding.

Since Parker was sound asleep, Kayleigh slipped out of bed and put on shorts, a tank top and running shoes. She headed out to the beach for a long run and didn't stop until she got to the end of the stretch of white sand. Then she turned around and jogged back to their villa.

"Kayleigh Jemison. My God, how long has it been?"

Aidan Brennan called as she reached the top of the stairs that led up from the beach.

He'd grown his red hair out past his ears, and his beard was longer than she'd ever seen it. There were lines around his vibrant blue eyes.

"It's been a long time, Aidan." Kayleigh turned to face him as he approached. "Seven years, at least."

The day before, she'd been picture perfect. But of course she would run into Aidan while she was drenched with perspiration, her hair was pulled up in a messy topknot and she smelled like sweat and sand.

"It's been too long." He pulled her into a hug, his ginger beard scraping her shoulder. Aidan released her and sighed as he took a step back and shoved his hands in his pockets. "I hear you're engaged now."

"I am." She dropped her gaze from his, then forced a smile. "And I hear you're an old married man with two beautiful children."

"I am the father of two handsome boys." Aidan frowned and ran a hand through his longish hair, which rustled with the gentle breeze and covered one eye. "But I've been divorced for the past two years. The boys live in Ireland with their mother and her new beau. I try to see them as often as I can...which is why I didn't arrive until today. I'd hoped to bring them back with me, but my ex-wife wouldn't permit it. She's afraid if I bring the boys stateside, I won't bring them back."

"Aidan, I'm sorry. I didn't realize—"

He waved a hand. "You couldn't have known."

Kayleigh breathed a sigh of relief. She hadn't wanted to hurt Aidan then, and she surely didn't want to hurt him now. They stood together in awkward silence. Neither of them seemed to know what to say.

"Aidan, if you don't mind me asking, what happened between you two? By all accounts, you were a perfect pair."

"On the surface, I s'pose you're right. But once we had the boys and I was consumed by my growing role in our family business…things changed. After that initial fiery passion died down, there just wasn't enough to sustain the relationship." He lowered his voice. "She and I were never as well-suited as you and I were."

Kayleigh's cheeks stung.

Was this what Kira was trying to tell her? That Aidan was single again and she'd wanted to give them a second chance?

Her chest ached and her head suddenly felt light. Fate had conspired to give her and Aidan a second chance at love, and she'd countered it with a fake-fiancé scheme.

Maybe the day Kira had made that call, she would've jumped at the chance to try again with Aidan. To tell him the truth about what his mother had done. But the past three months with Parker had changed everything.

She'd loved Aidan very much back then, but that was ancient history. She'd developed deep feelings for Parker. And after the wedding was over, she planned to tell him just that.

"I'd invite you in for a cup of coffee, but my fiancé is still asleep. I don't want to wake him."

Kayleigh tucked a loose strand of hair behind her ear. "But I guess I'll see you at lunch later."

He gave her a sad smile. "Count on it."

Kayleigh heaved a sigh as Aidan walked away. Then she turned up the path toward the villa she shared with Parker.

Eighteen

Parker stared out the window of the villa at Kayleigh, who was obviously distressed about her interaction with her ex. He'd been tempted to rush out to her side and finally meet the esteemed Aidan Brennan. But it didn't seem prudent to admit that he'd been anxiously awaiting her return like some sad little puppy and eavesdropping on the entire conversation.

He divided a split of champagne between two flutes and then poured a little freshly squeezed orange juice in both.

"Hey." Kayleigh seemed surprised to find him up and among the living after the way he'd crashed last night.

"Good morning." He handed her a mimosa.

Kayleigh looked at the open bottle of champagne on the bar. "It's a little early to start drinking, isn't it?"

"Thought you might need it after running into your ex."

"You heard that, huh?" She sipped the mimosa.

"I just happened to be near the window and heard him call your name." So much for keeping his eavesdropping to himself. "He seems like a nice enough guy."

"I never said he wasn't." Her tone was sharp.

He'd evidently irritated Kayleigh, though he wasn't sure why. It seemed best to move on to a different topic.

"You're probably hungry after your run. I'll order breakfast whenever you're ready." He walked toward the patio.

"Parker, look, I'm sorry." Kayleigh set down her glass. "I guess I'm just feeling… I don't know what I'm feeling." She settled onto the barstool.

"Maybe you're wondering if you've thwarted fate by setting up this charade? Or if Aidan might've been your best shot at happiness?" Parker asked tentatively, hoping Kayleigh would deny it.

She shrugged instead. "Something like that. Mostly I regret not telling Aidan the truth about his precious mother. It's like you said—I took away his choice because I was afraid he wouldn't choose me."

"I can understand why you might have some regrets." He certainly did. Why hadn't he kept his observations to himself?

"I'm sorry if I was short with you earlier. Seeing Aidan again after all these years was more intense than I thought it would be." Kayleigh downed the remainder of her mimosa and stood. "Why don't you go ahead and order breakfast? I'm gonna hit the shower. I promise to be in a much better mood when I get out." She forced a smile and pressed a quick kiss to his cheek before ducking into the bedroom.

Parker sank onto the sofa and sighed, his gaze still fixed on the door she'd just closed behind her.

During the past few weeks, he'd discovered that beneath the mangled wreckage of his and Kayleigh's friendship lay strong feelings that ran true and deep.

But as strongly as he felt for her, it seemed she didn't feel the same. Hearing her regrets about Aidan was like a cannon ball being launched into his chest.

It was Aidan Brennan she truly wanted. Parker had only been a convenient substitute.

He finished his mimosa and set the glass down hard on a nearby table. He wanted to be with Kayleigh. Not as a sham relationship or just for sex. He wanted it to be genuine. Because he loved her.

He'd picked one hell of a time to have that realization.

Parker paced the floor. The memories of that day in middle school were still as fresh as the day they'd happened. He hadn't initially set out to make fun of Kayleigh's father. But he'd mentioned a fact about the man in passing and several of his popular classmates laughed hysterically. The kids who didn't normally give him and Kayleigh the time of day.

They'd wanted to hear more about her father's escapades, so he'd obliged. For once, he was the one telling the joke, rather than the joke being on him.

But he hadn't had long to relish his status with the popular kids. He could still see the heartbreak in Kayleigh's eyes and the tears staining her cheeks when she'd overheard him telling an especially embarrassing story about her father and the chorus of laughter that rang out in that hallway.

He'd selfishly ruined their relationship by putting his best interest ahead of their friendship, and he'd lost her. Now that they'd rekindled that friendship, he couldn't risk losing it again. Even if it meant sacrificing his desire for something more with her. Because more than anything, he wanted Kayleigh to finally have some of the happiness that had eluded her for most of her life.

If Kayleigh wanted a life with Aidan Brennan, he loved her enough to want that for her, too.

But Aidan's belief that he and Kayleigh were engaged had ruined the prospect of the two of them finding their way back to each other.

It was a monumental dilemma, but Parker would do whatever it took for her to be happy.

* * *

Kayleigh stood on the terrace overlooking the Caribbean, watching the waves crash against the shore. They'd had another lovely dinner, and the evening was winding down.

Parker had been incredibly supportive. He'd gone out of his way to be personable with Kira, Theo and their wedding guests. He'd even taken a liking to Aidan. She'd initially found it unsettling. But Aidan seemed grateful for the break from his overprotective mother and prying aunts and cousins.

"Hey, you. What are you doing out here all by yourself?" Kira slipped her arm through Kayleigh's and laid her head on her shoulder.

"Just enjoying the view." Kayleigh leaned her head against Kira's. "Why aren't you in there with your incredibly handsome husband-to-be?"

Kira sighed softly. "I just needed a little break, I guess. I swear, if one more of our relatives asks when we're going to start having babies, I'm going to scream." Kira lifted her head and turned to Kayleigh. "Is it terrible that I don't want kids right away? That I'd like to bask in being the center of Theo's attention for now?"

"Of course not." Kayleigh turned to Kira and squeezed her hand. "And don't let anyone tell you differently. It's up to you and Theo to decide what you want. Everyone else can take a flying leap."

"Thank you." Kira nodded and turned to look at the water, too. They were both quiet for a moment before she spoke again. "So, you've probably figured out the other reason I wanted you to be here."

"Aidan." Kayleigh said his name softly as she turned to her friend. "You were trying to fix what your mother had done."

"He's never stopped regretting the day he stood by and

let you walk away without a fight. I thought that once you saw each other…" Kira sighed heavily. "I know what you're thinking."

"How very *Parent Trap* of you?"

"Something like that," Kira said.

"But you knew that I was bringing my fiancé." Kayleigh shoved Kira lightly with her shoulder.

"Honestly? I figured he was some random guy you were bringing to make my brother jealous." Kira shook her head. "But then I met him and got to see you two together. There's no mistaking that look in both of your eyes. He's obviously in love with you, and you love him, too. So despite my little scheme backfiring, I'm really happy for you, Kayleigh."

Kira leaned in and kissed her cheek. "I'd better get back to the party before—"

"Kira! Kira, darling, what are you doing out here?" Colleen Brennan peeked out of the French doors that led to the terrace. Her thin lips pressed into a harsh line and her nostrils flared.

Kira exchanged a look with Kayleigh, then sighed. "Coming, Mother."

Kayleigh sat in a nearby seat, her heart racing as Kira's words turned over in her head.

He's obviously in love with you, and you love him, too.

Kayleigh swallowed hard and tears stung her eyes. Her feelings for Parker had been building so gradually over the past few months. There'd been a growing affection between them for sure, and a passion that sent tingles up her spine whenever she thought of him. But love?

She'd convinced herself that Parker Abbott wasn't capable of truly loving anyone whose last name wasn't Abbott from birth. Even then, she'd suspected he only tolerated them. But seeing the interactions between Parker and his family up close…there was no doubt about the love between them. And he'd gone out of his way to fulfill his duties as her fake fiancé. She couldn't have asked for anything more.

Was it because he honestly did feel something for her?

"Kayleigh, there you are." Parker joined her on the terrace and sat beside her. "I have some work to do tonight, so I'm going to head back to the villa. But Aidan promised to see you back safely."

"If you need to leave, I'll come with you." She started to get up.

Parker halted her with a hand pressed firmly to her arm. "Don't feel you need to leave on my account. Besides, I could use the alone time to get some work done."

"Oh. Sure." She tried her hardest not to sound as hurt as she felt. It wasn't just that night. Parker's mood had changed. The first day and night they'd spent there on the island, they'd made love every chance they got. But in the past couple of nights, he seemed to be slowly pulling away...physically and emotionally. Her gaze met his. "Parker, have I done something to upset you?"

"No, of course not." He kissed the back of her hand and gave her what felt like a forced smile. "It's nothing like that."

"Then it is something." She echoed his words to her that day at the cabin.

"I've got things to do—that's all. Will you be all right?"

She nodded in silence and he leaned in and kissed her cheek.

As she watched him walk away, it was clear that there was more to the story. But he obviously didn't trust her enough to share. Just as he hadn't been willing to share with her exactly why he'd wanted to purchase her building and what their plans for it were.

Kayleigh turned back to stare out onto the water. Kira was only half right. She had fallen for Parker, but he clearly didn't feel the same way about her.

* * *

Parker paced on the terrace, his palms damp and his pulse jumping in his temple. The wedding party was winding down with the rehearsal, and the rehearsal dinner would start soon. Tonight was the night.

It's now or never, Park.

His eyes drifted closed and he sighed heavily. He'd spent the week getting to know Aidan Brennan. He needed to be sure that he was truly worthy of Kayleigh.

By all accounts, Aidan was a good and decent man. Despite the unfortunate circumstances with his ex-wife, he was doing his best to remain in the lives of his children. And he'd proven himself to be a savvy businessman, expanding the family's company's reach considerably since he'd taken the reins over from his father, who'd died many years before.

Parker had watched Aidan's interaction with Kayleigh. He still adored her. Even Parker could see that. Kayleigh obviously still cared deeply for Aidan, too.

He reflected on the pain and loneliness in Kayleigh's voice and the hurt in her eyes after she'd first encountered Aidan. It was a look he'd never forget. He'd been the cause of that pain before. In a way, he was the cause of it now.

He loved Kayleigh and he wanted her to be happy. For the briefest moment, he'd believed she could be happy with him. But the truth was that the man he'd been with her these past three months wasn't the person he'd been most of his life.

He wasn't fun-loving and spontaneous. Wasn't outdoorsy or a dancer. Wasn't adored by pets or small kids. He wasn't the kind of man who cuddled and spent the night or who spent his days daydreaming about anyone.

But for her, he had been.

Shouldn't that have set off alarm bells in his head? They both deserved to be with someone who loved them just the way they were. Not someone who'd force them to become someone else.

Parker sighed.

Kayleigh hadn't pressured him to be someone else. She'd simply introduced him to life outside of his comfort zone. And as much as he hated to admit it, he'd found enjoyment in activities he'd never thought he would. Just as she seemed to appreciate the new, more organized processes he'd introduced her to when he'd helped her organize her storeroom cabinet and switch to a user-friendly accounting software she'd actually use.

Maybe each of them simply made the other better.

"Parker." Aidan had stepped out onto the balcony. "Kayleigh asked me to tell you that she and the other bridesmaids are in a last-minute meeting with my sister. They'll return before dinner."

Parker stared at the man, his heart racing.

"Everything okay? You don't look well." Aidan came closer.

"I'm fine. I just wondered if we could talk for a minute." He would never get a more ideal moment than right now.

"Sure." Aidan shrugged. He leaned against the railing. "You've been quiet today. Is something wrong?"

"When we first met, you said that I was lucky to be with Kayleigh, and that you envied our happiness." Parker walked over and stood beside Aidan. "Was that a platitude, or were you being sincere?"

Aidan cocked his head and folded his arms over his chest. "I'm not sure what you're getting at or that I like the direction of this conversation."

"I understand, but I really need to know how you feel about Kayleigh. She's an incredible woman and she deserves to be happy. I'll do whatever I have to do to make that happen."

"Whoa!" Aidan held up his hands as he backed away. "I don't know what you and Kayleigh are into, but—"

"Relax, man. What I'm trying to say is that I think Kayleigh regrets walking away from you, too. That given the chance to do it again…maybe she'd have stayed and fought for you."

"She's your fiancée, and she seems quite taken with you. So why are you telling me all of this?"

Once he crossed this line, he couldn't go back. There was no way to put the genie back into the bottle. Most important, he'd be risking the plans they'd worked so hard on.

"Kayleigh isn't my fiancée," he said quietly.

"What do you mean?" Aidan's expression morphed from confusion to anger. "What kind of game are you two running?"

"Let me explain." Parker sighed. "Kayleigh didn't want to show up here alone and face you with your perfect little family. She asked me to pose as her fiancé."

"You lied to my sister and everyone here." Aidan's fists were clenched at his side.

"And I'm sorry, but there was no nefarious plot. It was simply a matter of Kayleigh wanting to keep her pride." Parker sank onto a chair and tapped a finger on the patio table. "She didn't want you to know that she was still very much alone."

Aidan heaved a sigh and sat, too. Neither of them spoke for several seconds. Finally he asked, "And exactly what do you expect me to do with this information?"

Parker's chest tightened. He stared down at his hands, folded in his lap, his shoulders drooping forward. The world seemed to be spinning.

"That depends on how you feel about her. If you love her still and you're ready to give her another chance, then tell her how you really feel. If not, I'd beg you not to reveal this conversation to her or anyone. We can all just go back to the way things were."

Everything inside him hoped like hell that Aidan would choose the latter. That he'd get up and walk away, pretending as if they'd never had this conversation.

"Do you really believe she wants to try again?" Aidan asked.

Parker forced a bitter smile, his lips pressed together tightly as he collapsed against the back of the chair and swallowed hard. "I think she's been wondering if she blew a second chance for you two by bringing me here."

Aidan nodded his head. He stood, extending a hand to Parker. "Thank you for telling me this. It couldn't have been an easy decision. You obviously care a lot about her."

"I do." Parker shook the man's hand as he rose to his feet. "So don't fuck this up."

"I won't, and I won't mention this to my sister or mother. But please, don't tell Kayleigh that you told me."

Parker nodded without speaking and shoved his hands in his pocket as he watched Aidan walk away with a renewed energy to his gait.

He'd done it. Risked the deal. Risked losing her friendship again. Risked any shot of pulling ahead of Blake as the next CEO. But he couldn't stand idly by and do nothing, knowing he'd had a chance to give her everything she deserved.

He walked inside to the bar and ordered a glass of King's Finest bourbon, neat.

Nineteen

Kayleigh was exhausted. As beautiful as the wedding had been, it felt like the longest day ever. It had begun with a bridesmaids' breakfast, and then there was all of the primping. Manicures and pedicures. Getting their hair and makeup done.

Suddenly she remembered why she was so low-maintenance. She had neither the time nor inclination for all of the upkeep required for her to look like this every single day. But for this one magical day, she'd looked perfect. And the expression on Parker's face when their eyes met as she took her turn walking down the aisle was priceless.

Kayleigh smoothed down the front of her chiffon bridesmaid's dress with the high-low hem. She loved the vintage mauve color Kira had chosen. The formal length of the back of the dress created a nice visual as each of the bridesmaids walked down the aisle, while the shorter length of the front of the dress allowed her to move about freely. She'd ditched the strappy nude stilettos after the bridal party's intricately choreographed dance they'd spent three days learning.

Now all she really wanted to do was spend the rest of

the night with Parker. Something she hadn't done much of over the past few days.

"Hey, handsome." Kayleigh snuck up behind Parker, seated at his table, and wrapped her arms around his shoulders. She pressed a kiss to his cheek. "Care to dance?"

His expression was an odd mix of deep affection and abject sadness that startled her.

"Is everything okay? Did something happen back home?"

"Everything is fine." He kissed her hand softly. "And yes, I'd love to dance with you."

Parker took her hand and followed her to the dance floor. Kayleigh wrapped her arms around him and they moved to the music. The muscles in his back were tense and he barely spoke.

Kayleigh stared up at him. "Parker, are you sure everything is all right?"

He nodded, but his sad smile barely turned up the corners of his mouth. "You look incredible, Kayleigh. I couldn't take my eyes off you."

Some of the tension in her shoulders eased. "Really?"

"Absolutely." His smile seemed more genuine. "Kira was beautiful, but you were the star of the show for me."

"You look pretty handsome yourself." A full grin spread across her face. She stared up at him again as she ran her fingers beneath the lapels of his cream-colored suit. It was the perfect shade for an outdoor wedding in the Caribbean. "I'm sorry we haven't had much time to spend together the last few days."

"You came here to help Kira and Theo celebrate their big day. Besides, I had plenty to keep me busy."

"Remember when we had to dance together at Blake and Savannah's wedding? How different things were between us?" Kayleigh sighed. "I wish things could've been like this then."

"So do I."

Kayleigh wished she could lay her head on his chest, the way she had when they'd danced by the pool at the cabin in the mountains. But her makeup would ruin his white linen shirt.

"Parker, I can't thank you enough for doing this. All of it. You've been so accommodating and nothing short of amazing. You're going to make an awesome fiancé someday." She forced a smile, her eyes searching his.

"Thanks." He quickly shifted his gaze from hers. "So will you. As for this trip, I think I'm the one who owes you. I hadn't been on an honest-to-goodness vacation in so long. And this was one hell of a trip. I won't forget it or any of the incredible moments that proceeded it."

"You're wearing the watch." She touched the leather band and smiled. "You didn't have to, you know. But I'm glad you did."

The music ended and they played a faster-paced song. Kayleigh's eyes met his and she braced his arms, holding him in place. "You know what I'd really like to do right now? I'd like to go back to our villa and…" She lifted onto her toes and whispered the rest in his ear.

His cheeks and forehead turned bright red as his eyes searched hers. "You're not making this easy for me, Kayleigh."

"I thought you enjoyed a challenge." Kayleigh grinned.

It was a beautiful night as they danced beneath the stars. But all she wanted now was to go back to their villa and spend their remaining hours in paradise making love and lying in each other's arms. And before they boarded the plane, she would find the courage to tell him the truth. Somewhere along the way, she'd fallen in love with him.

Parker took Kayleigh's hand and led her to the pier overlooking the water, away from where the partygoers danced.

Kayleigh's heart raced. When they stopped, she studied his expression. He was distressed. So clearly, whatever news he intended to deliver wasn't going to be good.

"Oh, God. It's that bad, huh?" Kayleigh wrapped her arms around herself, suddenly chilled by the cool breeze blowing off the sea. "So it isn't my imagination. You've been intentionally distant for the past few days."

"Kayleigh, I—"

"I feel like I should've had a drink to prepare me for this little talk." She laughed bitterly.

"We just toasted with champagne." Parker leaned against the railing.

"I was thinking of something a little stronger…like a dirty martini. Would you mind?" She needed the space and a few minutes to clear her head as much as she wanted that martini.

"Don't go anywhere. We need to talk."

Kayleigh nodded without looking at Parker. Tears stung her eyes as she stared out onto the water.

A few minutes later, she felt arms slip around her waist and lips nuzzle the back of her neck. Her eyes, which had drifted closed momentarily, quickly widened when she felt the scrape of a thick beard on her skin and recognized the distinctive cologne.

She whirled around to face Aidan. "What in the hell are you doing?"

His blue eyes danced and there was a mischievous smile on his face. He ran his fingers through his hair. "Kissing your neck, which if memory serves me, is something you've always favored."

Kayleigh folded her arms. "Did you suddenly forget that I'm engaged to someone else?"

His smirk deepened and the amusement in his eyes was unmistakable. Aidan shoved his hands into the pockets of the beige suit the groom and his groomsmen wore for the ceremony.

Her heart suddenly pounded in her chest and the entire world seemed to be spinning faster and faster. A knot tightened in her gut.

"You know, don't you?"

Aidan's smile turned into a full-fledged grin as he cradled her cheek and leaned in to kiss her.

Kayleigh shoved her hands against his chest and stepped backward. "How did you find out? Let me guess, your mother had someone look into me. That's low, even for Colleen."

"No, why would you think my mother was involved?" Aidan wasn't smiling anymore. "And what do you mean by it being low, even for her?"

"If your mother didn't tell you, then how did you know?"

"Your 'fiancé' told me the truth." He used air quotes.

"Wait... Parker told you." Kayleigh felt a sharp pain in her chest and tears stung her eyes. "No." She shook her head. "Parker wouldn't." She uttered the words under her breath, more to herself than to Aidan.

Maybe Parker didn't care about the crushing humiliation of such a revelation, but what he did care about was King's Finest. And that her building was an important part of the company's future expansion. So Parker wouldn't have violated their agreement. He wouldn't have risked losing the very thing he'd gone through all of this to obtain.

"He did."

"Why?" Her voice cracked, even as she tried to keep her composure.

Aidan's expression softened, all of the teasing gone. He took her hands in his and met her watery gaze. "Because I still love you, Kayleigh. And because you obviously still have feelings for me. Why else would you go to such elaborate lengths to make me jealous?"

"You think I did this because I wanted to make you jealous?" Her tone grew more indignant and the corners of her eyes were wet with tears.

"Didn't you?"

"No." She jerked her hands from his grip and stepped farther away. "Maybe my reasons for it were silly or even a little petty, but I did *not* do this to make you jealous. I thought you were still married."

"Then if making me jealous wasn't your aim, what was it? Why would you manufacture a fiancé and bring him all the way here to my sister's wedding?"

Kayleigh angrily wiped at her eyes with her knuckle. "I didn't want to show up here alone and watch you and your runway-model wife playing with your two beautiful little boys while I'm still—"

"Alone?" Aidan sighed, placing a tentative hand on her arm. "Kayleigh, there's nothing wrong with being alone. I wouldn't have thought any less of you because of it, whether I was still married or not."

"Maybe you wouldn't, but your mother certainly would. I just couldn't bear the thought of proving her right."

"About?"

"About me not being a suitable wife for her precious son." She raised her eyes to his again. "Or anyone, for that matter." Her last words were practically whispered.

"Are you saying that you walking away back then had something to do with my mother?"

It was his sister's wedding, and it had been such a lovely event. She hadn't told Aidan or Kira about her conversation with Colleen Brennan that day. Nor did she want to talk about it now.

What would be the point?

"Look, Aidan, none of that matters anymore. Yes, when I first learned that you were no longer married, I wondered if I'd screwed up a second chance for us." Kayleigh dabbed at her eyes, which were brimming with hot tears. "But spending this week with your family…it reminded me of all the reasons that walking away then…and now…is the right thing to do. I'm sorry."

Kayleigh lifted onto her toes and placed a soft kiss on Aidan's whiskered cheek.

He held her there. His rough beard scraped the side of her face and his lips brushed her ear as he whispered into it. "I didn't fight for you then. I was devastated by your rejection and I was furious that you chose to just walk away. I didn't ask the right questions then. So I'm asking you right now. Is there anything I can do to make you reconsider?"

Kayleigh pulled away enough to look into his blue eyes. Her chest ached for the pain she saw there, knowing she'd been at least partially responsible for it. She slowly shook her head, her expression a tortured apology.

"Why not, sweetheart?" His sincere, determined gaze almost broke her heart. Aidan didn't deserve any of this.

"Because… I love someone else." She took a step away when he finally released her arm. "And because as wonderful as this week has been, it's also been a reminder that this isn't the life or the family I want. I love my life in Magnolia Lake. Maybe I don't have family or a fiancé there, but I have amazing friends and a really good life and future. I'm not ready to give any of that up, Aidan. I'm sorry."

"Okay." He shrugged, running a hand through his hair again. "At least I tried, right?"

"And I thank you for caring enough to." Kayleigh gave him a faint smile. "Please, don't tell Kira or your mother. I'd be mortified. Besides, it's been such a marvelous week, I don't want to ruin it for her. Not even a little."

Aidan nodded. "I promise."

"Thank you. Please make my apologies to Kira and Theo, but I'm not feeling well. I'm going back to my villa to lie down." She turned to walk away, but then glanced back over her shoulder. "It was good seeing you again, Aidan."

Kayleigh hurried back to her villa as quickly as she could, tears streaming down her face. She was furious with Parker for betraying her trust again, just as he had more than two decades ago. But most of all, she was disappointed in herself for falling for a man who clearly didn't want or deserve her.

Twenty

Parker settled into a chair in their villa, his elbows on his knees and his forehead cradled in his palm. His heartbeat had been elevated by his hurried retreat back to the villa, but mostly because of seeing Kayleigh and Aidan in a tight embrace as the man whispered something in her ear.

Parker shut his eyes, replaying the evening in his mind. He wasn't sure what had been sexier. The way Kayleigh had looked in that dress or the mind-blowingly sensual thing she had whispered in his ear, which evoked a visual he simply couldn't get out of his head now, even if he tried. Sadly, they wouldn't get to act it out.

More important, he'd never have her in his life or his bed again. She'd probably move to Atlanta to be with Aidan. Or maybe they'd even move to Ireland to be closer to his children. Either way, the most Parker could hope was that the friendship they'd slowly resurrected, brick by painstaking brick, would endure.

He heard the screen door slam suddenly and jumped to his feet. It was Kayleigh. She was furious. Her eyes were red and her face was streaked with tears.

"How could you do this to me again? Why would you do it? Were you that desperate to be rid of me? Or was this all just a big joke to you?" Her bare feet slapped against the tile floor as she stalked toward him.

His act of selflessness obviously hadn't gone to plan. She knew he'd told Aidan the truth and she was furious.

"Kayleigh, how could you think that, even for a moment, I wanted to hurt you?"

"Because you just fucking did. *Again.* And I let you because I was stupid enough to think…" Kayleigh shook her head, jaw trembling. "It doesn't matter what I thought. I was wrong. But what I don't understand is why you would go through ten weeks of this—" she gestured between them "—and then jeopardize our deal by doing the one thing I asked you not to do?"

It was a fair question. One he struggled to answer.

"You know what? Forget it. *Why* doesn't even matter." Kayleigh walked out onto the wraparound deck and stood against the railing that overlooked the beach and the waters of the sea beyond it.

"Kayleigh, let me explain." Parker followed her outside. She stood there in her bare feet, the long train of her dusty-mauve dress billowing behind her.

When he grasped her arm, she turned around, like she was five seconds away from swinging on him.

Her chest heaved, likely as much from her fury as from the exertion of trying to distance herself from him.

"Don't touch me." She yanked her hand free. Her eyes filled with fresh tears. "I can't believe I trusted you again. That I was stupid enough to believe we'd actually become friends again at the very least. Do you really hate me this much, Parker? Was this your grand plan all along? To wait until we got here so that you could utterly humiliate me?"

"I could never hate you, Kayleigh, and I didn't do this to hurt you. I swear."

"Even if you got some kind of sick enjoyment out of doing this to me again, I thought you were disciplined enough not to blow up our deal and let your family down." Kayleigh swiped the backs of her fingers beneath her eyes. "What was it? Did I get too clingy? Were you afraid that I wanted more with you?"

"No, of course not, sweetheart. I've enjoyed every single moment we spent together over the past three months."

"Then why, for God's sake, would you do this?"

"Because I hated seeing how much it hurt you that things worked out between you and Aidan the way they did. You seemed to genuinely want a second chance with him. I could never have forgiven myself if I'd stood in the way of you *finally* being happy. I thought that if I told Aidan the truth—"

"That you could just pass me on to him because we were done? I'm not a baton, Parker." Her eyes blazed with anger and her voice dripped with disdain. "You don't get to decide who I love or what I do. That's *my* choice."

Parker stammered, his heart hammering against his breastbone.

"It was stupid of me to think I could make this work." She sniffled, looking out at the water. "You said you didn't want to do this. That you *couldn't* do it. I just wouldn't listen."

"I'm so sorry if I hurt you. That honestly wasn't my intention. I thought you *wanted* to be with Aidan."

Her eyes widened with indignation and her nostrils flared. She shook her head as if discussing the matter with him any further was pointless. "Go away, Parker. Just leave me alone, please."

She stalked into the bedroom and slammed the door behind her.

Parker's gut burned and his chest ached. He'd tried to give Kayleigh what he thought she wanted. Even though it was the one thing in the world that made him feel like his heart had been ripped in two.

Because he loved Kayleigh Jemison, and he couldn't imagine going back to life without her.

Kayleigh wanted to get out of the dress and makeup and maybe go for a run on the beach. Clear her head and pull herself together.

In the three months that she had been seeing Parker, she'd turned into a hot mess. And she hated herself for it. Before now, the only emotion she'd voluntarily let others see was anger. Everything else she'd kept concealed neatly below the surface. Out of sight, where they couldn't use those weaknesses against her. It was a neat trick she'd learned in middle school and had used ever since.

Concealing those painful emotions from others had kept her from feeling vulnerable. But it had isolated her, too. That had changed when she allowed Savannah in. And over the past few months, she'd let Parker in.

A few weeks ago, she'd seen the beauty of allowing someone else in and permitting them to see those vulnerabilities. But now she was reminded of the importance of choosing more wisely who to let in.

Kayleigh heaved a sigh and stood in front of the full-length mirror. She reached over her shoulder to unzip the back of her dress. Then she reached behind her to tug it down the rest of the way.

"Let me." Parker was suddenly there, standing behind her as he stared at her reflection in the mirror. "Please."

Kayleigh sighed, nodding as she dropped her gaze from his.

Parker unzipped the dress, then stepped away.

She allowed the fabric to pool around her on the floor, then tossed it onto the bed before going into the bathroom and removing her makeup.

Kayleigh stared into the mirror of the elegant bathroom, scrubbing the makeup from her skin as Parker leaned against the doorway in silence.

She met his gaze in the mirror. "What is it, Parker? Haven't you done enough?"

"I need to tell you how sorry I am that I hurt you. I was a little jerk when we were kids. Maybe I still am. But then and now, I didn't deliberately try to hurt you. My motives back then were selfish. But I swear to you that what I did today was the most selfless thing I've ever done. And I did it because I thought that's what you wanted."

"To be embarrassed?"

"To be loved and cherished and treated like the phenomenal woman you are." His voice grew faint and he took another deep breath. "I honestly just wanted you to have everything and to be happy, and if I can't be the man who gives that to you... I wanted to see you with someone who will."

"That's exactly what I'm talking about, Parker. I know you think it's your job to fix everything, but you don't get to decide who... Wait..." Kayleigh lowered the finger she'd been emphatically jabbing in the air. She tilted her head to one side as she studied him. "Are you saying that *you* want to be the one who makes me happy?"

"Not very well, I'm guessing. But yes, Kayleigh." Parker stepped closer, cradling her face in his hands. "I want to be the only man who truly makes you smile. I want to be the guy you walk Cricket with at night. The one you go riding and camping with. The guy you volunteer beside at the youth center each month. The one you go skinny-dipping with in the middle of the night." Parker traced her cheekbone with his thumb. "I want to be the only man you make love to."

Kayleigh closed her eyes and leaned into his touch as tears spilled down her cheeks. She sniffled, finally opening them. A wide smile spread across her face. "I want that, too, Parker. But I need to know I can trust you. That you won't betray my confidence for *any* reason."

He nodded. "I promise. I love you, Kayleigh. I've adored you since we were kids. And I never stopped thinking of you and wanting you back in my life. I've never felt this way about anyone before. So forgive me for screwing up."

"You love me?" Her voice trembled as she stared into his dark eyes, which were filled with emotion.

The corner of his mouth curved in a smile. "Very much. But it's more than that. I need you, Kayleigh. When I saw Aidan holding you in his arms, I felt physical pain. Like an elephant was standing on my chest and my lungs were about to collapse. If someone had said that to me a few months ago, I would've accused them of being melodramatic. But being heartbroken is a real thing because I felt every ounce of that pain."

"So did I when…" Kayleigh couldn't finish the words. She didn't want to be reminded of the pain she'd felt in that moment. She pressed a gentle kiss to his lips. "I love you, too, Parker."

Parker took Kayleigh in his arms and kissed her again. He needed to feel the warmth and comfort of her body. To show her exactly how much he needed her in his life. That he'd never hurt her again.

He stripped her of her pink lace panties and bra and laid her on the bed beneath him as he claimed her mouth in a heated kiss that made his body ache to be inside of hers.

Kayleigh ground her hips against his as she tugged his shirt from his waistband and helped him remove it and his linen pants.

Parker grazed one firm nipple with the backs of his fingers until it strained against his touch as he kissed her.

He closed his eager mouth over the beaded tip and sucked roughly. She gasped and arched her back.

His eyes drifted closed as ripples of need rolled down his spine in response to her soft whimpers. His pulse raced and body vibrated with his desire to be buried inside of her, but he needed to take his time. Focus on pleasuring every inch of her remarkable body.

He pressed a kiss to the space between her thighs. Laved her slick folds with his tongue as she shuddered in anticipation of each stroke. He lapped at the sensitive flesh surrounding the distended bundle of nerves, giving her pleasure while denying her the sensation she was so desperate for.

Until she begged for it.

Kayleigh applied the slightest pressure to the back of his head. "Parker, please. Don't tease me. I need you."

He grinned, his eyes meeting hers as he licked, then sucked on her slick bud.

Her head lolled back and she moaned with pleasure. She arched her back and her hips rocked forward. "Yes, yes. Right there. Just like that."

He increased his speed and intensified the pressure, bringing her to the brink. She was almost there and he was painfully hard when he halted his motion just enough to allow her to draw a breath. Then he drove his tongue inside her.

Kayleigh's body tensed and her eyes widened as she cried out with pleasure. Her heels dug into the mattress and her hips glided back and forth until she came hard, her muscles tensing and her core pulsing. His name on her lips.

He lay beside her, his lips brushing the shell of her ear when he spoke.

"I want to be the only man who gets to do that. The only man who gets to hear you call his name in that breathless tone while you shatter to pieces."

Her eyes were watery as she pressed her palm to his cheek. "That's what I want, too."

Parker kissed her again, made love to her. As much as he'd enjoyed each of their previous encounters, there was something about this time that was so much more intense. Maybe it was because neither of them was trying to delude themselves into believing that this was anything other than love.

Kayleigh lay with her cheek pressed to Parker's chest as he slept, breathing softly. It was nearly two in the morning and they had an early flight, but she couldn't sleep.

As happy as she was that she and Parker were a bona fide couple now, she couldn't help worrying about how things would change between them once they returned to Magnolia Lake.

She'd been able to forgive Parker and let go of their painful past, but being part of Parker's life meant being a part of his family members' lives, too.

She'd managed to be civil to Duke Abbott during their business negotiations and during the party at his home. But she'd been tense and her stomach had been in knots the entire time. How could she spend casual Sunday afternoons across the dinner table from the man who'd capitalized on her father's impending death and her mother's illness to swindle her family out of their land?

She still wasn't ready to forgive Duke Abbott for what he'd done. Maybe she never would be. If she couldn't, she and Parker would be over before they'd even begun.

Twenty-One

Parker realized that they were both tired after their late night and early flight. Still, Kayleigh had been unusually quiet. Every time he'd asked if she was all right, she'd said she was. Then she'd gone back to mindlessly bouncing her knee as she stared out the airplane window.

Parker squeezed her hand. "Kayleigh, I'll make you a promise. I'll always be straight up with you, but you need to do the same. So if something is bothering you, I need to know. You can trust me."

She turned toward him and met his gaze. "These past few months together have been amazing. I want this—I really do. But being with you means I'll be spending a lot more time with your family. Which is great, except… I don't know if I can get past what your father did. I thought making him pay dearly for my building would satisfy the debt, but I honestly don't know if I can forgive him for taking advantage of my mother at the lowest point in her life. Especially when your family has so much."

"Thank you for being honest, sweetheart." Parker threaded their fingers together and squeezed her hand.

"Kayleigh, I love you. I don't want anything to ever come between us again. There's only one way for you to resolve this thing with my dad. It's time you two talk and get everything out in the open."

"What could he possibly say that would make me feel better about what he did?" Kayleigh stared at their joined hands. "Other than camping, my best memories of my dad were those sober moments when we'd visit that old farm and he'd talk about all the things he wanted to do. He wanted to make it a working farm again. But my mother always dreamed of starting a little inn there."

"I know you don't think it'll help, but I need you to trust me. All I ask is that you give it a chance."

Kayleigh nodded and gave him a sad smile. "I promise to hear what he has to say."

Parker kissed Kayleigh's forehead and wrapped his arm around her. Now he would need to convince his father that it was time to tell Kayleigh the truth.

Parker had taken Kayleigh to her apartment to rest and settle in after they collected Cricket from Blake and Savannah's house. Then he went straight to his parents' home. After he hugged and kissed his mother and his sister Zora, who were working on dinner for later that afternoon, he found his father in the den. He was reading the newspaper with the TV on in the background.

"Hey, Dad." Parker sat on the opposite end of the chocolate-brown leather sofa, where his father was seated. "Kayleigh is prepared to finalize the paperwork for the sale of her building. She can come to the office tomorrow morning."

"Well done, son." His father patted his knee. "I know it wasn't fair that the lion's share of the responsibility fell to you, but I'm thrilled we could do this for your mother."

"Me, too. Only it turned out that this was the best possible thing that could've ever happened to me, Dad. I'm in love with Kayleigh, and she loves me, too. We might never have gotten together if it wasn't for this project. So thank you for pushing me."

"You and Kayleigh are an item now?" The elder Abbott's expression indicated that he was genuinely happy for him, but his brows furrowed with a hint of concern. "I'm glad to hear it, son. Kayleigh is a wonderful young woman."

"She is, and I want her to feel the same way about you, Dad." Parker scooted to the edge of his seat. "But you know what she thinks of you."

"We can't control the things people believe about us, son. We can only make sure they aren't true." His father sipped from the large glass of sweet tea that left a condensation ring on the newspaper he'd been reading.

"Most of the time," Parker agreed. "But in this case, we both know that isn't true."

"What are you talking about, son?"

"I know everything, Dad. I've seen the original paperwork. After the incident with Savannah going through our archives, I started reviewing them a little at a time. I wanted to make sure there weren't any other family secrets I should know about. That's when I discovered the truth. Now it's time that Kayleigh knows, too."

"Whatever you think you know, son, is best left in those archives." His father clicked the remote off, lines forming between his furrowed brows. "Things are the way they are for reasons you don't understand."

"Dad, whatever promises you made back then, I'm sure they were made for noble reasons. But circumstances change. I love her, Dad, but we both know there's no way that this relationship can work unless she learns the truth."

"Parker, you'll just have to find another way to convince her." His father walked over to the bar and refilled his glass.

"No, Duke, Parker is right. Kayleigh needs to hear the

truth, and she needs to hear it from you. Please." His mother stepped inside the room and squeezed his arm.

"But I made a promise," his father insisted.

"That promise was made to protect Kayleigh, but it hasn't. It's isolated her and left her feeling resentful and alone. That isn't what her mother wanted for her. And it isn't what I want for Parker," his mother pleaded. "This secret will keep the two of them apart."

Duke sighed and nodded begrudgingly. "If you really think it's in the girl's best interest, I'll tell her."

Parker gave his mother a long hug. "Thanks, Mom."

She smiled and kissed his cheek.

"Thanks, Dad." He gave his father a quick hug, then pulled out his phone to call Kayleigh. He didn't want to wait another minute to make things right between two of the people he loved most in the world.

Kayleigh clutched Parker's hand as he led her into his parents' home. He'd been adamant that she and Duke needed to talk right away. So she'd agreed to come to dinner and to listen to what his father had to say.

He led her inside the den, where his father was watching TV. Duke turned off the television, his shoulders tensing. "Have a seat, Kayleigh."

She shifted her gaze to Parker, who'd released her hand. "You won't be joining us?"

"I think you two should talk alone. But I'll be right down the hall in the kitchen if you need me. I promise." Parker gave her a quick, reassuring kiss.

It felt odd with Duke staring at them.

Parker left, closing the door behind him.

Kayleigh sank into a chair, her hands folded in her lap and her gaze not meeting Duke's. "Parker said that we should talk."

"Can I get you a glass of tea or lemonade? Maybe a bottle of water?"

"No, thank you. I'd really just like to hear what it is you have to say for yourself." Her voice wavered slightly.

"Fair enough." He nodded gravely. "Kayleigh, I don't know if your mother ever told you that I was sweet on her back in high school. But she was head over heels for your father."

"I know." It was one of the things her mother had reminded her father of whenever he was feeling sorry for himself or jealous of Duke and the Abbotts. *I chose you, not him.* "She said you two were good friends."

"We were." He smiled sadly.

"If that's true, Mr. Abbott, how could you have treated her so cruelly." Kayleigh maintained a respectful tone though she didn't mince words. Parker said he wanted her to have an honest conversation with his father. She'd taken him at his word.

Duke grimaced in response, as if her accusation had caused him physical pain.

Good. She'd drawn first blood.

"I realize this is an uncomfortable conversation for both of us, Kayleigh. And I know that you're angry because the money I paid your mother wasn't nearly the value of her property. But what you couldn't have known is that it was your mother who insisted I only give her a small percentage of the land's value."

"Why would she have done that? My father was dying and the medical bills had sucked up what little she and my father had managed to save for our college tuition." Kayleigh gripped the armrest of the chair. She'd promised to be civil, but she wouldn't stand for lies, not even from the high-and-mighty Duke Abbott.

"My father had offered to buy her father's land several years before. So she struck up a deal. She only wanted one

quarter of the land's value in cash. The rest was used here."
Duke handed Kayleigh a yellowing manila folder. "You'll
find the answers to all of your questions in there."

Kayleigh reluctantly opened the folder. Her and her sister's names were all over college-scholarship paperwork.
She recognized their signatures. "How'd you get my financial information?"

"It's typical that the organization granting a scholarship
maintain a record of all documentation."

Kayleigh's eyes widened and she stared at Duke for a
moment. She reviewed the documents again. Her heart
pounded in her chest.

"Are you saying that King's Finest paid all of our college
tuition and boarding through these scholarships?"

He slid back in his seat and crossed one leg over the
other. "Initially the money came from the difference between the price I paid for the land and what it was actually
worth, as well as interest. But your mother implored me
to see to it that you girls were cared for throughout your
college years. So when that initial infusion of cash ran
out, yes, King's Finest kicked in. You and Evelisse were
our first scholarship recipients, though you didn't know it.
And you're the reason we've done a scholarship program
ever since."

"I don't understand, Mr. Abbott." Tears stung her eyes
and her voice broke. "Why didn't she just leave the money
to Evvy and me?"

"Your mother was afraid that neither of you was ready
for that kind of responsibility. That you'd squander the
money within a year and be left with nothing."

Kayleigh wiped away tears. As much as she hated hearing that, she knew it was probably true. And, it seemed,
her mother had played on Duke's affection for her, knowing he'd make up the difference once the money from the
sale of the land ran out.

"So you've been our benefactor all this time? Why didn't you say something?" Kayleigh's chest ached and her stomach was tied in knots as she recalled all the awful things she'd thought and said about Duke Abbott.

"I made a promise to your mother that I wouldn't tell you where the money came from. She knew how you felt about Parker and our family by association. She knew her baby girl well enough to know you'd never accept what you felt was a handout. So she asked me to handle it anonymously. I promised I would, so I kept my word." Duke sighed, leveling his gaze with hers. "Even though it was one of the hardest things I've ever had to do."

"Why are you finally telling me now?" Kayleigh asked through tears.

"Because my son loves you something fierce. And he and my wife believe your mother wouldn't have wanted me to continue keeping this secret when it's doing you more harm than good." Duke squeezed Kayleigh's arm. "I only hope, now that you know, that you feel my decision was justified."

Kayleigh nodded, eagerly, tears streaming down her face. They both stood and she hugged the man tightly. "I'm so sorry, Mr. Abbott. I can't thank you enough. I hope you can forgive me for mischaracterizing you the way I did."

"There's nothing to forgive. You didn't know the whole story. I would've felt the same way, too."

There was a tap at the door and Parker stuck his head inside. "Just checking on you two. Everything okay?"

Kayleigh nodded. She kissed Duke on his cheek, before he excused himself and left them alone in the room.

"Thank you, Parker. For everything." Kayleigh threw her arms around him and hugged him tightly. Then she lifted onto her toes and planted a soft kiss on his lips.

He wound his arms around her waist. "I love you, Kayleigh."

Her mouth stretched in a wide grin; her heart was so full of love for him. "I love you, too, Parker."

"Good." He nuzzled her neck. "Because I have a request."

"No, Parker, we are not going down to that workroom." She laughed, remembering when they'd kissed for the first time there.

He smirked. "Fine, then I have another question."

"Shoot."

"It's about that ring. I promised my friend I'd ship it back as soon as we returned."

"Aww." Kayleigh pouted as she held out her hand and studied the ring's intricacies. "It's so gorgeous. I'm going to miss it."

"Well, that's the thing. Since it's so well-suited to you, and since we're two misfit toys best suited for each other and we've finally nailed this whole fake-fiancé thing… maybe instead of returning the ring, we keep it. On the condition that you agree to graduate from being my fake fiancée to being my real one."

"Parker, did you just ask me to marry you?"

"Not very well, apparently." He grinned. "So let me try again."

Parker got on one knee and held her hand. "Kayleigh, I've never been happier than I have these past three months. You've made me see myself and the world in a different light. Every corny romantic comedy where the guy declares that the woman makes him want to be a better man… I get it now. Because you truly make me want to be my best self. Most importantly you've shown me how much better my life is with you in it. So Kayleigh Jemison, I am formally asking you to please be my wife."

Kayleigh nodded, tears streaming down her face as she pressed her lips to his.

Epilogue

Kayleigh had just finished up with a customer who'd commissioned custom jewelry sets for her bridesmaids when Parker came into the shop with Cricket on his heels.

"If it isn't my incredibly handsome fiancé." They'd been engaged for less than a month and it still made her giddy to call him that. "What brings you here in the middle of the day with Cricket in tow?"

Kayleigh stepped out from behind the counter. She petted Cricket and accepted a kiss from Parker.

"I brought you a little something." He grinned.

"Another offer?" she teased.

"Of sorts." He held out a large brown envelope.

Kayleigh raised a brow, accepting the envelope and opening it. The smile quickly faded from her face as she read the document.

"Is this a quitclaim deed for my family's land?" The type had gone blurry through her sudden tears.

"Not all of it, of course." She knew the Abbotts had developed some of the land, so that made sense. "But our family took a vote. We won't expand any farther on the land. We have plenty of additional property to work with, when the need arises."

"Why?" Her voice broke as tears wet her cheeks. "Why would your family do this?"

"Consider it an engagement present from my father."

"To us?"

"To you." He cradled her cheek. "It's yours, free and clear. Regardless of what happens between us. Your family's land, at least some of it, belongs to you again."

"This is a truly incredible gift… Thank you, Parker." Kayleigh swiped at the tears staining her heated cheeks.

In light of everything Duke had already done for her and Evvy, it didn't feel right for him to gift the land to her. Especially when they had generously paid her far more than her building was worth.

"As much as I appreciate the gift, and I truly do appreciate it, I don't expect charity from your family. I'd like to pay for the land. What does Duke think is fair?"

"This isn't charity, babe. You're family now." Parker pressed a quick kiss to her lips. "My dad wants to do this for you, and he's firm about this. He won't take a penny from you for it."

Kayleigh couldn't stop the tears from sliding down her cheek. She jumped into Parker's arms and gave him a big kiss. One that made her contemplate locking the door and turning the Closed sign so they could have an informal celebration.

"There's something I forgot to mention." He interrupted their kiss before she could float her idea of an afternoon romp in the storeroom.

"What is it?" She tried not to sound aggravated.

"The land is yours to do with as you please. So no pressure. But what we think would be really lovely there is a little inn. Maybe just five or ten rooms. We'd even be willing to invest in such a venture."

"That would've made my mom so happy." Fresh tears spilled down her cheeks. "It's a fantastic idea, babe. I love it. And I love you, Parker."

He cradled her to his chest, her head tucked beneath his chin. "Love you too, Kayleigh. Always have, always will."

* * * * *

VENGEFUL
VOWS

YVONNE LINDSAY

To my blind-date hero,
thank you for all your years of
support and encouragement.

One

Alice Horvath—matriarch of the Horvath family, former CEO of Horvath Corporation and creator of Match Made in Marriage—surveyed the candlelit, flower-bedecked room and tried to ignore the trepidation that filled her. She didn't know why she was so nervous about the union of her third-eldest grandson, Galen, to a woman who was so perfect for him it had actually brought tears to her eyes when she'd made the match. But for some reason, despite all her usual attention to detail, she felt as though she didn't have quite her usual grip on what would happen next.

Their future happiness was her only goal, but for once she couldn't see that far ahead for them as clearly as she did with the others. If they made it, it would require hard work and commitment from them both. Had she taken an unnecessary risk? Galen had said he didn't want a grand passion, but everyone deserved that, didn't they?

She thought of her late husband, Eduard, and tonight

missed him more keenly than she had in a long time. But she wasn't ready to rest in peace with him yet. She still had too much work to do, and the success of this marriage was a part of that, no matter what secrets it brought out of the woodwork.

Galen closed his eyes briefly then started as he felt a small hand take his and give it a squeeze.

"It'll be okay," Ellie whispered. "She's going to love you."

He squeezed back gently. "She's going to love *us*," he affirmed.

He flicked an imaginary piece of lint from his suit sleeve and looked sideways at his best girl. Ellie grinned back up at him, and Galen felt his heart swell. Both his brother, Valentin, and his cousin Ilya had offered to stand here at the altar with him but this wasn't about a traditional marriage. This was about providing security for nine-year-old Ellie, so it made sense that she stand up with him as he married a total stranger. Poor kid; she deserved so much better than him, but he was doing his best by her, and would continue to do so for the rest of his life.

When he'd assumed guardianship of Ellie after her parents' shocking and sudden deaths in a car crash just over three months ago, his life as he'd known it had come to a screaming halt. No more wild parties. No more playboy lifestyle. All the commitment he'd dodged for most of his adult life had come to him in one complete package. He hadn't been ready for it, but then neither had his best friends, Ellie's mom and dad, expected to die, either.

He cast one more look around the room, ensuring everything was as it should be. He wouldn't be the CEO of Horvath Hotels and Resorts without triple-checking everything all the time. He knew how to keep people happy—all kinds of people. Surely, that would help when it came to keeping his new wife happy, too?

"She's here!" Ellie whispered hoarsely. "And she's so pretty."

Galen looked to the door at the end of the carpeted aisle in the function room and, honest to God, felt his breath catch in his lungs. Pretty? No, that didn't even begin to describe the woman paused there at the end. Her face was a picture of serenity, her head poised on a long, graceful neck. Her hair was pulled back in a loose updo that made his fingers itch to extract each and every pin and let her hair fall down over the slender bare shoulders exposed by her strapless gown. Her skin glowed. A diamond drop necklace sat low on her décolletage, drawing his eyes to the rapid rise and fall of her chest—to the hint of the soft swell of her breasts, framed by the gown's neckline. His gaze drifted lower, to the tiny waist cinched in a satin sash with a cluster of silk and diamanté flowers and then to the three tiers of flowing shimmering fabric that spread like a cloud around her.

"She looks like a princess," Ellie said, loudly this time so that everyone in the room turned their heads and a collective gasp of awe filtered through the air.

"Let's make her our queen, shall we?" Galen said and, still holding Ellie's hand, he walked toward his bride.

As they drew closer, he noticed the flickering pulse in her neck. So perhaps she wasn't quite as serene as she projected. That was fine by him. In a way, he'd have felt some reserve about marrying someone who *wasn't* just a little rattled at the prospect of meeting their future life partner for the first time at the altar. And while he'd seen his brother and his cousin make successful matches that way, he'd never for a moment considered it for himself. Truth be told, he'd never even considered marriage before Ellie.

The woman's eyes flared slightly, her bluish-gray irises almost consumed by her pupils in the candlelight.

"My groom, I presume?" she said in a voice that was a tiny bit husky and a whole lot of nervous.

"Galen Horvath, at your service," he said, taking her free hand and lifting it to his lips.

Her skin was warm and lightly scented. Something sweet, with a hint of vanilla and a slightly headier spice. A slight tremor of her hand made him release his hold.

Never one to be shy, his best girl piped up. "And I'm Ellie. Will you marry us?"

A smile tweaked the woman's lips. "Both of you? Now, there's a bargain," she said as her smile widened and her eyes sparkled with obvious delight. "The answer is yes. I'm Peyton Earnshaw, and I would be delighted to marry you."

Galen felt something shift deep inside as he watched her. Her smile, her manner, her scent. It all coalesced into something powerful inside him. Lust, he told himself. Pure physical attraction; that was all it was. And it was far, far more than he'd anticipated experiencing on meeting his bride. The tension that had gripped him all day began to ease. This was going to be okay. *They* were going to be okay, he corrected himself.

Peyton had done a lot of things in the pursuit of investigative journalism, but she'd never gotten married before. When she'd decided to do an exposé on Alice Horvath she'd been delighted to discover an old college acquaintance among Alice's staff. And when she'd learned the matriarch's own grandson was searching for a bride, she'd called in an old debt and secured Michelle's assistance gaming the system to match Peyton's profile with the grandson's. The fact that the matchmaking results could be manipulated like that lent weight to Peyton's argument that Alice Horvath's company was a complete fraud in the first place.

Peyton swallowed her nerves as, flanked by Galen Horvath and Ellie, she walked down the aisle toward the celebrant, who waited with a benevolent smile. She'd been prepared to do anything to achieve her goal—even marry a stranger—and now here she was.

Acutely aware of the warm strength of Galen's hand holding hers, she tried to calm the unaccustomed racing of her heart. He was just a man. Seriously, her groom could have been anyone—but he wasn't. He was one of Alice Horvath's many grandchildren. He could have been short, tall, thin, full figured, hirsute. He was tall, more handsome than any star she'd seen at the movies lately, and he exuded a charisma that she felt pulling on her in ways she'd never expected. And his touch was doing weird things to her insides. Things that she prided herself on not feeling. Things she'd inured herself to—by choice. She wasn't some naive creature full of unrealistic expectations. Oh sure, she knew you could fall in love, but she also knew the pain of a stupid decision made in the heat of the moment, and she wasn't going to make that kind of mistake ever again.

"Everything okay?"

A soft whisper of breath caressed her ear as Galen leaned close to her.

"Just peachy," she said with a bright smile that she was far from feeling.

His eyes met hers and he stared at her a moment before his face broke into a smile that literally stole the breath from her lungs. He gave her hand a gentle squeeze before letting go. She was going to have to be careful around this guy, she told herself as she composed her features and faced the celebrant.

The service was simple. She'd have liked to have said it

was honest but she was here under false pretenses. It gave
her a moment's pause when she considered that what she
planned to do would not only affect the man she was marrying, but also the little girl, who looked up at him with trust
and adoration. Well, she just wouldn't let anyone, herself
included, become too attached; that was all there was to
it. And when her in-depth article exposing Alice Horvath
for the manipulative and cruel woman she truly was hit the
newsstands, no one would be hurt but the woman who'd
destroyed Peyton's father and, in turn, her entire family.
Even the baby she'd been forced to give away.

Peyton blinked back the sudden burn in her eyes. Show
no weakness. That had been her mantra then and it remained her mantra now.

"Congratulations!" the celebrant announced with
warmth and enthusiasm—as if this was a real wedding
and as if they were planning a real future together. "I now
pronounce you husband and wife. You may kiss the bride."

Oh, no.

Peyton froze as Galen took both her hands in his and
leaned toward her. A sense of inevitability seeped through
to her bones as she instinctively closed the final gap between them and allowed his lips to brush hers. Except it
was more than a brush—it was an enticement. The gentle
press of his mouth against hers sent her pulse thudding
out of control, and when she parted her lips—to protest,
she would tell herself later—he took advantage and tasted
her with a practiced sweep of his tongue. She should have
pulled back, she should have ended it, but she didn't. Instead, like some sappy lovestruck teenager, she leaned even
closer and kissed him back as if this was a real marriage
and they'd been anticipating this moment for months.

When he withdrew she felt oddly bereft, even shaken.
She looked up at him and saw the same kind of expression

reflected back at her and instantly knew keeping Galen Horvath—her *husband*—at arm's length was going to prove a great deal more challenging than she'd hoped.

"Yay, we're a family!" Ellie said excitedly as she wrapped her skinny little arms around them both and gave them a big squeeze. "Nothing bad can happen now."

"Nothing ba—" Peyton started.

"I'll explain more later. Right now we have some celebrating to do."

And they did. They took photos with their guests, including a few of her friends from college she'd kept in touch with. The Horvaths had been suitably sympathetic when she'd explained that her mother had died when she was a child and her father was unable to make it for the wedding.

After they were done with the formal photos, they toasted and ate and danced and toasted some more. And with every step perfectly in tune with her new partner, Peyton kept a smile on her face and acted as if this was exactly what she'd wanted all her life.

When the lights dimmed in the reception room and the music slowed to a dreamy romantic number, Galen took her back into his arms and led her out onto the dance floor.

"Don't you ever get tired?" Peyton teased. "You haven't been allowed to sit down yet."

He flashed a brief grin at her before his expression grew more serious. "I wanted to let you know what was behind Ellie's statement earlier."

"Do tell," she encouraged when Galen fell silent.

If she wasn't mistaken, a shimmer of moisture appeared in his eyes. He tilted his head back slightly and blinked hard before meeting her gaze again. Then he drew a deep breath and his words came in a rush.

"Ellie's my ward. Her parents died in a car crash at the beginning of the year. They were my best friends."

Galen's voice cracked and Peyton was instantly flooded with compassion. She knew what it felt like to have your world ripped apart unexpectedly. But to lose both parents at the same time? That was almost too awful to contemplate. She waited, not wanting to fill the new silence between them with platitudes.

After a couple of minutes he continued. "I think she's done really well coping with her loss. Often, she's coped better than me. She's had grief counseling and we haven't made any changes to her lifestyle that she wasn't ready to make. In fact, it was her idea I buy a house in her old neighborhood for us both to live in. She said being at her old family home made her too sad."

"So you did that?"

"Well, it's a work in progress. For now we're staying here in my apartment at the hotel. I hope you can help us choose our home together."

"Our home together. Right. That's a big thing to ask when we've only just met, don't you think?"

He nodded. "True, but if we're going to make our marriage work properly, we need to be living under the same roof, right?" When she didn't answer, he continued. "Anyway, I thought Ellie and I were doing okay but she blindsided me one day. I found her crying in her room and when I managed to get to the root of the problem it floored me. It wasn't something I could just throw money at, or tease a smile out of, or distract away."

"What was it?" she prompted.

"She told me she was terrified about what would happen if I died like her mom and dad. If one day she was completely alone." He drew in a deep breath and looked around the room at the revelers. His voice was low and intense when he spoke again. "I knew then that I needed to get married, to find a wife who wanted to share Ellie's life with me. To help her feel secure and loved and needed, the way her parents did. I want to be totally honest with you, Peyton. This marriage didn't start out in a traditional sense, but I'd like to think we can work together to achieve that eventually. We've both come to Match Made in Marriage with the same goal. Finding a life partner. I'm being clear and up-front about my reasons for needing to find a wife. Right now Ellie is the most important person in my world, and I will do whatever I can to make her happy. I need to know you'll commit to that, too."

Two

Peyton didn't know where to look or what to think. She was consumed by guilt. Suddenly, this assignment was skewing out of her control. Not only did she feel like she was constantly fighting with her instincts to just let go and enjoy being with the man who held her so capably in his arms as they did another turn around the dance floor. This also wasn't what she'd signed up for. She'd expected an uncomplicated union, a chance to dig for more dirt on Alice Horvath and eventually the opportunity to extract from her the apology her father and her late mother had been due for far too long.

And now what? Now she was married; that was what. It wasn't the wedding she'd dreamed of as a child, where her father would proudly walk her down the aisle, but one engineered by a stranger so she could marry a stranger. She had been confident she could handle it. How hard could it be?

But now she was a stepmom, too. And not just a stepmom, but to a child who already knew far too much about loss and how the whole world could be upended in the blink of an eye. Already Peyton felt a pull toward the girl—how could she not? Ellie was bright and engaging and demonstrative. Everything she herself had been at that age. Except when Peyton's world had turned upside down she'd retreated into herself. She'd been nothing like Ellie. Did she dare risk crushing Ellie's spirit? Could Peyton enter into this debacle of a marriage and then exit it without causing harm? It was doubtful. And she was in, whether she liked it or not, for at least the next three months under the terms of the agreement she'd signed only a few weeks ago. Signed, secure in the belief that this would be a simple matter of going through the experience, writing her story and leaving without looking back.

Galen watched her, obviously expecting some kind of answer. He'd been open with her about his expectations and it was only fair that he expected openness in return. But honesty was something she couldn't give him, even if she wanted to. Her entire adult life she'd been gearing up for this moment. To exact the revenge for Alice's unfounded accusations against her dad of improper record keeping and misappropriation of funds. Accusations that had cast a permanent pall on his professional career and made him untrustworthy in the eyes of every potential new employer. Accusations that had put additional strain on her mother's diminishing health—she'd developed complications from her multiple sclerosis—which had subsequently drained what little they had in the bank and left them living on handouts and whatever sporadic income her father could earn. They'd been unable to pay medical bills for treatment that might have eased her mother's condition and had ended up having to move from California to Oregon, where the cost of living was lower, but which put her mom even far-ther from the medical team who'd overseen her care.

A little of the anger that had driven Peyton all these years sparked back to life, blanketing the guilt so there was little more than a pang left.

"I committed to marrying you, Galen. I will do my part."

He tensed as if waiting to hear more, but she wasn't pre-pared to outright lie and make false declarations. She was here to do a job and to close a chapter in her and her fam-ily's life. And then there was the other reason. The reason she barely allowed herself to think of. The child she'd been forced to give away. Had her family's circumstances been different, she would have been able to keep her. Circum-stances she could lay fully and completely at the feet of the woman walking toward them right now. With no money left in her college fund, Peyton had had to take out student loans to go to college. No matter how carefully she'd crunched the numbers there was no way she could afford food, rent, utilities and childcare on top of her loan repayments and her parents had had no way to help physically, emotionally or financially. After all these years, and all her painstak-ing planning, it was coming to fruition now. She couldn't afford to take her eye off her goal, for anyone.

"I guess that's all I can ask," he said. "And look, here's Nagy to check on her new chick."

"Nagy?" Peyton asked, quietly bristling at the idea of being one of Alice Horvath's *anything*.

"It's Hungarian. A diminutive of *nagymama*, for 'grand-mother.'"

And then Alice was upon them. Though she was slightly built and petite, there was a steeliness to her gaze, and her back was ramrod straight. It was clear this woman didn't suffer fools gladly; Peyton could tell the woman who'd controlled the Horvath Corporation at its head office in

California for many years after her husband's death was formidable. But as Alice drew nearer, a smile appeared on the old woman's face. It softened her and made her look entirely approachable. This wasn't the face of the monster Peyton had always believed her to be.

Galen's arm tightened around her waist and she involuntarily nestled closer. She had to look and act the part of newlywed, no matter what. And it wasn't so difficult, was it? He was hardly unattractive and the lean, hard lines of his body beneath his suit felt uncommonly right against her, confusing her even more.

"Congratulations, you two," Alice said warmly as she reached up and kissed Galen on the cheek then took Peyton's hands in hers. "You look wonderful together. I'm sure you'll be very happy."

Peyton smiled, or was it a snarl with her nemesis standing right in front of her? She couldn't be entirely sure. "Thank you," she managed, her voice sounding stiff and unnatural.

"We're a bit overwhelming en masse, aren't we?" Alice said with a conspiratorial smile. "But you'll get used to us. Everyone does."

By decree of Alice Horvath, Peyton thought bitterly. Get used to them and play by their rules, or get out. She forced herself to hold that smile on her face and took in a deep breath of relief when Alice let go of her hands and turned once again to her grandson. Peyton watched, intrigued by the genuine affection between them. There was nothing stilted or fake about the fondness they showed one another. She let their conversation wash over her and surveyed the rest of the room. It almost looked like the celebration of a real wedding as people laughed and danced and ate and drank. And yet she felt completely separate from all of it. Had she bitten off more than she could chew by taking this assignment?

* * *

Galen sensed his new bride's disengagement and hastened to end the conversation with his grandmother. It was important to him that Peyton feel she'd made the right decision. He was very good at making other people feel good—about their choices, about themselves, about him. He aimed to please, always, and it had stood him in good stead with his career choice and drew a lot of people to him. But he had the distinct impression that Peyton was not going to be an easy sell. He wouldn't be able to simply waltz her off into this new happily-ever-after life. There was a reserve about her, even though she was going through all the motions and smiling in all the right places. And he was determined to break that wall down, brick by brick if he had to.

He stroked the curve of her waist but her body remained rigid. Maybe his touch was too much, too soon. He told himself to let her go but the thought of doing so held no appeal at all. He was genuinely attracted to her and mentally gave his grandmother a thumbs-up for their pairing. And he'd have bet that Peyton was attracted to him, too, though she was doing her best not to show it. As soon as this party was over, things would be different. They could all relax. He thought about the Horvath resort in Hawaii where they'd be heading by private jet tonight. Hopefully there, soothed by the balmy breeze and the lush beauty of the landscape, Peyton would unwind a little more and allow him to get to know her better.

"Nagy, could you give Peyton and I a little time alone? We'll need to get ready to leave soon. Perhaps you could mind Ellie for me and we can collect her before we head to the airport?"

"Of course. It would be my pleasure. Ellie is such a delight. When you're back from honeymoon, I'd love it if she could stay with me in Ojai for a weekend."

His grandmother gave Peyton and him both a kiss on the cheek and went off in search of the nine-year-old.

"Ellie is coming with us?" Peyton asked with a surprised expression on her face.

"I hope that's okay. She's on spring break right now, so it made sense to me to include her and, as we weren't permitted contact between one another before the wedding, I couldn't exactly ask you."

"No, it's not a problem at all," Peyton answered, looking more than a little relieved.

Was it because she wouldn't be left alone with him, that they'd have Ellie as a buffer between them? Galen gave an internal shrug. Whatever; it didn't matter as long as this worked out. Ellie already liked his new bride. She was a bright kid and knowing she liked Peyton was half the battle won. If they could cement that into something strong and lasting—a family unit that would make her feel loved and secure for the rest of her childhood—then he would have succeeded in fulfilling the promise he'd made to his two dead friends as they were laid to rest. Failure was not an option.

"Are you curious about where we're going?"

"I'm assuming it's somewhere warm. I was told to pack light clothing and swimwear."

"It's perpetually warm. We're off to a Horvath resort a little over two and a half thousand miles east-southeast of here," he teased.

"That would be your resort on Maui, right?"

"You've been doing your research on us," he answered, surprised at her very specific response.

Her cheeks colored. "Research? What makes you think that?"

She sounded defensive. Definitely not what he'd been hoping for just before they left to change for travel.

"Let's just say I'm not used to people being as well-informed about my business as you apparently are," he said, attempting to soothe her.

"Information is my business," she said smoothly, her demeanor relaxing slightly.

"And your business is?"

"I'm a reporter, freelance."

"A travel reporter? We've been featured in quite a few magazines and blogs. Maybe you've been our guest before?"

She shook her head. "No, not travel. Didn't you say we needed to go and change?"

Her subject switch was about as subtle as dropping an old typewriter from the top of a tall building onto the pavement below. But he wasn't slow to take a hint and he had plenty of time to get to know her better.

"We do. A chopper is taking us to SeaTac in about an hour."

"It doesn't take me an hour to get ready," Peyton answered with a gurgle of laughter. "Do I look that high-maintenance?"

Her laugh was intoxicating, the first sign of unfettered emotion he'd seen in her so far. He knew he wanted more of it, more of her being natural, being herself.

"Well, we might be able to go earlier, provided we can say goodbye to our guests without too many holdups. It won't change our departure time from SeaTac, though—the flight plan has already been filed. We're taking one of our company jets."

"How the other half lives, huh?" she said, softening her words with a smile.

"You're a part of that now. Flight time is about six hours once we're wheels up."

"How late will it be when we arrive?"

"Hawaii's three hours behind us, so, all going smoothly, about seven p.m."

"It's going to be a long day for Ellie."

"She'll be okay. She was used to traveling with her parents and can sleep on the flight if she wants to. You can, too."

She shook her head. "Sadly, I'm one of those who can never sleep on a plane."

"Always vigilant?"

"Something like that. Well, I guess we'd better get on our way, then?"

"Let me see you up to your room," he said, taking her arm. "Did you want to throw your bouquet first?"

She shrugged. "Sure."

"Give me a minute to get it organized."

"I'll go get the bouquet."

He watched as she glided across the room toward the main table where she'd left her flowers. The gentle sway of her hips totally mesmerized him.

"Nice wife," his brother, Valentin, said as he approached.

"It's a good thing you have your own, or I'd be making you keep your eyes off mine."

"And I wouldn't trade her for the world."

Galen heard the intense emotion in Valentin's words. He and Imogene had been married once before, and until Nagy had reunited them in a Match Made in Marriage wedding, they'd both been unhappy. Now they were together again, for good this time, and Galen felt a glimmer of envy—wishing he, too, could experience the kind of relationship they had. But his bed had been made for him when he'd agreed to be Ellie's guardian and then signed up to find a wife so Ellie could feel safe again. He wasn't expecting romance and roses. What he needed for his best girl was stability, and hopefully, he could achieve that with Peyton.

"Peyton's going to toss her bouquet soon. I need to let the emcee know so he can make the announcement."

"Watch out for the stampede of cousins." Valentin laughed, but then his expression grew serious. "Galen, I just wanted to say a few private words."

"And they are?"

"We only get one shot at life, so we need to make the most of every minute. You're going to hit some roadblocks in this marriage, that's a given, but you need to be prepared to work through every one of them."

"I'm not afraid of hard work. You know that."

"Yeah, I know. I wish you a lifetime of happiness."

Valentin wrapped his arms around him in a fierce hug and Galen gave him back as good as he got. "Thanks, Val," he said, his voice suddenly thick with emotion. "I'm going to do my best."

"You're going to need to. Marrying someone you already know and love isn't always easy, but marrying a stranger…"

Galen looked across the room to where Peyton had been corralled by some of his aunties. "Yeah, but what a stranger, right?"

His brother slapped him on the back with another laugh then left him to find the emcee.

Valentin hadn't been wrong about the stampede. All their female cousins together with several women he'd never met before tonight, mostly Peyton's guests, jostled for the moment she released the bouquet. The scramble was both undignified and highly amusing, but Galen was shocked when he saw his nerdy IT expert cousin, Sophia, emerge triumphant at the end. He took advantage of the ensuing chaos to take Peyton by the hand and, calling out a good-night to everyone, lead her away.

"Ellie knows we're coming back for her, right?" Peyton looked worried.

Galen was touched at her concern for a child she'd only just met. "Of course. Her suitcase is already in the chopper. She knows I won't leave her behind. Ilya, my cousin, and his wife, Yasmin, will bring her to the helipad just before we're due to depart. For now she can party it up a little with my younger cousins."

"You do have a big family," Peyton commented.

"Yeah, I do. And you? Brothers? Sisters?"

She shook her head. "Just me…and my dad," she added.

"He couldn't come today?"

Her lips firmed into a straight line. "It's difficult—we barely talk. I'd rather not discuss it."

He wanted to press for more details, but one look at her face made him file that away for another time. Bit by bit, he was learning there were going to be a hell of a lot of layers to peel through to get to the core of what made up his new wife. It was probably a good thing that he was a patient man.

Three

Peyton pushed her hair off her face for the hundredth time. The onshore breeze delighted in tangling her hair at every opportunity, but it wasn't all bad. At least the wind was warm and gentle, not damp and biting cold like it so often was back home in Washington. After their arrival last night she'd been bone weary and had barely paid any attention to their luxurious surroundings. She didn't know what she'd expected exactly, when Galen had said they'd be honeymooning at a Horvath resort, but this certainly hadn't been it. It wasn't a hotel, although there apparently was one here somewhere in the many sprawling acres of the complex, but a large and airy house that faced the water and was full of dazzling sunshine. She'd been relieved to discover they each had their own bedroom, too, along with their own private beach, where Ellie was busy digging holes and creating roads and moats and tunnels, and squealing happily at the rising tide as it demolished her hard work.

"Can I braid your hair for you?" Galen asked from the sun lounger beside her.

"You?" Peyton was surprised by the offer.

"I'll have you know I've become quite adept at styling long hair. I don't even have to use a vacuum cleaner hose to get Ellie's ponytail perfect anymore."

"A what?"

"Check it out online. I tell you, YouTube is king when it comes to learning new skills."

She couldn't help but laugh at the idea of Galen even knowing how to use a vacuum cleaner, let alone having the skills to use a vacuum cleaner to tie Ellie's hair in a ponytail. But she was always up for a challenge and, heck, let's face it, she was curious to see how he proposed to tame her tangled locks.

"Okay, then. Show me your talents," Peyton said, sitting up on her lounger and turning her back to him.

"Now, there's an invitation I don't get every day," he said, his voice dropping an octave.

She couldn't help it; her body reacted with a shimmer of desire. She had no words to describe it, this stupid reaction to a tone of voice, but suddenly she was hyperaware of the man as he moved closer behind her. She dug into her beach bag for her hairbrush.

"You might want to use this first," she said, passing it back to him. "There's a hair tie on the handle, too."

He took the hairbrush, and the next moment his fingers were working their way through her hair, touching her scalp and skimming the back of her neck as he eased the hairbrush through the knots. She'd never in her life believed that having her hair brushed by a stranger could feel erotic. But there was something deeply sensual about the way Galen followed each stroke of the brush with the touch of his fingers on her scalp. It made her want to sigh with pleasure.

When he was done, she was on the verge of becoming putty in his hands. She felt a moment's relief that she was facing away from him so he couldn't see the way her nipples had become taut peaks against the thin fabric of her one-piece swimsuit in response to this most innocent of touches. But then he started to run his fingers through her hair again and every muscle in her body clenched.

"You okay? I'm not hurting you, am I?" Galen asked.

He was so close she felt his breath on her shoulder and shivered a little.

"I'm fine," she said in a voice that was tight with control.

He was simply doing her hair, for goodness' sake. Not seducing her. How this normal, everyday act could be playing such havoc with her senses was beyond her but she needed to get herself under control. She focused her gaze on Ellie and for a moment envied her the freedom of not caring who she was or what she looked like or what hurts had been visited upon her. Instead, she could just be carefree and in the moment. Industrious one minute, lying flat out on the sand the next, then laughing as she got to her feet and plunged into the water to wash off the sand five seconds later.

Galen began sectioning her hair.

"Do you want under or over?" he asked.

"I beg your pardon?"

"Your braid. Under, so it sits flat, or over, so it sits on top?"

"I never knew there was a difference."

"Your mom never did this for you?"

"My mom was sick for a long time, and my dad, well, let's just say he didn't have the benefit of online videos when I was growing up."

She swallowed against the surprising wave of emotion that choked her. There'd been days when her mom could meet her at the front door of their rented home with a smile and then there'd been others when she couldn't even raise a hand to wipe a tear from her cheek. The disease that had plagued her had taken its toll on everyone, and the fiercely guarded memories of those times always shook Peyton to the core.

"Anyway, does it matter?" she said a little more sharply than she'd intended.

"Over it is. And tomorrow we can go into the intricacies of the herringbone braid. Now, be still. I need to concentrate on this."

He fell silent as he worked. When it was over, he rested his hands on top of her shoulders. His palms were warm and his fingers gentle, but to her they felt like brands on her bare skin.

"Admiring your handiwork?" she asked with a note of sarcasm.

"Something like that. Did you know that you have these really soft curls of baby hair that grow at the nape of your neck?"

She shivered as he touched them, winding one around a finger. His knuckle brushed the back of her neck, sending her body into sensation overload. Who knew the back of her neck was so sensitive? Then her whole body went into shock as she felt the imprint of his lips right there at her nape. She bolted up from her lounger in an instinctive attempt to create more distance between them and adjusted her sunglasses on her face as she turned around and looked down on him.

Galen looked up at her unashamedly. "Sorry, couldn't help myself."

He flashed her another of those devil-may-care grins and rose from his lounger before jogging along the beach to where Ellie was fashioning a turtle sand sculpture. Peyton watched him join his ward with an enthusiasm she envied. Even in the short time she'd begun to get to know him, she recognized he had a knack for making everything look so uncomplicated. No doubt he was the life and soul of every party he attended, she thought with a touch of venom. The charmed billionaire who never had a care in his privileged world. He'd never had to come from school to a quiet house and wonder if today would be the day that he'd discover his mom dead in her bed. Or that the next knock on the door was from the sheriff to evict them from another home.

And then again, he'd known loss, she reminded herself with an effort to be fair. Ellie's parents' deaths had obviously affected him, and her research had uncovered he'd lost his own father when he was in his early teens. That must have been hard. Maybe his carefree act was just that. An act. She shrugged, picked up her sarong and knotted it at her hip before pushing her feet into a pair of crystal-studded thongs and walking along the beach to supervise the sculpting. Whether it was an act or not, it didn't matter to her because she wasn't here to enjoy Galen Horvath's company. She was here to do a job and she needed to remember that.

It was midnight, and Galen was mentally worn out and physically uncomfortable. There ought to be a law against suits and ties in tropical climates, he thought as he unknotted his tie and entered the villa that was home for the duration of their honeymoon.

"Good of you to come back." An acerbic voice came from the depths of the overstuffed couch facing the moonlit water. "I was beginning to wonder if you'd left us for good."

"Did you miss me?" Galen said, refusing to rise to Peyton's bait.

The woman had been so intent on keeping her distance

from him that he'd almost begun to wonder if she'd even miss him when he had to work. Of course, working on honeymoon was not ideal, but the resort was on the verge of signing an agreement for a major expansion with an overseas partner, and certain things needed to be dealt with right here, right now.

"Ellie missed you," Peyton said, rising from the couch and facing him with her hands on her hips.

Galen's throat went dry as he took her in. She was silhouetted in the light behind her, exposing the slim, lean lines of her body beneath the sheer cream on the lemon-patterned sundress she wore. He'd seen her in her swimsuit and, yes, she was incredible to look at. But like this? She was mystery and mayhem all in one package. The sharp sound of her voice dragged him into reality.

"I was beginning to wonder if you'd married me just so you could have a babysitter. I have to say, if that's your parenting style, I feel sorry for Ellie because she deserves better than that."

Deserved better than him, too, perhaps? Galen felt his anger rise but, as ever, he pushed a lid down firmly on it and deflected her words with a smile. "Ellie knew I would be tied up all day."

"It doesn't mean she didn't miss you. She gets really anxious when you're not around. Did you know that?"

A shaft of guilt struck him in the chest. The last thing on earth he ever wanted to do was cause Ellie any distress. "What do you mean exactly?"

"She sounded tense at dinnertime, asking when you'd be back. I tried to distract her. Let her beat me at cards."

"Let her?" He cocked a half grin. The kid was a demon at cards.

"Okay, so she thrashed me. But when you weren't home

by bedtime she got really upset. She was terrified something had happened to you, no matter what I said."

Galen nodded, accepting that he should have reached out to let her know he wouldn't be home until very late. Even though she'd been in his care for several months now, he was still adjusting to the responsibility. But they'd already been here on Maui for three days and Ellie had seemed equally happy to be with Peyton as with him—he'd been certain she'd be okay. Clearly, he'd been wrong.

"I'm sorry. I'll talk to her about it tomorrow."

"Would that be before or after your next business meeting?"

A kernel of warmth sparked to life deep inside him. Peyton might be angry at him but she was very firmly in Ellie's corner and that was what he'd hoped for all along—that he'd marry a woman who'd be comfortable in a maternal role with Ellie.

"There won't be any more business meetings. I promise. Not while we're on honeymoon, anyway."

"Until the next emergency arises and you need to offload your responsibilities again?"

He fought to keep his features neutral as he replied. "I don't make a habit of offloading anything. I'm sorry if caring for Ellie was such a burden to you."

Color flamed in her cheeks and her eyes grew bright. She looked like she was about to light off like a firecracker. Before she could respond, he put up a hand.

"Look, I'm sorry—that was uncalled for. I shouldn't have assumed that you'd look after Ellie when I couldn't."

"You don't even know me," Peyton said, a grimace twisting her beautiful face.

Galen walked closer to her and took one of her hands. "You're right. I don't know you, yet. I do, however, know you're trustworthy. We wouldn't have been matched if you weren't."

Peyton nodded ever so slightly. "She was upset tonight, Galen. I hated it."

Compassion flooded him and he squeezed her hand gently. "You feel so helpless, don't you?"

The anger that had been holding her rigid dropped out of her just like that.

"Yes, and I didn't like it. I'm sorry I took it out on you. But don't think I'm letting you off the hook."

"I know, and I'll make it up to both of you. I am a man of my word, Peyton. No more business on this vacation."

"Thank you."

She pulled her hand free and started to gather up her things, including some handwritten notes and a laptop computer.

"You were working?" he asked.

"Not until Ellie went to bed, which was only a couple of hours ago because she was so upset."

"I didn't mean it like that—no need to be defensive."

She raised her brows at him.

"I didn't. I'm merely interested. Is this a new article you're working on?"

"I don't discuss my work until it's published."

Peyton hugged her things to her as if hiding them from his gaze. Fair enough, but she was making it very difficult for them to find common ground for discussion and to get to know one another. So far both family and her work were off-limits. So what did that leave them? Not a lot.

"I can respect that. Your work is sensitive, then?"

"Usually, and this is particularly so. I'm not being obstructive. It's just the way I work. Okay?"

"Like I said, no problem. Hey, would you like to put your

things away where my prying eyes can't see them and come and join me on the patio for a nightcap?"

She hesitated. He was beginning to brace himself for a flat no, when she nodded and said she'd be right back. Galen shrugged out of his jacket and yanked the tail of his tie through his collar. Valentin had been right. This marriage thing wasn't easy, especially when you were married to a stranger.

The other day, brushing her hair, he'd felt as though they'd reached a new level of closeness. But apparently going to work today had thrown all of that out the window and he was back to square one. He had to make this work, for Ellie. He felt a pang of guilt as he threw his things on a chair and went down the hallway toward Ellie's bedroom.

Since her parents' accident she'd been sleeping with a night-light and her door slightly ajar. He entered her room and settled gently on the edge of her bed. Ellie's eyes flashed wide open in an instant.

"You're home!" She sat bolt upright and her little arms wrapped around his neck.

His heart squeezed tight and he hugged her back. "Yeah, I'm home, so no more worrying, okay? I thought we had a deal. You're supposed to talk to me about the things that make you feel upset."

"I know," she said softly as she pulled away. "It's just hard when you're not here."

"I'm sorry I was gone so long today. It won't happen again while we're on vacation, I promise, but it will probably happen again when we're home. But I promise you this, too. I'll make sure you're never alone and you can always get whoever is with you to text me at any time."

"Even when you're in an important meeting?"

"Even then. Nothing and no one is more important to me than you, Ellie. I'm here for you. Always."

"Okay," she said on a yawn.

"Now, back to sleep, young lady. Tomorrow is a new day."

"Thanks, Galen. I love you."

"I love you, too, kiddo."

Galen pressed one more kiss to her forehead and then rose from the bed. She was already asleep by the time he got to the door. He looked back on her, his heart so full of love for this little girl it sometimes took his breath away. Moments like this reaffirmed he had done the right thing in marrying Peyton. Ellie had endured more upheaval than any child her age should have to bear. She deserved a family that could love and support her through life. He only hoped that Peyton's defensiveness on Ellie's behalf this evening showed she felt exactly the same way.

Four

Peyton slipped back into her room, worried that she might be caught eavesdropping on the tender exchange between Galen and Ellie. She hadn't expected it of him, and that shocked her a little.

She reached for a tissue and brushed away her tears. Theirs appeared to be a very special relationship and for some stupid reason it left her feeling as if she was very much an outsider. That had never bothered her before. She'd always been an outsider after the shame of her father's dismissal from Horvath Corporation. Then in the new town they eventually settled in on the Oregon coast, she hadn't fit in, either. She'd had city girl written all over her in the tight-knit community where fishing and tourism were the main industries. Even when she'd gone to Washington for college she'd been an outsider, a fact that had worked in her favor when she'd hidden her pregnancy and subsequent adoption of her baby. Being an outsider came naturally to her now. It afforded her powers of observation she wouldn't have enjoyed otherwise. She even preferred it, she told herself as she reapplied her lipstick before returning to meet Galen for that drink.

But then why did it still have the capacity to hurt so much? Was it that her own child would be around Ellie's age? Was it because each day she was facing all that she'd given away? Peyton slammed a lid on those thoughts before they could drive her crazy. She'd made her choice, the best one she could for her child at the time. Even in the years immediately after the adoption there was no way she could have supported a child. Things had changed now, of course. Her work had paid extremely well at times. And the payday from the exposé on Alice Horvath would be huge, too. Horvath Corporation was global, but the company itself had never been her target. Just Alice. She'd been the one to arbitrarily destroy Peyton's father's career and, consequently, everything about Peyton's life that she'd held dear.

Keep focused, she told herself, sealing away her emotions behind the virtual locked door she always kept them in. She didn't have time to dwell on the child she'd given away; she didn't have time to dwell on the sense of living on the outside edge of everything she'd thought she'd wanted as a child. She had a job to do and she was going to do it. She straightened her shoulders and gave herself a brief nod in the mirror. She had this.

The night air out on the patio was balmy and redolent with the scent of frangipani. Peyton inhaled deeply and sighed out loud.

"Is it always this blissful here?" she asked.

"Yes. Even in the worst weather there's a raw beauty about the place that always gets to me and soothes me deep inside. It's my refuge when life gets too crazy."

"I had no idea you needed one," she commented as she

lowered herself into a rattan chair and stared out at the dark purple and midnight blue sea.

"Everyone does from time to time. It's all about having a coping mechanism."

"Then you're luckier than most to have this." She flung her arm out to encapsulate the view beyond them. "I'm sorry about before," she said, deciding to take the bull by the horns. "For implying you were derelict in your duty toward Ellie."

"Apology accepted."

"I was pissy because I missed you, too."

Where the heck had that come from? Peyton swallowed hard, barely able to believe the words she'd just spoken. But she knew they were true. She hated realizing that she'd come to look forward to seeing his sunny smile. The man was addictive and she now totally understood his popularity with her sex. It didn't mean she wanted to jump his bones, but she'd be lying to herself if she didn't admit she found him attractive.

Okay, she was lying to herself that she didn't want to jump his bones. If their circumstances had been different, a brief fling with Galen Horvath would have been an amusing breath of fresh air. But that wasn't possible and she needed to keep her mind on the game.

"I'm flattered," Galen responded with a slight duck of his head.

Was that a flush of color on his cheeks she discerned in the gentle patio lighting? Surely, she hadn't embarrassed him with her unexpected honesty. Definitely time for a subject change. "So, what do you recommend for a nightcap?"

"Whatever you fancy. I like to unwind with a good cognac from time to time but an Irish whiskey cream on ice works, too."

"I'll go with the Irish whiskey cream on ice."

She watched him as he moved to the small bar off to one side of the covered patio. All his movements were inherently masculine yet graceful at the same time. Her insides clenched on an unexpected wave of need. No matter how sternly she spoke to herself, it seemed her body had a completely different agenda.

Staring at the sea was infinitely safer than staring at her husband, so she turned her gaze back to the water. The clink of ice against the side of a glass heralded his return.

"Tell me more about you," Galen said as he handed her a drink, then pulled a chair up close to hers and sat.

All she had to do was point her toes and she'd be touching him, she realized as she accepted the glass. It would take a minimum of effort to run her foot up his calf, then higher still. She curled her bare toes tight against the warm tiled floor of the patio before she could act on her imagination.

"What do you want to know?" she hedged before taking a sip of her drink.

"Where did you grow up?"

This could be tricky and potentially lead her into a discussion she wasn't ready to have. "Oh, California for a bit, then Oregon."

"I grew up in California, too, not far from Santa Barbara. You?"

"Oh, nowhere near there," she lied. "Is everyone in your family expected to work for the Horvath Corporation?" she asked, changing the subject.

"Not necessarily, but we all benefit from the company's successes, so it makes sense to contribute to them, too. Some of my cousins work in other fields, though, like Dani. She's a vet in Ojai. But you were supposed to be telling me about yourself."

Peyton had the grace to look abashed. "Sorry, I have
a habit of taking charge of conversations. Occupational
hazard."

She'd gone too far, too quickly, and hastened to lighten
the mood before he closed up on her completely.

"You have a big family. Have you all always been close?
I can't imagine what that's like. Part of me envies you. The
other part shrinks in horror at the thought of having to share
everything with everyone and not having privacy."

Galen laughed. She liked the sound and wanted to make
him laugh more. "Well, the only thing, or person, we ever
had to share was Nagy, and our grandfather, too, when he
was alive. We all lived fairly close to one another, so it was
normal for us to cross each other's paths at school or be on
the same sports teams. Every Sunday Nagy had an open
invitation for everyone to come and visit and eat with her.
Still does. It's always slightly chaotic, but it's good to be
together when we can attend—to be around the people you
know will always have your back, no matter what."

"That must be nice," Peyton said with a touch of envy.

It was one thing to grow up with privilege like Galen
had, but another to have that close sense of family, too. Her
father had alienated his own family in the early years of
his marriage to her mom, who had in turn been disowned
for marrying him. Once her mom was gone there had only
been the two of them. Her father's bitterness about the circumstances of his life had made him a hard man to live
with. Happiness didn't come easily to him even now. Peyton
had always hoped that she'd get glimpses of the man he'd
used to be before he was let go from Horvath Corporation.
The one who'd played with her before dinner and tucked
her into bed at night. But after her mother's diagnosis of
multiple sclerosis, he'd changed. He'd become intense and
driven and distant—and he'd never shaken those traits off

since. His bitterness had become such an intrinsic part of him she'd almost forgotten the lighthearted man he'd been so long ago.

"Deep in thought?" Galen prompted her.

"Yeah, not good ones, either. My upbringing was very different from yours. My mom became ill when I was still in elementary school. It changed things at home. Then when we moved to Oregon she got worse."

"I'm sorry."

His simple words, genuinely spoken, struck at her heart. He was a good man. Empathetic without being intrusive.

"It was all a long time ago. I coped."

"So what made you want to be a journalist?"

She laughed. "I used to drive my parents nuts by always wanting to know the why of everything. That need to know and expose everything at its root has never left me."

"That would explain your interrogation style," he teased.

"Hey, I apologized for that."

"No problem. It's good for people to be passionate about what they do."

Passionate. She could so easily be passionate about him. He was a good listener, all too easy on the eye, and he made her want to do things with him she hadn't done in a long time. Her relationships with men were usually short-lived. She didn't give a lot of herself. Physically, sure, no problem, but she wasn't into emotions. And yet, with Galen, she'd already begun to run the gamut of them. She'd expected this to be a very personal assignment and she'd taken strength from the fact that she'd never had trouble keeping her mind on the job before. But there was something about Galen that all too easily distracted her.

She swirled the melting ice in her drink then lifted the glass to her lips to finish it off. "Well, I'm feeling tired. I think it's time to call it a night."

"Yeah, me too. Thanks for helping me unwind. I appreciate it."

"It was a tough day?"

"Yeah, but tomorrow's all about you guys. We'd better get some sleep so we can make the most of it."

"Good idea. What were you thinking for tomorrow?"

"Not sure. Maybe we can let Ellie plan the day."

"She'd like that."

They both stood and Peyton took their empty glasses to the kitchen.

"Leave it," he said, following her. "We do have staff."

"I know, but I'll never get used to people picking up after me. It was drilled into me from an early age to take responsibility for myself. It stuck."

She rinsed the glasses and put them in the dishwasher.

"Good night," she said as she straightened from the dishwasher and started to leave the kitchen.

"Yeah, see you in the morning."

As she passed close by him, she caught the faint scent of his cologne and felt her body react to it. That all-too-familiar tingling in her muscles. The hyperawareness of his proximity. All she had to do was stop in her tracks and turn and face him and she had no doubt he'd do the rest. Instead, she kept walking until she reached her room. Her heart pounded in her chest as she closed the door and leaned against it, trying to understand his effect on her. He was just a man, right?

Peyton pushed away from the door and got ready for bed with the words *Yeah, right* echoing in the back of her mind.

Five

"Come on, sleepyheads!" Galen knocked on first Ellie's and then Peyton's bedroom doors. "We've got a gorgeous day. Let's make the most of it."

"I'm ready!" Ellie said, bounding out of her room and wrapping her arms around his waist in a big hug.

A lump formed in his throat. This kid, she'd been through so much and her strength never failed to amaze him.

"And what exactly are you ready for, kiddo?" he asked, hugging her back.

"Shopping!"

"You want to go shopping today? Anywhere in particular?"

"Ala Moana," Ellie piped up excitedly. "Then lunch on the beach at Waikiki."

"Sounds like a grand plan," Galen answered with a smile.

He made a mental note to book a chopper to fly them

over to Oahu after breakfast. As if Ellie could read his mind, she piped up again.

"What's for breakfast?" she asked. "Where's Peyton?"

"Leilani is making pancakes. You want to go help? I'll check on Peyton."

"Pancakes! My favorite!"

And she was gone, just like that. Some days he envied her energy and wondered how on earth he would keep up with her. Galen turned back to Peyton's bedroom door and knocked again. When there was no answer, he carefully opened the door. Her bed was empty, the sheets tangled as if she'd had a restless sleep. Her laptop was open on the desk facing the ocean. Maybe she'd been working during the night, he thought as he went into the room and wandered over to the desk. He started as he heard the bathroom door open behind him.

"Galen? What are you doing in here?"

"Sorry to invade your privacy," he said quickly. "I hope you're decent?"

"Decent enough," Peyton said from close by.

Her arm snaked out and she pushed the laptop closed before he could read what was on the screen. Her bare skin was still sprinkled with droplets of water from her shower, he noted. His mouth dried as the urge to lick those tiny droplets from her flooded his mind.

"Ellie's gone to breakfast. I just wanted to make sure you were up," he continued, turning to face her.

"As you can see, I am."

She was wrapped in nothing but a towel. Granted, the towel was huge, but the knowledge that she was naked beneath it made every cell in his body jump to urgent attention.

"I'll, ah, leave you to get dressed, then. We'll probably be taking off in forty-five minutes."

"Taking off?"

"Ellie has prescribed shopping followed by lunch on the beach at Waikiki."

Peyton shook her head slightly.

"You having second thoughts about today?" he asked.

"No, I just can't quite get used to the idea that you can island-hop on a whim. Don't mind me."

But he did mind her. A gentleman would leave her to dry herself off and get dressed. He did not want to be a gentleman right now.

"Stick with me. You'll get used to anything," he teased with a fake salacious twirl of an imaginary mustache.

She smiled but he noticed it didn't touch her eyes, which had shadows under them. She looked weary. Without thinking, he reached up to cradle her face with one hand.

"You didn't sleep well?"

"Are you saying I look like a hag?"

He chuckled. "That would be the definition of impossible. But you do look tired. Everything okay?"

Her eyes shuttered for a moment. Then she looked directly back at him. "Everything is fine, really. I had a lot going through my head last night, so, no, I didn't sleep well. I decided to do some work instead."

"You're okay for today, though, right?"

"Wouldn't miss it for the world."

He wasn't imagining it. She was saying the right words, but there was no inflection, no meaning or enthusiasm behind them.

"Okay, this time I'm really leaving you to get dressed. I'd better go and make sure Ellie doesn't hoover up all the pancakes."

Peyton nodded and turned back to the bathroom. He watched her go. The woman was a puzzle. And his wife. She was so different from what he'd been expecting in a bride. What had Nagy been thinking when she'd approved their match? On the surface they looked good together; he knew that as surely as he knew his nose sat in the center of his face. But what lay beneath the surface? She wasn't the easiest person to get to know and sometimes he felt as if she didn't want him to know who she was deep down. If that was the case, why had she married? Surely, marriage, especially an arranged marriage, was built on a foundation of common ground. If you couldn't find that common ground because one partner was flat-out withholding everything about themselves, then where did you start?

Galen slid his phone from his pocket as he walked from Peyton's room and called the pilot on standby for the resort to schedule their flight to Oahu. Once that was done, he joined Ellie in the kitchen. He hadn't been there long before Peyton joined them. She must have applied some kind of concealer because the shadows under her eyes weren't so obvious now. She stroked Ellie's hair as she sat down at the table with them.

"Did you leave me any pancakes?" she said, leaning over to bump shoulders with Ellie.

"Of course I did. And bacon, too. Do you like bacon?"

"Everything's better with bacon," Peyton said, nodding fiercely.

Galen felt himself smile. Even though they hadn't known each other long, Ellie and Peyton appeared to have formed a bond already and, he realized, it made him feel less alone on this new journey of parenting a youngster. Quite frankly, this whole parenting thing terrified him. He loved Ellie as if she was his own daughter, had from the moment he'd held her in his arms the week Nick and Sarah had brought her home. He hadn't expected to feel that bond with someone else's child. He hadn't expected to feel that bond with any child, because deep down he'd never expected to have a family of his own.

After seeing Ilya lose his dad and then losing his own father less than a year later to the same congenital heart defect that had also robbed them of their grandfather, Galen had learned firsthand how loving and losing someone could damage a person. Destroy them, too. It had made him fearful of this thing called love and caused him to shield his emotions, to keep things very much on the surface when it came to relationships. He never allowed himself to actually fall in love. But with Ellie it had been different. He'd held that tiny, helpless babe in his arms and known that for her whole life he would be at her service.

He watched Peyton interacting with Ellie as he sipped his coffee and wondered if his love could grow for this woman, too. Attraction certainly had. Even now he felt hyperaware of her and could barely take his eyes from her as she ate her breakfast.

Every movement Peyton made had a purpose; there was nothing about her that was wasteful or flamboyant. Most people he knew talked with their hands to a degree, but Peyton was always physically composed, giving off a sense of calm that he suspected was a front for a much deeper and more complex mind than she had revealed to him yet.

"Earth to Galen!" Ellie's voice intruded on his thoughts. "You know you're staring. Mommy always said that's not polite."

"And she was right, except when a man stares at his wife," Galen said, putting down his coffee mug on the tabletop with a click. He was a little embarrassed to have been caught out by the nine-year-old and met Peyton's gaze across the table. "Isn't that right, Peyton?"

"I guess so. I never gave it much thought."

Galen's phone beeped, distracting him. "Excuse me,

ladies, I believe that's our reminder to be at the helipad in about fifteen minutes. Is that long enough for you both to finish getting ready?"

"I'm already ready," Ellie declared. "Although I haven't got any money. It's going to be hard to shop without money, isn't it?"

"I'll take care of that for you," Galen assured her. "First stop, an ATM. I'll give you an allowance that you can spend on whatever you want."

Peyton's brows drew together and she looked as if she wanted to say something.

"What?" he asked as Ellie got up and left the table to go brush her teeth.

"It's nothing."

"Clearly, it's something. You look as if you disapprove of me giving Ellie an allowance."

"I just wonder how she'll ever learn the value of money if you just give it to her."

"So you think I need to make her work for it? Kind of mean when we're on honeymoon, don't you think?"

"Look, it wasn't my place to say anything but you did ask."

"I did, and don't worry. This is an indulgence, but she won't grow up expecting handouts every five minutes. I never did and I'd like to think my parents set a good enough example to me that I can continue that with Ellie."

"I've offended you. I apologize."

Offended him? Yeah, maybe. She sure knew how to push his buttons, but he wasn't going to make a big deal of it.

"It's okay. You need to know you can talk to me about anything, Peyton. We're a couple. We should be able to discuss stuff. As time goes on, we'll learn to make decisions together. It's new for us both."

She pushed her chair back and picked up her plate, knife and fork. "You're right. I overreacted. I just—"

He waited for her to continue but she shook her head and took her things to the kitchen counter. Galen stood and followed suit.

"You just…?" he prompted.

She shook her head again. "No, it's nothing. I had a very different upbringing, is all."

Peyton pushed by him and he was left watching her retreating back, again. It seemed to be a trend. Just when he thought he was making headway with her and carefully peeling back a layer to expose some truth about her, she slammed that layer back down with superglue. That made him want to try even harder to understand what made his new wife tick—and he was nothing if not persistent.

Peyton watched Ellie skipping just ahead of Galen and her as they meandered along the white sand of Waikiki Beach. The shopping expedition had gone better than she'd expected. Instead of Galen just peeling off bills and giving them to Ellie, he'd made a point of buying her a cute little shoulder bag and a wallet and then given her some cash he'd drawn from an ATM. Then they'd discussed what she wanted to shop for and traipsed around the mall while she compared prices and eventually made a few purchases. He'd been so patient and Peyton found herself admiring his manner with the girl, even going so far as wishing her dad could have been more like him when she was growing up.

But her circumstances had been vastly different and her father had never had the kind of money at his disposal that Galen had.

"I've made a reservation at the restaurant up there." He gestured at a spot up the beach. "I hope you're both hungry."

"Surprisingly, even after that massive breakfast, yes, I am," Peyton answered.

"Galen! Look out there. Can we do that after lunch?" Ellie was pointing to a wharf jutting out from the sand.

"What is it?" Galen asked.

"The boat takes you out to a submarine and you get to go a hundred feet under the water. Can we do it, please?"

"I don't think—" Peyton started.

"Sure," Galen said at the same time.

"You're not serious, are you?" Peyton said.

"Oh, please, Peyton. It'll be such fun," Ellie pleaded, pointing to the giant sandwich board showing pictures of the underwater experience. "Please?"

"You guys can do it without me," Peyton said firmly.

Silence fell between them and Peyton could feel Ellie's disappointment. When the restaurant's maître d' showed them to their beachfront table, Galen snagged Peyton's arm and held her back a little. Ellie looked at them.

"Let me talk to Peyton a minute. You go on to the table. We'll be right there, okay?" Galen suggested to the girl. "It's okay. I've got my eye on you."

Peyton felt her entire body stiffen. What did he plan to do? Persuade her that she had to do this thing that Ellie so keenly wanted to do. Hell, no.

"Look, you two can go together. I'm quite happy waiting on the beach."

"No, if we do it, we'll all do it. Can you tell me why you're so afraid?"

"I'm not."

"Don't lie to me, Peyton. I saw the way you reacted the moment Ellie suggested it. It's quite safe, you know. They run operations like this in a few locations."

"And I'm sure they can manage to continue without my patronage."

"You don't want to disappoint Ellie, do you?"

Peyton glared at him. "She won't be disappointed if you take her, will she?"

Galen's voice took on a cajoling tone. "Seems to me that yesterday you were all about us spending time together. The three of us, right?"

"You spending all day at work does not compare to me staying on the beach while you and Ellie do the tourist thing."

"Tell me, Peyton. What is it that freaks you out so much? You strike me as an incredibly brave woman. One who wouldn't let the little things get in your way. After all, you agreed to marry me, sight unseen."

"This isn't the same."

She watched as he waved to Ellie, who'd been settled at an umbrella-shaded table and was staring at the two of them.

"We should go and join her," Peyton said, keen to end the discussion.

"Why won't you tell me?" Galen said softly. "Is it really that bad?"

She shivered in the balmy temperature and tried not to think about the incident soon after her mother's diagnosis that had made her so afraid of enclosed spaces.

"Fine, I'll do it."

"You don't need to make it sound like I'm leading you to imminent doom."

"I said I'll do it, okay?"

"I'll be there with you. You won't regret it."

She doubted that very much. At the very least, she hoped she didn't do something to shame herself. Being shut in an old refrigerator by the neighborhood kids growing up had been one thing, but that sense of being closed in, in the dark, and feeling like every last breath of air was being squeezed out of her lungs had been quite another. All she could think about was what her dad had told her the night before. That her mom was slowly dying and one day they'd have to say goodbye to her, so they had to make the most of every minute she had above ground. Thinking about her mom being in a coffin—with no light, no air—had freaked her out and she'd panicked and begun frantically hammering on the door. And then the unthinkable had happened. As she'd begun to believe she was really going to die, she'd peed herself—a fact that didn't go unnoticed when the other kids finally let her out.

The shame of that moment had been bad enough, but her father's disapproval when she'd run home to tell him what had happened had been what had struck deepest. She could still see the disgust on his face when he realized she'd wet herself. He wasn't interested in why. Wasn't interested in drying her tears. He'd curtly told her to clean herself up and to make sure nothing like that ever happened again. So she had. And she'd avoided enclosed spaces ever since.

"Come on," Galen said, taking her by the hand. "Let's eat."

"I'm not sure that's a good idea before going in the water, is it?" she said half-jokingly, but in actual fact, wondering how the heck she was going to choke anything down at all.

"Hey, sailors do it all the time. It'll be fine, trust me."

"Trust you? I barely know you."

"But we're working on it, right? Building memories together. Getting to know one another. That's what it's all about, isn't it?"

Was it? Maybe for normal people in a normal relationship. But she wasn't there under a normal pretext, and she'd do well to remember that.

Six

He had understood her reluctance to enter the submarine. After all, everyone had their thing that they hated. But he'd underestimated the level of sheer terror that Peyton would experience. The entire journey, her body had been rigid beside him, her hands clenched on her knees—to stop the trembling, no doubt. While Ellie had been wide-eyed with amazement at the world beneath the sea, his gaze had been fixed on Peyton. Eventually, he'd reached across and taken one of her hands in his and begun to gently stroke his fingers across her white knuckles. In tiny increments, he felt the tension in her begin to ease, but even so, she was not relaxed by any standard.

Afterward, on the top deck of the vessel taking them back to shore, he kept their conversation light, alternating between quizzing Ellie about what she'd seen and making sure that Peyton was taking part in the conversation. To give her credit, she was, but he could see her heart wasn't in it and she looked exhausted.

Once they were back at the house, they went down to the beach for their usual afternoon swim, except this time Peyton stayed on the sand watching from behind large sunglasses as he and Ellie cavorted in the gentle waves. When Ellie had had enough, he sent her up to the house to help Leilani bring some drinks and snacks down to them. Once she was merrily on her mission, he flopped down in the sand beside the recliner where Peyton was sitting.

"You okay?" he asked, looking up at her and noting she was no more relaxed now than she had been on the way back from the submarine trip.

"Fine," she answered succinctly.

"Would that be fine-fine, or just fine?" he pressed.

"I'm okay. All right?"

"You did a brave thing today," he said, deciding to take a different tack.

"I wasn't brave. I was terrified."

"And you did it anyway."

"Well, you weren't going to take Ellie unless I went, too. I had to go."

"I'm sorry. I shouldn't have put you through that."

"No, you shouldn't have."

"Peyton?"

"Hmm?"

"Why were you so scared?"

"I told you. I don't like enclosed spaces."

"The jet that got us here was an enclosed space. The chopper we took to Waikiki was an enclosed space. Why the sub?"

She shivered and reached for her sarong, wrapping it around her shoulders as if she was genuinely cold. Kind of hard to believe, given the perpetually warm air that surrounded them.

"I'll go and see if I can help Ellie."

She swung her legs over the side of the lounger, but before she could stand, he caught her hand and held her in place.

"No, stay, please. Leilani will help her. Why won't you open up to me, Peyton? We're husband and wife. We're supposed to learn to understand one another. If you won't let me understand you, how can we make this work?"

He stared at her, watching the emotions that flickered in her troubled blue-gray eyes—noting the taut lines of her body and how she tightened her hands into fists again, the same way she had on the submarine.

"We only met four days ago, Galen. You can't expect to know all my secrets immediately. A woman needs some mystery about her," she said, deflecting the seriousness of his question.

"Mystery is one thing. What you do is probably spy level ten."

She laughed, and he felt his whole body react to the sound. Joy, yes, that he'd brought a smile to her beautiful face, but more than that. A deeper, more intense reaction that made him want to reach out and touch her. To trace the fine line of her collarbone with his fingertips, then his mouth.

"Spy level ten? What are you, twelve years old?"

"Okay, level ten is probably a bit too high. Six, maybe. But seriously, Peyton. I want to get to know you, to understand what makes you tick. To make you happy."

A tinge of color flushed her cheeks. She blinked hard and swallowed before turning her face away from him.

"Look at me, Peyton. Don't keep hiding from me."

She slowly turned back to face him and he reached out to touch her cheek with his forefinger.

"I didn't mean to upset you," he said softly, catching one tear as it spilled from her lashes.

"It's not you—it's me. I'm just tired, that's all. Look, I had a bad experience as a kid. As part of a dare I was shut in an old refrigerator. I panicked. It left me feeling more than a little fragile when it comes to being shut in small spaces."

"How old were you?"

"A little older than Ellie."

"And your parents didn't help you through it?"

"We had just learned my mom had an incurable disease. My dad was all about working hard and trying to keep a roof over our heads."

She hadn't said much but he could read between the lines. They hadn't been there for her. She'd had to deal with the traumatic experience all on her own. It made his heart ache for the little girl she'd been.

"Again, I'm sorry."

"It's not your fault. It's not anyone's fault, to be honest. You just get on with things. Do what you need to do."

"Is that how you deal with everything in life? Do what you need to do?"

"Mostly."

"Is that why you married me?"

"No!" she protested. "That's different."

"Tell me, Peyton. What do you expect from our marriage?"

"What everyone expects," she hedged without going into any details. "Oh, look, there's Ellie and Leilani."

He wasn't mistaken—there was a distinct note of relief in her voice as they watched the two approach from the path leading to the house. Okay, he'd let her have her retreat, but he wasn't going to stop delving beneath the surface of what made her tick. Because at some point today, he'd realized that he really wanted to understand his new wife properly. Understand her and, hopefully, make this a proper marriage.

* * *

The next morning Peyton gave herself a stern pep talk in the mirror. No more weakness, no more frailty. Certainly no more exposing any softness to Galen. He'd been so persistent down on the beach yesterday. She couldn't afford to allow any further cracks to show. She was here for vengeance, nothing else.

She settled her features into what she hoped was a serene expression and squared her shoulders, ready to face the day. Ellie was just outside her door as she left her room.

"Good morning. Did you sleep well after yesterday? No bad dreams about sharks and shipwrecks?"

Ellie laughed. "No, I loved it. I don't remember dreams most times I wake up. Sometimes I dream about Mom and Dad, though. That they're still alive. When I wake up from those dreams I always feel sad. Sometimes I wish I could stay asleep just to be with them again."

Peyton reached out and stroked Ellie's hair. "I can understand that. I still dream about my mom, too, and she died a long time ago. You can always talk to me about it, if you want to."

What the heck was she doing? She didn't want to establish too strong a rapport with Ellie because she wasn't planning on sticking around. The poor girl had already had her world ripped out from under her—she didn't need to begin relying on someone who didn't plan on being around for longer than the requisite three-month trial period of the marriage.

"Or Galen, you can always talk to him," she added hastily.

"Who's talking about me?" Galen asked as he came down the hallway. "Ah, my two best girls. That's okay, then."

Ellie giggled and skipped toward him to give him a hug. "What are we doing today?"

"Well, as luck would have it, I think I've found the perfect escape for you."

"Escape?" Ellie looked confused. "I'm not a prisoner. Why do I need to escape?"

"I know you're not," Galen said. "You can totally leave at any time."

"No, I can't!" Ellie laughed.

"True, but today you can, if you want to, have some company from someone your age."

"You won't leave me there, will you?"

"Of course not. I don't plan on leaving you anywhere you don't want to be. The resort manager here has a daughter your age and she's really looking forward to meeting you. She has a pony."

Peyton watched as the caution on Ellie's face was replaced with rapt attention.

"A pony? When can we go?"

"After breakfast. We'll take you there, and if you're happy with it, we'll leave you to your girlie stuff and come back and pick you up after lunch. Deal?"

"Deal!"

Ellie flew down the hall toward the kitchen, where she would no doubt scoff her breakfast and be ready in record time.

"Well played," Peyton said.

"What do you mean?"

"Mentioning a pony. I don't think there are many girls Ellie's age who aren't enamored of ponies."

He shrugged. "I didn't want her getting bored, is all. She could do with a bit of fun with someone her own age."

"What about you? What do you plan to do?" Peyton asked.

"I thought I'd take my wife sailing."

She loved to sail. The freedom of being on the water,

as opposed to yesterday's expedition under it, held huge appeal for her. Skimming the waves, the wind in her hair, the crack of the sails as they caught the wind—she loved every aspect of it. It was a freedom she'd been introduced to as an adult but didn't get to experience often.

"Okay. I'll come, but only if you let me take the helm."

"Control freak," he goaded gently.

"Maybe," she replied with a grin.

"You drive a hard bargain but never let it be said I'm a man who won't let a woman take charge."

Was that a hint of innuendo in his voice? Peyton looked sharply at him, trying to ascertain whether or not to take his words at face value. "Are you patronizing me?" she asked slowly.

"I would never be so rude. No, I merely meant what I said. You forget, it was my grandmother who ran Horvath Corporation after my grandfather passed away. I'm not afraid of strong women. I revere them."

He was right about his grandmother being a strong woman. Knowing how much he respected the old lady, maybe she could get him to open up a bit more about her while they were sailing?

"Good to know," she said with a semi-smile.

Ellie had finished her breakfast by the time they joined her.

"Whoa! Hold on a minute. Are you sure you've actually eaten?" Galen teased her before she raced off to brush her teeth.

"I did! Should I get changed in case we do ride? I don't have any gear with me." All of a sudden Ellie looked unsure of herself.

"You look gorgeous as you are but maybe take a day pack with your swimsuit as well as jeans suitable for riding. I know there are spare helmets and boots at the stables, so you'll be fine."

Confidence restored, Ellie took off back to her room.

"You're really very good with her," Peyton observed.

"We're a work in progress. I'm constantly worried that I'm going to mess up but at least now I have company in this parenting thing."

Peyton felt a sudden pressure on her chest. "If our marriage works out."

"Why wouldn't we work out?"

"Well, you know. We might find we can't stand the sight of each other after three months. Earlier, even."

She knew she sounded like she was grasping at straws, but it had to be said.

"Cold feet already, Peyton?"

His face had grown serious and his blue eyes bored into hers as if he could see past the facade and deep into the secrets she was keeping.

"Not exactly. Just being practical."

Galen took a step closer to her. "For the record, I really enjoy the sight of you every morning and every evening, too, not to mention the hours in between."

His voice caressed her like a physical touch and Peyton set her nerve endings on edge. How did he do that? The sound of his voice had a power over her she'd never experienced with anyone before. She caught the subtle scent of his cologne and, despite herself, inhaled deeply.

"In fact," he continued, "I like a lot about you, and I really want to know you better. You just need to let go a little."

"Let go?"

"Yeah, you hold everything about yourself so tightly inside. You don't let people in, not even Ellie."

"I don't want her hurt if this doesn't work out."

"Why focus on the negative? Why not think about the benefits to all of us if it does work out?"

There was something about the way he said *benefits* that sent a surge of need through her body. She swallowed against the involuntary sound that rose in her throat and silently prayed that her hardened nipples were not painfully obvious through her light T-shirt.

"I'm ready!"

Ellie's voice behind her made her start and come back to her senses. Of course Galen hadn't meant anything like the benefits her runaway hormones wanted. Or had he? There was a mischievous gleam in his eye now that wasn't there before. Oh yes, he was well aware of the train of her thoughts, and their effect on her body.

"Excellent work, kiddo. I'll drive you over to their house in a moment. Just let me get my keys."

He was back in under a minute. "Okay, let's go."

"You haven't had your breakfast yet," Peyton pointed out as she settled at the table and helped herself to toast and scrambled eggs that Leilani had left on a covered warmer for them.

"I'll be back in ten. I'll eat then."

"Galen?" Ellie said.

"Hmm?"

"Why don't you and Peyton kiss when you say bye, like Mommy and Daddy always did?"

A sensation, not unlike icy-cold water, ran down Peyton's spine.

"Maybe Peyton can answer that," Galen offered, looking at her with the light of challenge in his eyes.

"We don't know each other as well as your mommy and daddy did," Peyton said awkwardly.

"My mommy said that Daddy kissed her on their very first date and she knew then that she was going to marry him. You two should kiss, too, and hold hands. That's what married people do, right?"

"I, ah…" Peyton's voice trailed off as she tried to think of something suitable to say.

"Like this?" Galen asked.

Peyton stiffened as Galen bent down and brushed her cheek with his lips. She felt a sense of intense relief when he left it at that.

"No, silly, like they do in the movies," Ellie said with a giggle.

"Oh, like this, you mean?"

Peyton wasn't ready for it. In fact, in a million years she'd never be ready for it, but he did it anyway. Galen bent down again and, tipping her chin up with one hand, took her lips in a kiss that honestly made her toes curl and her gut clench on another of those irritating surges of desire. He teased her lips open, deepening their kiss as her senses went into overdrive. Their only points of contact were his fingers at her chin and his lips on hers and yet her entire body went up in flames. For a moment she lost all sense of where she was, not to mention who was watching, and when Galen pulled back she was left feeling breathless with her mind spinning out of control.

That shouldn't have happened. The kiss. Her reaction. Any of it.

"Exactly like that," Ellie chortled from the other side of the room.

"Good to know," Galen replied with a quick grin before directing his next words to Peyton. "I'll be back soon. Try not to miss me too much."

And then, with a wink, he was gone.

Seven

Galen listened to Ellie chattering excitedly to him all the way to the resort manager's house and knew he was making the right responses, but internally he was in turmoil. Kissing Peyton like that had started as a bit of fun, and maybe to put a lid on Ellie's questions. But what the hell had he been thinking? What was supposed to be a sweet kiss had rapidly turned into a full-on assault on his equilibrium.

Yes, he'd begun to think he wanted more than a simple companionable marriage with Peyton, but this was something else entirely. That kiss had ignited a hunger in him that, now woken, would only continue to demand. And what if those demands weren't met? He wasn't about to force Peyton into anything that she didn't want. The very idea turned his stomach. But she'd been a willing participant in that kiss they'd just had, and that gave him hope— a great deal of hope—that with careful handling, theirs could become a real marriage. One with a strong physical connection.

He'd observed Valentin with his wife, and Ilya with his. When they were in the same room with their respective spouses it was as if there was an invisible current that ran between them. A link that couldn't be broken. He'd never thought for a minute that he wanted that kind of link with someone else. Oh, sure. He'd enjoyed relationships in the past, but he'd never wanted the depth of connectedness that his brother and cousin shared with their wives—until now. And now that he wanted it, he needed to figure out how to get it because, on the surface, Peyton had entered their marriage on similar terms to his. She hadn't mentioned wanting a grand passion; getting her to say what she wanted was a mission in itself.

It was a good thing he was man enough for the mission, he told himself as he pulled up outside the resort manager's house. He and Ellie got out of the car and were greeted by the resort manager and his daughter. When Galen was certain Ellie was comfortable with them and had arranged the time to pick her up, he headed back to the house feeling oddly nervous.

As far as he could see, no one remained happy in a marriage without some form of physical closeness—whether it was a grand passion or something more companionable. Based on how Peyton had reacted to their kiss, he knew she was capable of the former, although it left him wondering why she'd want to settle for anything less.

Peyton was in the kitchen when he got back. She'd obviously been busy. A packed hamper and cooler sat on the table.

"I wasn't sure what you wanted for our boat ride, so I just made sandwiches and grabbed some fruit and snacks and drinks."

Normally, Peyton appeared serene, untouchable. Right now she looked uncertain, as if she needed his reassurance. He hastened to give it to her.

"Sounds perfect. I was going to ask Leilani to do that for us, but since you've already done it, we can head straight to the marina. Have you packed your swimsuit?"

"I'm wearing it under this," she said, gesturing to her clothing.

He spied the ties of a halter snaking up from the neckline of her T-shirt. Did that mean she was wearing a two-piece today? His blood pressure kicked up a notch. Until now she'd been wearing a one-piece, and he had the distinct feeling that seeing her in a bikini could well undo him.

He grabbed the hamper and cooler and led the way back out to the car.

"You don't need us to grab towels or anything?" Peyton said, hanging back a little.

"Everything we need is on the boat," he answered.

"Just how big is this boat?" Peyton asked.

"She's thirty-six feet. Good for blue-water sailing but I rarely have time for that these days."

"Wow, that's a lot bigger than I was thinking."

"You'll love it. If you've enjoyed sailing on a smaller yacht, you'll really have fun on this one."

She fell silent and he could almost hear the cogs turning in her head.

"What is it?" he prodded her.

"Nothing, except… I guess I just can't quite get used to everything you seem to take for granted."

He frowned slightly. "Hey, don't get me wrong. I might be accustomed to a high standard of living, but trust me, I don't take one moment of it for granted. I saved darn hard for *Galatea* and bought her when I was in my early twenties. She was my first ever major acquisition and I felt so incredibly proud of myself the first time I took her out."

"Galatea is the goddess of calm seas in Greek mythology, isn't she?"

"Yeah, that's right. You're a fan of Greek mythology?"

"I did some papers on it in relation to classical literature in college."

"Sounds heavy," he said as he approached the car and opened the passenger door for her.

"It was. I think I preferred the fairy-tale versions of mythology told to me when I was a kid."

There was a wistful tone to her voice that prompted him to remain silent. Was she starting to open up a little more? He watched as she wrinkled her nose and grimaced briefly.

"But life's not about fairy tales, is it? Mythology is based on many brutal and sad stories."

"Some would say modern journalism isn't far different."

"Except it's based in exposing truth, not make-believe."

"Is that what appeals to you about your work? Getting to the core of things?"

He'd done some Google searches at night when he couldn't sleep for wondering about the woman sleeping down the hallway from him. Several of her articles were online and he'd been struck by the raw honesty in them. She didn't hold back from telling the truth, which was why she presented such a conundrum to him in real life. If writing in nitty-gritty detail was such an intrinsic part of her, why was she so selective about what she chose to reveal to him in person?

"You could say that. I hate injustice on any level. It needs to be exposed and the people perpetrating it held accountable for their actions."

Galen put the car into gear and headed down the driveway, surprised at the simmering anger in her tone.

"I read your piece on migrant workers. It was good," he said, opting for conversational safe ground.

"Thank you. I was rather proud of that assignment."

"So you're completely freelance?"

"Yes, I prefer being able to pick and choose my projects. It's a freedom that I worked hard to attain. Now I feel like I'm really doing what I was called to do."

"I'm glad for you. Everyone should be able to do what they love, right?"

Peyton felt the familiar anger toward Alice Horvath bubble in her veins. Yes, everyone should be able to do what they loved and not be persecuted and have false accusations made against them. She closed her eyes and took a steadying breath. She couldn't let her emotions get the better of her or she might slip up. This particular assignment was all too close to her heart and she wanted to give it her best. Her best meant never letting her guard down around the man sitting next to her, steering the sleek convertible toward the marina.

"It's a privilege to be able to do so. Not one I take for granted. I guess I'm a bit like you in that regard."

"Good to know we have some things in common," he answered lightly.

He pulled up in a parking lot beside rows and rows of berthed vessels. The sheer wealth exhibited here should have disgusted her but she couldn't help thinking of how much joy each of these symbols of exclusivity brought to the people who owned them, not to mention the jobs created building and outfitting them.

"We both breathe air, that's another thing," she said, her voice dry.

As she expected, Galen burst out laughing. "I would hope we have more in common than that," he said, still chuckling as he retrieved the hamper and cooler from the trunk and led her down one of the jetties toward a gleaming white-and-blue yacht.

"She's beautiful," Peyton said, pointing out the elegantly scripted name on the back of his yacht.

"My first true love."

"And your second?"

He stepped across onto the deck and held a hand out to assist her. His eyes met hers. "I'll let you know."

Peyton's throat dried and she swallowed hard. Was he implying he was falling in love with *her*? Surely not. It was too soon. Besides, he'd said at the wedding he wasn't looking for that kind of relationship.

But then there was that kiss. Peyton assured herself he had only done that to satisfy Ellie. It wasn't as if he had wanted to do it; he'd been coerced. And she certainly hadn't wanted it, either. She'd been taken completely by surprise. She couldn't lie to herself, though. It had been one heck of a kiss. Even now, just thinking about it made her press her lips together as if she could re-create the sensations he'd drawn from her.

She followed Galen through a hatch that led to a well-appointed galley and seating area below deck. He stripped off his shirt and dropped it on a squab in the dining area. In the close quarters, with him now wearing nothing but a pair of boat shoes and swim shorts, and without Ellie here as chaperone, Peyton was almost afraid of what she might do. Repeat the kiss of this morning, perhaps? More, even? Like, reach out and touch him—discover if he was as hot to touch as she felt right now?

"How about I put everything away for you," she blurted. "You get us going."

"Sure, but before we do, could you put sunblock on my back? I did everywhere else this morning."

Couldn't he just keep his shirt on? She mentally rolled her eyes. She didn't even know why she was reacting like this. She'd done it for him already a few times when they'd been down on the beach. But that was before they'd kissed.

"I promise I'll return the favor," he said, handing her the tube of lotion.

"I, ah… I thought I might keep my shirt on today," she said, taking the lotion from him and squirting a liberal amount into her palm.

"Sure, that works. As long as you don't mind that scratchy feeling of wearing it home after we've been snorkeling."

He had a point. Why did he have to go and kiss her like that this morning? It had changed everything. She began to rub the lotion onto his back, smoothing it along his lean, powerful shoulders and massaging it down the long muscles that lined his spine. He stood there like a statue, seemingly immune to her touch, while all the time her palms and fingertips tingled and her hands ached to travel around his waist to his belly and up to his chest—and then lower. So maybe the kiss had only changed everything for her.

She slapped him on the shoulder. "You're done."

Galen turned slowly. Okay, so maybe she wasn't the only one feeling the heat.

"Take off your shirt," he commanded.

Her eyes flicked back up to his face. Yes, that had been a command. The man looked determined. She spun slowly around and slipped off her T-shirt. The contrast of cold lotion and his very warm hands made her gasp as he began to apply the sunblock to her skin. His long, smooth, sure strokes made every muscle in her body tense in anticipation.

"Lift your arms," he instructed, his voice not sounding as confident as usual.

She did as he said and her breath caught in her throat as he smoothed sunblock on her sides, almost, but not quite, touching her breasts as he did so. Her nipples had bunched into aching peaks and every nerve was attuned to his touch. And then he stopped. She didn't know whether to rejoice or be disappointed.

"I'll go start up the motor and get ready to cast off."

Again, his voice held that strange note. At least he could speak. Words totally failed her. If he'd turned her around and kissed her again she doubted they'd have made it out of the marina today.

She looked toward the stateroom beyond where she stood. To the very large bed that stretched from one wall of the room to the other. She snatched her gaze away and schooled her thoughts.

She heard the sound of his feet on the steps leading to the deck and finally allowed her body to relax. It was no good, though. She could still feel the aftereffects of his touch on her skin. The sureness of his long fingers. His heat, which had ignited a simmering cauldron inside her. She stared unseeing at the picnic hamper to be unpacked. She needed to move but it was as if she was locked in a sensual trap, held captive by her own wants.

Eight

Galen kept his hands fisted around the wheel as he guided *Galatea* from her berth and out of the marina. Walking away from Peyton just now was one of the hardest things he'd ever had to do. Every instinct in his body and his mind had urged him to turn her around and pull her to him. To feel the heat of her skin against his. To lower his lips to her mouth and kiss her again. To find out whether those crazy fireworks that had ignited this morning were nothing more than an aberration.

But he knew if he'd done that, he wouldn't have known where to stop. They'd likely have ended up in the bed on board the yacht, and he wanted to know that when they came together she came willingly and with as much hunger for him as he had for her.

That day would come, he consoled himself as he fought to get his body and his thoughts back under control. He needed to keep his focus on the job at hand, which was negotiating past the breakwater out into the sea. Galatea had woven her magic, he noted, as the sea was serenely calm today. A complete contrast to the way his mind felt right now.

He saw Peyton come up on deck. "Can I get you anything?" she asked, looking hesitant.

"Perhaps you'd like to take the wheel while I get the sails ready."

"Sure."

Even with the gentle sea breeze brushing past his body like a lover's caress, he could feel the warmth that came off her as she came to stand beside him.

"I have a confession to make," she said ruefully as she stared at the wheel.

"And that is?"

"I've never steered a boat as big as this before."

"You'll be fine. The principle is the same."

He quickly gave her a few instructions, concluding with, "So when I give you a shout, you can turn off the motor."

She was a quick study, he noted, when a short time later the sound of the engine died away and the only noise around them was the wind catching in the sails.

"This is incredible," Peyton said with a laugh.

He looked at her beautiful face and smiled in return. For the first time since he'd met her, she looked completely relaxed. He wanted to see her like this more often. Open and carefree, instead of closed and, dare he say it, suspicious. He realized the latter attitude may come with the territory in her line of work. But right now she was happy, and he'd bask in that for as long as it lasted.

After sailing for an hour or so, they took down the sails and put down anchor near a small, sheltered bay. They ate their lunch and lay on the deck for a while, soaking up the sun.

"This is blissful. Ellie would have enjoyed it," Peyton

commented, shading her eyes from the sun as she rolled over onto her back.

"The last time she came out on *Galatea* was with her mom and dad. She has happy memories on the water. I might see about bringing the yacht back to Port Ludlow for the summer."

"You can do that? It's a long way to sail. Doesn't it scare you?"

"If I plan it right, nothing will go wrong. I bring a small crew with me on repositioning trips. You could come, too."

"I think I'll take a pass on that."

"Chicken?"

"No." She shifted to a sitting position and wouldn't quite meet his eyes. "I can't make plans that far in advance. I don't know what I'll be doing by then."

It was as if the sun had disappeared behind a cloud. He sat up, too. "What do you mean?"

"Well, I could be away on an assignment," she said, sounding slightly flustered.

"You're still planning to work away from home?"

"I still have a job to do, Galen. You'll still be doing yours, won't you? That requires business trips from time to time, doesn't it?"

She had a point but deep down inside he knew he'd be putting Ellie and Peyton's needs before any business trips going forward. At least that was his plan. Peyton, it seemed, didn't intend to change her life even though they were now married. So what had she been looking for in this marriage?

"We're going to have to coordinate our schedules carefully now that we're married," he conceded. "We can't leave Ellie holding down the fort alone. But we'll figure it out. I wanted to talk to you about having a live-in housekeeper anyway, once we find a new home."

"I guess I'd have to be okay with that, wouldn't I?"

"You mean you could get used to someone picking up after you, after all?" he teased.

"Or we could all get used to pulling our weight around the house to help her out, right?"

The tension that had built between them began to fade and a companionable silence took its place. After a while Galen got up and headed below deck. When he came back on top, he had snorkeling gear in his hands.

"This is a beautiful bay for snorkeling. Have you tried it before?" he asked, passing her a mask, snorkel and pair of fins. "I think these should suit you. Let's try them for fit."

"Can't say I've had the pleasure."

"There's nothing to it. All you need to remember when you go under water is that when you resurface you have to blow out hard to clear the pipe before you breathe in again. And if you don't want to go under water, you can float along the surface and still see a lot."

"That sounds more like my style," she said, trying the mask on for size. "How do I look?"

"Like a mutant goldfish, but that seal around your face looks good."

He quickly showed her how to clear the mask if water seeped in and helped her put on her fins before doing the same himself. Then he showed her how to step off the transom at the back of the yacht and into the sea.

Half an hour later they were back on board and Peyton was voluble in her delight.

"Did you see that turtle? That was incredible!"

He smiled indulgently. Yes, bit by bit he was starting to see the real Peyton Earnshaw. And the more natural and unforced she became, the more he wanted to know about her.

They were back at the marina tidying up the yacht when Galen's cell phone began to chime. It brought home to Peyton exactly how long they'd been out alone together today. The earlier sexual tension had eased off—not completely, but certainly enough for her to be able to relax and enjoy the experience. There were definitely some benefits to being married to a man who appeared to have everything, she conceded to herself with a grin.

"Peyton? It's Ellie on the phone."

Suddenly, her sense of well-being was put on hold. "Is everything all right?"

"Yeah, she's fine. She wanted to know if she can sleep over with Caitlin. Seems they're getting on like a house on fire. Caitlin's mom and dad are cool with it."

"Well, it's your call, isn't it?"

"We're in this together," he reminded her.

"It's okay by me," Peyton said stiffly, uncomfortable to be included in what was obviously a very parental decision.

Galen turned his attention back to the call, which lasted another two minutes. "Well, that's one very happy little girl," he said as he came below to collect the hamper and cooler.

"I take it she isn't usually a fan of sleepovers?"

"Not recently, no. This break away from home has been good for her. It's a relief to see her feel relaxed and trust that everything will be okay with us while she's with Caitlin and her parents."

"I hated sleepovers as a kid."

Oh heavens, why had she blurted that out? Now he'd want to know why. Of course, that was the very next question out of his mouth. Peyton gathered her thoughts together before answering, deciding brief and honest was probably the best approach.

"I guess, at the heart of it, I was always scared I'd get home and find out my mom had died and I wasn't there."

The words hurt to say and she wished she'd never opened this can of worms.

"That must have been hard."

"You get used to it. Your dad died, too. That can't have been easy."

"No, it wasn't, but I was in my teens, and while his death came as a shock, we didn't have the fear of it constantly hanging over us. We probably should have, though. My grandfather and my uncle both died of the same congenital heart defect before him."

"Did he never get checked out?"

"He always said he was too busy. Of course, Nagy made sure everyone in the family had a full medical workup after my father's death. Only one of my cousins has inherited the same problem but it's well managed now they're aware of it."

"Must have been worrying, wondering if you all carried the same time bomb."

"It was, but Nagy took care of it—of all of us. As she does."

Peyton felt the customary bristle of anger when she heard him speak of his grandmother in glowing terms. But this was a natural opportunity to find out more about the woman who'd had such a devastating effect on her family.

"She's very much the matriarch, isn't she? Does everyone obey her?"

Galen laughed. "You say that as if she sits on a throne and dictates orders to us all."

"Well, doesn't she? From what you say, she's omnipotent."

His face took on a softer look. "No, she's human, just like the rest of us. And she makes mistakes, with her own health, no less."

"So it's a matter of do as I say, not as I do?"

"Kind of like that. You probably heard she had a serious heart attack a few months ago. We're all so grateful that Valentin was there when it happened. He did CPR until an ambulance could get there. She's been different since. As if she thinks she's living on borrowed time but she still has so much to complete before her time is up. There's a weird urgency about her. It's kind of hard to explain."

"I guess a near-death experience will change a person."

"That's for sure."

They went up on deck. Galen locked the cabin door behind them before they left the yacht and headed back to the car. Peyton rued the fact she'd lost her opportunity to keep the conversation on Galen's relationship with his grandmother but filed away the snippets he'd already disclosed.

Once they got back to the beach house, she showered and changed, then typed up her notes from the conversation. When she was finished, she walked out onto the patio.

Through the open doors she could hear Galen on a call, so she settled on a sun lounger in the shade and let the beauty of the day and her surroundings lull her into sleep. She was surprised to see how low the sun was when she woke to the sound of the tinkle of ice cubes in a pitcher being put on the table in front of her.

"That had better be margaritas," she said sleepily.

"How did you know?" Galen asked, putting two chilled, salt-rimmed glasses down on the table beside the pitcher.

"Because that's just what I feel like. After a big glass of water, anyway."

"Then it's just as well that's what I made. Predinner cocktails. Did you have a good sleep?"

"I can't believe I slept that long. Why didn't you wake me?"

He shrugged with a casual elegance. "You looked like you needed it. A day on the water can be tiring."

"I bet you didn't sleep."

Again, that shrug. He poured the drinks, handed her a glass and held his toward her in a toast. "Here's to more days like today."

She clinked her glass to his. "Indeed."

Then she remembered the kiss. Did he mean *all* of today? She met his gaze as she took a sip of the perfectly blended cocktail. Oh yes, he totally did.

Suddenly, this whole marriage thing felt too complicated. She honestly hadn't thought this through. She'd imagined that she'd cruise through the first three months without worrying about fighting off a growing physical attraction or having to ignore the magnetism that steadily grew stronger between them, and she'd write her article then extract herself as neatly as she'd gotten into it.

He was a Horvath. A direct descendant of the person who'd upended everything that was safe and secure in Peyton's world and set her up for hardship. Yes, she'd clawed her way beyond that hardship now, but it had been a hard road and full of sacrifice.

For the briefest moment she allowed herself to think of the beautiful baby girl she'd had to give up and felt the all-too-familiar pain those thoughts always brought. That was what she needed to keep front and center in her mind. Pain. Loss. Disappointment. It was the only defense she had against the almost overwhelming enticement that was Galen Horvath.

Nine

It was a good thing they would be heading home in two days, Peyton thought as they finished their dinner on the patio. It was far too easy to be seduced by the stunning beauty of both this place and the man sitting opposite her.

The meal he'd prepared for the two of them while she'd been sleeping was perfection. The shrimp kebab appetizer had been mouthwatering, and the baked fish he'd served with a Greek salad as their main course had been outstanding.

"Do you feel like dessert? Leilani left a mango cheesecake in the refrigerator."

"Oh, no. I couldn't fit in another bite," Peyton protested. "In fact, I may never need to eat again. That was truly amazing. I had no idea you could cook."

"One of my hidden talents. To be honest, as a bachelor, I learned to cook food I enjoyed a long time ago. Now cooking is more of a way to relax for me than a necessity."

She narrowed her eyes a little. "And you needed more relaxation after today?"

He laughed and she felt her lower belly tighten. It didn't matter how many times she heard the sound; his laughter always had this effect on her.

"You can never have too much relaxation. How about a nice slow stroll on the beach?" he asked, holding out his hand to her as he stood up from the table.

She accepted his hand and let him help her up, expecting him to let go as they started on the path down to the beach. But he kept her hand clasped lightly in his and, despite her earlier reminders to herself to keep her distance, she liked it. The waves murmured softly against the sand as they strolled along the beach. The night was so perfect. It was a shame everything about being here was fake, she told herself, trying desperately not to fall under its spell.

But it was impossible not to, especially when Galen stopped and dropped to the sand, tugging her down with him so she was cradled between his legs and leaning against his strong chest and tight stomach. She tried not to relax, to keep herself ever so slightly apart from him, but she failed miserably. The lure of his warm body against her back—the feeling of being sheltered, protected—it was all too much. Galen traced his fingers along her arm, sending a rash of goose bumps along her skin.

"Cold?" he asked.

"No."

She was anything but cold. In fact, his every touch heated her blood more and more. To distract herself she tried to dig more information out of him about his family.

"Tell me about growing up," she asked. "Were you a little beach boy?"

"I've always been drawn to the water, that's true. Growing up was, well, fun. As a kid we didn't know what trouble was unless we broke a window or talked back to an adult."

"Sounds idyllic."

"Isn't that what childhood is supposed to be? Free of adult worries? How about you? You've mentioned a few dark spots, but surely it wasn't all bad?"

Had it all been bad? Not if she was honest. Before her mom got ill, and her father was disgraced, their life had been so very different. She searched her past, latching on to one particular memory that had brought her incredible joy.

"My happiest memory of my childhood was the day my dad brought home a puppy," she said softly.

"That sounds like it would have been a very happy memory. What was the puppy like?"

"He was a mutt, medium sized and very boisterous. I loved him so much."

"And?" Galen coaxed her a little more.

"And when my mom got sick and my dad lost his job, we had to move and surrender him to a local shelter. We couldn't afford to keep him anymore."

And just like that, the rift in her heart opened up again. She'd suppressed memories of Bingo and the part he'd played in her life. When her mom had gotten sick, Bingo had been her confidant. Listening faithfully as she poured out her worries, letting her cry into his springy fur when it all got too much.

"That was rough," Galen sympathized, pressing a kiss on her head.

"I got over it. At least I knew at the no-kill shelter my mom insisted on, he'd be rehomed, and he was such a lovely dog. He didn't stay there long."

But it was yet another loss she could lay at Alice Horvath's door, Peyton reminded herself. Yet another reason to expose exactly how far Alice's cruelties extended.

The breeze picked up, blowing strands of hair onto Peyton's face. Galen brushed them behind her ear. His touch was a sizzle of electricity across her skin. Peyton didn't want to talk anymore. Right now she wanted to forget the memories that had reopened old wounds and lose herself in the man who was here with her. She shifted slightly so she faced Galen. His eyes locked with hers as she lifted her hand to cup his cheek. And then she leaned forward to kiss him.

The shock of touching his lips with hers, of taking charge and of giving in, shot through her like a bolt from above. Soon, both her hands were locked behind his head as she kissed and nibbled at his lips. He kissed her back. Hot, wet and everything she needed to obliterate her painful past and live in the moment.

Somehow, they ended up lying on the sand, his body half over hers. She pressed her hips up, grinding against him and earning a groan from deep in his throat in response. He was rock-hard, his body straining toward hers, but even though he so clearly wanted her, he didn't press home the advantage. Instead, he held himself away from her slightly. Leaning on one elbow, he stroked her with his free hand, slowly moving the fabric of her skirt up over her thighs.

She shivered at his touch, wanting more. Wanting him. She'd been fighting this attraction from the moment she first saw him, but right now she was incapable of pushing him away.

His fingers softly caressed her inner thighs and she moaned, her hips involuntarily pushing upward again. Her hands still clasped his head, and his mouth was still on hers, their kisses long and drugging, sending a sensual spiral through her brain. She felt his fingers trace the edge of her panties and the hollowed curve at her groin. It was one of her most sensitive places and she moaned again, her body tensing for that moment when he'd move aside the fabric and touch that part of her that ached for his possession.

Galen shifted slightly, taking his lips from hers and kissing a line along her jaw, then down her throat and across her collarbone. Her body went liquid as he continued his sensual assault; her skin was ultrasensitive, her mind focused on the pleasure he drew from her. She lifted her hips again, silently urging him to touch her where she most needed, her hands moving to stroke the back of his neck, his shoulders, down his back.

Beneath her fingertips she felt the corded muscles of his body, their tension a mark of his restraint as he touched and kissed her—his focus purely on her pleasure alone. And then his hand moved to her mound, cupping her through the lace, his finger pressing unerringly on her clitoris and sending a piercing pleasure through her. She felt herself grow wet with need.

A particularly large wave suddenly crashed onto the beach, the sound roaring through her consciousness and reminding her of where they were. Of what they were doing. She stiffened, pulling away immediately.

"What is it?" Galen asked, his voice husky with desire.

"We can't do this," Peyton said abruptly and shoved him away for good measure.

"Okay," he answered carefully. "Shall we go back to the house?"

"I don't know about you but I'm going back."

Peyton scrambled to her feet and began to stride as fast as she could down the beach, dusting the sand off her as she went. How could she have been so stupid as to give in to her personal needs? This whole exercise was not about her. She couldn't afford to indulge in her desires. She was here to collect information.

But even as she worked her way through the soft whispering sand and to the path that led to their holiday house, her subconscious was urging her to stop and look back. To see if Galen followed her. To turn back to him and continue what they'd started. She shut down the treacherous thoughts before they could take a firm hold and bloom into something she knew she'd regret.

When she got to her room, she slammed her door hard and locked it for good measure. She didn't for one minute believe that Galen would try to enter her room or ever dream of forcing himself on her, or anyone, for that matter. She might symbolically be shutting him out, but if she was being truly honest, she was shutting herself in because right now she could barely trust herself around him anymore.

Today had been a mistake from start to finish. First the kiss, then the sailing, then the idiotically romantic walk on the beach after an equally romantic meal together. Even just thinking about it made her want to turn around and head back out that door and find him again. Pretty much every cell in her body was calling her every kind of stupid for leaving herself hanging like that when Galen had been so close to giving her the pleasure her body craved.

Peyton stomped across her room and into the bathroom, snapping on the shower faucet and shucking off her clothes, leaving them at her feet. She had to scrub this urge out of her right now, before she did something idiotic like follow her instincts. She wasn't here to fall in lust with the man and she certainly wasn't going to allow herself to do anything as dumb as fall in love.

All love ever did was hurt people and she wasn't going down that road ever again.

The flight back to SeaTac was smooth but Galen still couldn't shake the questions that filled his mind over Peyton's desertion the other night. Things had been coming along nicely between them. He knew she'd been there with him every step of the way. After all, hadn't she been the one to start it in the first place? And then nothing. It was as if she'd turned herself off like a tap. The next time he'd seen her, over breakfast the next morning, she'd been even more distant than before and she'd made every effort not to be alone with him again during the rest of their honeymoon.

And now they were nearly home. The helicopter that had transported them from SeaTac to the hotel landed smoothly and Galen assisted Peyton and Ellie off the aircraft. A porter from the resort came forward with a luggage rail to relay their cases to his apartment.

"Home sweet home!" Ellie said as they entered the private apartment at the top of the residence wing of the hotel.

"Speaking of home, I've contacted an agent to give us a private viewing of a few places tomorrow. You both up for that?"

He'd taken the liberty of organizing it without consulting Peyton or Ellie. He knew Ellie would be excited to check out potential new homes but he hadn't wanted to give Peyton time to find an excuse not to come with them. Telling her about their appointment tomorrow in front of Ellie, where she could scarcely say she was unavailable, was probably underhanded, but he was determined to get her input on the subject.

"Yippee!" Ellie said. "What time?"

"First thing, so make sure you get plenty of sleep and are up early tomorrow. It shouldn't be a problem with the time difference between Hawaii and here. In fact, you'll feel like you're sleeping in."

His gaze clashed with Peyton's. She didn't look impressed. The moment Ellie was out of the room she started in.

"I won't be coming with you. I have work to do now that we're back. I'm behind on my project."

"Surely, you can spend a few hours with us. It's the weekend, after all. Can't you get back to work on Monday, like regular people?"

"Galen, I'm self-employed. My hours are my own and sometimes that means I work on the weekends."

"So tell yourself you need the time off. This is important for us—as a family."

He let the last three words hang on the air between them, saying nothing more. She shifted uncomfortably before responding.

"Fine, but don't expect me to enjoy it."

"And why wouldn't you? Doesn't every woman want to create a home?"

"I can't believe you actually said that."

He shrugged. "Hey, I'm not being deliberately sexist here. I want to create a home, too. I just think it's important that if we're going to create one together, we all need to have some input on the subject, okay?"

"Whatever," she said, completely unimpressed. "Where am I staying? Does this apartment of yours boast more than two bedrooms?"

"Luckily, it does. You can take the master, though. I can sleep in the guest bedroom. I impressed upon the agent that we needed to look at houses that were ready for immediate, or near-immediate, occupancy."

"Then it won't matter if I take the guest room, will it?"

He looked at her, prepared to argue the point, then decided that he needed to pick and choose his battles if he was going to get past that solid wall of ice she'd erected between them since the night on the beach. His hands tingled at the memory of touching her the way he had. He'd been so lost in the moment, lost in her, that when she'd shoved him away he'd been slow to react. Certainly too slow to persuade her not to run away from him again.

"If that's what you want. By the way, remember the welcome home party tonight."

Would she attempt to find an excuse to skip that, too?

"Ah, yes. That."

"You don't sound thrilled. Some of the family is flying in specially for it."

"Well, they needn't have on my behalf. To be honest, it's a bit over-the-top, isn't it?" She sounded irritated as she began to pace the room. "They only just saw us a week ago."

"And they want to share in the joy that we're married."

"Your grandmother only wants to make sure she hasn't made a mistake matching us."

"You don't seem too fond of Nagy. Why's that?"

"I don't even know her."

Peyton crossed her arms and planted her feet in what he took as a more aggressive blocking stance. As if to say, *You can ask me all the questions you like, but you're not getting anything out of me.* He sighed.

"Look, after this we don't need to see them all until Christmas, if you don't want to."

"If we're still together by Christmas." She lifted the handle on her suitcase and started to roll it down the hallway. "I'm assuming my room is down here?"

"Yes, third on the left. Can't miss it," he said in defeat.

Whatever had come over her that night on the beach hadn't changed. In fact, there was a bigger distance between them than on the day they'd met and married. He shook his head and walked over to check his phone messages. He didn't know what had come between them but he had to get past it.

He didn't want Ellie to be disadvantaged by his decision to find a partner the way he had. The last thing he'd wanted to do was parade a string of girlfriends by her while he searched for a suitable wife, which was why he'd used

Match Made in Marriage in the first place. Nagy's hit rate had been 100 percent—pretty damn impressive in this day and age. She didn't make mistakes.

So why did Peyton already want out? Obviously, she didn't think they stood a chance. But why wasn't she prepared to at least try? Maybe he'd moved too fast while they were in Hawaii, but she'd been the one to put the moves on him that night. He'd held himself back until he could hold back no further. And he knew she'd been as invested in their lovemaking as he. More, in fact. The sounds she'd made, her physical responses… All of it had driven him to near madness. He groaned out loud in frustration. For the first time in his life he'd found the one woman he couldn't charm, and he didn't like it one little bit.

"At least try to look as if you're enjoying yourself," Galen whispered in her ear as she stood to one side surveying the room full of Horvaths.

A small gathering, he'd said. She growled internally. There were at least twenty-five people here, all of them close relatives of his. Ellie was in her element, showing off her tan and telling everyone who'd listen about swimming and pony riding and her new friend she'd made. It seemed she knew and loved everyone at the party and that those feelings were strongly returned.

"I'm enjoying myself," she retorted.

"Then would it kill you to smile a little?"

"Like this?" She bared her teeth at him.

"Well, I guess that's better than looking like you'd like to barbecue us all on the nearest spit. You know you could have invited your family, too. This wasn't supposed to be a one-sided thing."

"My father was otherwise occupied," she answered.

Or at least he probably would have been if she'd even told him about this.

"Look," she continued, "I'm just tired and cranky. Go, enjoy the crowd. I'll be fine here for now."

"Are you sure? You're not going to run out on me, are you?"

"Of course not. Go, please."

She felt her body sag with relief when he did what she said. The past couple of days had been a trial. While she'd determinedly kept away from him, her body tormented her by being on high and hopeful alert for whenever he was near. It left her exhausted during the day, and then at night, a recurrent dream of being on the beach with him, of finishing what they'd started, plagued her. Every darn time she had the dream, she woke hovering on the edge of orgasm and feeling as unfulfilled and frustrated as it was possible to feel. This morning she'd given in and brought herself to climax, but while the physical stimulation had brought her release, it certainly hadn't brought her satisfaction. If anything, it had only left her even more aware of Galen's proximity and of how often he brushed by her with a casual touch that seemed to leave him unaffected but reduced her to a taut set of jangling nerves every time.

Ten

Alice watched the newlyweds. All was not well in the state of Washington if their body language was anything to go by. Again, she felt that frisson of foreboding that had struck her before their wedding. Something wasn't right, but they couldn't give up. She detached herself from the group she'd been talking to and made a beeline for Peyton, who submitted to Alice's kiss on the cheek.

"Mrs. Horvath," she said in acknowledgment.

"I thought we'd discussed this before, my dear. Call me Alice, or Nagy. We're family, remember."

"Of course," she replied with a smile that was more caricature than genuine.

"If you don't mind me saying so, you're hardly the picture of a blooming bride. What's wrong?" Alice asked bluntly.

"Wrong? Why should anything be wrong?" Peyton hedged.

"Based on our analysis of your suitability to be matched

with my grandson, absolutely nothing. However, it's clear that you're not happy. What is it?"

While Alice knew Peyton was hardly likely to tell her the real reason why she was so out of sorts, she couldn't help but ask. She watched as the girl shifted her gaze and sought Galen across the room. He lifted his eyes and met hers. Peyton visibly stiffened and a bloom of color filled her cheeks. Good, Alice thought. There was a connection between them. There was hope this would still work out.

"I guess it's hard to put into words," Peyton finally admitted.

"Of course it is, dear. Look, do you mind if we take a seat over there? My stamina isn't what it used to be."

"Sure."

Alice led the way to a group of chairs and sat down heavily in the nearest one. "I'm not as spry as I used to be," she said as Peyton settled down opposite her. "Now, tell me what's wrong."

"Nothing you can help with, I'm sure."

"I have a fair bit of experience behind me, my dear. Try me and see."

"Look, I'd rather not talk about me. Can we talk about you instead?"

"Me?" Alice feigned surprise.

"Yes, you. You're fascinating. You built a successful business into an empire. That's not a feat many women get the opportunity to achieve." Peyton was full of admiration but to Alice's ear it sounded forced. "I imagine you made some tough decisions along the way."

"I worked hard and I made sure that I never lost contact with the heartbeat of the business. Every department reported to me personally. Plus, I made sure I had the right people in those departments. Those that weren't right, left. Thankfully, there were only a few."

She watched as Peyton chewed over her words for a moment.

"You must have made some enemies along the way."

"One or two. No one ever reaches the top of their field without upsetting a few apple carts. There are some things I regret and they weigh on me now that I'm older, but I stand by my decisions." She met Peyton's gaze head-on.

"You'd retired from Horvath Corporation. What led you to establish Match Made in Marriage? Was it a financial decision or did you do it just out of boredom?"

Alice laughed out loud. She adored how blunt Peyton was. "Oh, my dear, you are priceless. I have to admit, I admire your forthright nature. It reminds me of myself, actually. In answer to your question, once I retired from Horvath Corporation I found I lacked a challenge. Since so many of the couples I'd introduced over the years went on to form lasting partnerships, I decided I may as well enlist the help of some experts and make it official.

"It's not every dating agency that can boast a one hundred percent success rate. I don't hold with these modern notions of dating apps and swiping left and right based on a few words and a photo. It takes strength and fortitude to build a marriage, together with like-minded thinking and a fair amount of physical attraction. My grandson is a handsome man, yes?"

"Oh, yes," Peyton agreed automatically. "When you say one hundred percent success rate, are you basing that on couples who have continued to stay together for years, or merely on couples who have survived the three-month minimum marriage period?"

"Continued to stay together for years, of course." Alice contemplated Peyton seriously. "It's a wonderful thing, you know, to find someone's perfect match. I was thrilled when your profile came across my desk. I knew you were perfect for Galen, and he for you. And Ellie?" Alice nodded across the room. "Well, she's just the icing on the cake for you both. Such a delightful child—I love her dearly. A family isn't only about those born into it, Peyton. It's about everyone."

After a little more small talk Peyton excused herself. Alice stayed where she was, watching her walk away. Had she done enough? she wondered. Or was it already too little, too late?

"I think I'll stay home today," Peyton said at breakfast the next morning.

"Don't you like us anymore?" Ellie asked quietly from across the table.

Galen watched for Peyton's response.

"Of course I like you," Peyton protested.

"You're acting different since we're back," Ellie persisted.

"That's because now that we're back, I need to return to work. Life isn't a perpetual holiday, you know."

"What's *perpetual* mean?"

Galen interceded before Peyton could respond. "It's something that's never-ending. How about you look it up in your dictionary and see if you can use it in a sentence when you get back to school tomorrow?"

"Good idea," Ellie said and, fired with purpose, she pushed away from the table and went to her room.

Galen took her seat and turned it to face Peyton.

"Your opinion is important. It's going to be home to all three of us, so of course we need your input. Please come."

He watched as she waged some internal battle.

"Fine, I'll come," she grumbled.

They both rose from their seats at the same time, bumping into one another. Galen put out his hands to steady her and she looked up at him. He saw confusion in her eyes and then a flare of something else—quickly masked as she pulled away. He let his hands drop down to his sides, wondering why she was so determined to continue creating as much distance between them as possible.

"Peyton, what have I done to upset you?"

"Upset me? You haven't upset me," she said, taking another step away.

"Really? Because it feels like you can't stand to be in the same space as me anymore and, to be honest, I thought we were making progress."

She looked startled but at least she didn't leave the room immediately.

"Progress?" She spoke the word as if she was feeling it on her tongue, as if it was a foreign concept to her. "Correct me if I'm wrong, but you married to create a more stable home environment for Ellie, did you not?"

"I did," he agreed.

"And you said you weren't looking for the heights of passion or anything like that."

"I may have said words to that effect, but that doesn't mean that given the clear attraction between us we can't make something of that and build on it."

"To be honest, Galen, I don't think it's a good idea. It'll send a confusing message to Ellie if she sees us embarking on a romantic relationship when we barely know each other."

Galen wanted to argue but he could see she had a point. "Yes, that's true, but she took delight in us kissing a couple of days ago. To her it's normal to see the people who care for her care for each other, too."

"I can't believe you're using that to try to get me into bed."

Peyton's words hit him like a bucket load of icy-cold water. "You're accusing me of using her?"

She stared back at him for a moment before answering. "Well, aren't you?"

"Look, you're taking this out of context. Yes, all I wanted was an uncomplicated union with a like-minded individual. Match Made in Marriage promised me that. I was unexpectedly delighted to meet you and marry you." He paused, unsure whether it was a good idea to lay his cards on the table now, or to hold them close to his chest. He opted for the former. "I won't lie, Peyton. I'm so fiercely attracted to you that I can barely think straight. That night, on the beach, that was magical. Yes, I can understand we probably moved too quickly for your liking. I get that you don't want to race into that side of marriage, but at least give a man some hope for the future. If we were matched it was because we had similar interests, similar likes and dislikes. Please don't tell me that I'm wrong, that we have nothing in common, or that you don't find me attractive, too, because I can't believe that."

Peyton had grown pale during his speech.

"Are we ready to go?" Ellie said as she bounded back into the room.

"I just need to get my bag," Peyton said, leaving the room as quickly as humanly possible without breaking into a sprint worthy of a cheetah.

"Yeah, kiddo, we're just about ready," Galen answered as Ellie looked from Peyton's retreating back to his face.

"You talked her into coming, didn't you?" the nine-year-old said, beaming at him with great pleasure.

"Looks like it."

The apartment phone started to ring and he answered it. The real-estate agent had arrived, ready to escort them to the properties. He'd just hung up as Peyton rejoined them. Her color was back, he noted, and she'd applied some lipstick and combed her hair, but he could see by the look in her eyes that she wasn't entirely happy to be involved in this little jaunt.

"Thank you," he said sincerely as she came to a halt.

She shrugged in response. "Let's get this over with."

Galen couldn't help but smile. "You make it sound like we're leading you to your execution. Trust me—it won't be as bad as that."

"It had better not be," she said firmly. Then, letting Ellie take her hand, she led the way out the front door.

They'd already looked at two houses, both beautiful, but both completely unsuitable for their requirements. Galen had been adamant that he didn't want Ellie to be too far from her school or her friends, and the agent assured him that the last property on the list for the day would meet their needs. When they pulled up in the driveway outside the multibay garage, Peyton began to think the woman might be right. This property looked big enough for all three of them; the bedrooms weren't too close together and they wouldn't be bumping into one another all the time, like they seemed to do in the apartment. Here, Peyton could definitely have her space while she finished her article. Better yet, the property was vacant and ready for immediate occupation and had a stunning view over Puget Sound.

She couldn't believe how quickly things went after that—after a few phone calls they were told they could take possession the following weekend.

"I can arrange a truck to collect your things for you," Galen offered as they drove back to his apartment.

"No, that's okay. I thought I'd keep my apartment for now."

He shot her a glance before putting his attention back on the road, and she noticed his hands tighten ever so much on the wheel. To her relief, he didn't raise the subject again during their ride home.

But once Ellie went to bed that night and before she could escape to her own room, he asked her to join him for a nightcap. She was on the verge of saying no, but he pre-empted her by pouring two snifters of brandy and gesturing toward the sofa where he'd been sitting earlier. Feeling trapped, she took the glass he'd poured and chose one of the easy chairs opposite the sofa.

"What is it?" she said, coming straight to the point.

"You never mentioned you were keeping your apartment."

"Look, it's still early days—you can't blame a girl for being a little cautious."

"Peyton, we're married. That takes a level of commitment I'm not seeing from you."

"Wow, talk about making me feel like I've just been sent to the principal's office," she said, trying to lighten the mood.

But he was right. She wasn't as committed because she *was* using him. So how did she play this? It was becoming harder to stay focused when every time she was alone with him, all she could think about was how his mouth had felt on hers. The taste of him, the feel of him beneath her hands. She was shaken by the swell of sheer need that bloomed from deep inside her and knew if she allowed herself to capitulate at that final barrier and let him make love to her, let herself make love to him, she'd never be able to complete this task she'd set for herself.

She decided to approach their conversation from another angle. Perhaps a blend of honesty, a few select words about her past and an appeal to his chivalry would get her out of this awkward mess.

"Look, Galen, I've avoided commitment for a long time

because of a really traumatic experience in my past. I—"
She paused, partly for effect but also because of the massive lump that suddenly appeared in her throat. "I loved someone very much once. Losing them broke me apart. I don't know if I'm actually capable of feeling that level of love for another person again."

He leaned forward, concern painted clearly in his beautiful eyes. For a moment Peyton felt a shaft of guilt. He was only trying to do the right thing and she, most definitely, was not.

"Can we at least try?" he asked. "It's clear we're attracted to each other. You chose to get into this with me. No one forced your hand. You had to know that intimacy would come up at some stage."

"But not this soon!" she blurted without thinking. "I don't want to put myself at risk of being hurt like that again. Please respect that."

"So you want all the appearances of a good marriage, without the trimmings?"

A crooked smile pulled at his lips and she felt that all-too-familiar tug deep inside. He was so easy to fall for, so easy to want to get to know, so easy to *want*, period.

"Isn't that what you wanted, too?" she asked, remembering his words during their wedding reception.

He sighed and sat back again, his hands now resting on the tops of his thighs, fingers splayed. Somehow, she couldn't take her eyes off them. Couldn't stop herself remembering their gentle, sensual touch on her skin.

"It's what I thought I wanted but here we are, just over a week out and, to be totally honest with you, I want more."

Peyton lifted her gaze to his face, to the entreaty in his eyes.

"I can't give you more. Not yet."

Even as she said the words she felt guilt slice through

her. If the circumstances had been different then, yes, maybe she would have grasped what he was offering her with both hands and run with it. But they weren't. It was as simple as that.

"Well, I guess I have to thank you for your honesty and hope that at some stage your feelings about the matter will change. It won't, however, change how I feel about you."

She nodded and took a sip of the brandy. It warmed a trail down her throat. "Your own feelings about me might change, too," she said, mindful of how he would probably react when he discovered her true reason for marrying him.

She doubted he'd be quite as keen on making theirs a real marriage in every sense when that happened. In fact, she doubted he'd even be able to stand the sight of her anymore. That knowledge seared into her heart like a burning arrow but she forced herself to ignore the sensation. People hurt people. She'd been on the receiving end of it often enough to know she didn't want to go through that ever again.

"I need an early night. Thanks for the drink."

But as she stood and took her glass through to the kitchen, leaving Galen in the semi-dark of the lounge room, she couldn't help but acknowledge that somehow he'd wended his way through the labyrinthine corridors that protected her emotions and that when she did walk away from him, it would hurt her, too.

Eleven

"But I don't want to go. Why do I have to?"

Peyton heard Ellie's vehement words as she made her way downstairs to breakfast. They'd been in the house a week and each morning had presented some drama or another as they settled into a new routine.

"It's to earn your next Girl Scout achievement, isn't it?" was Galen's response. "Besides, all your friends are going. You don't want to be left out while they're away having a great time. It's just one night, Ellie, and you love the museum."

"I'm not going," Ellie said again, just as forcefully as the first time.

"Oh, yes, you are, young lady," Galen responded with equal determination.

Peyton walked into the breakfast room just as Ellie's lower lip began to wobble.

"Hey, guys. What's going on?"

"Galen says I have to go but I don't and I'm not going to," Ellie said with a tremor in her voice.

"She does and she will," Galen said, sounding more adamant than Peyton had ever heard him.

"Whoa, take a breath, everyone, will you?" Peyton said, holding her hands up for further effect. "First, Ellie, tell me what this is about."

Peyton gave Galen a stern look, warning him to stay quiet, as Ellie began to tell her about the overnight camp at the museum.

"That sounds really fun. Why don't you want to go?" she coaxed.

"What if something happens to you?"

"Happens? Like what?" Even though she asked, she had a feeling she knew exactly where this was going.

"Like, y'know."

Ellie's shoulders slumped and a tear trickled down her face. Peyton squatted down and took her hands in hers.

"Like what happened to your mom and dad?" she asked, confronting the giant elephant in the room.

Ellie nodded. Peyton pulled her into her arms.

"Oh, honey, I can see why you're afraid. Would it help if I tell you that Galen and I will do everything we can to look after each other while you're away? Maybe we can speak with your Scout leaders and see if they'll let you call us at bedtime. Would that help?"

"Maybe."

Peyton looked up at Galen, who nodded. "I'll call them right now, okay, Ellie?" he said, sliding his phone from his pocket.

He left the room and Peyton could hear the low tones of his voice as he made the call. She realized she was still hugging Ellie to her, and realized, too, that while she'd avoided being overly affectionate with the little girl, it somehow felt right to hold her like this—to be the one offering her comfort when she most needed it.

She wondered if whoever had adopted her little girl comforted her like this when she was distressed. Most of the time, Peyton barely allowed herself to think of the daughter she'd signed over to the private adoption agency. It simply hurt too much. But somehow, holding Ellie like this filled a hole inside her that she hadn't even wanted to acknowledge was there.

She gave the little girl one last squeeze then let her go. Offering Ellie comfort was one thing. Taking it for herself was quite another and she couldn't allow herself to fall into that trap. She'd spent most of her adult life avoiding people with children because she hadn't wanted to suffer the questions she knew it would raise in her mind. Questions about her own child's growth and development. Questions about the sound of her voice, the color of her hair, whether she was sporty or bookish or both.

Peyton couldn't help herself. She reached out to smooth back a lock of hair that had fallen forward on Ellie's face.

"Okay, we have a meeting after school with one of the leaders who will be on the trip with you," Galen said as he reentered the room. "We'll work out a management strategy together, okay?"

Ellie looked confused. "Management what?"

Peyton brushed the girl's cheek. Now that she'd allowed herself to comfort her, she simply couldn't seem to stop. "Don't worry, Ellie. It just means we're going to get together to discuss making you feel safe and secure on the trip. Honestly, we'd hate you to miss out on something that we know you're going to love."

"And if I still don't want to go?"

"We'll cross that bridge when we get there, okay? Let's not make any decisions right now," Peyton reassured her.

"Okay, kiddo. Get your bag. The bus will be at the end of the driveway in a few minutes," Galen said, gently coaxing Ellie along.

Ellie grabbed her bag and started out the breakfast room but stopped, turned and raced back to Peyton. Wrapping her arms around Peyton's neck, she whispered in her ear, "I love you."

Before Peyton could gather her thoughts together and answer, Ellie had let her go again and was racing out the door, with Galen close behind her. It was part of their morning ritual, waiting for the bus together, and to be honest, Peyton was now glad of the moment to herself to gather her thoughts together.

Ellie *loved* her? Did a child fall in love with an adult that fast or were her words merely an expression of thankfulness for bringing the argument she'd been having with Galen to a close and pushing him to find a new solution? Whatever it was, it terrified her. She wasn't here to be Ellie's mom. In truth, she wasn't here to be Galen's wife, either. And what she had planned to do would hurt them both. What was she going to do?

A week later they gathered with all the parents to bid farewell to the bus as the kids loaded aboard. Galen rested his arm across Peyton's shoulders and he was glad that, for once, she didn't pull away. And, judging by the glimpse of tears he'd seen in her eyes as Ellie had turned on the bus steps and waved to them, his wife wasn't quite as unmoved by this moment as she'd tried to portray. It was a side of her he hadn't expected to see. Peyton was normally so contained when it came to her emotions. The only time he'd seen her lose her iron grip on her control was that night during their honeymoon. Right now, however, she looked as vulnerable as any parent sending their kid away to an overnight camp.

"She'll be fine," he murmured in her ear as the bus started up and the windows were filled with young faces and waving hands.

"I know."

"I was thinking—maybe we could go out for a drive together today and have lunch somewhere."

He didn't realize quite how much he was hoping she'd say yes, until she pulled away from him.

"That sounds like a nice idea, but I have some calls to make."

She'd had a private line installed to her office at the house and she'd been spending a whole lot of time in there. He respected anyone with a strong work ethic, but he had the suspicion that a good part of her office hours were spent very determinedly staying out of his way.

Galen nodded. This was obviously a battle for another day. "Okay, maybe another time, then."

She visibly relaxed, showing she'd obviously expected him to push back.

"Yeah, sure, another time."

"I'll drop you back home then head into the office for a while."

"Thanks."

He cringed internally. Things between them were so damn stilted. He hated it. They walked together to the car. Together, yes, but apart, as well. No touching, no accidental brushing of their bodies. *It'll work out*, he encouraged himself. *It's still early days.* They'd only been married a month; they were still getting to know one another. But even as he gave himself the little pep talk, he knew the problems went deeper. Peyton was deliberately shielding herself from him. Was it really because of her long-lost love, or was it something more?

After dropping her home and getting to Horvath Hotels and Resorts head office, he settled himself at his desk and tried to turn his attention to work. It was hopeless. All he could think about was Peyton and how little he knew about her. There was someone who could help with this, he realized—his grandmother. Did he want to ask her advice on the situation, or should he turn to his brother or cousin Ilya instead? Or did he simply try to work this out himself? He twiddled his pen end over end between his fingers before slapping it onto his desk with a hard smack. He had to do this himself. Running to anyone else when he had a problem wasn't his style. He solved problems, period.

So, he and Peyton didn't know each other that well yet. She'd opened up a little when he'd cooked her a meal in Hawaii. Maybe he'd try that tactic again tonight and see where it led. He'd noticed that when she was working she was oblivious to the world around her, even to the point of needing to be reminded to have meals. She wouldn't even notice him coming home and cooking for her. But he might need a little help preparing for the meal.

He picked up the phone and called the new housekeeper. Peyton had been adamant she didn't want live-in staff in the house, so they'd compromised. Galen had hired a woman who was happy to come six days a week to do cleaning and some meals along with supervising Ellie after school as necessary.

When Maggie answered the phone he told her what he had in mind. She was more than happy to do the shopping for him and told him everything would be waiting in the fridge when he got home. He hung up satisfied that he finally had a plan in action.

* * *

Galen made it home early and went upstairs to change, noting that Peyton's office door was firmly closed—a good indicator that she was in the zone and working hard. Once he'd changed into jeans and a T-shirt he went down to the kitchen and opened the refrigerator. As good as her word, Maggie had made sure everything he'd asked for was there. He took out the butterflied chicken and prepared a honey-and-rosemary marinade to paint it with. Once he'd done that and added some seasoning, he took the bird in its dish outside and set it in the barbecue to roast. He quickly scrubbed some baby potatoes and put them in a pot, ready to cook. Then he set to dicing zucchini, mushrooms, onions and bell peppers, and pushed them onto metal skewers ready to add to the barbecue before the chicken was done.

Preparing their meal was wonderfully relaxing. He'd never really been one to just sit, preferring active relaxation instead. As a kid his parents had teased him for having ants in his pants, but no matter how much people urged him to stop and smell the roses he'd always needed to be doing something, anything, to feel good. And he felt good now. Anticipation thrummed a steady beat through his veins as he set the table, adding some flowers from the garden and a couple of squat white candles set on colored sand in glass bowls. He'd always had a certain flair for setting the tone of a room—it was something that had stood him in good stead as he'd climbed through the ranks at Horvath Hotels and Resorts.

Thinking about those years reminded him of his friends Nick and Sarah. A few years older than he was, they'd been quick to take him under their respective wings and show him the ropes here at the offices and resort in Port Ludlow. When he'd assumed the top role as CEO of the chain, they'd been as supportive of him then as they had back in the early days. He missed them every single day. Bestowing him with the responsibility of raising their daughter had been a gift he accepted with an immense sense of sadness and duty blended with a whole lot of love.

Despite appearances, he wasn't as free with his feelings and emotions as people thought. Yes, he had always been that good-time guy who made everyone around him laugh and made everything feel like a party. But overall he was rarely deeply invested in another human being to the extent that he was with his family, or with Ellie and her parents.

And now there was Peyton. He'd thought he could go into marriage keeping things light. How wrong could a man be? Yes, he'd wondered if Peyton's constant pushback wasn't just making him want to try harder simply because he wasn't used to not getting his way. But when he considered it fully, he realized he'd been an idiot to think he could have a marriage without emotions getting complicated. Life was complicated. Their union no less so. And while he'd specified companionship over love everlasting on his application, and assumed she also must have for them to be matched, he now knew that wasn't enough. Nor would it ever be.

Deep in thought, he went down to the wine cellar and chose a bottle of wine to enjoy with dinner. He'd noticed Peyton had a preference for oaked chardonnay and he knew he had a particularly nice one from New Zealand in his collection. After finding the bottle he went back upstairs, surprised to find Peyton poking around the kitchen.

"Something smelled good, so I had to come downstairs and see what's cooking."

He smiled in response. Her office window was above the outdoor grill. There had been an ulterior motive behind his decision to cook the chicken outdoors.

"Did you have lunch?" he asked.

"Lunch? What's that?" she answered lightly.

"You don't take very good care of yourself, do you?"

"I do okay."

"Well, you'll be pleased to know I do more than okay in the kitchen."

He grabbed a large round wooden board from under the kitchen bench then went to the fridge and gathered up some tempting goodies to tide them over until dinner was ready. The Brie Maggie had bought at the store was perfectly ripe and Galen added some sun-dried tomatoes, olives and stuffed baby bell peppers to the board along with a few slivers of fresh French bread.

"That looks like a meal in itself," Peyton said, grabbing one of the peppers and popping it into her mouth.

"Just an appetizer. Shall we take it outside?"

"Can I carry anything for you?" she offered.

"How about you bring the wine and glasses."

He went and checked the chicken after putting the wooden board on the outdoor table. Peyton sat down and poured them each a glass of wine. He rejoined her, making a point to sit right next to her so they were both facing out to the Sound.

"To us," he said, lifting his glass toward hers.

"Yes…to us."

She didn't wholeheartedly join him in the toast but she made it. He'd take that as a win, he decided.

"Did you get a lot of work done today?"

She nodded. "I've spent most of the afternoon compiling my research. The actual writing comes next."

"I imagine it's difficult to decide on what you're going to use and what you need to leave out."

"Yeah, it can be. Especially when the subject is very close to your heart."

She helped herself to a piece of bread and spread some

Brie on it. He watched as she bit into it and felt his whole body grow taut as she groaned in appreciation.

"This is so good. Try some."

And just like that, she turned the conversation in another direction. He'd let her, for now, but sooner or later Peyton would begin to open up to him and he'd be right here to listen when she did.

By the time dinner was cooked and they went inside to the dining room to eat, he knew she was beginning to relax. Maybe it was the wine, or maybe it had been the morsels of food she'd picked at before dinner, but he sensed she had lowered her barriers a little.

After dinner they retired to the sitting room. It was a beautiful space, with a wooden cathedral ceiling and tall glass sliding doors that opened out onto the deck. The views of the Sound were spectacular. This had been one of the main features of the property that had made him want to buy it, and he'd come to look forward to relaxing in here in the evenings to unwind after work. It was all the better for Peyton's company tonight.

She sank onto the overstuffed sofa with a sigh of contentment.

"That was a truly beautiful meal. Thank you."

"My pleasure."

They lapsed into a companionable silence. Galen topped up their wineglasses and handed Peyton hers.

"It's quiet without Ellie," she commented.

"You're a natural with her. From helping her overcome her fear of the sleepover, to seeing her off today. You did great."

Peyton's face froze for a moment, but then she smiled. He watched her, realizing that when she smiled, there was no joy behind it.

"I'm glad you think so. Despite the fact you haven't

been her father all her life, you do a great job, too—you make it look so effortless." She sighed and pulled her feet up underneath her on the sofa. "Parenthood doesn't come naturally to me."

Galen sensed she had a lot more to say, but was just finding the right words. Rather than prompt her, he maintained his silence and watched the emotions that played over her face. She drew in another deep breath and let it go slowly as if she was gearing up for something really important. He felt his whole body tense in anticipation.

"I—" The word came out as a croak and Peyton cleared her throat before starting again. "I had a baby once. I gave her away."

Twelve

Her heart hammered in her chest. There, she'd said the words out loud. The secret she'd never disclosed to anyone other than her dad and those immediately involved in the birth and subsequent adoption of her little girl. To his credit, Galen didn't look as shocked as she thought he might. When he spoke, his voice was incredibly gentle.

"How long ago?"

"Nearly ten years."

"So your baby would be Ellie's age now?" He caught on quickly. "That's got to be difficult for you. I had no idea."

"Well, I didn't exactly include the information in my application," she said, trying to make light of it. "It's not something I like to talk about."

But the lump in her throat grew thicker and she swallowed hard against it, worried she might do the unthinkable and actually cry in front of Galen. She always fought to keep her emotions in check. Life was messy enough without them. But right now it was more difficult than usual.

"She was absolutely perfect," Peyton managed to say, allowing herself a brief moment to remember the rosebud lips, the soft downy blond hair and the sweet scent of her child.

"And her dad? Was he supportive?"

"He was dead."

"Did he know about the baby?"

She shook her head. "He was a marine. He died on his first deployment. Not active duty—a car accident. I didn't find out until quite a while after. I thought, when I contacted him to tell him I was pregnant, that maybe he was just ghosting me. Y'know, it was a good time while it lasted but now it's over kind of thing."

She saw she had shocked him. He rose from his seat and joined her on the sofa. "Peyton, I'm so sorry. Did you have any help from home?"

"My mom died when I was in junior high. My dad, well…"

She let her voice trail away. How did she describe her dad? Bitter. Angry. Resentful. He had told her she could sort out her own problems.

Peyton didn't notice the point at which Galen had taken her hand, but right now his warm, steady grip was grounding, something she could focus on rather than the words that tumbled from her.

"It was hell. I was still in college, nearing the end of my degree. I didn't know what to do or where to turn. A few weeks before she was born I finally accepted that no matter what happened, I couldn't keep her. I just couldn't offer her the opportunities she deserved. I looked into adoption and through a counselor I received additional information about private adoption. I went for that in the end."

She didn't mention how choosing to go with that option had made her feel as though she'd been a womb for hire.

As if her baby was a commodity to buy and sell, and not a living, breathing human being. But she'd still have been paying off her student loans now if she hadn't agreed to her costs being covered by the adopting family.

"Do they share information with you about your daughter?"

She shook her head. "No. I wanted it that way. I didn't think it was fair to give her away and expect to still be a part of her life."

"And if she wants to find you one day?"

Peyton shrugged. "The option is open to her. Her adoptive family insisted on it."

"They sound like decent people."

"I certainly hope they are, and that she's happy."

Her voice broke on the last word and she closed her eyes, not wanting to give in to the feelings that threatened to swamp her. There was a reason she'd kept everything locked deep down inside and that reason was self-preservation. If she'd allowed herself the luxury of indulging in her emotions then the memories would rise up and swallow her, much as they appeared to want to do now. It was too much. She needed a distraction.

"Galen?"

"Hmm?"

"Would you make love to me?"

She felt shock ripple through him, his fingers tightening on her hand in a grip that was almost painful.

"Are you sure about this, Peyton?"

She shifted on the sofa so she was facing him, so his mouth was only a hairbreadth from hers.

"Yes," she whispered.

Then she leaned forward and kissed him. She didn't want any more words. Words only reawakened the pain and sorrow she'd pushed so deep down inside. Now she wanted actions, feelings, sensation. Anything and everything so she could just stop hurting again.

His lips were smooth and supple against hers and she wasted no time, rising onto her knees and straddling his lap. She held his head and angled her face so she could kiss him more deeply and felt his body's answering heat and desire flame to life beneath her. Then his hands were on hers, holding them away from him, and he pulled away slightly.

"What is it? Don't you want this?" she asked, breathless with the desire that pulsed through her.

"Oh, I want this. I want to be certain you do, too. This isn't a one-shot deal, Peyton. As much as I want to let you use me to push away your past, I can't just make love with you and then go back to where we were this morning."

He was asking for her commitment. It was only reasonable. When it came to her, the man was so fiercely astute it was frightening. But right now her body and her mind clamored for the relief she knew being with him would bring. She didn't want to think past this moment. And the idea of commitment? It was too much. But he needed a response and she owed it to him.

"I understand," she forced herself to say.

She'd deal with the outcome of tonight's choice later. Right now she wanted him and she wanted oblivion, in that order. She kissed him again, shifting her pelvis this time so her body ground against his, letting him know how much she wanted him.

"You're not being fair, Peyton," he said against her lips. "You're tormenting me. In fact, you've been a torment since the first time I laid eyes on you."

"Then let's ease our torment together. Let's go upstairs."

She wriggled off his lap and stood in front of him, holding out her hand. She'd made the invitation; it was up to him to accept it. Whatever came next was all down to him.

He didn't hesitate. He took her hand and rose to his feet, then led her through the room and up the stairs and along the gallery to the master suite.

"Now is the time to leave if you don't want to go any further, Peyton. I'm serious."

"Then let's not pretend," she answered, stepping closer and reaching up to stroke his face. "So solemn. Let's see if we can't change that," she murmured before going on tiptoes and kissing him again.

"I can't think when you do that," he protested.

"And when I do this?"

She slid her hands under his T-shirt and up to his chest, where she found the flat discs of his nipples and squeezed them gently.

"And when you do that," he affirmed.

"And what about this?"

Peyton let one hand slide down his torso, to his belly, to the waistband of his jeans. His sharply indrawn breath allowed her to slip beneath the waistband and to his boxer briefs, where she stroked him through the fabric.

"Most definitely when you do that," he groaned. "In fact, pretty much when you do anything."

She gently gripped him, squeezing slightly before letting him go and pulling her hand out. "You're wearing far too many clothes for what I want to do to you."

"To me? Or with me?" he asked.

"Both, either. Does it matter?"

"It matters. When it comes to you, Peyton, everything matters."

There was something in the tone of his voice that gave her pause, made her question whether or not she was doing the right thing. But the steady thrum of her pulse and the deliciously building tension of her body told her more than anything that she was in the right place at the right time.

They would find pleasure in one another, that was a given. The man lit her up like the Fourth of July when he kissed her. And when he touched her...

She didn't want to think anymore. Instead, Peyton reached for his T-shirt and tugged it over his head before letting it drop to the bedroom floor. Then her hands were at his jeans, clumsily undoing the fastenings. She shoved her fingertips under the waistband of his briefs and eased them down over his hips. He stood there in front of her, gloriously naked. She wanted to touch all of him, taste him, feel him. She drew in a shaky breath before tugging away at her own clothes. The moment she was naked she wrapped herself around him, drawing in his strength and heat. His hands spread across her back, holding her even tighter to his body.

Peyton lifted her face to his and welcomed the fierceness of his kiss, the plunder of his tongue. This was what she needed. Him. All of him. Everywhere.

They backed up to his bed and he fell back on the mattress. She straddled him again, pushing his shoulders down until he was flat on the bed. Her hands molded the muscles of his shoulders as she bent her head to his throat and kissed a wet trail down the strong column and farther, to his chest. Her nostrils flared at the scent of him: heat and spice together with the fresh scent of the sea. She'd never be able to smell the ocean again without her mind being filled with him. They were intrinsically combined now. She shifted a little so she could continue her trail of kisses, her fingertips tugging gently at the spear of body hair that arrowed below his belly, her lips and tongue following.

His erection strained against her, brushing her breasts as she moved lower. She took him in her hand again and slowly stroked his hot, silky skin. His flesh jerked against her palm and she tightened her hold.

"You like this?" she asked.

"I like everything you do to me," he growled in reply.

She smiled and arched a brow. "Everything?"

"Everything." His voice was adamant.

She lowered her mouth to the swollen head of his penis, her tongue darting out to flick against him. Beneath her, he shuddered.

"Especially that," he said, his voice trembling.

She stroked her hands over his strong thighs and nuzzled the base of him before licking a path along his length and taking him into her mouth. His fingers caught in her hair as she swirled her tongue around him, taking him deeper into her mouth and sucking hard. His entire body tensed and she knew he was on the verge of losing his mind when she eased the pressure of her mouth and rose above him.

She settled herself over his glistening shaft.

"I'm glad we can dispense with any interruptions," she murmured as she began to take him into her body. "We're both clean and I'm on birth control."

He groaned as she sank down on him and rocked her pelvis. "I'm glad you're glad," he teased in return, but by the tone of his voice it took every ounce of effort he had left.

She knew how he felt. Right now all she wanted to do was bounce and buck and wring her pleasure from his body. But first, she wanted to pleasure him. She started to move, her motion gentle, deep and slow. Galen lifted his hands and cupped her breasts, his fingertips playing with her nipples—at first gently, then squeezing just a little more tightly until the delicious pain of it made her internal muscles clench on an involuntary wave of pleasure so intense she thought he'd make her come, just like this.

She fought against the urge to give in; when she came, it would be with him and because she wanted to. She increased her movements, leaning her body weight onto his upstretched arms as she got faster, and faster still. His eyes remained locked on hers, staring into her as if he could see past all her walls and into her very soul. And then she felt him buck beneath her, his climax rocketing through him, his body straining against hers, and she let go, allowing herself to disappear on the rolling crescendo of satisfaction that stole the breath from her body and the memories from her mind.

This was what she'd wanted, needed. Oblivion.

Thirteen

Making love with Peyton had been everything he'd dreamed of, and more—every single time. And yet, while they'd reached physical perfection together, there was still a disconnection between them. She'd blindsided him last night. Both with the news about the child she'd surrendered for adoption and then with their lovemaking.

He'd willingly let her take the lead, instinctively understanding that was what she needed, but while he'd made it clear that if they took that step in their relationship it meant they couldn't go back, he wondered if she hadn't simply been paying lip service to get what she needed right then.

So what happened next? He knew what he wanted out of their marriage, even if he hadn't exactly gone into it with an expectation of falling in love. But if how he was feeling right now was any indication then it was clear his expectations had done a U-turn.

Peyton shifted in the bed, her body suddenly tense.

"You okay?" he asked.

She stretched and rolled over to face him. "I'm good. And you?"

He reached out and smoothed her hair from her face, enjoying the intimacy. "I'm great. No second thoughts?"

He had to ask, needed to know what she was thinking, what she planned to do now that the cocooned world of night had been shattered by day. Peyton's eyes were slightly shadowed as she sat up abruptly, the sheets falling from her body and exposing her naked form to his hungry eyes.

She shook her head and looked back at him over her shoulder. "Not me. I'm going for a shower. Then I'll cook us a huge breakfast. I'm famished."

He smiled back, feeling the tension in both his mind and body ease. "That sounds like a great idea. Need help washing your back?"

She laughed. "If you do that, breakfast might be more like lunch."

"I can wait," he said.

He watched her as his words sank in. Her pupils dilated and her nipples tightened into dark pink buds. Buds that had felt perfect as he'd rolled them with his tongue last night. She'd been a very open lover, giving as well as receiving. Last night had been exceptional and, under other circumstances, would have left him sated. But there was something about Peyton that drove him to want more—physically and emotionally. He swung his feet to the floor, stood up and walked toward her. Her gaze roamed his body, coming to rest just below his hips.

"I see that you have something else in mind," she said with a saucy smile.

As her lips curved he felt something pull tight in his chest. Was this what love was? he wondered. This sense of being knocked sideways by something as precious as a smile? This overwhelming need to touch her and be touched by her? This wanting to know and understand her every thought? To make her happy? If it wasn't love, it was pretty darn close.

Galen held a hand out to Peyton and tugged her forward, aligning her naked body against his and relishing the heat in those areas where their bodies touched. He didn't think he could ever have enough of this, of her.

"Oh, I have a lot of things in mind right now. Every single one of them centered on you."

Her breath hitched and he saw a look of yearning on her beautiful features. A yearning that was swiftly masked by something else. She was good at that, he realized. Far too good. His wife was an expert at masking her true thoughts and feelings. In fact, the only time he thought she'd been 100 percent open and honest with him had been last night, in the sanctuary of his bed. Well, if that was what it took to get to know and understand her, then he'd gladly step up to the task. Keeping her loved up and satisfied would be both an honor and a pleasure.

"C'mon," he said, his voice just a bit gruff. "Let's shower."

"We're going to have to hurry if we're to meet Ellie's bus," Peyton said with a laugh as she whisked eggs in a bowl.

"I can do the bacon on the outdoor grill if you like. It'll be quicker."

"Thanks. These will only take a few minutes."

"I'm onto it."

Galen snagged the packet of bacon with one hand and started to whistle as he went out onto the deck. He hadn't felt this happy in forever. Maybe it was the sense of letting go of his control over his emotions that left him feeling like he'd just been on the most incredible roller-coaster ride of his life. Whatever it was, he liked it.

He looked through the window to the kitchen and watched Peyton as she moved around. It was quite the scene of domestic bliss. Something that had been sadly lacking in the weeks prior. She'd been so wary, but then again, he had been, too. Last night, when she told him about her daughter, it had opened things up between them. But he knew she was still holding back. Peyton was complex, with multiple layers. He'd only uncovered one—a very important, deeply scarred one.

She was scarred, but strong, as well. A person would have to be, to get through that without becoming a wreck. He didn't know if, in similar circumstances, he'd have been able to face the same thing.

He thought for a minute about his female cousins. Each one of them strong and independent, benefiting from their grandmother's example. But if any one of them had faced a situation like Peyton's she'd have had a wealth of support behind her. Peyton hadn't had any of that. No wonder she was so reserved and aloof. No wonder she feared love. The more he began to understand her, the more he realized that it was fear holding her back, whether she knew it or not.

"Are you planning on burning that bacon?" Peyton called out from the kitchen, snapping him out of his reveries.

"As if I'd do such a thing," he called back and quickly snatched up a set of tongs and a plate to take the strips off the grill. "I hope you like yours crispy," he commented wryly as he reentered the kitchen.

A gurgle of laughter bubbled up from inside her, the sound making him stop in his tracks and simply drink in the joy of watching her unguarded, happy. Hell, he'd almost burn the bacon every day if it meant he could hear her laugh so honestly.

"You're lucky I do," she said, spooning a generous serving of scrambled eggs onto his plate.

"Hey, leave yourself some," he protested.

"Oh, I won't miss out, don't worry."

He looked at the clock. They had half an hour to eat and clean up before collecting Ellie at the pickup point. If only they had more time alone together. Somehow, the dynamic of having Ellie around changed things between them. He didn't regret having the little girl in his life one bit, but he suspected that sometimes being around her was like rubbing salt in the wound for Peyton. Some of the looks she'd given Ellie began to make sense now. The looks that spoke of longing and regret. Looks that were tempered with a please-don't-love-me vibe because she was too afraid to love in return. He had to break through those barriers. Somehow, he and Peyton and Ellie would become a real family.

Peyton stood with Galen's arm draped around her as they waited with the other parents for the bus to arrive. It all felt so normal and so foreign at the same time. Things had changed since they'd been here in the same spot yesterday. Then, she'd been full of trepidation for Ellie, an emotion that had been swiftly chased by pride in the girl as she'd shouldered her anxiety and climbed on board the bus.

And hadn't she done something similar herself last night? She tightened her hold on Galen's waist, taking strength in his nearness and his solid presence beside her. Was this what marriage had been like for her parents before her mom had gotten sick—before her dad had changed? The sad thing was, she couldn't even ask him. He'd been so filled with seething anger, even going so far as destroying the photo albums her mom had so patiently and lovingly made up for Peyton as a way of remembering her when she was gone.

She wondered where Ellie's parents' pictures were and made a mental note to ask Galen. While she knew that Ellie's old bedroom from her parents' home had been faithfully replicated at his apartment and then more recently in their new house, she had no idea what had happened to everything else. Maybe it would help Ellie to feel more secure and connected if she had access to more of her happy memories with her mom and dad.

And when you move on, what then? Her conscience pricked sharply.

Beneath her hand, she felt Galen's body tense.

"There's the bus," he exclaimed. "And there she is!"

With his free hand he began waving madly. Peyton felt her heart constrict. They had been very occupied during Ellie's absence, but it was clear Galen hadn't stopped worrying about her.

The next half hour was filled with a blur of retrieving the overnight bags and girls saying goodbye to each other until, finally, they were able to climb into the car and get back to the house.

"You had a good time?" Galen asked after Ellie did up her seat belt.

"I had the best time."

"So you're glad you went?" Peyton pressed.

"Yeah, thank you for making me go. It was really cool."

Their ride home was peppered with Ellie's excitement, which stretched out into the afternoon. Peyton helped her unpack and put her things in the wash, teaching her how to do each step.

"My mommy used to do this but at the hotel apartment Galen just sent our laundry out. Do I have to do this all the time now?" Ellie asked as she turned on the washer.

"If you want to. It's good to know how to take care of yourself."

"But what if I don't want to?"

"Well, you have me and we have Maggie."

"Did your mommy teach you?"

"No. My mommy got sick and wasn't able to do a lot of stuff."

"I'm sorry."

"It was a long time ago."

Ellie enveloped her in a hug. "I'm glad you're with us now. You don't need to be alone anymore."

The child's simple words cut her to her core. Alone? She felt like she'd spent her entire life alone from the day of her mom's diagnosis. And now that she actually had something, she was gearing up to leave it all behind her again. She awkwardly returned Ellie's hug and then pulled away.

"C'mon, you can help me prepare a salad for dinner. Galen's grilling steaks and baking potatoes."

"Yum!"

And just like that the moment changed. Kids were so adaptable, she thought as she followed Ellie through to the kitchen. Maybe she needed to be a bit more like that.

The evening went quickly and it wasn't long before Ellie was drooping with exhaustion. After Galen had seen her to bed, Peyton went into her office to work on her article. She read through the opening paragraphs, but instead of the sense of triumph she expected, she ended up with a knot in her stomach. She sighed in frustration and dropped her head in her hands. Why was writing this so hard? She'd planned it for years, relished the opportunity to depose Alice Horvath from the heady pedestal on which everyone put her. This should be the easiest thing in the world to her. It didn't involve political upheaval; it didn't involve genocide or massive environmental damage—all of which she'd written about to great acclaim in the past. So what was wrong with her? Was it that she was too close to the subject matter? Too biased, perhaps?

No, it wasn't personal bias. She'd found others, like her father, who'd been summarily dismissed from their jobs at various Horvath Corporation branches. Locating them had been like finding needles in haystacks, and a handful had signed nondisclosure agreements on their termination, so they had politely, but firmly, rebuffed her attempts to interview them. But the others backed up her father's experience.

Peyton had always prided herself on balanced reporting. Up until now all she'd accumulated was one side of the story. And there was her answer. She needed to go straight to the source. She needed to interview Alice. Her stomach knotted in anticipation. Would the grand matriarch grant her an audience? It was well known that Alice didn't do interviews. Hey, she could ask, right? But what would be the best way to approach her?

A sound behind her made her minimize her open computer window, swivel in her chair and look at the door. Galen stood there, one arm casually propped against the frame and looking far too sexy for his own good. Her body tightened on a surge of remembrance. This afternoon had been about Ellie, but right now her mind was crammed with all the things she and Galen had done together last night.

"Everything okay?" Galen asked.

"Yes, and no," she admitted. How could she approach this? she wondered. Just ask him straight-out if his grandmother would talk to her, perhaps? But for what reason? An idea sprang to her mind. "A part of my article focuses on strong women in business. Would Alice agree to an interview, do you think?"

What she'd said wasn't a total lie. Galen straightened and took a step inside her office. He frowned a little.

"She's not a fan of interviews. You probably know that already."

"I had heard something like that," Peyton said lightly. "But there's no harm in asking her, right? If she says no, it's no." She shrugged as if it didn't matter.

Galen stroked his chin thoughtfully. "I could talk to her for you."

"No, I wouldn't ask you to do that. Using you as a go-between would be cowardly."

"You're probably right. In fact, I know you're right. Nagy would probably see it as a weakness and dismiss the idea immediately."

Peyton nodded. "I'll call her tomorrow, and just get straight to the point."

Galen moved closer and rested his hands on her shoulders, massaging the knots of muscle that had formed there while she worked. "Good idea. What will you do if she says no?"

"Move on to the next person on my list. Alice's input isn't vital to my article, but I'd be keen on hearing her out."

"Then let's hope she's in a magnanimous mood tomorrow," he said on a chuckle. "Jeez, you're so tight. Is this what working on your articles does to you?"

"Sometimes, especially when things aren't going as well as I'd like. But y'know what?"

"What?"

"I know something that loosens me up like nothing else."

His hands stilled and she heard his sharply indrawn breath. "And that might be?"

"Oh, I think you know what I mean," she answered as she rose to her feet. "Or have you forgotten already? Perhaps I need to refresh your memory."

She entwined her arms around his neck and lifted her face to his, taking possession of his mouth in a kiss that she knew would leave him in no doubt of what she was talking about. Thankfully, he was a quick study. She felt his body's instant response to her invitation, and when he scooped her in his arms and stalked with her across the landing toward the master suite, she allowed herself to thrill in the anticipation of what she knew would come next.

Fourteen

"Thank you so much for agreeing to see me, Mrs. Horvath."

Alice forced herself to smile. "Please, dear. I've asked you already to call me Alice or Nagy. If you keep referring to me as Mrs. Horvath I'll think you're not really a part of the family."

She had kept the censure from her voice but she didn't miss the swiftly masked expression on the younger woman's face. Was it irritation, perhaps, or embarrassment? Or maybe something else? Since her operation she didn't feel quite as sharp as she used to be and it annoyed her intensely. Getting old certainly wasn't for sissies. Luckily, she'd never been a sissy in her life.

"I'm sorry, Alice," Peyton apologized.

"That's better, dear. See? It didn't hurt a bit, did it?" Alice allowed herself a small smile. "I hope you enjoyed your flight?"

"Having a company jet at my disposal isn't something I think I'll ever get used to but, yes, it was a smooth trip."

"Good. Now, please, take a seat and tell me what this article is about. It must be important to bring you all the way to California. You know I don't usually give interviews."

"Yes, I do, and I really appreciate you making time to see me."

"Time seems to be something I have a great deal more of than I wish to these days."

"Oh, isn't Match Made in Marriage keeping you busy enough?"

Alice waved a hand in front of her. "Oh, yes, that's fun. But it's hardly the cut and thrust of the corporate world, is it? And I have to say, since my surgery earlier this year, I've been forced to slow down a little. A temporary thing, I've been assured."

She firmed her lips before she said any more. She didn't like exposing her infirmities to anyone, least of all this newest member of her family. "Tell me, how is Ellie doing now that you're settling into your new home? It must have been a big adjustment for all of you—getting married and living together. But you're doing all right, I trust?"

She listened as Peyton filled her in about the little girl, nodding and smiling where necessary. She wondered if Peyton knew how her expression changed when she talked about Ellie, about the small elements of pride that shone through when she mentioned Ellie's bravery at going on the overnight visit to the museum and her latest school results. And then, how her expression became softer when she talked about Galen. Yes, Alice had made the right choice here. It had been a risk, thrusting a husband and child onto a young woman for whom career appeared to be everything, but as with so many things in life that were worthwhile, you had to take a leap of faith at some point.

Much of the tension that had been apparent on Peyton's face when they'd returned from their honeymoon had eased, but she was clearly very driven. It was a trait Alice both identified with and admired, but she knew firsthand that that drive had to be tempered or it would take over any chance for true happiness.

Peyton brought her conversation back to the point of her being there. "So, as you can see, our lives are busy. But no less busy than your life must have been with your much larger family and juggling your children's needs with the demands of the Horvath Corporation after your husband passed away."

"We women do what we do." Alice shrugged.

"That's true," Peyton agreed. "Which is what I wanted to speak with you about. I want to talk about women in business. About the balance of life and work and how that affected your decision-making."

"Affected my decision-making? You mean emotional versus rational, that sort of thing?"

Peyton looked slightly uncomfortable. "I guess, yes. We are emotional creatures, aren't we?"

"You're testing me, aren't you?" Alice said with a little laugh. "Okay, I'll give you your interview, Peyton. I respect you for both asking me directly and for coming to me, face-to-face, to conduct it. I should have expected as much from you."

"Expected as much?"

"Oh, I'm well aware of your successes in your field, young lady. I should be flattered, I suppose, that you wanted to interview me, too. That you thought my life worthy of inclusion in one of your articles. Although, I have to say, this is a shift for you, isn't it? Women in business instead of your usual David versus Goliath style of reporting?"

Peyton shifted in her chair. "Yes, it is. But you have to admit, it's a subject dear to a lot of women's hearts."

Alice smiled. It was clear that Peyton was only revealing half of her intentions. Perhaps by offering Peyton her trust, it would convince the girl that she truly was a part of the family. And if it didn't? Alice rubbed absently at her chest, a habit she still found herself indulging in even now that her heart was so much better.

If Alice had miscalculated, it might mean she'd made the first serious mistake of her life and endangered the happiness of both her much-adored grandson and the little girl he had taken responsibility for. But Alice Horvath didn't make mistakes, she reminded herself. She relaxed her features and put a smile on her face.

"Ask me your questions, my dear. And then we can enjoy lunch together and get to know each other a little better."

Peyton wondered if a butterfly caught in a net felt the same as she did right now. This interview was no different from anything she had done before, so why did she feel like a rookie reporter covering her first school event and worrying if she'd get the names right? It was ridiculous. She smiled back at Alice and took out her notepad and pen from her leather bag.

"No recorder?" Alice asked, raising one brow.

"I prefer to make notes as I go, but if you'd rather I record, I can do that using my phone."

"One of the reasons I don't usually grant interviews is because I have a deep dislike of being misquoted. At least if you have a recording, there can be no mistakes, correct?"

Peyton averted her gaze. There was something about Alice's tone that made her uncomfortable. As if she was being challenged. Or maybe it was merely her own guilt that was making it seem so. She pulled her phone from her bag, put it on the coffee table between them and selected the voice recorder app.

"There we go," she said as brightly as she could manage. "No mistakes."

"Thank you, my dear. It's good of you to indulge an old woman."

Now there was a trap laid before her if ever there was one. Peyton couldn't help it; she laughed. "You may be older than me, Alice, but you're likely as sharp as you ever were."

She met Alice's blue eyes across the table and saw the glimmer of humor reflected there; she also noted the subtle nod of her head.

"More people would do well to remember that. Now, ask me your questions."

Peyton skimmed through what she mentally called the fluff questions, all of which appeared to bore Alice if her lackluster responses were anything to go by.

"Don't you have questions with more meat to them? I thought you wanted this article to be as hard-hitting as your usual work. Or are you targeting a new audience?" the older woman asked her with a dash of acerbity to her tone.

Peyton was a little taken aback. This was her interviewing style—fluff to soften up her subject before rounding out the interview with the serious questions that gave her the kind of answers she really wanted. The technique had served her well in the past, lulling most of her interviewees into a sense of security before she got to the point of what she wanted to know. Alice, it appeared, was not one of those people.

"No, it's not for a new audience. This will be as serious a work as anything I've done before, perhaps even more so," she replied, feeling slightly defensive.

"Then kindly get to the point."

Alice's words were delivered with a smile but Peyton

was left in no doubt whatsoever that she was treading on thin ice.

"So, Match Made in Marriage. What drove you to establish the company and how successful is it, really?"

"I believe I already mentioned to you once, I have a knack for introducing people to one another. It made sense to formalize that with a company that specialized in creating introductions."

"But they're not just introductions, are they? Not when people meet for the first time at the altar," Peyton pressed.

"You approached us. You know the format."

Was that a note of censure or warning in Alice's voice? Peyton felt a tiny thrill of excitement. Was she finally getting to her? Riling up the ever-serene and much-loved Nagy, who appeared incapable of doing any wrong to her doting family.

"That's true—I did. And you delivered exactly what I asked for in my assessment questionnaire. How can you be certain, though, that every match will be a success?"

Alice narrowed her eyes a moment. "Are you speaking as a reporter now? Or from a point of fear for your own relationship with my grandson? You were unsettled when you arrived back from your honeymoon. Are things not improving?"

Peyton shook her head. Oh, the old lady was good. She'd managed to turn the tables on Peyton with next to no effort. She girded herself to take back control of the interview once more.

"We aren't talking about me and my situation. I'm curious about the science behind the matches you make."

"It's not all science, although since I've established the company I've enlisted the assistance of psychologists and relationship experts to ensure that we're on the right track. We've had no failures so far, which is more than I can say for most dating options available to people these days. We take a lot of pride in our matches—there's a lot at stake."

"This is true," Peyton agreed. "A great deal is at stake on many levels, including the legal assurances in the agreements your clients sign. But is it true that, science and probabilities aside, you always have the final say on whether or not a couple are to be matched?"

Alice's voice had lost all its warmth when she spoke this time. "As I said earlier, I have a knack for making introductions. The science merely supports this. Our track record now speaks for itself."

"So basically, and let's be totally honest here, you're it. You're the one manipulating people's lives and potential happiness with your matches. And, despite your 'knack,' as you call it, you weren't a hundred percent on track as a younger woman, were you? After all, didn't you keep two men dangling for your attention before you chose to marry Eduard Horvath?"

Peyton knew she was taking a risk by raking up that old coal, but she wasn't here to pussyfoot around. Alice sighed and straightened her skirt over her legs.

"You didn't set this interview up to discuss Match Made in Marriage, or my past," Alice said pointedly.

"The matchmaking business is a part of who you are as a businesswoman, but if you're uncomfortable talking about Match Made in Marriage we can move on to something else. Okay, as far as I can tell, Horvath Corporation has a very high staff retention rate. But no workplace is ever perfect. Tell me about the people you've fired. Who were they, and why did you fire them?"

"Telling you who they were would be a breach of confidentiality," Alice responded smoothly.

But Peyton didn't miss the stiffening of the woman's spine.

"Without stating specifics, then. What kind of thing would lead you to release a staff member?"

"Theft and disloyalty are generally the only reasons I have been forced to let people go. And it never failed to surprise me that despite all the benefits we offered, together with very competitive salaries, there'd always be a few who thought they could dip their hands in the pot, so to speak."

"How did you deal with it?"

"How does anyone deal with theft? The consequences are clearly spelled out in staff employment agreements. The offender is terminated."

"And what process of investigation do you follow? Surely people are assumed innocent until proved guilty?"

Peyton held her breath. She still vividly remembered the day her father had come home from work, furious that he'd been dismissed without a chance to defend himself.

"The staff member is generally put on leave with full pay until an independent investigation is conducted. Depending on the outcome of that investigation, they either return to work or they go on to find work elsewhere."

"And what about the rumors I've been told, that you've interfered with some former staffers' ability to find other work?"

Alice's eyes narrowed. "I don't address rumors."

"Okay, let me rephrase that. Have you ever interfered with an ex-employee's ability to find other work in their field?"

"I believe this interview is over." Alice rose to her feet. "I look forward to seeing your article when it goes to print. Will you furnish me with an advance copy?"

And give the old lady time to file an injunction preventing its publication when she saw what the article truly held? Peyton smiled and shook her head.

"That's not my usual practice. I can't be seen to make an exception. I'm sure you understand."

"Oh, I understand, Peyton. Be careful where you tread."

"I beg your pardon?"

"I said for you to be careful where you tread. You don't know what you may inadvertently step into. Now, let's adjourn to the dining room. I believe our lunch is ready."

Peyton watched the woman as she walked slowly and carefully across the room. The interview had left her with a bitter taste in her mouth—there were still so many questions Peyton wanted to ask. At least Alice hadn't kicked her out, but she had the feeling she'd come mighty close to it. Best not to poke the tiger any further today.

One thing, however, was crystal clear. She needed to wrap up the feature and get out of this marriage—this family—as quickly as possible.

Fifteen

Galen watched Peyton as she got ready for bed that night. There was something about her bedtime routine that he found unbelievably sexy. He rose from the bed and walked toward her where she sat at the bedroom vanity, brush in hand. He was only wearing his cotton pajama bottoms.

"Let me do that," he suggested.

She didn't protest as he took the brush from her hand and began to run it through her hair. But rather than relax her, as it usually did, she appeared to grow even more tense.

"How did the interview go with Nagy today?"

"She's the queen of stonewalling, isn't she?"

"Ah, so it didn't go well, then." He kept up the steady strokes of the brush.

"No, it didn't. Not for me, anyway. I have some quotes I can use but I didn't get near to what I really wanted."

"Do you want me to try for you? Perhaps she might be more amenable if I ask—"

"No!" Peyton blurted. "I'm sorry, but no," she repeated more gently this time. "I will work with what I have."

Galen met Peyton's gaze in the mirror. She showed obvious signs of strain around her eyes and there were shadows beneath them, too. He put down the brush and rested his hands on her shoulders.

"I only want to help you, Peyton, to make your life easier where I can."

"I know that, but you have to understand, I'm used to relying on myself. That way I have only myself to blame if something goes wrong."

"Why should anything go wrong?"

She gently shook her head and gave him a slightly pitying look. "You really have no idea, do you?"

Her words stung. Did she think he'd never known hardship or sorrow or difficulty? As if she suddenly realized how her words must have sounded, she shook her head again.

"Look, I'm sorry. Of course you know what it's like."

"Everyone has their battles to face. But you don't have to face anything alone anymore, Peyton." His fingers tightened on her shoulders and he leaned down until his face was even with hers. "I'm here for you now. All you have to do is let go and trust me to help you."

She lifted a hand to one of his, her fingers lacing in between his and squeezing them. "Thank you. It's an adjustment learning to rely on someone else. I'm not sure I'm very good at it."

"Hey, practice makes perfect, right?"

He dropped a kiss on her shoulder, then shifted her hair to expose the back of her neck and pressed his lips there. A tremor ran through her and she dropped her head forward.

"It does crazy things to me when you do that," she said softly.

"Want me to distract you some more?"

"Please."

The heartfelt plea in that single word made him want to stop and ask more about what had happened today between her and his grandmother. That it hadn't gone well had been evident in every line of her face and the way she'd carried herself when she'd arrived home a quarter of an hour ago. But now was not the time. Now was all about shifting that tiredness from her eyes and putting life and energy back in them while revitalizing her body to a point where she could forget what troubled her. She'd said she didn't want his help, but she'd accept this, so he'd give it to her.

Galen's hands slid to the straps of her nightgown and gently eased the thin strips over her shoulders and down her arms. The silky fabric of her nightie slipped down her breasts, slowly exposing them to his hungry gaze. He bent his head and kissed a line along her shoulder while his hands slid down, tugging the fabric away from her breasts completely. Her nipples had grown into taut points and the creamy flesh of her breasts rose and fell as her breathing quickened in response to his touch. He cupped her breasts with his hands, massaging them gently and watching his actions in the mirror. There was something incredibly erotic about seeing their reflections in the mirror like this and feeling the weight of her in his hands, inhaling the subtle scent of her fragrant skin and feeling the rising heat that came from her body.

"Are you playing voyeur tonight?" she asked.

Her voice was husky, and when her eyes met his in the mirror, they shone with arousal.

"Do you like that?" he countered.

"Only if I get to watch, too," she replied, her voice catching on a hitch of breath.

Desire surged through him, making his fingers tremble as he touched her, clouding his mind to the point where he could barely think. Her hands closed over his, pressing them more firmly into her soft, malleable flesh and guiding him to gently squeeze her nipples. Her head fell back on his shoulder, her eyes glittering as she continued to watch their hands on her body. A flush spread across her chest and her cheeks. She guided one of his hands down over her belly to the apex of her thighs. He felt her shiver in response as his fingertip brushed against her clitoris.

"Again," she demanded.

Always a gentleman, he did his best to oblige. She let go of his hand and threaded her fingers up through his hair, her nails scraping his scalp as he circled the nub of nerve endings—occasionally touching it, pressing it, grazing it ever so slightly before letting his hand sweep away to dip into the core of her. She was wet, so wet, and he was equally as hard.

"Stand up," he directed. He helped her to her feet and pushed the stool away. "Good. Now put your hands on the dressing table."

"You're so bossy," she teased.

He ran his hand down her back to her buttocks and gave her a little slap. Her eyes flared in the mirror and she bit her bottom lip.

"And you're cheeky," he said with a smile as he loosened the tie on his pajamas and let them fall to his feet.

He stroked himself, letting her watch his reflection in the mirror.

"Oh no, that can't be what you plan to do," she said with a smile and swayed her hips sensuously. "Not when there are much better options available."

"I like being a man with options. What would you suggest?"

"You're a clever kind of guy. I think you've got this, don't you?"

He stroked one hand down her spine to the cleft of her buttocks and felt her body grow taut beneath his touch. He stroked the lush globes of her bottom, then delved lower, deeper, to where the heat and moisture of her body awaited his possession.

"This, you mean?"

He slid one finger inside her and stroked her deeply—feeling her body clench against him.

Her voice shook when she spoke. "Something like that, yes. But I think you can do better."

"She wants better?" he murmured. "Then her wish is my command."

He positioned himself behind her and guided the swollen head of his penis to her, pressing himself gently until he was only just inside the entrance to her body. He forced himself to hold back, his hands now resting on the curves of her hips. Her inner muscles tightened around him, driving a groan from him and sending a bolt of pleasure rocketing from his tip through his entire body.

"Galen, please. Don't tease me, not about this, not anymore. I want you deep inside me. I need you."

It was those last three words that proved his undoing. He threw restraint to the wind and allowed his body to surge within hers. Peyton's hands tightened into fists on the dressing table as he filled her. A gasp of pleasure escaped her. She pressed against him and the sensation of her buttocks against his groin made him move again, and again, until all he could think about was the pleasure filling his body, filling hers. On the brink of letting go, he paused and reached for her, his fingers deftly finding her pleasure spot and massaging her right there. It took the lightest touch to set her off and he felt every paroxysm of pleasure as it swelled through her body and he gave himself up to his own release.

They were both shaking when he finally withdrew from her moments later. She rose and turned to face him, her arms sliding around his waist. The skin-to-skin contact, their racing hearts and the perspiration of their bodies gleaming in the light of the room seemed like the perfect denouement to their joining.

"C'mon," he whispered against her hair. "Let's go to bed."

Shortly afterward they were cuddled up in bed together, her head resting in the curve of his shoulder and his arm around her body, his hand absently stroking her silky skin. Galen flipped the master switch that plunged the room into darkness and was beginning to slide into sleep when she spoke.

"Galen?"

"Mmm-hmm?"

"I think you should brush my hair more often."

He smiled and pulled her even tighter to him, his heart filling with the words he suddenly wished he could say. He loved her. The realization hit him with a solid thump to his solar plexus as he turned the thought around and around in his head. He loved her. But did that mean anything if she didn't love him in return?

She couldn't concentrate because her treacherous mind kept spinning back to the way Galen had made love to her last night. And it had been lovemaking, not just sex. There'd been something about the way he'd touched her, the way he'd lavished attention on her, that had been more than what they'd done together before. The knowledge both thrilled and terrified her. She'd barely dared consider that she could let another person get this close to her. She could feel herself wanting to let him inside every part of her, not just her body but her mind, as well, so they could truly be one together. But she couldn't let that happen. It wasn't what she'd set herself up to do and she'd learned a long time ago that deviation from her chosen path only led to heartbreak and disappointment.

Peyton saved her document again and stared blindly at the computer screen. This feature was no less aggressive than anything else she'd done. Oh sure, as Alice had so adroitly pointed out yesterday, it wasn't about anything as topical as an environmental or political issue, nor did it tread along the battlefields of far-flung places. But it did reflect the battlefield of her childhood, and the woman who'd single-handedly ensured that Peyton's life would never be the same again from the moment she'd fired her dad.

She thought for a moment of the bitter man he still was today. Of the blame and anger that had become his constant refrain, which had, in turn, pushed away anyone who'd tried to love or care for him, including Peyton. How different her life would have been had Alice Horvath not destroyed the very fabric of her family. Peyton sighed and rested her hands back on the keyboard. She had to somehow remove personal bias from this profile of the Horvath matriarch. Let the facts speak for themselves.

She printed out the document and rose from her chair, pacing her office as the papers began to stack up in the printer tray. Once the article was printed, she grabbed one of her favorite red pens for editing and the bunch of papers and went downstairs onto the deck.

She hadn't been editing for long when she felt her cell phone vibrate in her pocket. A quick glance at the screen confirmed it was Ellie's school. She put down her pen and answered the call.

"Ms. Earnshaw, I'm sorry to bother you. I did try to get hold of Mr. Horvath but he's apparently in a meeting."

"Not a problem. Is it Ellie? Is something wrong?"

"She appears to have an upset stomach. We feel it best if she went home for the rest of today."

"No problem. I'll be right there."

Peyton disconnected the call, shoved her phone in her jeans pocket and reached for the stack of papers she had on the table in front of her. Just then, a massive gust of wind caught the papers and ruffled them across the table and the deck. Peyton frantically picked them up, counting them to ensure she had them all. Yes, every last one accounted for. She closed the glass sliding door behind her as she raced to the breakfast room, where she'd left her bag and car keys yesterday, and shoved the papers in her bag before shooting through to the garage, getting her car out and heading toward the school.

Ellie was very definitely the worse for wear when she got there, tearful and pale with a sickly cast to her skin that made Peyton glad she always carried a spare towel or two in her car.

"C'mon, sweetheart, let's get home and into bed," she said, putting an arm around Ellie and picking up her school-bag.

Ellie fell asleep in the car on the way home, a sign she definitely wasn't feeling well because she was usually full of energy and chatter right up until bedtime. Peyton felt her heart tug in sympathy for the child. As she drove down the driveway to the house, she saw Galen's car up ahead outside the garage. She hadn't expected him home this early and thanked her lucky stars she hadn't left the unproofed article lying anywhere.

She parked, hooked her bag over her arm and went around the car to open Ellie's door. The poor kid was still out cold and Peyton didn't want to wake her. There was nothing else to do but to carry her inside. She unhooked Ellie's seat belt and lifted the little girl into her arms. She was heavier than she looked, Peyton realized as she made her way to the door.

To her relief, the door swung open the moment she approached.

"I got a message from the school," Galen said, stepping forward. "I called back, but they said you'd just left with her, so I came here instead to wait for you both. Is she okay?"

"Probably just a tummy bug," Peyton said. "She doesn't seem to have a fever."

"Can I take her for you?"

"I think I can manage, but maybe you could take my bag before I drop it?"

The minute the words were out of her mouth she regretted the suggestion. She hadn't zipped her tote shut in her hurry and her article was jammed right there at the top, in full view of anyone.

"Just leave it here in the foyer. I'll grab it later," she said quickly as Galen reached to slide it off the crook of her elbow.

At that moment Ellie stirred in her arms and groaned. "I'm going to be sick!"

Peyton rushed toward the guest bathroom, thankfully only a few steps away. Galen dropped her bag to the floor and followed in hot pursuit.

So this was parenting, Peyton thought as she brushed her hand over the exhausted little girl's forehead after they'd changed her into pajamas and settled her in her bedroom.

"Will you stay with me?" Ellie asked weakly.

"Sure."

Galen hovered at the end of Ellie's bed, watching the little girl with a worried expression on his face. "Would you like me to stay, too?"

"I want Peyton," Ellie grumbled listlessly.

"I'm right here," Peyton said. "I'll sit with you until you fall asleep, okay?"

Ellie nodded. Galen moved away from the bed.

"It seems I'm not needed," he murmured.

"For now."

"You'll be okay?"

Peyton looked at Ellie, whose eyes were already drooping closed. "Yeah, we'll be fine. I'll just stay with her a while until she's fast asleep again."

Galen put a hand on her shoulder and she instantly felt the warmth of his fingers through her thin shirt.

"You're good with her, y'know?"

"Thanks," she managed through a throat that was a little choked up. She'd never had the chance to soothe her own baby's tears or illnesses.

As Galen left the room, Peyton turned her gaze back to the little girl in the bed. She looked so very small right now, so helpless. Peyton was swamped with emotion. Was this what parenthood was like? This overwhelming fear that something could go wrong at any time and snatch your precious child away combined with a love that constantly grew and evolved as the child did? She'd given away her chance at experiencing all of this and hadn't allowed herself to ever grow close enough to another person to risk having to face doing such a thing again.

Peyton reached out a hand to gently brush Ellie's brow, telling herself she was just checking for fever. She didn't want to love this little girl and yet the thought of leaving had begun to fill her with dread.

But she couldn't turn back. She'd set her path. The words Alice had spoken the other day came back to ring in her ears—*be careful where you tread*—and sent a shiver down her spine.

Sixteen

Galen changed out of his suit, took a quick shower and put on jeans and a T-shirt before heading downstairs again. He felt conflicted. For several months it had just been him and the kiddo, and he'd liked that. But, he reminded himself, getting married was something he'd chosen to do so that Ellie would always have someone to fall back on in those times when he couldn't be there. Times like today.

When he got downstairs he saw Peyton's bag where he'd dropped it. He'd teased her about being Mary Poppins the first time he'd seen the size of the thing. Smiling at the memory, he went over to pick it up but, as he did so, a sheaf of papers spilled from inside onto the tiled floor. He gathered the papers up and was about to shove them back in her bag when a name caught his eye. Alice Horvath.

Was this the article she was so busy working on lately? Peyton had refused to discuss it with him and he knew, out of respect for her, he should put the papers back in her bag and forget about them. But the mention of his grandmother had piqued his interest. Galen went into the sitting room, sat down on a couch, telling himself he was just going to skim but the content forced him to read them in earnest. His temper rose as he realized that the article was very specifically about his grandmother and it wasn't flattering. Galen put the papers very carefully back in Peyton's bag and fought the urge to thunder up the stairs and demand she explain what the hell she was up to.

He got up and went outside. Staring into the distance, he wondered what had driven Peyton to write such a piece. He knew his grandmother had to have made some enemies along the way; a person didn't carve out the success she had without making a few. But this article had taken a very dark look at Nagy's business practices, even drawing into question her methods for matchmaking with Match Made in Marriage.

The sense of betrayal he felt ballooned as he considered how Peyton had been welcomed with open arms into the family. It was all the worse for the fact that he now knew he'd fallen in love with her, prickly nature and all. There had to be a very specific motivation behind Peyton's actions and he needed to work out what that was and stop her from sending this piece out. Given Nagy's heart surgery and her age, he was prepared to do anything to protect her and knew the rest of the family would close ranks around her, too. But he couldn't alert any of them to this yet—if he did, they'd shun Peyton immediately. And if he could turn Peyton around to see the Nagy he, his family and most of her employees loved devotedly, then there'd be no damage done. First, however, he needed to understand why she'd done this.

He had no idea how long he had to investigate his wife, but he knew he had to act swiftly. Galen went into the office he kept downstairs, fired up his laptop and did a basic search on Peyton. Very little came up under her maiden name aside from her publishing accolades. It made him suspicious that there was no mention of her prior to her career as a journalist. Normally, there was something, somewhere, about people. A sporting achievement, an award given while at college. But it was as if she'd popped into the world fully formed and hard at work from the age of about twenty-one. Which probably meant she had legally changed her name at some point.

There was one person who likely had the information he sought. The very person he was trying to protect in all this—Alice. But how on earth would he get it out of her? She guarded the information surrounding the people involved in her matches zealously—and would continue to do so even knowing she was under attack. He shook his head. Somehow, he had to find a way that didn't involve his grandmother.

It took several days before the investigator he'd engaged got back to him. What he read was disturbing. It seemed that on graduating college, Peyton had assumed her mother's maiden name. He could understand why. From what the investigator had uncovered, Peyton's family life, if it could be called that, had been grossly dysfunctional. He could understand why anyone would want to turn their back on that. But even though she'd changed her name, and for all intents and purposes appeared to have little to no contact with her father, she still supported the man financially. As if she was trying to make up for something when, as far as Galen could see, she had nothing to make up for. In fact, she'd been very much the victim.

And no wonder she'd had such empathy for Ellie. She'd been a similar age when her mom had been diagnosed with multiple sclerosis and her mother's downturn in health had been unexpectedly rapid, exacerbated, no doubt, by the fact they had no medical insurance once Peyton's dad had been fired from Horvath Corporation. That little snippet had come as a surprise.

Learning that Peyton's father had been the chief financial officer at Horvath Corporation but had been let go on suspicion of embezzlement had shocked him. The evidence against the man had been damning; in fact, Alice would have had every right to have pressed criminal charges against him. But given the man's situation at home, Galen had no doubt his grandmother had chosen the high road. Getting rid of Magnus Maitland had been her only choice.

The PI had done a little background search on Maitland, discovering that he'd held a raft of short-term positions over the years since his dismissal. Not one of them had approached the salary he'd earned at Horvath Corporation, which must have been galling to a man with his qualifications, let alone worrying financially. It seemed that his wife's illness had eaten up every penny of savings they'd had, but there was strong evidence that they'd lived well outside their means while he was at Horvath Corporation, which had only made matters worse for them when he was fired.

Galen shook his head. Poor Peyton. She hadn't stood a chance with her father's white-collar crime, her mother's illness, being torn away from the home she'd grown up in and moving out of state. And then, to cap it off, to have had a brief and obviously intense relationship with a young man on the brink of deployment and to find herself pregnant and alone after his death. Was it any wonder she'd developed a hard shell of distrust and caution?

But to have written this article the way she had? That spoke to a level of planning years in the making. And had she somehow manipulated their marriage match? The idea was outrageous and yet made perfect sense. Was it possible that his grandmother had been tricked by someone with access to the Match Made in Marriage systems? Had Peyton married him purely to get better access to information about his grandmother?

And after she released her article to the world, what then? Did she plan to simply up and leave him and Ellie? Did she not care for either of them one bit?

He thought about the woman who'd spent the night sleeping in a chair beside Ellie's bed after the tummy bug incident. That didn't match up with the woman who'd written the vile piece of journalism he'd read the other day. But the woman who'd written that article was well capable of doing the things he suspected. Of manipulating and using others to her advantage. And right now Galen was feeling very used.

There was only one thing for it. He had to confront her.

Galen had been distant these past few days and Peyton couldn't help feeling she was responsible for that, somehow. Even tonight, his office door remained firmly shut, and when Ellie went to tell him their dinner was ready, he'd asked her to tell Peyton to leave his plate covered and he'd get to it later. It was only after Ellie had retired for the night that she dared knock on his door and beard the lion in his den, so to speak.

"What?" he said, looking up.

He'd been running his hands through his hair, which stuck out every which way in complete contrast to the smooth executive who'd left the house this morning. Peyton gave him a smile.

"Is everything okay? You sound distracted."

"No, everything is not okay. Take a seat. We need to talk."

She felt a knot form in her stomach. He'd never spoken to her in that tone before. From day one, Galen had been lighthearted, teasingly coercive or passionate. Never this serious. She settled on the small sofa tucked against the wall and waited for him to speak. He rubbed at his eyes a moment and then drilled her with a look that made her feel like an insect on a pin.

"I'd like you to tell me about your article."

"I told you before," she hedged. "It's about strong women in business."

"Peyton, we both know that isn't true."

"Have you been sneaking into my computer?"

"No, I haven't. But I will admit I have read your article about Nagy." He briefly outlined what had happened the afternoon Ellie had come home sick.

"You had no right to read that," Peyton said firmly.

"You had no right to write lies about my grandmother."

"Everything I've said in that article is true."

"Really? Are your sources legitimate? I notice you don't refer to anyone by their real name. Not even your own father."

"Alice fired my father without adequate proof and without an independent investigation. Have you got any idea of what that did to my family?"

"So this is about revenge, then." His voice was cold and his face set like stone.

"You had better believe it. Not everyone has the chance to see the world through rose-tinted glasses like you Horvaths do. You don't even see the truth in one another. When your grandmother fired my father, she as good as murdered my mom. Without Dad's benefits we couldn't afford to stay near her doctors, let alone afford her ongoing care when she started to suffer from seizures. What Alice did to us was unspeakable. The shame of what she'd accused my dad of was bad enough for Mom without having to sell our home and move away from everyone we knew. But your grandmother couldn't resist going one step further, could she? She had to go and smear my father's name so it became impossible for him to find a decent job.

"Do you know what it did to him to have to take on work detailing cars and cleaning bathrooms in office buildings just so we could eat? It crushed him that he couldn't provide for Mom's health care. It wasn't her MS that killed her. It was a broken spirit. Broken by your grandmother."

"Your father made his choices."

"Oh, of course you'd say that," Peyton spit in disgust. "All of you are the same. I had begun to think you were different. That maybe I was making a mistake. The article you saw, that was a draft. I'd even begun to wonder if I was doing the right thing. But your attitude right now is typical of what I'd always believed your family to be. You're so damned self-righteous. You don't believe for a second you could be in the wrong. You've never had to struggle and fight for anything. You have no idea what it's like for the rest of us, and you never will. Yes, your grandparents built a dynasty. But they did it at the cost of other people's happiness, and it's past time people got to see the real Alice Horvath. She's not the warm, friendly character you all portray. She has a backbone of steel and ice water runs in her veins. She had no compassion for my family, none, and that killed my mother! My father struggled to raise me and, because of your grandmother, I couldn't raise my own daughter."

Galen stiffened under her verbal assault. His face, already stern, now looked as though it had been carved from granite, and his blue eyes turned glacial. In this moment he looked more like his grandmother than Peyton had ever seen him, and it shocked her.

"I think you had better stop there," he said very carefully. "Before you say anything more you might regret."

"I regret nothing," she answered, determined not to give an inch.

"Really? And what is this all for? You already told me you and your father barely speak."

"We never got the chance to have a normal father-daughter relationship thanks to Alice!"

"Did you really think that writing this muck about my grandmother would turn back the clock for him and you? That you'd be able to rebuild the relationship you think you should have had with him?"

Peyton couldn't speak for the pain that had built like a giant burr behind her breastbone.

"Tell me, Peyton, what did you hope to gain from our marriage?" Galen continued. "Material for that article? Was that all?"

She nodded and pursed her lips. She didn't trust herself to speak right now, not when she could hear the note of hurt beneath the anger in his voice. She'd told herself from the start that the end justified the means. Her parents deserved to have their truth be told, both them and the others who'd been unfairly dismissed from Horvath Corporation. She was their crusader, their voice in the darkness, their right from wrong. She wasn't about to let some stupid emotions get in the way of all of that.

"So the whole thing is a sham for you—is that what you're saying?"

"Don't put words in my mouth."

She thought it wouldn't matter—that she'd be able to keep her feelings secure behind the rock-solid walls she'd erected around her for all her adult life—but faced with his anger, his disappointment, his hurt, she knew those walls would never be high or deep enough to save her from the pain that had begun to unravel inside. By attacking Alice Horvath, she'd hurt Galen deeply, and by hurting him, she'd hurt herself.

"Oh, I think we've probably both said enough for today, don't you?" His voice vibrated with pain and fury. "I want you out of here, out of my life and away from Ellie before you can poison her, too."

His words stung her like the lash of a whip. Logically she knew he had every right to demand she leave this house immediately, but the reality of it was excruciating.

"I'll pack and leave in the morning after Ellie's gone to school."

"Thank you." He bit the words out as if they left a bad taste in his mouth. "I'll sleep in one of the other rooms to-night."

"No, don't. I'll go back to my room."

He acknowledged her offer with a lift of his head. Silence stretched between them interminably. Peyton felt as though she should say something but she was frozen in place, still filled with shock that he'd discovered what she was doing before she could extricate herself from what had become a messy situation. She snapped herself out of it, spun on her heel and left Galen's office to go upstairs.

In her old room she sat on the bed. She'd never imagined he'd find out. Somehow she'd always thought she could just do her thing, release her article and walk away. But it turned out nothing was simple anymore. People complicated things. Which was one of the reasons she'd never allowed anyone to get close to her since her baby's father had died, she reminded herself.

But Galen had looked stricken. Not just because of what she'd said in her article, but on another level. As if he'd begun to develop feelings for her that went deeper than being bed buddies and coparenting Ellie. She felt the sharp pain behind her breastbone again.

Peyton tried to do what she'd always done: default to anger. Anger was a useful emotion—not like love or sorrow or any of the weaknesses that left you exposed to other people. Anger was something you could work with. She sat where she was and allowed it to grow, stoking it with the list of Alice's transgressions, which had broken her family into tiny splintered pieces.

The list was long—from her mom's inability to pay for treatment to the dog they'd had to give away. From her father's bitter emotional distance to Peyton's desperation to find love with a stranger. From finding out she was pregnant by a man she barely knew, but believed she'd loved, to learning of his death and having to give up custody of her newborn daughter. Oh yes, and then there was all the financial hardship in between. Being that child at school wearing clothing from the thrift store, clothing that one of the popular kids' moms had left there, and being ridiculed for it. All of it could be laid squarely at Alice Horvath's feet.

So, Galen wanted her gone from here. Her hands curled into fists at her sides. She couldn't wait to leave.

And Ellie? Would leaving Ellie behind be easy? No, of course not. But she'd said goodbye to her own baby—a child she'd nurtured and carried for forty weeks and three days before giving birth. A child she'd left in the nursery as she'd walked out of the hospital and turned her back on motherhood forever. This idyll with Ellie had been a taste of what she might have had—but she couldn't afford to dwell on that. Instead, she had to let the black hole that had opened deep inside her consume the love she'd developed for the little girl.

And what about Galen? No, she couldn't think about

him. Couldn't give words to how she felt about him—how he'd made her feel. She'd known from the start that getting married would be a risk. That was what her work was about. Taking that risk. Pushing that envelope. But it came at a very high cost.

Seventeen

Peyton stripped the bed in her room and balled the sheets up in her arms. She'd barely slept a wink during the night and at about 4:00 a.m. she'd given up entirely and begun to pack her things. She hadn't brought much—knowing in the back of her mind that this wouldn't last forever.

And now it was over. She felt as if she'd suffered a bereavement. There was no triumph in the piece she'd written. No sense of completion. Just this yawning, aching hole deep inside her, knowing that today she was walking away from Galen and Ellie forever. She'd spent a lot of last night thinking about Galen's reaction, about his anger. Not to mention his protectiveness toward Ellie.

She'd known the article would affect everyone associated with Alice in one way or another. Even Ellie viewed Alice as a much-loved great-grandmother. The knowledge that the fallout would hurt the little girl pricked like needles under Peyton's skin. Hurting Ellie had never been on her agenda. She'd just wanted the world to see Alice for who she really was. And yes, as Galen had suggested yesterday, maybe rebuild a better relationship with her father.

A knock at her bedroom door startled her. "Yes?"

"It's me. Can I come in?" Galen's voice sounded strained.

"Of course," she said.

Her body clenched on a wash of pure physical reaction as he came into her room and shut the door behind him. Dressed in a dark navy suit and pale blue business shirt and tie, he was the epitome of a Horvath—power and success exuded from every pore. He looked tired, with shadows beneath his eyes, and she felt a spiteful tinge of satisfaction that he'd probably had no more rest last night than she had.

"Look, about our discussion last night."

"I think you made your wishes perfectly clear. I'll leave as soon as Ellie's safely at school."

"Yes, well, there's been a change in plans. I've been called to go to Japan for urgent meetings. I had hoped that perhaps Maggie could live in while I was away so Ellie's timetable wouldn't be disrupted, but she is unable to do so. Can I ask you to please stay on, at least until my return?"

"Well, make up your mind, won't you?" Peyton couldn't help the irritated tone in her voice. "First you want me out of here, now you want me to stay?"

"This isn't my preference, Peyton. You're the one who made a mockery of our marriage, our family."

Oh, he knew how to hurt her and, she reluctantly admitted, she deserved it.

"Fine. I could do with the time to make some arrangements anyway. How long will you be gone?"

"A week, possibly ten days." He shifted, looking uncomfortable. "If I could have had anyone else here, I would. But Ellie is bonded to you and without me here…" His voice trailed off.

"I'll stay."

"Thank you." He turned to leave but then turned around and faced her again. "And you will say nothing to Ellie about us separating. I will deal with that myself on my return. Understood?"

"Understood."

Her throat closed up. She could barely breathe, let alone speak. While his face remained as implacable as it had been last night, in his gaze she could see the turmoil and hurt. Turmoil and hurt she'd caused. He closed his eyes briefly and when he reopened them all those feelings had been wiped away and replaced with a resolve that reminded her very much of his grandmother.

"I'll call Ellie before bed every night."

She nodded and watched as he opened the door and left. She waited until she heard the front door slam before she managed to pull herself together and head downstairs. Ellie was perched at the breakfast table, finishing her cereal. Maggie was humming happily in the kitchen. It was like any other morning, except it wasn't.

Galen was exhausted. The return flight from Tokyo had been full of turbulence, and while that didn't normally bother him, Ellie's fears related to losing her parents had weighed on his mind and made him anxious to get home.

His driver dropped him at the front door of the house and he grabbed his case and let himself inside. The house was quiet, so quiet that he wondered whether or not Peyton had already moved out. He shook his head. She might be a devious piece of work but she'd never abandon Ellie. He was sure of that.

He heard a sound on the staircase. Peyton.

The sight of her was like a punch to the gut. Every cell in his body went into overdrive. He'd missed their physical connection with an ache that had been present the entire time he'd been away. Ten long days and even longer nights. But, he reminded himself, he'd better get used to it. She was out of here very soon. In fact, now that he was back, it may as well be today.

"All packed?" he asked, dispensing with any of the usual greetings.

"Not quite," she answered.

He could see his words had irritated her. Good, because he was irritated, too. Why did this all have to be such a debacle? He'd talked to his grandmother while he was away, probing for information about Peyton without telling Nagy exactly why he couldn't just ask his wife directly. Nagy had been tight-lipped, advising him to stop beating around the bush and to speak to Peyton. But how did he tell Nagy that Peyton would be out of all their lives very soon, and that they'd need to collectively batten down the hatches as a family if the fallout from Peyton's damned article was as bad as he suspected it might be?

Galen dragged his thoughts back to the woman in front of him.

"I'm back. You don't need to be here anymore," he said bluntly.

"Your grandmother is coming to visit. Tomorrow. Would you like me gone before or after she arrives?"

Galen bit back the frustrated retort on the edge of his tongue. "My preference doesn't matter. She will obviously expect to see us both. You'd better stay until we find out what she wants."

"Fine."

He watched Peyton stalk away and heard a door upstairs slam soon after. Then he dropped into the nearest chair. What a damn mess—and what the hell was Nagy up to, making a spur-of-the-moment visit like this?

* * *

Peyton heard the car pull up in the driveway and straightened herself before going to open the front door. Maggie had been instructed to make up the downstairs guest suite in preparation for Alice's arrival and had even agreed to extra hours to ensure that every whim that Alice might express could be met. Ellie had been over the moon with excitement when she'd heard the old lady was coming to stay. Peyton certainly didn't feel the same. And there Alice was, standing in the doorway, looking a little older, a little frailer than she had a few weeks ago, when Peyton had interviewed her.

"Alice, welcome. Please, come inside," Peyton said stiffly.

"Are you the sole member of the welcoming committee?" the older woman asked, offering her cheek for a kiss.

Peyton bent and brushed her lips against the wrinkled skin, and was surprised to feel the press of Alice's lips against her cheek.

"It's good to see you, my dear. How have you been? Working too hard, by the look of you."

"I could say the same about you," Peyton responded in kind and was rewarded with a chuckle of approval.

"I like you, Peyton. I wasn't sure I would, but I really do."

Peyton took a step back—Alice's words were both a surprise and a shock. Well, she might like her now, but that was sure to change.

"Now, where are my grandson and my great-granddaughter?"

"Ellie will be home from school shortly and Galen is on his way here as we speak. An unexpected call held him up."

He'd texted her earlier, saying he'd been delayed. Texting seemed to be the only way they were able to remain civil to one another these days.

"Will Ellie be joining us at dinner tonight?" Alice asked, giving Peyton a sharp look.

"No, it's a school night. We thought it best if she not stay out too late."

Alice nodded. "Hmm, probably just as well."

"Just as well?"

"We have a lot to discuss. Now, if you don't mind, I think I'll take a little beauty rest. You could do with following my example."

Peyton blinked in surprise at the insult. Then she realized Alice was teasing. She didn't quite know how she felt about that but opted for a smile. "Have a good rest, Alice. The bed in the guest room is all made up. I'll make sure Ellie doesn't disturb you."

She rolled Alice's suitcase into the bedroom and hoisted it onto a stand for her, then left the old woman to her devices. Probably casting spells and mixing up potions, she thought with an uncharitable smirk. But then she stopped herself. Alice had said she liked her, and the woman was known to be painfully blunt about things. The knowledge that she'd somehow broken past the barrier of acceptance was bittersweet and filled her with unaccustomed warmth. That was rapidly quenched with the icy reality of how this family would treat her once her article went out. She'd delayed sending it to her editor, telling herself she needed to triple fact-check every word. But she knew that everything was perfect and ready to go. All she had to do was push Send. Yet, somehow, something held her back.

Was it the fear of how it would affect Ellie? she asked herself as she settled on one of the loungers on the deck. Or was it the fact that when it went to publication, she'd be closing the door on any chance of ever mending fences with Galen? She'd never felt a single qualm about any word she'd written before. Why was this different?

She felt that all-too-familiar tug at her heart when she considered what it would be like when she walked out that front door and never came back. Never saw Galen or Ellie again. Grief swelled inside her, threatening to reduce her to tears. But she wasn't a crier, she told herself. She was strong. She'd made the tough decisions and survived before and she would again. But this time it was different. This time she'd be walking away from the man she loved.

Peyton closed her eyes and allowed herself to finally admit that she was in love with Galen. She'd never expected to fall for him, never wanted to. But now that she'd admitted it to herself, she found she couldn't neatly box up her feelings and hide them away like she'd always done in the past. She loved him and she knew this article was hurting him, and yet she still owed it to her mom and dad to put it out there.

You could cut the air between Galen and Peyton with a knife, Alice observed as they were seated at a waterfront table at one of her favorite restaurants in Port Ludlow. Time was not making this match any easier. Alice sighed inwardly. This wasn't how she imagined things progressing at all. These two would regret this for the rest of their lives if she didn't step up and fix things. She only hoped she wasn't too late.

After they'd placed their orders, Alice settled herself more comfortably in her chair and stared at the two of them.

"Which one of you is going to tell me what's up between you?"

Silence, although her question did make them look at one another.

"Peyton, how about you start?" she coaxed.

She knew the girl was unlikely to sugarcoat anything.

"We've decided to separate. Things are not working out."

"Really?" Alice frowned. "Is that all you have to say on the matter?"

Peyton started fiddling with her napkin, then her water glass, then placed her hands in her lap and looked straight across the table at Alice. "Really. I need to be honest with you. Galen discovered that I lied about my motives for entering our marriage."

"Is that so?" Alice raised a brow and looked at her grandson. "Galen?"

He nodded, clearly not trusting himself to speak.

"So your motive to marry my grandson to be able to get dirt on me has upset him?" Alice stated calmly and reached for a breadstick. She snapped the end off and popped it in her mouth, chewing thoughtfully as she took in Galen's and Peyton's identical, somewhat comical, looks of disbelief.

"You knew?" Peyton blurted.

"Of course I knew. But the facts are the facts. You and Galen are the most compatible match for one another. Once you get this bee out of your bonnet, I think you two will be very happy together."

"You can't expect us to remain married after this," Galen spluttered. "She has manipulated us and outright lied. I certainly can't trust her and I don't want her around Ellie, either."

"Ah, yes. Ellie." Alice looked down at her plate, searching for the right words. This was such a sensitive situation. Had she overreached herself?

"What about Ellie?" Peyton sounded truly concerned and had paled considerably.

"Have a sip of water, dear. I don't want you fainting on us," Alice said. "The situation with Ellie is complicated. Peyton, I've followed your life carefully since your childhood. I know it wasn't easy for you and you struggled at times, but when I discovered you were alone and pregnant, I knew I had to step in and offer help."

"You what? You've spied on me since childhood? You arranged the private adoption? What is this? Some kind of *Twilight Zone* episode?"

Peyton was incredulous and Galen equally dumbstruck.

"It does make me sound like a meddling old woman but I knew your parents well. I owed it to your mother to keep an eye on you. You see, your father not only betrayed our company, he betrayed a friendship, as well."

"You were no friend of my mother. You left her to die."

"And I will regret that for the rest of my days. Your father cut off all contact between us when you moved to Oregon." Alice blinked hard and fought to compose herself. "Now, regarding the adoption—Nick and Sarah had been in our employ for quite a while and they befriended Galen and made his transition from upstart college graduate to astute and compassionate CEO a much easier one than if he'd had to work with anyone else. I knew of their struggles to have a child. I knew of your predicament. It seemed to me to be the best solution at the time, and it cleared your student loans and medical bills, did it not? Made the path easier for you to truly get ahead in your career? A career you have done exceptionally well in, too, I might add. And while I'm on the subject, how is your latest work coming along?"

Peyton just stared at her, dumbstruck. Galen was not so stricken.

"Her latest work is a pack of filthy lies!" he interjected.

"It is not! Can't you even hear your grandmother now? She's been pulling strings and meddling in everyone's lives for years! Mine included." Peyton slapped her hand on the table. "I can't do this. I can't sit here and pretend to be civil and enjoy dinner."

She stood up and started to walk away. Alice reached out and caught her hand.

"Sit down, my dear, please. I have something to say to you and you *will* do me the courtesy of listening. After that, stay if you want to, or leave. The choice is entirely yours."

To Alice's relief, Peyton sat down again. All eyes in the restaurant were turned to them. Alice gave the other diners a quelling glance and all turned back to their meals immediately. In the meantime a waiter hurried over with their plates and another poured their wine. Alice lifted her glass and tipped it to the others.

"To your good health," she said.

Galen and Peyton automatically followed her lead but she noted that Galen didn't sip his wine, instead placing the glass back on the table with careful deliberation. Her poor boy. He was in turmoil. She could see it as plain as the nose on his face. He'd fallen in love with Peyton, too; she could see that. It was why he was hurting so badly now. A pang of regret flicked along a nerve in her back and she flinched before taking a steadying breath and preparing to make her statement to Peyton. Maybe after this Galen would be free to admit his love and to fight for his woman. She could only hope.

"Now, Peyton, I imagine that you have written what you believe to be the truth."

"I know it's the truth. I've done my research. I've checked my sources," she said stubbornly.

"The thing is, there are always many sides to a story. If you aren't careful, my dear, you will end up repeating your father's mistakes and, like him, end up irrevocably hurting the ones you love most."

Peyton's nostrils flared as she drew in a sharp breath. "You are the one who hurt our family."

"My dear, I suggest you need to rely a little less on personal memories and go straight to the source of all your discontent. I tried to protect you and your mother then, and once you've checked your research more carefully, you will find that you've allowed your father's somewhat skewed version of the events of that time to overcome your usual reason and ability to report rationally. I know you're at the top of your profession, Peyton, but I fear you are well off the mark with your current assignment.

"Can I also say that I found your approaching and exploiting your old college friend Michelle beneath the caliber of reporter I have always thought you to be."

"You haven't fired her, too, have you? It wasn't her fault," Peyton interjected.

"No, of course it wasn't. Michelle came to me right away and told me exactly what was going on. I allowed her to give you access to specific information because you deserved at least that. But twisting that information to suit your own needs, that is not what I expected of you. I know you think you circumvented the matchmaking process with Galen, but I can assure you that you did not. Michelle had no control over the outcome of who Galen was to marry that day. You and he are the perfect match for one another. It is my goal to see my grandson and my new great-granddaughter happy. You also deserve to be happy, Peyton. But your happiness, and now that of Galen and Ellie, is entirely up to you and what you decide to do next."

Eighteen

Peyton parked her car on the bluff of the windswept beach and got out to scan the sand that stretched out below. This was a lonely and godforsaken stretch of the Oregon coast. It suited her father perfectly. In the distance, she could make him out, a large surf rod embedded in the sand next to him. He stood there, oblivious, the wind buffeting him, a light rain soaking him. Self-contained in all his animosity and resentment at the injustices of the world. She swallowed hard. This wasn't going to be easy. The last time she'd seen him, after she'd given Ellie up for adoption, he'd basically told her not to bother visiting again.

His words had been calculated to hurt and do as much damage as possible. But here she was, nearly ten years later, gearing up for another onslaught of his vitriol and unhappiness, all in the pursuit of truth. Would he even give her that much? she wondered. Or would he just retreat back to his basic cabin off the beach and continue to wallow in his misery?

She never understood how a man who'd appeared to have it all when she was a child could have come this low. But now that she was older and, she hoped, wiser, she could begin to understand.

Peyton locked her rental car and started down the weathered steps that led to the beach. The wind whipped around her, throwing sand at her skin with stinging intensity, while waves crashed loudly on the beach beside her. He must have seen her approach, but he didn't react until she was almost upon him.

"You're back."

He didn't sound happy about it.

"Yes, I'm back, Dad. How are you doing?"

He shrugged. "What do you want?"

"Some answers."

"Have you done that article yet?"

Peyton sighed. The last time she'd tried to talk to her father he'd been about to hang up on her, until she'd told him what she was planning to do. "Not yet, no."

"What's taking you so long? I told you what that bitch did to me. About time she got a taste of her own medicine."

Peyton shoved her hands in the pockets of her jacket and stared out at the waves and their inexorable assault on the sandy beach. She weighed the questions she'd been practicing in the back of her mind on the long drive here. It was time to ask them, even if it may well end up being the last time her father ever spoke to her. She turned to face him.

"Dad?"

"What?"

His response was abrupt. Hardly an invitation to open up for a deep and meaningful conversation, but she had to press on. She deserved to know the truth.

"What really happened when you lost your job at Horvath Corporation? Did you steal from them?"

Her father stared out at the sea and the lines on his face appeared to deepen beneath her gaze. His lips firmed, then trembled as they parted on a huff of breath. He seemed to grow physically smaller in stature, his shoulders more bowed, his head more bent. His hands curled into fists at his sides.

"It was only meant to be a loan," he said so softly she barely heard him speak.

"A loan?" she prompted when he fell silent again.

"Your mother deserved the best of everything. It's what she grew up with and I'd promised her that if she chose me, her life didn't have to change. I was overstretched financially, but once I was on the treadmill, I just couldn't get off it. It gave me a buzz to give your mom the latest gadget, the best garden, the latest model car, everything. At first I only borrowed a little bit to tide us over from paycheck to paycheck. I'd reimburse it and no one was any the wiser. But then your mom got sick and I got behind in returning the money, and eventually I had to borrow greater and greater sums. It became harder to hide it and I had to adjust some of the financial reports to ensure that no one would pick up the discrepancies."

"Why didn't you just tell Mom we were living beyond our means? Why didn't we downsize sooner, before you needed to take money from the company?"

He laughed but it was a bitter and twisted sound. "And lose your mother's love? I couldn't bear to see the disappointment on her face if I told her I wasn't what I pretended to be. It was my role to provide for you both. She was the love of my life, my whole reason for being on this earth. I had to be able to offer her the moon and the stars and more. She came from a wealthy family, she had everything, but she chose me. I had to show her I was as good as the people who'd cut her off when she married me. The people who, even when she became ill, would have nothing to do with her. No help, not a letter, not a phone call, nothing. I had to be everything to her. I wanted to be everything to her. And I turned out to be nothing, after all."

A solitary tear worked its way down his weathered cheek and Peyton felt her heart twist in compassion to see her proud, if misguided, father let down his guard this way. What he'd done had been incredibly wrong, but he had done it for love. Peyton had grown up believing her mom's parents had died, but this revelation from her father made her realize that she had a whole other family out there. More people who didn't want her. But she couldn't afford to dwell on that now.

"Dad, I think she would have loved you anyway. I never saw her love for you falter or change, even when she got really sick and we had to move from California."

He just shook his head. "If that bitch hadn't fired me, we'd have managed. It's her fault your mom died the way she did. If I could only have stayed in my job and kept my benefits, your mom would still be alive today."

"We don't know that."

"I know that. And I want Alice Horvath and her sanctimonious family to pay for what they did to us. They deserve to be taught a lesson. They could've afforded a few hundred thousand here and there. There was no need for them to punish me the way they did. I need vengeance, Peyton. I deserve it. Your mother deserves it. You deserve it. I can't do it myself, so you have to do it for me. You have to!"

His eyes took on a haze of fury and Peyton realized it was very possible that he wasn't entirely sane. Maybe he never had been. He'd always been prone to irrational outbursts. And his love for her mother had bordered on obsessive; she could see that now. But his choices and actions, they were all on him, whether he could admit to them or not.

She felt as if the scales had been ripped from her eyes. All these years she'd believed him to be the innocent party, somehow unfairly wronged in the process that had seen him lose his job and their lifestyle. And now she knew the truth. He had stolen the money from Horvath Corporation. He had falsified reports. The knowledge that he'd been guilty all along, while proclaiming his innocence and acting the injured party, was devastating. All these years she'd been coached by her father to hate the Horvath family, when all along they'd been innocent. The very people she'd been brought up to vilify, the people who'd welcomed her into their family with open arms, had been the victims all along.

"I'm not doing it, Dad."

"You have to," he repeated.

"No, I don't. It's time to let go of your anger, if you can. You know you did wrong and I'm grateful you've finally told me the truth."

"The truth is they deserve everything they get. They need to be knocked down a peg or two."

"No, Dad, they don't." Something Alice had said to her last night about protecting her and her mom tickled at the back of her mind. "They could have pressed criminal charges against you back then, do you realize that? Alice Horvath chose to only fire you because she knew if she pressed charges that Mom and I would suffer even more."

"She should have let me keep my job." He remained adamant.

"Would you have done that in the same position?"

"I always meant to give the money back," he said sullenly.

"I'm sure you did," Peyton answered sadly. "Dad?"

"What now?"

"I have a daughter."

"That child Galen Horvath is looking after?"

"Yes. She's my daughter."

Finally, something in her tone made her father look at her and meet her eyes. "The baby you gave away?"

"Yes."

"More meddling from that bitch, I suppose."

"No, more *care* from Alice Horvath. She made it possible for me to finish college, Dad, without loans. She made sure my baby went to a loving home with people who cared for her as if she was their own. And when they died suddenly, she gave me a second chance at motherhood."

Magnus looked away from her and toward his surf rod, noting it was bucking away with a fish on the line.

"I've got to go," he said.

"Dad? Don't you want to see her? My daughter? Your granddaughter?"

He shook his head. "No. I want to be left alone."

If he'd taken his filleting knife out and sliced her heart from her chest he couldn't have done any more harm than he'd done with his words right now. Choking back the tears that threatened to fall, she nodded in response.

"Fine, I'll go. I love you, Dad."

No response. She turned and walked down the beach toward the stairs that led up the bluff to her car, unaware of the wind that tugged at her hair, whipping it across her face until she could barely see. She shouldn't have expected any different, she told herself. He'd always been this way. But not to even want to see a picture of his own granddaughter? That was a blow she hadn't been expecting.

As she drove the two-and-a-half-hour journey back to the airport in Portland she mulled over the exchange with her dad. It had gone exactly as she'd expected, even if it hadn't gone as she'd hoped. But he'd finally told her the truth about what he'd done and, in doing so, had rendered her fight with the Horvaths to be null and void. She had no bone to pick with them. Her article, as Alice had so rightly pointed out last night, had been slanted by her father's twisted version of events and was now not even worth the kilobytes of space it took up on her hard drive.

After her flight from Portland to SeaTac, she headed to the parking garage. Before starting her car, she took her laptop and a clean USB drive from her bag and transferred the article she'd written to the drive before wiping it from her computer hard drive and from her cloud storage. Then she drove the two-hour journey home.

By the time she pulled up in front of the house it was dark and she was absolutely shattered. But there was one last thing she had to do today. Despite the late hour, Alice responded to her knock on the guest suite door looking composed and elegant with a string of lustrous pearls around her lined neck, her makeup perfect and not a hair out of place.

"Peyton? Are you all right, my dear? You look worn out. Come in."

"No, I won't come in. This won't take long." Peyton drew in a deep breath and began to talk. "I… I wanted to apologize for what I've done. I was wrong and I… I have something for you." Peyton held the USB drive out to Alice, who took it automatically. "It's the article. The only copy. It's up to you what happens to it."

"Ah," Alice uttered, her tone filled with a wealth of understanding. "I see. You've been to see your father today?"

Peyton nodded.

"Then," Alice continued, "I think you should have this back. You will do with it what is right. And, Peyton?"

"Yes?"

Alice frowned for a moment before shaking her head briefly. "No, it's not my place to say anything. I've said and done enough. Sometimes life puts us on a path we didn't mean to take, but only we can make the decision to take a new course or to attempt to forge on the way we're going. Just trust your heart, my dear, and you won't go wrong."

Nineteen

Ellie had long since gone to bed and Peyton assumed Galen was watching TV upstairs in the lounge off the master bedroom. She went up to her office, closed the door and set her laptop on the desk and started to write.

The sun was rising as she finished proofreading what she'd written. Finally satisfied, she attached the file to an email to her editor and pressed Send. There, it was done. Whatever happened next was out of her control.

She could hear Ellie stirring as she passed the girl's bedroom, so she knocked gently on the door.

"Good morning," she said as a sleepy face with tousled hair popped out from the covers. *Her daughter*, she thought with a sharp tug at her heart. She fought to keep her voice even. "Sleep well?"

"Yes. I missed you last night, though."

"You were already asleep when I got back."

"Are you wearing the same clothes you wore yesterday?" Ellie asked.

"Yeah. I haven't been to bed yet. There was something I had to finish. Now it's done."

"Was it really important?"

Peyton nodded. "I'm going to catch a few hours' sleep now, but I'll see you after school, okay?"

"Okay. Sweet dreams, Mom."

Peyton felt her heart shudder in her chest. Mom? Had that been a slip of the tongue, or had Ellie begun to truly see Peyton as her mother? She wanted with all her heart to rush into Ellie's room, scoop her into her arms and hold her as tight as she could, but she forced herself to blow a kiss instead and close Ellie's door behind her.

She turned around and came to an abrupt halt when she realized Galen was standing on the landing, waiting for her. As tired as she was, Peyton couldn't control the swell of desire that rippled through her body at the sight of him. Fresh from the shower, his hair wet but combed, his suit and shirt crisp and clean, he was the personification of the successful businessman. But she knew that beneath the layers of his corporate attire was a complex man with complex needs and desires that equaled her own. How was she ever going to bridge this distance that she'd created between them? Would he ever trust her again?

"So? Did you speak to him?" His tone was not in the least welcoming or friendly.

"I did. And I've apologized to your grandmother. Now I want to apologize to you."

Behind her, Ellie sprang from her bedroom. "Last one down to breakfast is a rotten egg!"

She danced away down the stairs and Galen's eyes followed her. Peyton looked at him, drinking him in, wondering if this would be one of her last chances to do so.

"We need to talk," he said abruptly. "But not now. This evening."

She nodded and watched as he went down the stairs after Ellie, before stumbling to her room and falling into her bed fully clothed.

Peyton slept heavily, only waking when she heard the front door slam to announce Ellie's arrival home from school. She shoved her hair out of her face and looked at the clock for confirmation. She hadn't meant to sleep this late—she'd even missed saying goodbye to Alice, who had flown home at lunchtime. She shucked off her clothes and dived into the shower, thankful that they had Maggie to welcome Ellie home and see to her post-school day needs. There were some distinct advantages to wealth on the scale that the Horvath family enjoyed, she forced herself to admit.

She spent the afternoon with Ellie, marking time until Galen was home from work and they could have that talk. By the time Ellie had gone to bed, he still wasn't home and Peyton's stomach was tied up in knots. She couldn't settle—alternately pacing the downstairs sitting room floor, or opening the refrigerator door for something to eat even though she couldn't bear the thought of food in her stomach. It was close to ten o'clock when she heard the front door open.

Peyton walked to the main entrance and stopped in her tracks as she saw Galen standing there. He looked exhausted. Every cell in her body urged her to welcome him home, to comfort him—but she'd lost that right, and the realization tore through her with a visceral pain.

"Thanks for waiting," he said. "I have a lot I need to say to you. I'll just go put my case in my office and I'll meet you in the den, okay?"

The den, not the sitting room? It was cozier in there. Was that a sign that this discussion was going to be kinder than she deserved? She didn't know how she'd handle kind. She certainly didn't deserve it. She went to the bar and poured a couple of brandies and went to wait.

She didn't have to wait long. Peyton handed Galen his drink, momentarily basking in the thrill of her fingers brushing against his as he took the glass from her.

"Before you say anything," she said, determined to pre-empt him, "I want to apologize for my actions in using Match Made in Marriage and, in particular, marrying you to further my own agenda. I shouldn't have been so cavalier with you or with Ellie and I'm deeply ashamed that I was. I went to see my father yesterday and I learned some painful, eye-opening truths. They made me realize exactly what I've done here, to you and to Ellie. Made me realize, too, that somewhere along the line I'd become as harmful and toxic as my father. I didn't like having that mirror held up to me. So—" she sucked in a deep breath and rushed the words she'd been practicing all evening "—I'm leaving. I have a new assignment coming up and there's no point in me staying here when we both know we can't go on. I won't contest a divorce. In fact, I'll begin proceedings if that's what you prefer. And Ellie…"

Peyton blinked hard against the burning sensation in her eyes. "I won't fight you for custody of Ellie. You were right. I gave her up before, I made my choice then, and I have no right to change my mind now that I've been fortunate enough to find her again. I have no right to usurp what you two have together, what her *parents* wanted for her. I don't want to unsettle her when she's already been through so much. With your agreement, however, I would like visitation rights, to see her and get to watch her grow up—" Her throat dried up completely, making further speech impossible.

She took a sip of her drink, letting the brandy burn a

path down her throat to the pit of her churning stomach. Galen hadn't said a word. He just sat there, watching her, his expression inscrutable.

"I've already packed and loaded my car. I can't face saying goodbye to Ellie again, so please don't expect it of me. In fact, it's hard enough to say goodbye to you. We had some good times, didn't we?"

Galen looked pained. "Is this really what you want? To just walk out and pretend we never happened?"

She nodded, her eyes awash with tears. "Please don't say anything. I just... I...have to go."

Peyton carefully put her glass down on the coffee table between them and stood. "Thank you again for everything you've tried to do for me. And thank you for looking after Ellie. She's so lucky to have you. I... I hope that one day you find a woman who can give you the family you and Ellie deserve."

And with that, Peyton fled from the room and down the passageway. She heard Galen's voice behind her but she didn't dare stop or look around. She went straight for the front door, down the main steps and into her car. She struggled to put the key in the ignition and saw Galen's form loom in the front door just as she managed to insert the key and turn it. Her car fired to life and she put it into gear and pressed on the accelerator. And then she was on her way—her child, the man she loved and all her unspoken dreams left behind.

Galen stood at the entrance to the apartment and checked the address he'd been given, then knocked firmly at the door. He heard sounds from inside, then the scrape of a chain on the door and the turn of a lock. The door opened a few inches and he caught his first glimpse of Peyton's face in three endless weeks.

"I've read your article," he stated. "Can I come in?"

"What? How? It's not even in print yet." She narrowed her eyes.

"It wasn't what I was expecting."

"I'm assuming you had some kind of injunction on my work?"

"I did, and I make no apology for that. I protect what's mine. Peyton, let me in."

"Ever heard of freedom of the press?"

"I was especially impressed how you showed that even through her grief over my grandfather's death, and the subsequent deaths of my father and my uncle from the same heart condition, she kept a firm hand on the running of the business. And how she maintained her leadership of the corporation with compassion and a fair hand. It was far more than I expected. No lies. You did good work."

"Damned with faint praise," she muttered, but she closed the door a little and he listened as she slid the chain off. "What do you want?"

"To talk. You left without hearing me out."

"That was three weeks ago," she pointed out, her tone bitter.

He let his gaze roam over her. She'd lost weight she could ill afford to lose in the past three weeks.

"Peyton, let me inside. I'm not having this discussion on your doorstep."

"Fine," she said. "Come in, then."

"I took the time to think about what you said that night. About you leaving us. And—" he reached into his suit pocket to withdraw the petition to dissolve their marriage "—I received this."

"I'm glad to see my lawyers are worth their exorbitant fee."

He looked around the apartment. Spartan with the bare

minimum of furnishings. The only thing that he saw that contained an ounce of her personality was a framed picture of her and Ellie on the beach in Hawaii. He remembered that day vividly and remembered taking that photo. He realized that it was probably at that point that he'd begun to fall in love with her. How had he not seen the similarities between her and Ellie then? They were like peas in a pod with their sandy-brown, sun-kissed hair, the tilt of their noses, the clarity in their gray-blue eyes. For that moment in time they'd been happy, a family.

"Nice place," he commented.

"Don't lie, Galen. What do you want from me?"

"I wanted to know why you changed the article."

"I told you the night I left. I found out the truth from my father. I couldn't send the article as it was anymore. Alice deserved better. You all did."

"Why didn't you tell me you had changed it?"

She shrugged. "I didn't think it would change anything between us. I'm sorry, Galen. When I researched and wrote the original piece, I believed that what I'd been told was the truth. In fact, growing up, it was *my* truth. It was all I ever heard from my father, and I saw nothing that made me believe any differently...until I met you."

"And now?"

"Now I'm back where I was at the beginning. Alone, but wiser." She gestured to the divorce papers. "Have you come to bring these back? You could have used a courier. You've signed them?"

"I haven't. And I'm not going to."

"What? Why not?"

"Because I want you back. Come home."

"What?"

"Come home. I want you back. In my life, in our marriage, in my bed. Ellie wants you back, too. She misses you and she has every right to understand that you're her birth mother. She needs you in her life."

"I asked if I could see her sometimes—"

"No. Not sometimes. She deserves better than that. You both do. We all do. Come home. You say you changed the article because you learned the truth, but you never stopped to discover the rest of the truth about us. I love you, Peyton, even with all your prickles and barbs and the walls you constantly keep trying to raise between us—and I believe you love me, too. I'm happy to wait for when you're ready to admit it. I can wait until my dying day if I have to, but I cannot wait another moment to have you back in my life. Unless, of course, you can convince me you don't love me, or *can't* love me. If that's the case, then I'll turn around and walk out your door, but I believe that somewhere in our crazy, mixed-up marriage we both did something right, that we found something together that we can build on and grow to last a lifetime.

"Please, Peyton, say you'll come home to us. To me."

"I don't know, Galen. I'm terrified to give in to love. I saw what it did to my father. How his love for my mom drove him to do stupid things like stealing and lying. He's a broken man. He didn't even want to see a photo of Ellie when I went to see him. How can I be what she needs when I don't even know how to be a good parent?

"All these years, ever since I gave her up for adoption, I've strived not to love, not to let go of my control over my life. Being with you and Ellie was tough at first because I kept fighting my feelings for both of you. But then I started to relax. I let go of those reins and I allowed myself to begin to love Ellie. Finding out she was really my daughter was terrifying to me, while being the greatest gift of my life at the same time. I wanted to grab her and run, but I knew I couldn't do that—to her or to you. I knew being with you had started to strip away the barriers and safeguards that I had built up ever since childhood. It frightened me."

She took a deep breath and then looked directly into his eyes. "I love you, Galen. I didn't want to. I fought against it. I even used sex to try and distract myself from it."

"Well, you can feel free to distract yourself anytime you want. Just saying."

She laughed at his attempt to lighten the seriousness of the moment. It was a sound of pure joy.

"Thanks," she said when she got her laughter under control. "I'll take that under consideration."

"So you're okay if I do this?" He held the divorce papers in front of him and tore them in half.

"Yeah, I'm okay if you do that."

Galen tossed the scraps onto a nearby chair. "And you're okay if I do this?"

He stepped closer, took her in his arms, bent his head and took her lips with his. She remained still for a split second, making him wonder if he'd taken a step too far, too soon, but then she softened in his arms, her mouth responding beneath his. Their lips meshing, tongues grazing. He forced himself to pull back, to allow her to make the next move, and prayed that it would be the right one for them both.

"I'm very okay if you do that," she answered breathlessly. "In fact, I'm okay if you do that again, just to be sure."

Ever a gentleman, Galen did, and when he broke off the embrace he looked deeply into her eyes.

"Peyton, will you come home with me? Will you be my wife in every sense? Be Ellie's mom? Be our lives?"

"I will. These past few weeks have been hell. I can't seem to function without you and I don't want to anymore."

He allowed himself a smile. His proud, fiercely independent wife had just admitted more than she probably realized. "Then let's go home."

"Yes, I'd like that. For good this time."

"Forever."

* * * * *

COMING SOON!

We really hope you enjoyed reading this book. If you're looking for more romance, be sure to head to the shops when new books are available on

Thursday 4th April

To see which titles are coming soon, please visit

millsandboon.co.uk/nextmonth

LET'S TALK
Romance

For exclusive extracts, competitions
and special offers, find us online:

- f facebook.com/millsandboon
- 🐦 @MillsandBoon
- 📷 @MillsandBoonUK

Get in touch on 01413 063232

For all the latest titles coming soon, visit
millsandboon.co.uk/nextmonth